W9-BDA-461

DEATH'S EXCELLENT VACATION

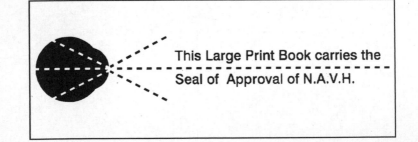

This Large Print Book carries the
Seal of Approval of N.A.V.H.

DEATH'S EXCELLENT VACATION

EDITED BY CHARLAINE HARRIS AND TONI L. P. KELNER

WHEELER PUBLISHING
A part of Gale, Cengage Learning

GALE
CENGAGE Learning

Detroit • New York • San Francisco • New Haven, Conn • Waterville, Maine • London

GALE
CENGAGE Learning

LIBRARY OF CONGRESS CATALOGING-IN-PUBLICATION DATA

Death's excellent vacation / edited by Charlaine Harris and Toni L. P. Kelner.
    p. cm.
    ISBN-13: 978-1-4104-3442-5
    ISBN-10: 1-4104-3442-7
    1. Occult fiction, American. 2. Short stories, American. 3. Vampires—Fiction. 4. Demonology—Fiction 5. Vacations—Fiction. 6. Large type books. I. Harris, Charlaine. II. Kelner, Toni L. P.
    PS648.O33D43 2011
    813'.708037—dc22   2010044286

Published in 2011 by arrangement with The Berkley Publishing Group, a member of Penguin Group (USA) Inc.

Printed in the United States of America
1 2 3 4 5 6 7 15 14 13 12 11

*This book is dedicated to Alan Ball,
who has given the supernatural world a
huge boost by bringing it to the
screen in a gloriously sexy and bloody
hour of entertainment.*

CONTENTS

7

INTRODUCTION

After we'd done as much damage to birthdays (*Many Bloody Returns*) and to the Christmas holidays (*Wolfsbane and Mistletoe*) as we could, we started brainstorming about our next anthology's theme. What hadn't we covered? We're sort of saving Arbor Day, and so many paranormals don't celebrate the Fourth of July.

Toni brought up the summer holidays. Since we're both moms with kids in school (albeit kids of very different ages), the idea made us gleeful. But we decided to broaden it a bit to include all vacations, because we didn't want to leave out the possibility of a really good vampire skiing story. Unfortunately, as it happened, none was turned in to us by our stellar list of authors.

But we got some great stories, with settings as varied as a hotel in California, a family reunion in Ireland, the headquarters of a mysterious sect in Paris, and other

9

interesting locales ranging from the exotic to the ridiculous . . . and we love them all.

Now, if you'll excuse us, we've lined up house sitters, and we've packed our sun-screen and paperbacks. We're officially on vacation. We'll send you a postcard!

Charlaine Harris
Toni L. P. Kelner

TWO BLONDES

CHARLAINE HARRIS

Charlaine Harris, #1 *New York Times* bestselling author, has been writing for twenty-seven years. Her body of work includes many novels, a few novellas, and a growing body of short stories in genres such as mystery, science fiction, and romance. Married and the mother of three, Charlaine lives in rural Arkansas with her family, three dogs, and a Canada goose. She pretty much works all the time. The HBO series *True Blood* is based on Charlaine's Sookie Stackhouse novels.

"So why are we going to Tunica?" I asked Pam. "And what are we supposed to do when we get there?"

"We're going to see the sights and gamble," Pam said. The headlights of a passing car glinted on Pam's pale, straight hair. Pam was paler than her hair and approximately a hundred and sixty years old, give or take a decade. She'd become a vampire when Victoria was still a young queen.

"It's hard to believe you'd want to go to Mississippi. For that matter, it's hard to believe you'd want to take me along."

"Are we not friends, Sookie?"

"Yes," I said, after a little hesitation. Though it didn't seem polite to say so, I was closer to being a friend of Pam's than I was of any other vampire. "Somehow, I got the feeling you really didn't think enough of humans to want to claim one as a friend."

"You're not as intolerable as most," Pam said lightly.

"Thanks for the glowing testimony."

"Oh, you're quite welcome." She grinned, flashing just a bit of fang.

"I hope this is fun, considering I'm using my two days off to make this little trip." I sounded a little grumpy, with good reason.

"It's a vacation! A chance to get out of your rut. Don't you get tired of Bon Temps? Don't you get tired of hustling drinks at Sam's bar?"

Truthfully, no. I love my little Louisiana town. I feel as comfortable as a telepath can be among the people I know so well (better than most of them will ever understand). And I love working for Sam at Merlotte's. I'm a very good waitress and barmaid. My life brings me enough excitement without me having to leave town to get more.

"Something always goes wrong when I go out of town," I said, trying not to sound whiny.

"Such as?"

"Remember when I went to Dallas? All those people got shot? When I went to Jackson, I got staked." Which was pretty ironic, since I'm human. "And when I flew up to Rhodes with you-all, the hotel got blown up."

"And you saved my life," Pam said, suddenly serious.

"Well," I said, and then could think of nothing more to add. I started to say, *You would have done the same for me,* but I was by no means sure that was true. Then I started to say, *You would have been okay, anyway,* but that wasn't true, either. I shrugged, at a loss. Even in the darkness, Pam saw me.

"I won't forget," she said.

"So, we're really just going to see the casinos and gamble? Can we go see a show?" I wanted to change the subject.

"Of course we'll do all those things. Oh, we do have one tiny errand to perform for Eric."

Eric and I are — I'm not sure what we are. We're lovers, and in an unofficial vam-

13

pire way, we're married. Not that I had anything to do with that; Eric maneuvered me into it. He had good intentions. I think. Anyway, it's not a straightforward situation, me and Eric. Pam is gung-ho Eric, because she's his right hand. "So what do we have to do? And why do I need to come along?"

"A human is involved," Pam said. "You can let me know if he's sincere or not."

"All right," I said, not caring one little bit that I sounded reluctant. "As long as I get to see all the casinos and a good show that I pick."

"It's a promise," Pam said.

As we went up Highway 61, we started to see casino billboards flashing by in the night. Pam had been driving since darkness had fallen . . . That had been at five thirty, since it was February. Though I remembered February as being the coldest month when I was a child, now it was an eerie sixty degrees. Pam had picked me up in Bon Temps, then we'd gone through Vicksburg to turn north on Highway 61. There were a few casinos in Vicksburg and a few more in Greenville, but we kept driving up the western side of Mississippi. It was flat, flat, flat. Even in the dark, I could tell that.

"Nowhere to hide, here," I said brightly.

"Even for a vampire," Pam said. "Unless

one found a bayou and crouched down to bury oneself in the mud."

"With the crawdaddies." I was full of cheerful thoughts.

"What do people *do* here?" Pam asked.

"Farm," I said. "Cotton, soybeans."

Pam's upper lip curled. Pam was a city girl. She'd grown up in London. England. See? We couldn't be more different. City girl, country girl. Experienced and well traveled, inexperienced and stay-at-home. Bisexual, heterosexual. She's dead, I'm alive.

Then she turned on the CD player in her Nissan Murano, and the Dixie Chicks began singing.

We did have something in common, after all.

We saw the first turnoff to the casinos at two in the morning.

"There's a second turnoff, and that's where we're staying," Pam said. "At Harrah's."

"Okay," I said, peering at the signs. To find these street lights, this traffic, and all the neon in the distance in the middle of the Mississippi Delta was like finding out Mrs. Butterworth had pierced her navel. "There!" I said. "We turn there."

Pam put on her blinker (she was an excellent driver) and following the signs, we pulled up in front of the casino/hotel where we had a reservation. It was large and new, as everything in the casino complex seemed to be. Since there wasn't a whole lot going on at that hour, several jacketed young men made a beeline for the Murano.

Pam said, "What are they doing?" Her fangs popped out.

"Chill. They're just going to valet-park the car," I said, proud that I knew something Pam didn't.

"Oh." She relaxed. "All right. They take the keys, park the car, and bring it back when I require it?"

"Right." A high school classmate of mine had had that job at a casino in Shreveport. "You tip 'em," I prompted, and Pam opened her purse, a Prada. Pam was a purse snob.

She laughed when one of the young men wanted to carry her luggage. We both entered the hotel with our weekend bags slung over our shoulders. Eric had given me my bag as a Christmas gift, and I really, really liked it. My initials were embroidered on it, and it was red with blue and gold flowers. In fact, it coordinated with the coat he'd given me the year before, the coat I didn't need this unseasonably warm night.

Pam had reserved one of the designated

vampire rooms, a no-window space with two sets of doors. Our rooms were on the same floor at the back of the hotel. Of course, I'd gotten one of the much cheaper regular human rooms. I was glad we were here on a weekday, because one glimpse of the weekend rates had almost rendered me speechless. I *really* didn't travel much.

Very few people turned to look as we made our way to the elevator. Not only were vampires seen pretty frequently at casinos — after all, they were open all night — but everyone was absorbed in the gambling. The slot machines were in rows across the huge floor, and it was always night in here. Sunlight didn't have a hope of penetrating. The noise was incredible. The chiming and ringing and humming never came to a stop. I don't know how the people working there managed to stay sane.

In fact, one of the servers wending her way through the chaos in a slacks-shirt-vest uniform was a vampire. She was a thin strawberry blonde with such large boobs that I suspected she'd had a little augmentation before she was brought over. She was carrying a heavy tray of drinks and managing it with ease. She caught Pam's eyes and gave her a nod. Pam nodded back, giving her own head exactly the same degree of

17

inclination.

On the third floor, Pam peeled off to find her room, and I followed the numbers to mine. Once I'd tossed my bag on my bed, I didn't know what to do with myself. Pam knocked, and when I let her in she said, "My room is adequate. I'm going to go down and look around. Are you going to bed?"

"I think I will. What are our plans for tomorrow?"

"Do whatever you like during the day. There's a shuttle that runs between the casinos, so you can go to whichever one you like. There are shops, and there are restaurants. If you notice a show you'd like to see, book us for the first one after dark. After that, we'll run our errand."

"Okay. I think I'll turn in, then." You notice I didn't ask about the errand? That was because I wanted to enjoy myself the next day. I'd find out soon enough what Eric wanted us to do. It couldn't be too bad, right? He was my lover and Pam's boss. On the other hand, he was frighteningly practical about taking care of himself. *No,* I told myself. *He wouldn't risk both of us. At the same time.*

"Good night, Sookie." She gave me a cold kiss on the cheek.

"Have a good time," I said faintly.

She smiled, happy at having startled me. "I plan on it. There are plenty of us here. I'll go . . . network."

Pam would always rather hang with her own kind than grub around with "breathers."

It took me all of ten minutes to unpack and get ready for bed. I crawled in. It was a king, and I felt lost in the middle of it. It would be more fun if Eric were here. I pushed the thought away and turned on the television. I could watch a movie on pay-per-view, I discovered. But if I paid specially for a movie, I'd feel obliged to stay up. Instead, I found an old Western that I followed for maybe half an hour until my eyes wouldn't stay open anymore.

About ten the next day, I was eating a wonderful breakfast at a buffet that was as long as the Merlotte's building. I had sausage and biscuits and gravy, and some chopped fruit so I could say I'd eaten something healthy. I also drank three cups of excellent coffee. This was a great way to start the day, and no dishes to do afterward. That was the kind of vacation I could appreciate.

I retreated to my room to brush my teeth, and then I went outside to catch the bus.

The sky was overcast, and the temperature was as unnaturally warm as it had been the day before. One of the valet-parking attendants told me where the shuttle bus would pick me up to take me to the other casinos, and I waited for it with a stout couple from Dyersburg, Tennessee, who had cornered the market on chattiness. They'd won some money the night before, their son was going to the University of Memphis, they were Baptists but their pastor liked to visit the boats (all the casinos were theoretically boats, since casinos couldn't be built on solid land) so that made a little gambling okay. Since I was young and alone, these two decided I was applying for a job at the casinos. They assured me someone as young and perky and pretty as me would have no trouble.

"Now, don't you go to that bad place north of here!" the woman said, with mock admonishment.

"What place would that be?"

"Henry, close your ears," she told her husband. Henry good-naturedly pretended to hold his hands over his ears. "There's what's called a *gentleman's club* up there," she said in a stage whisper. "Though what someone calling himself a gentleman would be doing there, I don't know."

I didn't say that I was pretty sure real gentlemen had sex urges, too, because I understood what she meant. "So it's a strip club?"

Mrs. Dyersburg said, "My Lord, I don't know what all goes on in a place like that. I won't ever see the inside of one, you can bet. Listen, our oldest son is twenty-four, and he's single, got a good job. You dating anyone?"

Then, thank God, the bus came. Whatever casino the Dyersburgs chose, I'd pick another one. Luckily, they got off pretty quickly, so I waited to disembark at Bally's. I went in, to be assaulted by the newly familiar chiming and clicking of slot machines. I saw a sign for a huge buffet. I got a discount coupon immediately from a smiling older woman with elaborate brown hair and lots of gold jewelry. There were three restaurants in Bally's, and I could eat till I popped at any one of them, according to the material on the coupon. I wondered how much of an appetite I could work up playing a slot machine.

Out of sheer curiosity I walked over to an empty machine, looked at it carefully while I worked out what to do, fed it one of my hard-earned dollars, and pulled the lever. There, I felt it — a distinct frisson of excitement. Then my dollar was lost for good. Was I willing to spend my money on that thrill? No.

I wandered around for a while, looking at the people who were so intent on what they were doing that they never glanced at me, or smiled. The casino employees, on the other hand, were full of good cheer.

Over the course of the day, thanks to the shuttle, I discovered that all the casinos were basically the same. The "décor" changed, the staff uniforms were different colors, the layout might vary a bit, but the noise level and the gambling facilities . . . those were constant.

I had lunch at yet another casino in the middle of the afternoon. Each casino seemed to have two or three places to eat. I decided I couldn't face another buffet. I made my way to the lower-priced restaurant that offered menus. When I tired of people-watching, I pulled out the paperback I carried in my purse.

At the casino after that, I had to fend off a persistent admirer, a man missing an important front tooth. He wore his hair pulled back in a long, graying ponytail. He was sure we could have some fun together, and I was just as sure we could not. I got back on the shuttle.

I returned to Harrah's with a feeling of relief. I'd seen lots of new things, including a riverboat and a golf course, but all in all the casinos seemed kind of sad to me. The gamblers weren't people like you see in James Bond movies, rich people dressed to the nines who could afford losing. Some of the people I'd seen today didn't look like they could afford to waste even ten dollars. But I had to admit, they'd seemed to be having a good time, and after all, that was the point of a vacation.

It was lovely to shut the door of my room and enjoy the silence. I threw myself down on the bed and closed my eyes. It wouldn't be long until Pam rose.

Sure enough, she knocked on the door thirty minutes later. "Did you get some tickets?" she asked.

"Hi, Pam, good to see you. Yes, I had an interesting day," I said. "I got us tickets to the Mucho Macho contest."

"What?"

"It's a strongman competition. I wasn't sure you'd like any of the music acts. The groups I actually knew, they were all sold out for tonight. So I got tickets to see big strong guys. I thought you'd like that? You like guys too, right?"

"I like men," Pam agreed guardedly.

"Well, we have an hour before the show," I said. "You want to go get some warm blood?"

"Yes," she said, and followed me to the elevator, still looking dubious.

While Pam drank a couple of bottles of TrueBlood Type A, I had a bowl of ice cream. (Calories don't count while you're on vacation.) Then we went to the casino next door to watch the Mucho Macho contestants do their manly thing. I got to say, I really enjoyed it: muscular guys lifting heavy weights, swinging big hammers, pulling farm equipment with their teeth. No, I'm just kidding about the teeth. They used a rope harness.

It was like monster trucks, but with men. Even Pam got into the spirit, yelling encouragement to Billy Bob the Brawler from Yazoo City as he harnessed up for his second attempt to move the tractor a yard across the floor.

Of course, Pam herself could have done it easily.

She got a call on her cell phone as we were leaving the show.

"Yes, Eric. Oh, we've just finished watching big, muscular, sweaty men move large things around. Sookie's idea."

Her eyes went sideways to meet mine. She

24

grinned at me. "I'm sure you could, Eric. You could probably do it without your hands!" She laughed. Whatever Eric said next got her serious attention. "All right, then. We'll go now." She handed the phone to me. I didn't like the compressed lips and narrowed eyes. Something was up.

"Hey," I said. I felt a surge of lust down to my toenails just knowing that Eric was on the other end of the connection.

"I miss you," he said.

I pictured him in his office at Fangtasia, the nightclub he and Pam owned. He'd be sitting in his leather office chair, his thick golden hair falling in a waving curtain past his shoulders, and he'd be wearing a T-shirt and jeans. Eric had been a Viking, and he looked like it.

"I miss you, too," I whispered. I knew he could hear me. He could hear a cricket fart at twenty paces.

"When you return, I'll show you how much."

"I look forward to that," I said, trying to sound brisk and businesslike, since Pam could hear the conversation.

"You're not in any danger tonight," he said, sounding more businesslike himself. "Victor insisted you go with Pam. The vampire you're meeting has a human com-

25

panion. You will know if Michael is dealing with us in good faith or not."

"Can you tell me what this is about?"

"Pam will brief you on the way. I wish I'd had time to discuss it with you myself, but this opportunity came up very quickly." He sounded, just for a second, like he was wondering why it had come up so quickly.

"Is something funny about that?" I asked. "Funny strange, I mean?"

"No," he said, "I was considering that . . . but no. Let me talk to Pam again."

I handed the phone back. A glimmer of surprise crossed Pam's face. "Sir?" she said.

Whatever transpired in the rest of the conversation was lost to me, because the Ittabena Hulk plowed through the crowd in his street clothes, looking neither to the right nor the left. He was intent on the stacked brunette who was waiting for him by the "wait to be seated" sign at the entrance to yet another buffet. She curved in all the right places. She was wearing a tight leopard-print stretch top and a black leather miniskirt grazing the tops of her tan legs. Four-inch black heels completed the ensemble.

"Wow," I said, in genuine tribute. "I wish I had the guts to wear something that bold." The cumulative effect was literally stunning.

"I would look excellent in that," Pam said, a simple statement of fact.

"But would you want to?"

"I see what you mean." Pam looked down at her own silk blouse and well-cut pants, her low heels and conservative jewelry.

"So where are we going?" I asked, after the valet had retrieved Pam's car. We turned north on 61. The traffic was heavy. Though it was a weekday, everyone seemed to be in a great hurry to lose their hard-earned cash and experience something a little different from their everyday lives.

"We're going to a club that's just west of this highway, about ten miles north of here," Pam said. "It's called Blonde, and it's owned by a vampire named Michael."

I remembered my conversation with the couple on the bus. "This would be a 'gentleman's club'?"

Pam looked massively sardonic. "Yes, that's what they call it."

"Why are we going there? Eric said a vampire runs it. We're across the state line in Russell Edgington's territory." Russell Edgington was the vampire king of Mississippi. Though most humans didn't know it, there were other systems of government in the USA besides the one in Washington, D.C.

27

Not every state has its own vampire ruler; some states are populous enough to have two or even more. (New York City has its own king, I understand.) Visiting vamps were supposed to check in when they had to cross into another vamp's territory. I'd met Russell, and he was no joke.

"This must go no further, you understand?" Pam gave me a very meaningful look before turning her attention back to the road. The oncoming traffic heading south from Memphis was moving easily, but it was also nonstop.

"I understand," I said. I didn't sound enthusiastic. Vampire secrets are unpleasant and dangerous.

"Our new masters have been chipping away at Edgington's control of Mississippi," Pam said.

This was very bad news. Louisiana, where Bon Temps lay, had been taken over from its previous management by the vampires of Nevada. Since Arkansas had previously allied with Louisiana (long story), the king of Nevada (Felipe de Castro) had gotten two states for the price of one. His ambitious lieutenant, Victor Madden, had apparently decided to go for the trifecta.

"Why would they want to do that?" Felipe owned two poor states. If he added Mississippi, he'd have the equivalent of one prosperous state, but his people would be spread thin.

"The casinos," Pam said.

Of course. The big business in Nevada was casinos, and there were lots of casinos in Mississippi. Felipe had already acquired casinos in Louisiana, and had the state of Arkansas thrown in for free.

"Vampires can't own casinos," I said. "It's against the law." A powerful human lobby had pushed that legislation.

"Do you imagine that Felipe *doesn't* control what happens at the casinos in Las Vegas? At least in large part?"

"No," I admitted. I'd met Felipe.

"In fact, our king is bringing a lawsuit to challenge that legislation through the human courts, and I'm confident he'll win," Pam said. "In the meantime, Victor told Eric to use us as an advance team."

I had seen Victor much more often than the king himself. Victor Madden was Felipe de Castro's man on the ground in Louisiana, while Felipe stayed at his castle in Las Vegas. "Ah, Pam, do you think this is all on the up-and-up?"

"What do you mean?"

I thought she knew perfectly well what I meant. "Victor specified us. Why do *we* have

29

this top secret mission, instead of someone better at negotiation? Not that you're not a great fighter," I added quickly. "But you'd think if we're trying to pinch off parts of Mississippi, Victor would send Eric himself." Eric was the only remaining sheriff that the previous ruler had put in place. All the others were dead. I remembered Victor's adorable, smiling face, and I got worried. "You *sure* this Michael is willing to ditch Russell?"

"Victor says so."

"And Michael has a human companion."

"Yes, a man named Rudy."

"This is dangerous, no matter what Victor told Eric. We're in foreign territory. This isn't a real vacation. We're *poaching.*"

"Russell doesn't know why we're here."

"How can you be sure?"

"I told his headquarters that I was having a weekend here, so they wouldn't think my presence was caused by business of any kind."

"And?"

"Russell himself came on the phone to extend his hospitality. He told me to feel free to enjoy myself in the area, that Eric's second in command was always welcome."

"And you don't think that's fishy?"

"If Russell had any idea what Felipe was

considering, he would have counterattacked by now."

Vampires pretty much wrote the book on chicanery, double dealing, and what you might call drastic politics. If Pam wasn't worried, should I be?

Sure. Pam could take a lot more damage than I could.

Blonde was not an attractive edifice. No matter how much female beauty might be on the inside (and the billboards promised plenty), on the outside it was a metal building in the middle of nowhere. It had a huge parking lot, and there were at least forty vehicles there. The ground had risen as we approached Memphis and its bluffs, and the club stood on top of a hill with a deep ravine behind. The whole area outside the parking lot was covered with kudzu, like it had been carpeted in the plant. The trees were covered, too.

"We go to the back," Pam said, and she drove around the building.

The back was even less appealing than the front. The parking lot was poorly lit. Michael was not too concerned for the safety of his workers. *Of course,* I told myself, *maybe he walks each of the girls to her car every night.* But I doubted it. "Pam, I have a bad feeling about this," I said. "I want to be on record as letting you know that."

"Thanks for the pep talk," Pam muttered, and I realized that she had more misgivings than she'd revealed. "But I have my orders and I have to do this."

"Who issued those orders — Felipe, Victor, or Eric?"

"Victor called me into Eric's office and told me what to do and to take you. Eric was present."

"How do you think he feels about this?"

"He isn't happy," Pam said. "But he's under new management, and he has to obey direct orders."

"So we have to do this."

"I have to. I am Eric's to command." Eric had made Pam a vampire. "You aren't, though Eric pretends to Victor that you obey him in all things. You can leave. Or you can stay in the car and wait for me. There's a pistol under the backseat."

"What?"

"A pistol, a gun, you know? Eric thought you'd feel more comfortable with one, since we're so much stronger than you."

I hate guns. Having said that, I also have to admit that a firearm has saved my life in the past. "You're not going in by yourself, armed or unarmed," I said. I hesitated, because I was afraid. "Give it to me," I said.

32

We were parked at the very back of the lot, right by the kudzu. I hoped it wouldn't take Pam's car while we were inside.

Pam reached under the seat and drew out a revolver. "Point and shoot," she said, shrugging. "Eric got it for you specially. He says it is called a Ruger LCP. It fires six shots, and there's one in the chamber."

It was about as big as a cell phone. Good God Almighty. "What if I need to reload?"

"If you have to shoot that much, we are dead."

I got that feeling that had become familiar since I'd started hanging with vampires; the feeling that says, *How the hell did I get into this?* If you examined the process step by step, you could see how it had happened; but when you looked at where you'd ended up, you just had to shake your head. I was walking into a very dubious situation, and Eric thought I needed a gun. "Hey, at least we'll match the décor," I said at last.

Pam looked blank.

"Blondes," I said helpfully. "Us."

She almost smiled.

We got out of the car. I tucked the gun in the small of my back, and Pam checked to make sure it was covered by my fitted black jacket. I never looked as put-together as Pam, but since we'd been going to a show and then out, I'd worn my good black pants and a blue and black knit top with long sleeves. The jacket didn't look ridiculous, since the temperature had fallen into the forties. Pam pulled on her white trench coat and belted it tightly around her waist, and then off she went.

I trotted along behind her, second-guessing myself every step of the way. Pam knocked once on the employee entrance. After a pause, the door opened, and I saw that the male holding it was a vampire. Not Michael, though, if I was any judge at all. This male had only been a vampire for a few years. He had a Mohawk, colored green and gelled to a high crest on his otherwise bald head. I tried to imagine going through the centuries like that, and I thought I might throw up.

"We're here to see Michael," Pam said, her voice especially cool and regal. "We're expected."

"You the ladies from Shreveport?"

"We are."

"There's a lot going on here tonight," he said. "You going to try out after you talk to Michael? I'm in charge of the tryouts." He was proud of that. "Just come right to this door when you're ready." He pointed at a door to the right that had a hand-lettered sheet of typing paper taped to it. Straggly letters spelled DANCERS IN HERE.

We didn't say anything to that, and he cast a glance back at us that I couldn't read.

"Let me see if the boss is ready," Mohawk said.

When he'd knocked and been admitted through a door on the left, Pam said, "I can't believe they let someone so deficient answer the door. In fact, I can't believe anyone bothered to turn him. I think he's slow."

Mohawk popped back out of the door as quickly as he'd popped in.

"He's ready for you," he said, which I found an ominous way to put it.

Pam and I followed his sweeping gesture, which led into an unexpectedly luxurious office. Michael believed in treating himself well. The room was carpeted in dark blue and topped with a lovely Persian-style rug in cream, blue, and red. The furniture was dark and polished. The contrast with the bare corridor was almost painful.

Michael himself was a short, broad blond with a distinct Slavic look. Russian, maybe. A dull throb underlay all the polish of his office, and I realized the throb, which I'd been aware of since I entered the building, was the sound of the music playing in the club. The bass was turned up all the way. It was impossible to tell what the song was, not that the lyrics were the point.

"Ladies, be seated, please," Michael said. He gestured toward the two very impressive guest chairs in front of his desk. He had a heavy accent and a bad suit. He was smoking. It smelled just as bad when a vampire did it. Of course, he wouldn't suffer any consequences. An open bottle of Royalty Blended was on the desk by the ashtray. "This is my associate, Rudy," Michael told us.

Rudy was standing behind Michael. He was the human I'd come to read. He was slim and black-haired, with an extensively scarred face. He looked as if he was eighteen, but I figured he was at least ten years older than that. He gave off a very strange mental signature. Maybe he wasn't completely human. Everyone I know has a brain pattern: Humans have one kind, weres of all sorts have another, fairies are opaque but identifiable, and vampires leave a sort of void. Rudy didn't fall into any of those categories.

"You can leave," Michael said to Mohawk, his voice contemptuous. "Go back to organize the tryouts. We'll be there soon." Mohawk backed out of the room, pulling the door closed behind him. The noise level abruptly dropped, thank God. The boss's office was soundproofed. But the drumbeat was pulsing in my head, and I swore I could feel it through my feet even if I couldn't hear it any longer.

"Please let me offer you a drink," Michael said, smiling at both of us. Rudy decided to smile, too. His teeth were very sharp; in fact, they were pointed. Okay, half-human at most. I was suddenly and deeply frightened. The last time I'd seen teeth like that, they'd bitten bits out of me.

"You've never met anyone like Rudy?" Michael asked. He was looking directly at me.

I'm good at schooling my face. Telepaths learn that lesson early in life, or they don't survive, is my guess. How had he known?

"I sense your pulse speeding up," Michael said charmingly, and I knew I didn't like him at all. "Rudy is a rarity, aren't you, my darling one?"

Rudy smiled again. It was just as bad the second time.

"Half human and half what?" Pam said. "Elf, I suppose. The teeth are a giveaway."

"I've seen teeth like that before," I said, "on fairies who'd filed them to look that way."

"Mine are natural," said Rudy. His voice

37

was surprisingly deep and smooth. "What can I get you to drink?"

"Some blood, please," Pam said. She loosened her coat and leaned back in the chair.

"Nothing for me, thank you." I didn't want to drink anything Rudy had touched. I hoped the human-elf hybrid would leave the room to get Pam's drink, but instead he turned and bent down to a little refrigerator to extricate a bottle of Royalty Blended, a premium drink that mixed synthetic blood with a large dash of the real blood of certified royalty. He popped the top off the bottle and put it in a microwave sitting atop a low filing cabinet. There were odds and ends on top of the microwave: a bottle opener, a corkscrew, a few straws in paper wrappers, a small paring knife, a folded towel. Quite the home away from home.

"So, you come from Eric? How is the North man?" Michael asked. "We were together in St. Petersburg at one time."

"Eric is flourishing under our new ruler. He wishes you well. He's heard good things about your club," Pam said, which was outrageous flattery and almost certainly untrue. Unless there was a lot below the surface, this was a sleazy little club catering to sleazy little people.

The microwave dinged. Rudy, who'd been fiddling with the items on top of the microwave, took the drink out, putting one of his thumbs over the open top of the bottle so he could shake it gently. Not the most hygienic way of doing the job, but since vampires almost never get ill, that wouldn't make any difference to Pam. He came around the desk to hand the bottle to her, and she accepted it with a nod of her head.

Michael picked up his own bottle and raised it. "To our mutual venture," he said, and they both drank.

"Are you truly interested in having a further discussion with our new masters?" she asked. She took another sip, a longer one.

"I am considering it," Michael said slowly, his accent even heavier. "I am tired of Russell, though we share a liking of men." Russell liked men as fish like water. I'd been in his mansion, and it was full of guys who ranked from cute to cuter. "However, unlike Russell, I also like women, and women like me." Michael gave us an unmistakable leer.

This woman didn't like him. I glanced at Pam, who also enjoyed sex with either gender, to see her reaction. To my dismay, her cheeks were red — really red. I was so used to her milky pallor I found the effect shocking.

She looked down at the bottle in her hand. "This was poisoned," she said slowly, almost slurring her words. "What did you put in it, elf?"

Rudy's smile became even more disagreeable. He held his hand up so we could see the cut in his thumb. He'd put his own blood into the Royalty Blended. The human blood had disguised the taste.

"Pam, what's this going to do to you?" I asked, as if the men weren't there.

"Elf blood isn't intoxicating like fairy blood, but . . . it's like taking a huge tranquilizer or having lots of alcohol." Her speech was even slower.

"Why have you done this?" I asked Michael. "Don't you know what will happen to you?"

"I know how much Eric will pay me to get you two back," Michael said. He was leaning forward over the desk, his expression one of sheer greed. "And while he's getting the ransom together, Rudy will be drawing up a paper about your mission in coming here, which you and the vampire will sign. That way, when we return you to Eric, he can't retaliate. If anything happens to us, Russell will have the ammunition to

40

start a war. Your new masters will be quick to dispose of Eric if he causes a war."

Michael was as deep a thinker as he was charming. That was to say, not at all. "Do you have something personal against Eric, or are you always this double-dealing?" Keep 'em talking while Pam got in a little recovery time.

"Oh, always," he said, and he and Rudy laughed. They were certainly two peas in the same pod; they were relishing my anxiety and Pam's intoxication.

"Stand up, Pam," I said, and she laboriously worked her way to her feet.

Rudy laughed again. My insides were burning with a huge brushfire of hate.

My friend's face was mottled, her movements sluggish, and her eyes were frightened. I had never seen Pam scared of anything. She was a revered fighter, even among the vampires, who were known for savagery and ruthlessness. "Let's try walking it off."

"That won't help you," Rudy said with a sneer. He was lounging against the wall. "She won't be feeling herself again for a couple of hours. In the meantime, we'll have fun with you first, Michael and me. Then we'll have her."

"Pam, look at me," I said sharply, trying

not to picture their idea of fun. She did look. "You have to help me," I said intently, trying to get a message into her addled brain. "These men are going to hurt us." Her eyes finally focused on mine, and she nodded slowly. I moved my head slightly to the right, pointed a thumb at my own chest. Then I inclined my head oh-so-slightly toward Michael, pointing the same thumb at her.

"I understand," Pam said clearly, but only with great effort.

Michael was still seated, but Rudy had pulled away from the wall at the moment I drew the gun. They smelled it as I was drawing (and they might have sooner if Michael hadn't been smoking) and reacted with the quickness of their races. I fired into Rudy's face as he grabbed for me, and Pam threw herself across the desk to grip Michael's ears. He clawed at her arms and slammed her down onto the desk. Ordinarily she would have tossed him over her shoulder or something equally spectacular. But in her drugged state, she could only hold on to what she had. He was hitting her repeatedly, too angry to pry her hands away when he could be doing damage to her body. She'd have to loosen her grip, eventually.

While Rudy gurgled and grabbed at the

hole in his face under his left cheekbone, I said, "*Pull,* Pam!" and she obeyed.

She pulled Michael's ears off.

When he flinched back, his mouth open with the pain, she lunged again and stuck her thumbs in his eyes. Instead of throwing up, I shot Rudy again, this time in the chest.

Michael wasn't dead, of course, but he was rocking in silent agony. While he was distracted, Pam pulled out his tongue. I averted my eyes as quickly as I could and swallowed down the bile that rose in my throat. This was Pam on a *bad* night.

I checked on my target. Rudy was down, though he wouldn't stay that way. If elves were as tough as fairies, he'd be up within a half hour. I grabbed the towel from the top of the microwave and wiped off the gun, then tossed it on the desk. I don't really know why — I just had to get rid of it.

"We have to get out of here," I said to Pam, and she dropped the bloody ears. Slowly and deliberately, she wiped her hands on the chair cushion. The ears lying on the desk looked like discarded Play-Doh shells with red paint sprinkled on them. I wondered briefly if Michael could stick the ears back on, if the eyes and tongue would regenerate.

Whoops! Rudy was already up on his

elbows, trying to drag himself toward us. I kicked him under the chin as hard as I possibly could, and he collapsed. Pam had started to waver, but I put my arm around her again and she steadied.

"I took care of him," Pam said, enunciating with care. She smiled at me. Speckles of blood had landed on her pink silk blouse, so I told her to button her coat up again. I tied it shut. "That was fun," she said guilelessly.

"I'm glad you had a good time," I muttered, "since I planned all this for your benefit." We stepped out of the office in the corridor and let the door shut behind us. If we could just make it to the car . . . Mohawk was staring at us from his place on the stool by the back door.

Then that door opened, and two cops walked in.

And we'd been doing so well.

The pulsing noise of the stripper music and the office soundproofing had drowned out the shots. I knew this, because no employees had come to check on the gunfire. So no one had summoned these guys; therefore, they must be friends of the management, since they'd entered through the rear.

I was trying to think, and think fast, and

my brain was a little too crowded (what with shooting an elf, seeing a guy lose his facial features, and whatnot). One thing I was clear about was wanting to stay out of jail. These cops might not even be within their own jurisdiction, but we had to avoid coming to their attention.

After giving Mohawk a casual wave, they'd stopped to talk to a short, curvy stripper in a platinum wig, which meant they were blocking the rear exit. If we reversed direction and tried to walk out through the front, we'd attract even more attention, I figured.

"Whoops," said Pam cheerfully. "What now, my perky friend?"

"You girls ready to try out?" Mohawk called, and the cops glanced at us before resuming their conversation. Mohawk pointed to the DANCERS IN HERE sign.

I said, "We sure are, sugar! We go in there to put on our costumes?"

He nodded, and his Mohawk swayed. Pam giggled. I'd never heard Pam giggle like that. "Course, most girls don't even bother with a costume," Mohawk said, grinning.

"I think you'll find we're not most girls," I said, arch as all hell.

He was interested. "How're you two different?"

"We're always together," I said. "Get what

I mean?"

"Uh, yeah," he said. His eyes darted from the clearly sloshed Pam to me. "So, go change. It's audience night. They vote after you take your turn. You could end up on permanent staff."

Oh . . . *yay.* I knew there were speckles of blood on Pam. Vampires could always smell blood. As we passed him in the narrow hall, I didn't dare to meet Mohawk's eyes.

I steered my drunken vampire friend into the designated room. It was a huge nothing. There were about twenty folding chairs set around at random, and about six of those were occupied by women waiting their turn. The others had already had their stage time and left, I assumed. No screen to change behind, no makeup table, no hangers — no clothes hooks, even. There was a full-length mirror propped against the wall, and that was it. The glamour just overwhelmed me.

The aspiring strippers were all blondes: At least, they'd achieved blonde-dom by some means. They glanced at us and looked away. One face looked vaguely familiar.

I helped Pam to a chair. She sat heavily. Her complexion was still hectic, but at least the red patches were fading and she looked more like a regular vampire and less like cherry vanilla ice cream. Speaking of red dots, I hastily spat on a tissue and dabbed at the specks of blood on Pam's blouse. I'd been very fortunate; a quick glance into the full-length mirror confirmed that I was unbloodied. "All right, genius, what do we do now?" I asked myself, aloud.

Pam said, "I'll, I'll . . . appeal to her. She has two extra costumes." She nodded toward the woman I sort of recognized.

Pam was oddly sure about what the wannabe dancer — who I realized was a vamp — had in her huge tote bag.

"Pam, you did great in there," I whispered.

"So did you. You're so cute," she said. "No wonder Eric likes you."

I glanced out into the hall. The cops were still there, still having a lively conversation with the curvaceous stripper. Crap.

Pam rose cautiously and went over to the vamp, who was sitting by herself, looking bored. She had the requisite blond hair (so did the only African American applicant, by the way) and enormous boobs, and she was a few decades old, I figured. She was thin, with the sulky expression of someone who's used to being spoiled. She wore a yellow bikini top with a tiny pleated gray and yellow skirt, a take on the "naughty schoolgirl" image. Where had I seen her before?

As soon as Pam acknowledged her, the

vamp straightened in her chair, inclined her head, and dropped the sulkiness. When Pam murmured in her ear, she began rummaging around in the big bag. She handed Pam a handful of material and two pairs of shoes. I was amazed until I realized that she could have carried twenty costumes in there, if the size of the one she was wearing was any gauge.

Pam cocked her head at me, and I hurried to help.

"What you got?" I asked. She dropped the garments into my hands. She'd snagged a glittery gold spandex bandeau to go around the chest and a matching — well, it was flattering it to call it a thong. There was a pair of translucent heels to wear with it. Then there was a sort of sky blue leotard with black trim: a former leotard, since most of it had been snipped away. A little swath of blue for boob coverage, descending in a tiny strip to the bottom part, which was like an abbreviated bikini. Black heels and thigh-high black hose completed the look.

Pam sat down on a chair, hard. She giggled again. "Get ready, buttercup! I'll take the gold; you take the blue. It'll look great with your tan." She shrugged off her coat, and when the speckled blouse came into view, she read the alarm on my face

48

correctly. She turned her back to the room to unbutton it, then turned it inside out and tossed it on the floor, close to the vamp. To my amazement, the vamp waited for a moment, then in one quick movement picked up the blouse and stuffed it into her huge bag.

Pam was out of her clothes and into the costume as if it were her daily routine.

I turned my back on the room, though no one seemed in the least bit interested in my goodies. In the course of wriggling into the thing, I found out the descending strip Velcroed to the bottom of the costume. Convenient.

I looked at us together. "Wow," I said. "Pam, we look *great*."

"We do," Pam agreed, with no attempt at modesty. We gave each other a high five. "I'm coming down," Pam said. "Really, I'm feeling almost like myself."

Mohawk called from the door. "Okay, the doubles act!"

I had no idea how we were going to get out of this, so we started toward the door. Even drugged, Pam managed walking in her platform shoes without a wobble in her step, but I had to concentrate ferociously to master the spike heels.

"What's the names?" Mohawk asked.

"Sugar and Butterscotch," I said, and Pam turned her head to give me a look that clearly said she thought I was an idiot.

"Cause she's white and you're brown," Mohawk said. "Cute."

I hadn't spent all that time tanning for nothing.

"Okay, you're on," Mohawk said, opening the door at the end of the corridor to reveal a short flight of steps leading up into darkness. The noise surged out at us. A Latina blonde stomped down the steps, topless, followed by the sound of whistles and catcalls. She looked sweaty and bored.

The cops were still in the hall.

"Shepherd of Judea," I muttered, and Pam and I looked at each other and shrugged.

"New skills," she said. "Eric told me you are quite the dancer. You just have to try doing it naked."

So we went up the steps, teetering in our high, high heels, to begin our careers as strippers. Suddenly we were on the stage, which was simply wood painted black, punctuated with three stripper poles.

The emcee was a brunette guy with a big white smile. He was saying, "Remember, gentlemen! The applause each girl gets is measured with our applause-o-meter, and out of all our dancers tonight, the three girls getting the most audience response will be hired to appear right here at Blonde!"

So we were supplying the audience with free entertainment in the faint hope that we might get a job out of it. Michael was an even bigger asshole than I'd thought, which was saying something.

"Here, straight from their record-breaking engagement in Vegas, I give you Sugar and Butterscotch!" the emcee said, with considerable drama. I figured he took drugs.

I put on my biggest and emptiest smile, and managed to make it to the front of the stage without falling down, thanks to Pam's sudden grip on my hand. Together, we looked out at the men hidden in the darkness, catching a glint of beard here, shine reflecting off a belt buckle there. The hoots and whistles were deafening.

We hadn't specified a song, of course. Justin Timberlake's "SexyBack" came blaring over the sound system, and that was all right with me. "Move it," yelled a rough voice.

We had to *dance. NOW.* And then we had to get the hell out of here before Michael and Rudy recovered enough to come after us.

I half turned to look at Pam flirtatiously, and she stared blankly back at me until she got my drift. "The pole," I muttered, and she gave the audience a saucy smile and wound herself around the nearest pole. The cheering started. I felt the lust begin to dominate the men's minds as I hugged Pam from behind. Pam got with the program, and we swung around the pole together as if we'd been glued. I caught a glimpse of Pam's face. She was licking her lips in a lascivious way.

"You go, Pam!" I said.

"They want a show, we'll give them a show," she said. She bent me over her knee and pretended to spank me in perfect time to the music. In fact, Pam got a little carried away. But the guys loved it; oh boy, did they. I got spanked, licked in the ear, had Pam's hands running over my barely covered chest, and more stuff I just won't mention. We both ended up doing things the stripper pole had probably endured many times.

You know, it was kind of fun after I got the hang of it.

I wouldn't go close enough to the side of the stage to get grabbed. And since I already felt naked, I wouldn't take off my top. Since that was something the audience clearly expected us to do, it was lucky that at that moment the police pulled the plug on the music and switched on the house lights.

They weren't the cops who'd been in the hall. "All right, everyone!" called a tall detective in a blue Windbreaker. "There's been a murder here, and we need to talk with all of you."

"Murder," I said to Pam. "Murder?"

As our eyes met, I could see she was just as bewildered as I was. And I have to say here: With the lights up, we could see our audience, and they looked even worse than I'd expected.

Officer Washington, neat and shiny in his brown uniform, tried to look anywhere but at my chest. He'd been on the force long enough to have a kind of worn-out face, but he hadn't become so world-weary as to be able to completely ignore the abundance of Pam and me that was on display. I learned that the idea of being with a white woman didn't do a thing for Officer Washington, which helped him do his job.

"You ladies talked to the manager of this club earlier, I understand?" he asked. He had a pad and pencil out. By now we knew that the victims were Michael and Rudy.

"Yes, we had an appointment," I said.

"What for? None of the other strippers had to talk to the manager."

"We used to work at another vamp-owned club," I said, improvising. I could give Fangtasia's phone number. "We hoped if we told him that, we'd get the job. He said he'd take it into account."

Pam and I shrugged, at very nearly the same moment. Pam seemed to be a little high even now, but there was more control in her movements and she was keeping her mouth resolutely shut. She was still holding my hand, though.

We'd waited our turn in the bigger room where we'd left our clothes. We'd been allowed to change, thank goodness. Pam was still wearing her gold bandeau top. In sympathy, I'd only pulled on my slacks.

Our friend the stripper vamp had passed by the door on her way out. She was escorted by a cop. She glanced our way, her face composed and indifferent. I finally remembered where I'd seen her: working at Harrah's, carrying drinks, when we'd checked in. Huh. She had a sizable purse hanging from her shoulder; I wondered where the big bag was? Pam's bloodstained blouse was in it . . .

As the other strippers had been questioned, they'd been released. We were the last ones to be brought to this room, which I figured had been Rudy's office. Officer

Washington had been waiting for us there.

"What else happened while you were in there? They want you two to give them a free sample?" Washington was young enough to look faintly self-conscious.

"They seemed more interested in each other," I said carefully.

The policeman glanced at our linked hands and didn't comment. "So they were both alive and well when you left the room?"

"Yes, sir," I said. "In fact, they wanted us to hustle out of there because they were about to talk to someone else, had a guy coming in from out of town, they said."

"That right? Did they say anything else about this man? Vampire or human?"

"No," Pam said, opening her mouth for the first time. "They were just anxious for us to leave so they could get ready."

"Get ready? How?"

We shrugged simultaneously. "They wouldn't hardly tell *us*," I said.

"Okay, okay." Officer Washington snapped his notepad shut and stowed away his pencil. "Ladies, good night to you. You can go pick up your personal items."

But we didn't have any. Pam only had the car keys in her pants pocket and her white trench coat. We had nothing we could have brought costumes in. Would Officer Washington or Windbreaker Guy wonder about that?

Now that the big room was empty, it looked even more depressing. Only a litter of tissues and cigarette butts showed that the women had been here at all. That, and the big bag the vamp stripper had carried, sitting on the chair that was draped with Pam's white coat and my jacket. Windbreaker Guy was staring at the bag. Without hesitation, Pam strode across the floor in those incredible shoes and scooped it up by the shoulder strap.

"Come on, Butterscotch," she told me, "We need to hit the road." Her voice had no trace of the faint English accent I was used to.

And just like that, we left Blonde, doing our stripper walks all the way out to Pam's car.

Mohawk was leaning against the driver's door.

He smiled at us as we approached. His smile was not dim or goofy or naïve.

"Thanks for giving me the opening, ladies," he said, and there was nothing slow in his speech, either. "I've been waiting a year to have them down long enough for me to finish them off."

If Pam was as shocked as I was, she didn't

show it. "You're welcome," she said. "I take it you're not going to tell the police anything about us?"

"What's to tell?" He looked up at the night sky. "Two strippers wanted to tell the boss and his buddy something before they tried out. I'm sure you explained that. When you went on stage, that asshole Michael and his buddy Rudy were alive and kicking. I made sure the cops knew that. I'm betting you also told them something about Michael mentioning he was expecting someone else or expecting trouble."

Pam nodded.

"And stupid, slow me, I was cleaning the toilet, like my boss Michael had told me to do. No one was more surprised than me when I went in the office later and found Rudy dead and Michael flaking away." Mohawk rolled his eyes theatrically. "I must have just missed the killer." He grinned. "By the way, I threw the gun in the ravine back there, right down into the kudzu, before I called the local law. The skinny blond vamp did the same thing with your blouse — Sugar."

"Right," Pam said.

"So off you go, ladies! Have a nice night!"

After a moment of silence, we got in the car. Mohawk watched us as we drove away.

"How long do you think he'll last?" I asked Pam.

"Russell has a reputation for acuity. If Mohawk is a good club manager, he'll get away with killing Michael, for a while. If he doesn't earn money, Russell will make sure he doesn't last. And Russell won't forget that Mohawk is patient and wily, and willing to wait for someone else to do the dirty work."

We drove for a few minutes. I was anxious to get back to my room and wash away the atmosphere of the Blonde.

"What did you promise the vamp that helped us?" I asked.

"A job at Fangtasia. I had a conversation with Sara — that's her name — after you went to bed last night. She hates her job in Tunica. And she used to be a stripper, which gave me the idea of planting her here in case we needed some help. Besides extra costumes, she brought a number of handy items in her bag."

I didn't inquire as to their nature. "And she did all that for us."

"She did all that because she wants a better job. She doesn't seem to have much . . . planning ability."

"In the end, the trip was for nothing. It was a trap."

"It was a bad trap," Pam said briskly. "But it's true that because of Victor's greed, we were almost in serious trouble." She glanced over at me. "Eric and I never thought Victor was exactly sincere about his motives in sending us here."

"You think he was trying to hamstring Eric by getting rid of both you and me? That he knew Michael really wasn't going to defect?"

"I think we're going to keep a very sharp eye on our new master's deputy."

We rode in silence for a couple of minutes.

"You think Sara would mind if we kept the costumes?" I asked, now that Eric was on my mind.

"Oh," said Pam, "I'm planning on it. Without some souvenirs, it's not a real vacation."

The Boys Go Fishing

SARAH SMITH

Sarah Smith's YA ghost thriller, *The Other Side of Dark,* will be published in November 2010 by Atheneum. She has written the modern stand-alone *Chasing Shakespeares,* about the Shakespeare authorship controversy, and three historical mysteries: *The Vanished Child, The Knowledge of Water,* and *A Citizen of the Country.* Two of her books were named *New York Times* Notable Books of the Year. They have been published in twelve languages and have reached bestseller status in the United States and abroad. She is working on a novel about the *Titanic* and another YA thriller, *A Boy on Every Corner.*

for Yuki Miuma

Time could lie lightly on Mr. Green. He could choose to be young, his face smooth, his hair black. He could catch an explosion in a force-field container. But under the weight of loneliness he is just another old man.

His friends have gone. Robin grew up, came out, moved to San Francisco, he's in politics now. The Bat retreated into "scientific experiments." The last time Green saw him, the Cave smelled and the Bat looked like Howard Hughes: long fingernails, dirty beard. Iguana's dead. Atom, dead. Thunderbolt, dead.

And Lana. His girl, his only girl. He remembers every moment they spent together, but the good times are fading. They're places he's gone to in his mind so often he can't see them anymore. The bad times don't fade at all, the sonsabitches. Toward the last, when she could barely speak, he visited her in the hospital, changed his face and hair back to what he'd been, changed into the costume, the whole thing, the mask, the green cloak. "I remember you," she whispered. But she really didn't know him.

Sometimes it isn't worth getting up in the morning.

"I need your help," says the red-haired girl.

Her knocking wakes him. He squints out the door of his cabin into early-morning

61

sunlight, sees a face that reminds him of girls in old comics. The sultry Chinese villainess. But the sultry Chinese villainess would wear a red silk dress cut up the side and she'd have black hair. This one has hennaed hair, cut spiky, and is wearing a parka from L.L. Bean.

The Thompson brothers' rental SUV from town is parked by the fence. Whatever she wants from him, she drove forty miles on logging roads in the snow to get here.

Which means she's trouble.

"Whatever it is, I don't do it anymore."

"Hi, I'm from Worldwide Travel? I left you voice mail?"

He doesn't check his voice mail.

"I have a job for you. From some special fans."

Special has only one meaning for him now. "I don't do hospitals." Never hospitals.

"Not that kind of special."

"Or comic book conventions. Or" — he curves quotes with a finger — " 'media conferences.' And I don't talk with people who use the word *special*. Or *supernatural powers* or *superhero*. Town's back there, you can get going."

"You take people fishing," she says. "They just want to go fishing."

It's been his cover for the past forty years:

ice fishing. Up here, northern Maine, the lakes region. He doesn't do summers, never joined the Ice Fishing Association, doesn't have a Web site. People hire him, they don't, it's all the same to him.

Back when Lana was alive, he pissed clients off regularly, so none of the fishermen kept coming long enough to notice that Lana got old and he stayed young. Now he pisses folks off out of habit.

"They want to go fishing with you."

He stands in the doorway, keeping her outside.

"They're Talents," she says.

"No, they aren't. Those days are gone."

"They are real Talents."

"What do they do?" he jeers.

"They don't know."

This tugs at him. He knows about that kind of talent. Strength and special powers don't cure AIDS ,or end a war, and they don't keep a woman from dying. What does a Talent do, these years?

"I heard the story," she says. "I heard about you and the other superheroes going fishing, once."

For a moment he visits a worn old place in his perfect memory. He's among old friends, laughing friends. *Let's go fishing like superheroes, boys.* And they did, for the only fish worth having.

"Yeah? So?"

"They've heard, too," she says.

"We were showing off."

"Talents were heroes once," she says. "Talents knew what to do with their powers."

Super cleanliness isn't one of his talents. He points back into the cabin at the pile of gear in the corner. "Auger," he says. "Ice adze. Ice saw. That thing in the box, portable cabin. The ice gets thick. Fisherman bores holes in the ice. Cuts a bigger hole. Shines a flashlight through the hole. Waits for a fish to come investigate. Ice fishing. Boringest thing known to man unless you fall through the ice. 'S what I do now. That's what I know to do with myself. They want to go ice fishing? I'll take 'em ice fishing."

She crosses her arms, purses her lips a little, disappointed.

"No," he says. "They want pow, bang, thump. Big fights with big fish. Superhero fishing. There's no fishing like that anymore."

"Let's just say they want pointers," she says. "They're looking for advice."

"I don't give advice."

"What's your rate?" she asks.

"For Talents? There's a special rate."

She nods. "They have money."

"Not money," he says. He knows what he wants. It's what Atom got, the Captain. What Lana got.

"I want somebody to kill me."

The little cabin gets airless. She opens her mouth to protest. Shakes her head. Closes her mouth.

"All right," she says. "It's a deal."

He pads over to the stove, leaving her at the door. Pours cold coffee, scratches his bristly chin with his white china diner mug. (What does the last superhero drink his coffee out of? A diner mug. They really are unbreakable.)

"Yeah?" he says.

"I promise you. You will die."

"Who'll do it?"

"Me," she says.

He figures he has a foot of height on her, a hundred pounds, a thousand years.

"You and who else?"

"Me."

"How?"

She shakes her head. "No proof until it happens."

He figures he's being scammed.

Life is a scam.

Remembers his manners belatedly.

"You want coffee?"

"Do you have tea?"

"Nope."

She looks around. The back ends of her hennaed hair waterfall to her shoulders. Green eyes, strange for Chinese, a green that reminds him of the color of the cloak gathering dust in his closet. He becomes suddenly conscious of dirty laundry on the sofa back and a winter's worth of mud on the floor. He moves molecules, sorting for dirt, inching it toward a corner. He wonders where he put the laundry basket.

Special powers. Hah.

The Fort Kent airport has the welcoming charm of a VA hospital morgue. She's set up a chartered plane for them. The engines chatter like false teeth. They're alone in the passenger cabin.

"So where do you fit in this?"

"I'm their travel agent."

"Talents need travel agents?"

"It's not a full-time job."

"You fly up on this?" he says. He's asking if she can fly.

She smiles and shakes her head. "Yes, I took the plane." No, she can't fly.

"Hope it's safer than it looks."

Green eyes and red hair: Back then, if she wasn't the Oriental villainess, she would have been the sort of girl he'd have rescued from an airplane crash. Back then, he'd have cradled the plane in a force field, smiled for the cameras, never worried about air traffic controllers or incident reports or finding another identity someplace even farther off the map than the unincorporated townships.

Back then, he wouldn't have been in the plane. He hates flying.

"So what's your Talent?" he asks.

"Nothing really."

He waits.

"Organization."

He makes a noncommittal noise. Her cheeks go a little rosy.

"You try parking a tour bus outside Rockefeller Center at noon. Organization *helps*."

"Helps to kill me?"

"Maybe."

"You do lots of tour buses?"

He thinks about tour buses parked at the end of the driveway and shudders. See Mr. Green at home. See Mr. Green do his laundry. See Mr. Green tie one on.

She can't help him. But she could blow his cover. "One thing straight," he says. "It's —"

"Only this once," she says. "Right? You do this one thing, and even if I can't help you, except I can, I never bother you again.

That's OK. There won't be any more kids like these." She reaches into her purse, brings out a compact, powders her nose. He can't remember the last time he saw a girl do that; no call for powder in the townships. She smiles up at him. "Organization is the ability to foresee the future. Just a little."

"I foresee they'll be bored and you'll be pissed off and I'll be cheated."

Her eyes turn from green to the color of smoke over the woods in fire season: dangerous, challenging.

"Do you want a real foreseeing?"

Out of the purse — it's a little purse — she pulls a wooden flute. An old flute, dark and smooth with fingering, so long and thin and curved it looks like a piece of the edge of the world. Too big to fit in the purse. She puts it to her lips and begins to play. He looks out the scratched green plane window, out at the snowy fields. Barren lines of black. Dark and sparse like her music. The landscape of loneliness.

"Stop that," he says.

But she keeps playing. The flute song changes, creeps around him like green tendrils.

"Stop."

She takes the flute away from her lips.

"I won't cheat you," she says.

"Girls?"

"Young women," she says.

There are eight of them. Foreigners. Japanese. And five of them are teenaged girls. There are two older men, one tall with a mustache and long hair, one round and dense and lazy. One of the kids is a boy, he guesses, though the kid has a long pigtail down his back. The rest are wearing pink ribbons and plaid skirts, and they're giggling and nudging each other and pointing at him. They all look alike. Spiked hair. Pointed faces like foxes.

They're tiny. It'd take two of them to haul in a minnow.

"Talents?" he hisses.

"You'll see."

One of the older men comes forward and bows and says a name Mr. Green doesn't catch and says he's honored and all that, or something. Languages aren't one of Mr. Green's skills. "I am head of dojo 'Do Anything Martial Arts.' These my students. Also are my daughters."

The five girls giggle. High school at best. One of the girls curtsies and begins flailing around with a set of pink ribbons. "Flying Beauty Martial Arts!" she chirps. One of them has a pink backpack with a picture of a white cat and the words *Hello Kitty.* Hello Kitty Martial Arts? The girl blinks at him with big eyes and twitches her nose speechlessly. The other three try to hide behind each other. The boy preens like the only rooster in the henyard.

"We are very honor for you take us fishing," says the lazy man. He's wearing a too-loose Red Sox cap turned backward and a Red Sox jacket much too big for him. The effect is oddly dangerous, as if he's about to spring back to a much bigger size.

They gaze at him as if he's supposed to say something. *Pointers,* he thinks. *I'm supposed to give them pointers. Advice.* They all have big eyes. It's like being surrounded by black-velvet pictures of kittens.

They look at him.

He looks back. The only advice he can think of is *Don't eat yellow snow.*

He clears his throat. "Come on. You're going fishing. Don't fall in."

They all giggle. Aargh.

"Come get baggage," the tall man tells the kids, and he and the compressed man trundle off toward the baggage carousel. The kids follow him in a whispering herd, looking back at Mr. Green.

The girl with the pink ribbons whispers to

the boy-rooster.

"Secret-u identity," the boy whispers back.

Good, they're disappointed. Mr. Green scowls at the red-haired travel agent, prickly-proud of himself.

"Guess they expected —"

"Green mask and cloak, glowing force field —"

"I can finish my own sentences." They expected the Green Force, Atom, Astounding, the Bat, Iguana, all grinning with perfect teeth and washboard abs. They expected to go fishing for the Fish, the Monster. Not a weather-beaten old fisherman in a plaid shirt and jeans with a bucket full of farm-raised trout. "What do they do? Giggle the villains to death?"

"Please," she says.

He clears his throat, looking at the strutting boy trying to take all the heaviest luggage himself. "That boy and all the girls? I'm not having hijinks."

She looks at him like she's about to burst into laughter. There's something sad behind it. "Throw cold water over him," she says.

The kids and the men come back, lugging the gross national product of Japan on wheels.

In the plane, on the way up to the lake, the red-haired Chinese girl gets them all

71

singing old songs. He watches her. Red-haired like a flame, short-lived as a match. To care about humans is to care about leaves, about the frost on the glass in the morning. Breathe and it's gone.

Still, he surreptitiously cradles the over-loaded plane.

There is ice on the lake, thick, hard ice, no fog. The kids wrap themselves up like packages in parkas, hats, mittens. Mr. Green takes the girls out back and gets them to make a shelter. He does something he hasn't done in years, gestures a hemisphere of glowing green. "Pile snow over that." "Oooh," the kids go. *"Ano ne!"* When they cover it with snow, there's nothing but an igloo glowing faintly like a neon light in a snowstorm.

Advice: "Anyone know why we cover it up? You protect your secret identity. You don't want to advertise."

They bob their heads in agreement.

"People laugh," says the kid with the long braid bitterly, slouching out from the cabin. He has a butterfly on his jeans. Probably gay.

"No. Not just people laugh. Your enemies find you. People who are going to hurt you find you."

The kid considers.

"Same thing. Laugh. Hurt."

The kid knows nothing.

The boy and the men get settled down in the clients' loft, and the girls giggle in the new igloo.

The red-haired travel agent gets the spare room in the cabin. She uses the shower until the mirror is steamy. He showers after she's finished and smells lavender soap, woman smells. It's been twenty years since Lana died. It's been forever since he was a human man with Lana. He feels bothered and self-conscious with so many people in his privacy.

He pads out in socks to find the red-haired girl in front of the fire, toweling her wet hair from mahogany back to flame. She's wearing a green sweater that goes too well with her hair and jeans that fit her like a thin coat of paint. He realizes, embarrassingly, there's a question he hasn't asked.

"My name is Lan," she says.

He winces.

"I know," she says. "Your wife's name. I am sorry. My name is just Lan."

He pulls herself together. "That's your Talent name?"

She shakes her head, smiling. "Just my name."

"Funny name."

"Not as funny as the Green Force."

"Green," he says. "Bill. Bill was the name my foster parents gave me. The last name changes, but I'm always Bill."

He looks into the fire, remembering streams of fire, falling, falling, gravity screaming around him, catching and shaping it in his pudgy hands, turning it into a cradle —

"Bill," she says. "Nice. Why do you want to die, Bill?"

She's probably twenty, twenty-five. Before he gets to know her, she'll be dead.

He's told his own story a hundred times, seen it in the comics, until he almost believes that Mom baked pies for church socials and Dad drove a tractor round the farm. But he remembers the First World War and the Civil War and the Revolution, and before his name was Bill it was Will and Gwillhem and Willa-helm, and his parents were Mutti and Dadu.

Demon, the villagers called him. The villagers tried to burn him, drown him, stone him. Fire flowed around him. When they threw him into the pond, he shaped air in a bubble around him. *He is your angel,* the priest said. *Call him Willa-helm, Protector. Do not be afraid of him.*

74

For a long time he protected them from a distance, like a guard dog, half-angel, half-wolf.

Then he got involved.

He had friends.

He fell in love.

Now he fishes.

"Death is what people do." Not so long ago, a moment ago in his long life, the other Talents showed up. Each of them unique, wild, strange. Together, a gang. Friends. And Lana. He thought he was people. They proved he was wrong.

"What do those kids have for talents?" he asks.

"Oh, one thing, another. They look after each other," she says. "That's talent enough."

Yeah. "They got long life?" he asks. "Is that one of their Talents?"

She sits with the towel on her knees, looking into the fire. "No. I've known lots like them. The others are dead."

"What's their story? Born with Talent? Made?"

"Made."

"How?" Atom, an atomic explosion. Poor Elastic, a vat of chemicals. Himself falling like a star.

And he has touched something. The Chinese girl stares into the fire, her eyes dead black and her mouth widening into a grimace. Her hands tighten around the towel.

"I made them," she says. "I cursed them. Me."

And she gets up abruptly and leaves.

Four of them went on that long-ago fishing trip: Iguana Man, Astounding, Atom, and the Green Force, who kept the mortals safe and dry. In ordinary ice fishing you shine a light into the murk under the ice. At the bottom of the water, they shone Atom. They could barely see past the yellow ball of light that Atom threw. They were all wasted, laughing so hard they were falling down. Suddenly scales turned in the murk like ragged hands and a single dark eye glared at them before it flashed away into darkness. The world's last monster, trapped in her lake.

"*Shit,* boys," Iguana said.

"It'd be bad to be like that," Atom said soberly.

"No," the Green Force said. "Not us. We won't be like that."

He thought there was an *us*. They'd all live forever. There would always be big, colorful villains to fight, Nazis and Yellow Perils, and beings like himself to fight them.

He had seen something but it took him years to know it: the Great Fish, trapped in her size and strength, with no path out; too big to get out; without the talent to die.

It's two days into an endless fishing trip before he finds out what their talents are.

As far as he can tell, they're normal annoying teenagers. They bundle themselves up in parkas, stare into the ice hole for fifteen minutes, get bored, and move the light around so they scare the fish. They forget to watch the flags. They play with Game Boys and plug their ears with iPods. They giggle and bicker, and kick and punch, and yell "Pow! Wham!" like they are making up their own soundtrack. The boy with the long braid farts like an elephant; nothing worse than the smell of teenage boy. The fathers are polite and heat endless hot water for tea.

It's clear what Lan's talents are. She makes popcorn and sushi, cleans the trout they occasionally catch, braids pigtails, dries little-girl tears.

On the afternoon of the second day the fog comes in.

"We aren't going fishing today," Mr. Green says. "Probably not tomorrow. You can play with your Game Boys in the cabin."

They give him the big-eyed stare.

"Ice is dangerous. Can be a foot thick one step, two inches thick the next. Worse when there's a thaw. Where the Muskeag comes into the lake, the river water's eating the ice from below. Where the ice got broken up by our old fishing holes, where the fish gather, where there's a lot of weed, the ice is thinning out and not healing yet. By the shore the level of the water goes up and down and the ice breaks. But it's foggy, so you're not thinking about that, just trying to find your way to the shore. Unless you know to respect the ice, and you kids don't, you don't fish."

The kids mutter in Japanese.

He and Lan go outside, and she checks the weather report on her magic phone. "Above freezing for the next two days," she points out.

"You foresaw that, right? So it's your problem."

"Come on. They could have a more interesting time."

Their boots slush through the runny snow.

"You could do for them what you did," she says. "You and the others. Back then."

"That's what you want for your kids? Bam, pow, monster? I don't do that anymore."

"They can't even go out in this," she says. "Just can't fish."

"They can't. No. I mean they don't want to go out in this. It sets them off. Their Talents."

"Which are?" he says.

"They're shape-changers."

He waits for more. She doesn't say anything.

"You did it to them?" he prompts. He's given her plenty of chances to talk about it. They've been fishing from the same ice hole for two days. She hasn't said a word.

She doesn't say a word now.

"You cursed them?"

He doesn't believe in personal curses.

"None of my business, I guess," he says finally.

She turns away from him, looking off into the trees.

"What do they change into? Werewolves? Bats?"

"Various things," she says, turning back toward him, blinking. "Short-lived things. One of them changes into a cat. She'll live ten years."

Ten years is a moment.

"I did that to them," she says. "And I'm sorry. I want to help them."

"What are you looking for from me?" he

says. "How not to die? That's the kind of advice you want?"

"How to live!" she shouts at him. "Yes!"

"I move things. Air toward me, water and fire away from me. But I don't know why I keep on living."

"Teach me how you live," she says, "so I can teach them. And I'll find out how you can die."

When they get back to the cabin, the kids are gone.

She says something under her breath and starts running down the path toward the lake, her boots wallowing in the snow. He begins to run too.

It's three-quarters of a mile to the lake, and the footing is horrible, slushy snow over mud over frozen earth. For years he's made his body into an old man's. He slips and his arms windmill as he catches up to her.

"— *foresaw* this?" he pants.

She turns back to him, furious. "Are you a Talent? Does it always work for you? I was talking to you! And if you can push fire away, why can't you push earth and just fly?"

"I don't fly —"

He is a man. Men don't fly. He is a man, like others; he had friends; he had a wife; he was in love. He is Mr. Green, Bill Green. He is not something fallen from the sky, doomed to be alone. He doesn't fly.

He was mankind's Protector once, and he is too lonely to go back to that lonely place. A Protector flies. A man doesn't.

He hears screaming from the lake.

And he flies. Nothing superhero-like, rocketlike; he just pushes the force of gravity away. He's awkward, rising, wobbling. Too far at first; he thinks he'll be spotted and spends too much time scanning the sky for a plane. He ducks down into the trees, gets tangled and caught in a pine, flails at branches. He bullies his way through the treetops like a bear through shrubs, sticky with pine sap, whipped by branches.

There's light in front of him, a plain that looks like a wide white field.

The lake is smoking with fog. He can't see anything. He drops downward, shouting for her, for them, looking for the shore. In the fog, somewhere, they're shouting for him.

When he hits the ice, it tilts.

Broken ice. Open water. He runs across them both, light as a skater. He's never lost anyone on the ice, and he's not going to start now. The ice bobs under his feet, and suddenly, out of the fog ahead of him, he sees the kids. They're stupidly huddled all together by the edge of a fractured black hole, and thrashing in the water he sees two of them, the boy with the long hair and his father. Lan is already out on the ice, flattened on it, her red hair a shock in the grayness, holding her hands out to the boy. "I've got you," Green shouts at her. "It'll hold."

But it doesn't. He tries to extend a cradle of force all the way across the ice, over the hole, without trapping the boy and his father. But there are too many of them, the kids all together are too heavy on all that tipping ice, it's too far, it's been too long.

The ice cracks; she slips and flails and is gone. One by one the kids slide in after her and in a moment the ice is empty.

His giant invisible hands of force reach out and tilt the ice back, find a struggling body here, a furry parka there. His giant invisible fingers sieve the black water, hunting the kids. He shapes a globe of air and shoves a drowning kitten into it. A bear is grabbing at the ice, breaking more chunks away. A Red Sox hat, a Hello Kitty backpack, but no flaming red hair —

He touches something, touches her. Pulls Lan out of the water, her hair a river of blood down her back, her face blue. Throws her down onto the bank. How to get water out of lungs? He makes up something, moving air, moving water. Feels something in her dark and alien as death. Then feels her retching cough.

"What am I looking for?" he yells at her. Another part of him is a net, dredging. "Help me find them!"

In the end he recognizes them only because there are the same number of them as before. There were five girls, one boy, two men; now, one girl, a snake, a great brown bear, five little beasts. A bedraggled kitten stares up at him, a sobbing round badger clutches a girl's glasses in one wet paw. The girl has a long braid. The bear has a Red Sox cap.

They look at him with adoration, as if he could solve all their problems, and their superhero is so lonely he could howl.

He and Lan have sent the kids back to the cabin to bathe, and they stand outside to give the kids privacy. Lan says they want privacy. Lan's changed her clothes, but she's still shivering. He warms the air around her, moving it gently. Protector. They watch through the windows. Through the steamy glass he sees them, bedraggled, silt-smeared animals filing into his shower, little girls coming out wrapped in his towels. A kittenish girl, a round brown girl with a tilted chin and pointed nose. The bear has the lazy man's lumbering, rolling walk, the boy has a girl's shy smile.

"Cold water makes them — change. They change their shape. Hot water turns them back into human," Lan says, her teeth chattering still.

"How did you do that to them?"

"I don't know! As if I knew!"

"There's got to be some way to undo it."

"There was another spring. It's gone."

It's another kind of Talent from anything he knows. "I don't believe in this. It's magic."

"But you can fly," she says, half laughing and half shivering.

"I don't have to believe in myself."

She watches the kids through the window. "Maybe all kinds of magic exist. Somewhere, in a cave, a family of werewolves is reading old *Green Force* comics and saying, 'Of course he isn't *real*.' Ghosts are reading *Sir Gawain and the Green Knight* and saying what you're a metaphor for. And the bats sleep through the day and dream of all of us."

He thinks of the Bat in his Cave. "And we'd all rather be human."

"I thought you could make them human

again. Or at least give them time. *You* don't get old —"

"No," he says sharply. "No."

When his parents began to get old, he thought about fixing their aging bodies. "There are stories about things I did. Humans getting old but not able to die. People turning into trees. They weren't trees. You don't want me messing with those kids."

I want to die. I want to get old and older and oldest and die, and turn into a tree, into a rock. I've been a man.

She shudders, cold or dispirited. "What can you do, then?"

"When my wife got old, I did nothing. That's what I could do for her. I did nothing."

"No." She turns toward him. In the half dark where they are watching, her eyes have turned dark as prophecy. "What can you do?"

"I don't understand."

"Move the light," she says. "Move the light from the window. Can you do that?"

He moves it an inch to the right. Parlor trick.

"You can move *light*. But you got the kids to cover up the igloo because you were worried about satellites. You moved the water

85

out of my lungs, but you didn't move the fog off the lake. You heated the air for me, but you didn't cool it for them. Here we are standing out in the cold. What can you do? I mean, have you ever thought about it? In an organized way?"

She's shouting at him. *I can get old,* he thinks. *I can be old like a bitter old man. I can be bitter.*

But I can't be an old man.

I can't be a man at all.

The kids are looking out the window at him, adoring, hoping for miracles.

"Who are you?" he says. "What right have you to ask me to do anything? You and they will be dead by the time I've had my lunch. You want me to do anything for you? You want me to care about you? That's going to hurt me, and it won't help you or them."

"You have no idea what you can do, do you?"

He knows what he can't do.

"Then I've given you your wish, Green Man," she says. "You are dead. You care about nothing. You are a rock. A stone. An old man fishing until the end of the world."

I can't, he thinks. *I don't have the talent for that either.*

"Then let's try something else," she says.

■ ■ ■ ■

She could book a flight on her magic phone, but she doesn't. She makes him zip them across the Atlantic in a glowing green saucer a hundred feet long. She tells him he can make it invisible to radar and infrared and light, can't he? The kids scream and giggle and bounce around the inside of the flying saucer and ask him to turn off the gravity inside, which he does. The kids fly. He's a terrified protector, afraid of the villagers, helping them from a distance, a watchdog and not a man. He is bony ribs around the kids' beating hearts. He feels like someone in an airplane, speeding along too fast, cradled by something he can't control.

They land on the Mars-rocky shore of the loch, between the pines and the peaty water, Lan and Green and a luminous flying saucer full of giggling, flying teenage Japanese shape-changers. "Make it a submarine now," the kids tell him. He thinks about recirculators, scrubbers; he pushes molecules around. They sink into the brown darkness like into moving loam.

"Can you —" Lan says.

But he holds up his hand. He has been here.

Ice fishing: the seldom-seen, magical moment when the water under the ice is clear, when the fish can see light from a distance. When they gather. When, in the light, the fisherman sees muscular dark bodies turning. When the fish looks at the fisherman, curious, and the fisherman looks at the fish.

What can you do? Who are you?

He does like he did with the dirt on the floor, like at Lake Musky seining for the kids, but tinier, tiny. He sends out into the water nets that are no stronger than metaphors, trawling for the smallest pieces of drowned bark and leaf, gathering them together, dodging around any fish or eel or water snake. He thinks about Brownian motion. Why did they need Atom's light? The water clears. The water clears, leaving worms and little fish wriggling, surprised. The darkness recedes around them; a bigger fish bullets by, mouth open, and the small fry streak for safety in the blackness below them. Green globes light around the kids, and around them the fish gather, as if they are all in one great dark place under the ice together, with one flashlight to draw them.

The kitten-girl gives a little breathy scream.

Out of the blackness, out of the depths,

She comes. She strikes at the glow, but Green thinks slipperiness and the ball that holds them spins past her teeth. She mouths a man-sized fish and flips her body round, whirls around them, thrashing, stretching out her neck, trying to catch them. She is too big to see whole. Riffles of gills, a great round flat eye like a target, scarred scales.

He plays her. Green is the worm; Green is the net, the line, the hook. The great She-Fish worries at the green ball-light, her teeth an inch away from them, and he and Lan and the kids bounce away from her. She wraps her long neck and tail around them. He feints and slides away.

And then suddenly it is a dance. He knows what she wants. He morphs the ball in which they all float into a mirror-monster of her, a ghost monster of green and light. She rears back. He shapes the green fish to match her motion. And for a moment the two of them hang there, in the water clear as glass, a monster fish like ebony and a monster fish like emerald, and she is still, still, still, and she reaches out her long neck, sniffing, opening her mouth to taste the water with her tongue, tilting her head so she sees him out of one enormous eye. *Are you like me,* her outstretched neck says, her tongue licks, and Green's heart beats loud in his ears, *Are you like me?*

But she throws her head back with a cry of loneliness and disappears into the deep.

When they are back on dry land, the kids say nothing. They stand on the rocky shore, each of them alone for a minute. Then the boy goes from one to the other, touching them on the shoulder, bringing them together into a protective hug. They reach out for the two older men, for Lan. She reaches out for him. Green stands with them, embracing them and embraced.

Tonight he has done new things. Of all of them, that silent lonely hug is the hardest, and it's what he will remember, that and Nessie's tongue tasting the green monster made of force and silt, hoping she could find something like herself.

He takes everyone back to Japan in his invisible force-field UFO. They're quiet on the trip. Over Japan, the trees are pink and green with springtime. At the big Tokyo train station, the kids and the older men shake hands with him and Lan. Then the Japanese Talents wander away, down escalators. The station is a big mall, open in the center. Green and Lan can still see the group, past the escalator, two levels below them. The kids stand in front of a game store, huddling together.

"Guess they thought they'd be happier when the heroics happened," Green says. "Guess they thought they'd figure something out."

"They've seen monsters," Lan says.

He nods.

"We went fishing," he says. "Four of us. We were so jazzed about being Talents. That was the age of Talents. We thought we had it made. We were kings of the world. We were like each other. But Atom got sick, Astounding was going to get himself blown up someday and he did, I stole my wife from Iguana and pretended to be human. We went fishing and we caught loneliness. I can't help the kids, Lan. Badgers and cats don't live more than a few years. Someday there'll be only one of them left. And it'll see something it thinks is like itself or its friends, but the smell will be wrong and the taste will be wrong, and it'll know it's the only one of itself in the world. Being the one there's only one of, that's being a monster."

"I'll buy you a present," Lan says.

She makes him wait outside a shop full of statues of every description, from Buddha to the Virgin Mary. Here in Planet Tokyo you buy Buddhas in a train station. She

91

comes out with a little box. Not far away from them there's something like a food court with little tables. They take a table with pink plastic flowers embedded in its top. "Open your present now." She goes away and comes back with two drinks, something chewy and sweet with barley in it.

Green's present is eight little plastic statues in a row on a plastic base.

"The Eight Immortals." She touches their small heads one by one. "Immortal Woman He, whose lotus flower gives health. Royal Uncle Cao, whose jade tablet purifies the world. Iron-Crutch Li, who protects the needy." She takes the next one off the stand, a slim Chinese boy or girl with a woven basket and a flute, and stands it by her purse. Through the woven material of the purse he can see the outline of that long flute. "Lu Dongbin, whose sword dispels evil spirits. Philosopher Han Xiang, whose flute gives life. Elder Zhang Guo, master of clowns, winemaking, and Qigong kung fu. Zhongli Quan, whose fan revives the dead."

Green picks up the statue with the basket and flute, and looks a question at her.

"Immortal Woman runs a health food store in New Jersey. The Philosopher and Quan are dead, I think. The Philosopher's flute came to me in the mail one day. I saw Zhang Guo on the beach in Monterey but he wouldn't talk to me. Lu, Li, Cao, I don't know. Immortal Woman frightens me most. She didn't want to be a monster. She wanted friends and neighbors. She made herself forget she was immortal. I go in there once a year or so, and she says nothing but trivial things, *How do you like those Dodgers?* She never stops talking. She bores everyone and forgets to charge for newspapers. But she isn't a monster."

"You want to be lonely?" Green says. "You want to be alone?"

She touches the statue he has picked up, which means she touches his hand. "Lan Caixe. The shape-changer, the mysterious one. The minstrel whose songs foretell the future. No," Lan says, "I didn't want to be a monster. So I made other shape-changers, and I thought they would be like me."

"Yeah," Green says.

"Which made me a monster."

He doesn't move his hand, though he agrees with her. Her fingers stay lightly on his, ready to be rejected.

"I thought you could help," she says. "You would make me not a monster anymore."

"Wish I could have." Still their hands touch, in midair, but he doesn't pull away,

93

until it's awkward, or meaningful, or something, but neither of them pulls away.

"What are we if we aren't humans or heroes? Are we always monsters?" she asks.

No. We are, he thinks. *We just are.*

Immortal? Enduring. Like a rock, like an old man fishing — ?

"Organized, maybe," he says to her.

"Not very." But she smiles.

"You more than me."

"It's a talent."

The kids could use help. Not that he can give it. He has failed at being a Protector and failed at being a man. But maybe she can think of something he can do. Maybe together they can —

He wonders if she's foreseeing he'll think that.

He wonders what she's foreseeing.

That might bother him, her foreseeing him.

"I owe them," she says. "Thanks."

But maybe it won't bother him much.

"S'pose we go back to my place; we can have some coffee and talk about stuff."

"You don't have any tea?" says his red-haired Chinese immortal hopefully.

Nope, he's about to say; but here he is in Shinjuku Station, in Japan, on another planet, and it is spring. Nothing will bring back Mutti and Dadu, nothing will bring back his lost wife or his old friends. Even if Lan is one of the Eight Immortals, there are no guarantees. And nothing will make him a man.

But perhaps to be superhuman you need to have been human once, and failed.

Here is what I'd say to you, he thinks to those little Japanese kids he will probably meet again, *here's the advice I'd give. You little bits of frost, you falling leaves, you mortals? You're doing the important thing right. Keep hold of each other as long as you can. Hug each other and hang around to-gether.*

Nothing lasts forever. But Atom and Astounding and the Iguana and me?

We had a great time fishing.

"This is Japan. I bet we can buy us some tea."

ONE FOR THE MONEY

JEANIENE FROST

Jeaniene Frost lives with her husband and their very spoiled dog in Florida. Although not a vampire herself, she confesses to having pale skin, wearing a lot of black, and sleeping in late whenever possible. And although she can't see ghosts, she loves to walk through old cemeteries. Jeaniene also loves poetry and animals but fears children and hates to cook. She is currently at work on the next novel in her bestselling Night Huntress series.

ONE

I squinted in the morning sunlight. At this hour, I should have been in bed, but thanks to my uncle Don, I was traipsing across the NCSU campus instead. I strode up to Harrelson Hall, then climbed to the third floor to the class I was looking for. When I walked in, most of the students ignored me, either chatting with each other or rifling through

their bags as they waited for class to sta.
The room had stadium-style seating, wit
the entrance down by the professor's lec-
tern. My lower vantage point gave me the
same sweeping view of the students the
professor would have. I scanned every face,
seeking the one that matched the jpeg I'd
been sent. *No, no, no . . . ah. There you are.*

A pretty blonde stared back at me with
barely concealed suspicion. I smiled in a
friendly way and threaded up the aisle
toward her. My smile didn't soothe her; she
flicked her gaze around the room as if
debating whether to make a run for it.

Tammy Winslow, I thought coolly. *You*
should *be scared, because you're worth a lot
of money dead.*

The air felt charged with invisible currents
moments before a ghost burst into the
room. Of course, I was the only one who
could see him.

"Trouble," the ghost said.

Sounds of heavy footsteps came down the
hall while the air thickened with greater
supernatural energy.

So much for doing this the quiet way.

"Get Bones," I told the ghost. "Tell him
to be ready at the window."

That turned a few heads, but I didn't care
about my college-student ruse anymore. I

d to get those people out of here.

"I've got a bomb," I called out loudly. "If you don't want to die, get out now."

Several kids gasped. A few snickered, not sure if I was kidding, but no one ran for the door. The footsteps coming down the hall got closer.

"Get out *now*," I snarled, pulling my gun out of its hidden holster and waving it.

No one waited to see if I was kidding anymore. Scrambling ensued as the students ran for the door. I held on to my gun, shouting at everyone to stay away from me, relieved to see the room emptying. But when Tammy tried to dart away, I grabbed her.

A man barreled through the door, knocking the panicked deluge of students aside as if they were weightless. I shoved Tammy away and whipped out three of the silver knives that I had strapped to my legs under my skirt, waiting until no one was in front of him before flinging them at the charging figure.

He didn't try to dodge my blades, and nothing happened when they landed in his chest. *A ghoul, great.* Silver through the heart did nothing to ghouls; I'd have to take his head off to kill him. Where was a big sword when I needed one?

I didn't bother with more knives, but launched myself at the ghoul, bear-hugging him. He pounded at my sides, smashing my ribs as he tried to shake me off. Pain flared in me, but I didn't let go. If I were human, the punishment from his fists would have killed me, but I was a full vampire now, so my broken bones healed almost instantly.

I managed to put the gun's muzzle to the ghoul's temple and pulled the trigger.

Screams erupted from the few kids still left in the room. I ignored them and kept pumping bullets into the ghoul's head. The bullets wouldn't kill him, but they did a lot of damage. His head was in oozing pieces when I let go.

Tammy tried to run past me, but I was faster, knocking over desks in my way as I grabbed her. Scraping sounds let me know the ghoul was crawling toward us, his head healing with every second. I hopped over the desks, yanking Tammy along with me, and pulled out my largest knife from under my sleeve. With a hard swipe, I skewered the ghoul's neck.

The ghost appeared in the window, followed by another surge of energy coming from the same direction. Time to go.

Tammy screamed as she fought me, trying to break my hold on her. "I'm not going to hurt you," I said. "Fabian." I glanced at the ghost. "Hold on."

He wrapped his spectral hands around my shoulders. Tammy wasn't as trusting. She kept screaming and kicking.

I ignored that and ran right at the window. Tammy shrieked as we smashed through it with a hail of glass. Since her classroom had been on the third floor, we didn't have a long hang time before something collided with us, propelling us straight upward. Tammy's screams rose to a terrified crescendo as we rocketed up at an incredible speed.

"Somebody help me!" she shrieked.

The vampire who'd caught us adjusted his grip, flying me, Tammy, and the hitchhiking ghost toward our destination at the far edge of campus.

"Somebody has," he replied, English accent discernible even above Tammy's screams.

The Hummer was equipped with bulletproof windows, a reinforced frame, and a backseat that couldn't be opened from the inside. Tammy found that out when she tried to escape as soon as we'd thrown her in and sped off. Then she'd shrieked for another ten minutes, ignoring my repeated statements that we weren't going to hurt her. Finally, she calmed down enough to ask questions.

"You shot that guy in the head." Her eyes were wide. "But that didn't kill him. How is that possible?"

I could lie. Or I could use the power in my gaze to make her believe she hadn't seen anything unusual. But it was her life on the line, so she deserved the truth.

"He wasn't human."

Even after what she'd seen, her first reaction was denial. "What kind of bullshit is that? Did my cousin send you?"

"If he'd sent us, you'd be dead now," Bones said, not taking his attention off the road. "We're your protection."

I knew the exact moment Tammy got a good look at the vampire who'd snatched us out of thin air, because she stared. Her scent changed, too. That former reek of terror became a more perfumed fragrance as she checked out his high cheekbones, dark hair, ripped physique, and sinfully gorgeous profile.

Young, old, alive, undead, doesn't matter, I thought ruefully. *When Bones is around, women go into heat.*

But Tammy had just been through a very traumatic experience, so I ignored the vampire territorialism that made me want to grab Bones and snap, "Mine!" Instead, I handed her a pack of wet wipes.

She looked at them with an incredulous expression. "What do you expect me to do with these?"

"Nothing works better to wipe off blood, believe me," I said, showing her my newly cleaned arms.

Tammy looked at them, at me, and at Bones. "*What* is going on?"

"She already told you," Bones said, pulling over on the side of the road and putting the vehicle in park. "But you need more proof before you believe us, right?" He held up his hand. "Watch."

Bones dragged a knife across his hand, cutting open a line of flesh. Tammy stared as it closed moments later as if it had an invisible zipper. Fabian didn't even blink. The ghost was used to the healing abilities of the undead.

"I'm a vampire, that's why I can do this. Name's Bones, by the way."

"And I'm Cat," I added. "I'd introduce you to Fabian, but you can't see him anyway. We're your guardians until my uncle tracks down your cousin and arrests him."

Tammy's face was almost comical in its incredulity. "But it's daylight," she said at last. "Vampires can't go out in the sun, everyone knows that!"

Bones chuckled. "Right. And we shrink back from crosses, can't travel over water, can't enter a home unless invited, and always get staked in the end by the righteous slayer. Really, who'd be afraid of a creature like that? All you'd need is a Bible, a tanning bed, and some holy water to send us shivering to our dooms."

Tammy shook her head slowly. I watched with sympathy. Denial was how I'd reacted at sixteen when I found out my absentee father had been a vampire, and that it wasn't puberty causing my strangeness, but the growth of my inhuman traits.

"I know it's hard to believe since vampires and ghouls look human most of the time," I tried again, "but —"

"Let me get this straight," Tammy interrupted. "I asked some of my father's old government friends for help when 'accidents' kept happening to me, and someone sent a *vampire* to protect me?"

Fabian began to laugh. I gave the ghost a censuring look that silenced his chuckles, but even though he was partially transparent, it was clear his lips were still twitching.

"Actually, two vampires," I corrected. "The ghost was a bonus."

"I'm a dead woman," Tammy muttered.

Bones snorted. "Told you this job wouldn't be easy, luv."

He was right, but I owed Don a favor. Even if I hadn't, I would still be here. Last month, Tammy had almost been killed by a "freak" electrical surge. Two weeks ago, a drive-by shooting nearly took her life. Could've been unfortunate coincidences, except for the fact that if Tammy died before her twenty-first birthday, all her father's millions would go to her cousin, Gables. Tammy's late father had been an old friend of my uncle's, and Don didn't believe in coincidences. Then Don did some digging and heard that the next attempt on Tammy would involve an "exotic" kind of hit man who never failed.

Don knew what that meant. He ran a special Homeland Security division that dealt with the supernatural — not that taxpayers knew part of their money went toward policing things that supposedly didn't exist. I was retired from the unit, but that made it even better for my uncle. Don didn't need to use an active team member to look after his old friend's daughter. No, he could call me, knowing I wouldn't turn away a girl who had her head on a preternatural chopping block.

Tammy seemed to have gotten over her initial shock. She tossed her blond hair. "I offered to pay for protection, and if you're the ones protecting me, that means you work for me. So I'm going to lay some ground rules, got it?"

My brows rose. Fabian whistled, but of course Tammy couldn't hear the ghost. *You better hurry up and arrest her cousin, Don,* I thought.

Bones gave me a knowing look. "Told you not to answer your mobile whilst we were on vacation, Kitten."

I sighed.

Tammy ordered, "Take me back to my house," but Bones ignored her, pulling onto the road and continuing in the opposite direction of where she lived.

"It's only for a few days," I said.

Or so I hoped, anyway.

Two

Most people who'd had three brushes with death — one involving a ghoul — would be scared into a very cooperative state. Tammy appeared to be channeling her inner Paris Hilton instead. Evidently she'd never heard the word *no* before. She was outraged that we didn't let her go back to her house to pack, and then she was *really* upset once she saw the town we were hiding out in.

"You've got to be kidding." Tammy gave a disparaging glance at the rustic countryside and overgrown cherry orchard bordering the property where I'd grown up.

"It's in the middle of nowhere," Tammy went on. "You probably have psychotic in-breds living in the woods!"

She's suffered a traumatic experience, I reminded myself again, gritting my teeth. *Cut her some slack.*

Licking Falls *was* in the middle of rural nowhere, but that was the point. It might not look appealing to a young heiress, but for safety, it was ideal. No one would think to look for Tammy here.

We'd rounded the last turn and were heading down the long gravel road that led to my old house when Bones abruptly stopped.

"What's wrong?" I asked, feeling his tense-ness like invisible ants marching across my skin.

"Your house isn't empty," he stated low. "And the occupant isn't human."

"Let's get out of here," Tammy said, her voice rising. "Now!"

I had my hand over her mouth even as Bones slid soundlessly out of the car. All we

106

needed was for Tammy to start screaming to really alert whoever the undead intruder was. How the hell had someone beaten us here? We'd told no one we were coming! Instinct made me want to follow Bones, but that would leave Tammy unprotected. I glared at Tammy and ordered her in a low tone to be silent. The power from my gaze rendered Tammy mute at once. Then I let go of her mouth and pulled out a few weapons, all my senses directed toward the house half a mile up the road.

Relief rolled across my subconscious moments later, causing me to lessen my grip on my knives. Bones must have killed the intruder. Being connected to Bones this way was like hitchhiking on his emotions. In situations like this, it also came in handy.

I began to drive up the road again, ignoring Tammy's frantic pokes on my shoulders. I'd compelled her to be quiet, but not to be still, more's the pity.

When I was halfway up the road, Bones appeared, a bemused expression on his face.

"Your mum's here," he said.

I'd slowed on seeing him, but at that, I slammed on the brakes. "She is?"

Bones nodded and got into the passenger seat. "In the undead flesh."

"Catherine?" I heard my mother say,

107

sounding as surprised as I felt. Of course. Even a hundred yards away, with her new hearing, she'd pick up my conversation with Bones as easily as if she'd been in the car.

A lump made its way into my throat. "Yeah, Mom. It's me."

I hadn't seen my mother in months. Not since the night I killed the man who'd kidnapped her and forcibly changed her into a vampire. He'd done it just to hurt me, the bastard. It was a shame I couldn't kill him twice.

My mother was framed in the front door, watching me as I pulled up. The highlights had grown out of her hair, and her skin was already paler than it had been the last time I'd seen her. Feeling the aura of supernatural energy coming from her was something I didn't think I'd ever get used to.

"Hi," I said as I got out. I wanted to hug her, but I was afraid she might push me away. My mother had always loathed vampires. Now she was stuck as one, and it was all because of me. To say that strained our relationship was putting it mildly.

Her hands fluttered, like she wasn't sure what to do with them. "Catherine." A small smile creased her face. "What are you doing here?"

"We were going to use the house to hide

out, but since you're here —"

"Someone's after you again?" she cut me off, green tingeing her blue gaze.

"Not me," I hastened to assure her. "Tammy, the girl in the backseat. Bones and I are, uh, guarding her for a few days until Don squares things away."

"Hallo, Justina," Bones said, getting out of the car. "Certainly didn't expect to see you here."

"I wanted somewhere quiet to go for a vacation," she muttered.

He let out a sardonic laugh. "Seems we're not the only ones to have our vacation interrupted, then."

Bones took it for granted that we'd still be staying here. We'd decided this place was perfect to hide Tammy, and I'm the one who owned it, so to him it was settled. But after all my mother had been through, I didn't want to subject her to my current predicament.

"We'll go somewhere else," I said with an apologetic shrug.

"Is something wrong with the girl?" my mother asked, pointing.

I glanced at the backseat. Tammy was smacking at the door while her eyes bugged and her mouth opened and closed like a fish.

"Oh shit, I forgot about muting her!"

I let Tammy out and returned her voice with a flash of my gaze. The first thing she did was howl loud enough to make me wince.

"Don't *ever* do that to me *again!*"

"Then don't give away our position if we think there's danger, and we won't have a reason to," Bones replied with an arched brow.

"Mom, this is Tammy," I said, waving the blonde forward.

My mother smiled at her. "Hello, Tammy. Nice to meet you."

Tammy grabbed my mother's arms. "Finally, someone normal! Do you know what it's *like* with these two? They're worse than prison guards! They wouldn't even stop to let me eat!"

Bones snorted. "We were a bit busy keeping you alive, if you recall."

My mother glanced at Tammy and then back at me. "Poor girl, you must be starving. I'll make you something for dinner. You don't want Catherine to cook, believe me."

Under normal circumstances, I might have bristled at the implication. But that statement, plus the look she'd given me, said we would be staying here after all. Safety concerns for Tammy aside, I was happy. I'd missed my mother. Maybe our mutually interrupted vacations were a blessing in disguise for our relationship.

"After you, Mom."

My warm and fuzzy feeling evaporated after dinner, however. The house only had two bedrooms. My mother kindly offered to share hers with Tammy, but just as I was about to thank her for it, Tammy spoke.

"Shouldn't I sleep with *him* instead?" Tammy's gaze swept over Bones with unmistakable lust. "After all, since I'm the one paying, I should choose who I bunk with."

My mother gasped. I opened my mouth to deliver a scathing retort, but Bones laughed. "I'm a married man, but even if I weren't, you wouldn't stand a chance. Rotten manners you have."

"Your loss," Tammy said, with another toss of her hair. Then she looked around in frustration. "You can't expect me to stay here more than a couple days. I'll go crazy."

"But you'll be alive," I pointed out, which should have been her top priority, in my opinion.

"You killed that thing, didn't you?" Tammy asked. "Doesn't that mean the danger's over?"

Bones shrugged. "I doubt the ghoul was

111

the person contracted to kill you. Sounds like outsourced, cheap local talent to me."

Tammy gaped at him. "She had to cut his head off before he stayed down. *That's* what you consider cheap local talent?"

"No self-respecting undead hit man would take a contract on a human," Bones said dismissively. "Humans are too easy. Like getting paid to stomp on a goldfish. But in your case, probably a human hit man who knows about the undead got frustrated that his last two attempts didn't work, and gave some quid to a young ghoul to finish you. It's a practical solution; the ghoul gets money and a meal, the hitter still keeps the bulk of the contract payment, and the client's happy that you're dead."

"You would know, wouldn't you?" my mother muttered.

"How's that?" Tammy asked.

Bones smiled at her, beautiful and cold at the same time. "Because I was a hit man for over two hundred years."

Tammy gulped. I didn't add what I knew: that Bones had been very particular about his contracts. He killed other killers, not innocent people, and most of those people were his own kind. That hadn't won Bones any popularity contests in undead circles, but if Bones thought someone deserved to

112

die, he took the contract, no matter the danger.

"In a few days, Don should have your greedy toad of a cousin arrested, and then it will be safe for you to go home," Bones went on.

"If you're a hit man, why can't I just pay *you* to kill Gables?" she asked, recovering. "My birthday isn't for another two months. Who knows if my cousin might try to kill me again, even if he is in jail?"

My eyes widened at how causally Tammy broached the subject. *Pass the salt. Kill my cousin.*

Bones shrugged. "He might, but you'll have to look elsewhere for a hitter. I'm too busy for that now."

Tammy glanced at my mother, me, and then Bones before her face tightened up. "This sucks," she said, and ran up the stairs.

Considering I could have been spending the next two weeks on vacation with my husband instead of looking after a spoiled rich girl who was being targeted by killers, I agreed.

"It'll be all right, Tammy," I called out.

An expletive was her response. Bones arched a brow and tapped the side of his eye.

"Say the word, luv. I'll glare a whole new

attitude into her."

Vampire mind control would be the easy way out, but when did I ever take the easy way?

"She'll come around," I muttered. *Hurry up, Don.*

"I'll go talk to her," my mother said.

Both my brows went up. "You think you can make her see reason?"

My mother gave me a jaded look as she ascended the stairs. "You forget, Catherine — I've had a *lot* of experience dealing with a difficult child."

Bones laughed, with a knowing glance at me that made my mouth twitch despite myself. Okay. My mother had a point.

THREE

I'd been in life-and-death situations since I was sixteen, but those could be handled with some bravery — or recklessness, depending on who you asked — and my knives. A cranky, demanding heiress required a different set of skills. Ones I didn't seem to have.

Day two during a conversation with Tammy: "So you're married to Bones, huh? How'd you manage to snag him? You know, with your red hair and white skin, you look like a big candy cane."

Day three: "Boy, is Bones *hot.* If I were you, I'd be on him five times a day. If you two break up, send him my way, huh?"

Day four: "Let me out of this room! I'll call the police, the FBI. Let me *out!*"

By day five, when Don still hadn't located Gables, Bones and I were ready to take matters into our own hands. If my uncle, with all the resources of the military and the government behind him, couldn't find Gables, then he wasn't going to be found anytime soon. Putting our lives on hold for a few days was one thing, but Bones was Master of a large vampire line. We couldn't hide with Tammy for much longer. Soon we'd have to get back to our usual routine, dealing with the intricacies and dangers of life in undead society.

Not to mention, staying in a tiny house with my mother had ground my sex life to a halt. These walls were paper thin anyway, and with my mother being a vampire, anything we did would be as clear to her as if she were in the same room. The idea of her overhearing every last detail of me getting it on with Bones wasn't romantic, to say the least. Yeah, it was past time to be proactive about finding Gables.

We drove down a barely used road that

115

dead-ended at a large industrial warehouse. Judging from its exterior, you'd never guess this was a nightclub filled with creatures the average person didn't believe existed. It was called Bite. Bones had taken me here on our first date, but we weren't taking a trip down memory lane. We were here for information.

Parking was around the back, surrounded by a thick line of trees that concealed the number of cars from anyone who happened to stumble across the lonely single road. For a secluded spot where immortals could let their hair down, Bite was perfect.

Of course, the heartbeats coming from many of the people waiting to get in proved that Bite didn't cater only to undead partiers. *They're the menu, with legs,* Bones had said of the humans the first time he brought me here. It was a willing arrangement. A skillfully executed vampire bite could feel better than foreplay. Plus, some humans hung around vampires hoping to be promoted to the next level in the food chain. Even the undead had groupies.

My mother declined to come with us, stating that she didn't want to be around more vampires than necessary. Fabian stayed to keep her company, which seemed to make her happy. How far she'd come. I remembered when my mother would have run screaming away from a ghost, not looked forward to spending an evening with one.

So it was just Bones, Tammy, and I who walked past the people in line. Humans and new vampires might have to wait their turn, but a Master vampire — and anyone with him — could go straight to the door. As we approached, I felt Bones draw in his aura of power, suppressing it to a level far below the mega-Master that he was. It was a trick Bones had gotten better at during the past several months. Immediately, the connection I had with him was barely discernible. The last time he'd closed himself off like this, it was right before he'd almost died. Feeling that blank wall when I was used to tapping into his mood brought back bad memories.

"I hate it when you do that," I whispered.

He squeezed my hand. "Sorry, luv. I don't want to announce myself to anyone who doesn't already know me."

I understood. Muting his power level was a better disguise for Bones than dyeing his hair or making other changes to his appearance.

The entrance was guarded by a brawny, blond vampire who had to be six feet tall. She barely looked at Tammy, smiled when she saw Bones, and then laughed when her gaze flicked to me.

"I knew it. Wait until I see Logan. I told him Bones brought the Red Reaper with him years ago, but Logan didn't believe me."

I'd recognized the bouncer from that night, but I was surprised she remembered me.

"Trixie, luv, been a long time," Bones said, giving her a kiss on the cheek. She returned it before shaking my hand.

"Reaper. A pleasure."

"Call me Cat." *Red Reaper* might be my nickname among the undead, but I preferred to be called by the abbreviation of my real name.

Tammy gave Trixie a frank stare. "Is she dead, too?"

Trixie grinned, showing off the gold plating on her fangs. "Does that answer your question?"

"Ew," Tammy said.

I rolled my eyes and mouthed *Sorry* to Trixie, but she didn't seem to care about Tammy's comment.

"No fireworks inside," Trixie said, giving my hand a last, friendly squeeze.

I glanced at my hands and suppressed a shudder. One of my new tricks as a vampire was that when I got really pissed, flames shot from my hands. Guess word of that had spread. It shouldn't surprise me. Nobody loved gossip as much as people who'd had centuries of experience spreading it.

"We're not here for trouble," Bones said.

Trixie laughed. "That'll be the day when you don't leave trouble in your wake, Bones. Just keep it away from here."

"She knows you pretty well, huh?" I asked once we'd come inside.

Bones's mouth quirked. "Not as well as you're implying, Kitten."

It was a valid guess. Bones looked like temptation incarnate, and he'd been around the block for hundreds of years before he met me. If I assumed he'd slept with every female vampire he introduced me to, I'd be right more than I was wrong.

I pushed that thought away with all the other things I didn't like to dwell on. "Come on. I can smell the gin and tonic up ahead."

It was true. I smelled the different alcohols as the bartenders poured them, the myriad of other people's scents mixed with different perfumes, aftershaves, and the tang of blood. Add that to the pulsating music, the muted strobe lights, the crush of people, and the energy wafting from everyone without a heartbeat, and I felt almost drunk from sensory overload.

"You couldn't feel it the last time, but you can now, can't you?" Bones whispered. "How thin the line is here between the normal and the paranormal. I told you Ohio was a supernatural hotspot. This club was built on an even bigger one. Feels like a charge in your blood, doesn't it?"

It did. No wonder the undead flocked to hotspots. Alcohol and drugs couldn't affect me anymore, but being surrounded by all the inhuman occupants, where magic seemed to throb just below the surface, was sensual and exhilarating.

"Forget the drink. Let's dance."

My voice came out lower than I intended. Green appeared in the dark depths of Bones's eyes.

"Are you guys going to let me dance and have a little fun for once?" Tammy grumbled.

Bones swept out his hand. "By all means. Only don't leave the dance floor for any reason, or I'll lock you in your closet for a week."

Even if Tammy didn't know from experience that Bones never bluffed, his expression must have convinced her, because she gulped.

"Stay on the dance floor. Got it."

120

"Right, then. Off you go."

FOUR

Bones was pressed to my back, his hips swaying against mine while his hands slid down my sides with a slow caress. Our recent celibacy combined with the brush of his lips on my neck, the coiled power pushing at his aura, plus all the mystic energy swirling around us, made me want to find the nearest corner and commit unspeakable acts on him.

But even the headiness of the atmosphere and the sensuality of dancing with Bones couldn't make me endanger Tammy — or have sex in public, like some people did at these clubs.

"After this is over with Tammy, we're coming back here," I murmured. "I bet you know where the private spots are in this place, and I intend to molest you in every one of them."

He laughed, sending tingles down my neck where his breath landed. "What a scandalous notion. I vow I'm blushing."

I doubted Bones had blushed since the Declaration of Independence was signed. *In 1776, Bones would have been ten,* I thought hazily, shuddering as his fangs grazed my pulse in a tantalizing way. *Close. At seventeen, he was prostituting himself to the women of the English* ton *in order to survive.*

"Ready for that drink, luv?" Bones asked, turning me around to face him.

Yeah, I was ready for a drink, but not gin and tonic. I wanted to bury my fangs in Bones's throat and drain him until there was only enough blood left in him to keep him hard.

Hunger swelled in me at the thought. Changing from a half-breed into a vampire had had unexpected side effects. I was only *mostly* dead, as my occasional heartbeat evidenced, and I drank vampire blood instead of human blood. Problem was, I absorbed more than nourishment from the blood I drank. I also absorbed power. Found that out after I fed from a pyrokinetic vampire and then my hands sprouted flames. I didn't want to absorb more freaky abilities by feeding from vampires with unusual powers, so I stuck with drinking from Bones. So far, that had only made me stronger, not stranger.

Of course, Bones always looked good enough to eat. Whoever said *Don't play with your food* sure hadn't been a vampire.

Bones inhaled, his eyes changing to emerald green. I knew mine would have changed also, and I felt my fangs push at my lips. *Give us flesh,* they urged. *His flesh. Now.*

"Stay here. Keep an eye on Tammy," Bones growled, surprising me by shouldering his way through the other dancers. Had he spotted a threat? I glanced around, looking for Tammy's familiar blond head among the mass of living and undead gyrators. There. Dancing with *two* men, no less.

I made my way through until I reached Tammy, getting between her and one of the dancers. His scowl turned into a smile as his gaze swept over me.

"Hello, redhead," he drawled.

"I'm just getting my friend," I said.

Tammy didn't budge. "Hell no. I'm just starting to have fun!"

"Tammy," I gritted out, "don't make me carry you." If there was danger, I wanted our backs to a wall with me in front of her. Not where trouble could come from any angle.

Tammy glared at me but didn't object again. I led her to the closest corner, as if we were having an intimate conversation, but I was braced for action. No one looked as if they were stalking us. Still, appearances were deceiving.

I felt a stab of relief when I saw Bones striding toward us. A large ghoul with black bushy hair and a blindingly white smile followed him.

"Verses, this is my wife, Cat," Bones introduced me.

"Nice to meet you," I said, shaking his hand. I was surprised when Bones tugged me away a moment later.

"Follow me," he said, leading me past the DJ's booth and to a door behind it. It opened to reveal a staircase, and it was a good thing I could see in the dark, because there were no lights once Bones shut the door.

I expected to see a weapons cache, but we were in a room cluttered with old speakers, musical equipment, boxes, and tables. I was about to ask what we were supposed to do with this stuff when Bones yanked me to him. He kissed me, pushing me back against the table and reaching under my dress.

Clearly we weren't here to armor up against danger. "Bones," I managed, pushing him back. "Tammy —"

"Is fine with Verses," he cut me off. "Don't fret about her. Think about me."

He propped me up on the table as he spoke, pulling my underwear down past my knees. I gasped when he kissed me again, because he unleashed his aura at the same time. The waves of power suddenly flooding over me, combined with the rub of his desire on my subconscious, felt just as tangible as his tongue raking inside my mouth.

My objection vanished. Music boomed all around us, its throbbing beat mimicking the pulse I no longer had. I kissed him back, pulling him closer. A last tug on my underwear had them off, and Bones spread my legs, positioning himself to stand between them. I opened his shirt, tonguing his flesh from his neck to his chest, awash in the heightened sensations of supernatural energy, lust, and power that came from Bones and the club above us.

He squeezed my breasts, his fingers teasing my nipples rigid even through my bra and dress. Hard, bare skin rubbed me below as he tugged down his pants. I arched against him, moaning into his mouth. Need throbbed within me. The table and walls vibrated from music pumping above us. To me, it seemed like everything was shuddering with passion.

"Now," I gasped.

He pushed deeply into me, the merging of our flesh sending waves of pleasure through my nerve endings. The invisible currents of his power seemed to sink into me with each new stroke.

I sank my fangs into his neck, feeling him shudder with a different kind of enjoyment. Blood filled my mouth, bringing a rush of ecstasy that his strong, smooth thrusts only heightened. I sucked harder, feeling his pace increase as the tension inside me built. I bit him again, crying out when his grasp tightened and he ground himself against me.

A flood of emotions seared my subconscious. I could feel Bones's control crumbling under the jagged slices of pleasure assaulting it. Felt the rapture shooting up his body when he abandoned that control and let lust have reign. Felt passion blasting through me as he yanked me even closer, thrusting with a sensual frenzy that would have hurt me if I were human, but only felt incredible now. Then I felt his fangs pierce my neck and my blood being pulled out. The music swallowed up our cries as we rocked together, faster and harder, drinking each other's blood, until both of us trembled from orgasm.

"That was *really* inappropriate," I said several minutes later while I straightened my clothes.

Bones laughed, low and sinful. "After being denied a week, I haven't begun to get inappropriate with you, Kitten, but I will."

"I'm serious." I might have an excuse,

since decreased control over urges, food or otherwise, was a side effect of being a new vampire, but Bones had been dead a long time. "We're supposed to be guarding Tammy, not sneaking off for a quickie."

"Who knows how many more days we'll be holed up with your mum and Tammy? I wasn't wasting this opportunity. Besides, Verses is the owner of this club and he's a friend. Tammy's safe. He's probably twirling her around the dance floor as we speak."

That made me feel less guilty. We *were* supposed to be on vacation, after all, and the past week of sleeping together without anything else happening had been taking its toll on me, too.

I brought my attention back to business. "Time to mingle with the local lowlifes and see if anyone's heard about a hitter after a human?"

Bones grinned. "People do talk about all sorts of things when they're out having a bit of fun. Let's see if we can find out anything useful."

FIVE

True to Bones's prediction, we found Tammy on the dance floor with Verses. The ghoul could dance like nobody's business, too. Tammy looked happier than I'd seen her all week.

"It *can't* be time to go yet," she said once she saw us.

"Not yet," Bones replied. "Verses, mate, point out one of your most gossipy regulars, but someone who can still be taken seriously."

With his height, it was easy for Verses to see over the other people. After a few seconds, he gestured at a bar manned by a beautiful vampire covered only in dark blue body glitter.

"See the gray-haired vampire sitting on the end? Name's Poppy. He tells too many stories to be trusted with a secret, but he doesn't make up what he hasn't heard."

"Smashing. I'd appreciate it if you kept your staff from mentioning that I was here tonight — or my wife. Trixie recognized us. Maybe a few more of them, too."

Verses gave Bones a look. "Bite is a haven for our kind. You're not intending to break my rules, are you?"

Bones clapped him on the back. "I won't do anything on your premises. After all, I intend to come back here with my wife. We still have some areas left to explore."

If it were possible, I'd have blushed at the blatant innuendo. Verses just laughed. Tammy looked bored.

"Why don't you do whatever it is you're going to do while I stay with Verses and dance?" Tammy suggested.

I was glad to change the subject. "Verses might have other things to do, Tammy."

"Keeping a pretty lady happy always takes priority," Verses said, winking at her.

Bones tugged my hand. "This shouldn't take too long, Kitten."

We left Tammy on the dance floor with the ghoul to head toward the glittering blue bartender and the gray-haired undead gossip.

I sat a few seats away from Bones at the bar, dividing my attention between eavesdropping on him and keeping an eye on Tammy. So far, she seemed to be fine, and Verses had been right; the wrinkled vampire next to Bones didn't need much prodding to start chattering. Bones let him pick the topics for the first half hour or so, then he turned the conversation.

"Bloody economy's got us all buggered," Bones declared, draining his whisky in one gulp. "Take me. Three years ago, I'm living the posh life off my investments. Today, I'm guarding a human to scrape by. Like to stake myself and save the embarrassment, I would."

Poppy snickered. "What're you guarding a human against? Tax evasion?"

They both laughed, and then Bones lowered his voice conspiratorially. "No, mate, against her relative. In truth, I wonder if I shouldn't be on the other side of this coin."

Even across the bar, I could see the gleam of interest in Poppy's eyes. "What other side?"

Bones leaned in, lowering his voice even further until I could barely hear him. "The side that gets paid more if the whiny brat dies. Faith, if I knew how to contact the chit's smarmy cousin, I'd take that job instead of the one I've got. Then I'd get a meal out of it to boot."

Poppy chewed on his drink straw. "Can't ya find out from the girl where this relative is?"

"She doesn't know. Believe me, I asked with the brights on." Bones tapped under his eye for emphasis. "I can't take another month of this. I'll eat her and then get no bloody money from anyone."

Poppy glanced around. I looked away, pretending to study my drink. When I strained, I caught his reply.

"Had a fellow here last night. He's in the population reduction business, if you know what I mean, and he was laughin' about this job where hired meat tried to use a bone muncher to tidy things up on a contract that was runnin' long. You'll never guess what happened. Somehow, the bone muncher ends up dead. Dead! Then the mark disappears. The way I heard it, now the meat's worried about his contract gettin' canceled."

Forty minutes later, this finally pays off, I thought.

"You hear the name of this meat?" Bones asked casually. "I might be interested in helping him out once I'm finished with this job."

"Think I heard the fellow call him Serpentine. Isn't that funny? The meat renamed himself just like he's a vampire."

Serpentine. I'd have Don burning up the computers on that alias as soon as we got home.

"Ah, mate, I owe you. Next round's on me."

Bones stayed another twenty minutes, letting Poppy ramble more until I fantasized about wrapping duct tape around the vampire's mouth. Finally, Bones feigned regret over needing to leave, but told Poppy he'd be back next weekend. And complained about how he'd have the bratty heiress with him.

My brows rose. *What are you up to, Bones?*

Six

I pulled the clothes out of the dryer and stifled a curse. Bleach stains everywhere. Tammy was twenty; how could she *not* know how to do a load of laundry without ruining everything?

Still, at least Tammy was doing her own laundry now. Or trying to. That was the result of my mother's influence. Twenty years of spoiled rich bitch didn't stand a chance against forty-six years of farm-reared discipline. Even though I was much closer to Tammy's age and my mother made Tammy do things that caused the blonde to wail, to my surprise, my mother was the person Tammy seemed to have bonded with.

Perhaps that was my fault. Maybe I was so used to being in search-and-destroy mode that I couldn't tackle being in a nurturing one instead. The thought was oddly depressing. *Check my ovaries, Doctor, because maybe I'm not really a woman.*

After dinner — which my mother still insisted on cooking, not that I complained — we sat by the fireplace. It was time to fill Tammy in on what we'd found out.

"Tammy, here's what's going on: Don still hasn't found your cousin, but Bones found out that the original hit man who took your contract is dead."

Tammy bolted out of her chair. "That's great! Does it mean I can go home now?"

"Not so fast. The hitter died under unusual circumstances."

Tammy sat back down, her enthusiasm fading. "How?"

"His throat was ripped out," Bones said bluntly. "And his computer and other effects were rummaged through, so someone else might have taken an interest in his unfinished jobs."

Bones's connections from his bounty hunter days turned out to be faster than Don's computers, because he discovered Serpentine was dead before my uncle even found out his real name. Don did send a team over to examine the apartment where Serpentine — or James Daily, as the autopsy certificate read — was found. Even though the person was clever at covering their tracks, Don could tell someone had hacked into Serpentine's computer. Maybe it was a coincidence that some of the files that were accessed were about Tammy, or that Serpentine had been killed by a vampire. We knew Serpentine had undead connections since he sent a ghoul after Tammy. But maybe it was more than coincidence.

"I told you vampires normally don't

bother with contracts on humans, but life never fails to surprise," Bones said in a dry tone. "When we were at Bite, I told the gossipy bloke I spoke with that we'd be back tomorrow night. If we still go, it would allow me to dig for more information, but there's a chance it could prove dangerous to you."

Tammy scoffed. "How dangerous? I've almost been electrocuted, shot, and eaten by a ghoul, remember?"

"If another vampire did decide to get involved with the contract on you, he or she could follow us back here and try to take you out," I said quietly.

Tammy gave us a shrewd look. "And then you could catch them. Find out where my cousin is, I'd bet. I saw you in action against that ghoul, Cat. How about you, Bones? You're a tough guy, right? Because I want this over. I want my life back."

Fabian floated in the room. "I could be the lookout. No other vampire or ghoul would notice me. I'd help keep Tammy safe."

Poor Fabian, he was right. Vampires and ghouls were notoriously disrespectful of ghosts. They ignored them more than most humans ignored homeless people.

"Thanks, Fabian," I said. "We could really

use your help."

"It's so weird when you do that," Tammy muttered.

I hid a smile. Some part of me thought Tammy didn't believe Fabian existed and that we just pretended to speak with him to mess with her.

"I'll help protect her," my mother said. Her face was closed off, as if she were fighting back memories. Once again, I hated what had been done to her because of me.

Bones rose from his chair. "All right. If we're going to Bite tomorrow, it's time you learn to defend yourself, Tammy."

She gave him a startled look. "Isn't that what I'm paying you two for?"

I didn't correct Tammy by saying my uncle and his department were getting her money, not Bones or me. I hoped Don wasn't taking Tammy to the cleaners, but he *was* a government official.

"You should still know basic skills. After all, you're a pretty girl, and predators can have heartbeats, too."

Tammy brightened at the compliment. I hid a smile. Flattery would make her much more accommodating, as Bones would know.

Bones went into the kitchen and came out with a steak knife. He dangled it in front of

135

Tammy, who looked at it doubtfully.

"What do you expect me to do with this?"

"Stab me with it," Bones replied. "In the heart."

Her mouth hung open. It was the first time I'd seen her speechless. "You're kidding?" she finally got out.

"You need to learn how to protect yourself against a vampire. Granted, your odds would be dismal, but your advantage is that no vampire would see you as a threat."

"That's how I managed to kill so many of them when I was your age," I chimed in. "The element of surprise can save your life."

Tammy looked at the knife again. "I don't know . . ."

Bones let out an exasperated noise. "Justina, come here and show her how it's done."

My mother looked more surprised than Tammy had when the whole conversation began. I was taken aback, too.

"You want me to stab you?" my mother asked in disbelief.

Bones gave her an impish grin. "Come on, Mum. How many times have you dreamed about that?"

My mother got up, took the knife, and then stuck it right in the middle of Bones's chest. He never flinched or moved to block her.

"See, Tammy, this is how most people would think to do it," Bones said calmly. "But Justina knows the blade isn't in deep enough, nor is it in the right place. The heart's a bit to the left, not exactly in the center. And she didn't twist the knife, which is what you must always, *always* do to kill a vampire, unless you've stabbed the heart with more than one knife."

Bones took the knife out and handed it back to my mother. "Now, Justina, show her how it's really done."

My mother looked even more startled, but she took the blade, aimed more carefully this time, and shoved it in with a small shudder.

"Twist," Bones said, as if this didn't hurt him, which it would, even if steel through the heart wasn't fatal. Only silver was.

My mother gave the blade a turn to the right. Bones caught her hand and jerked it, hard, in a ragged circle. Tammy gasped at the blood that stained his shirt.

"That's how you do it," he said, voice as neutral as if pain weren't searing through him. I felt it, though, and it was all I could do not to yelp and demand he stop. "Rough, quick, and thorough, else you won't get a second chance."

He let go of my mother's hand and pulled out the knife, wiping it on his ruined shirt. "Let's show Tammy how it's done from the back now."

Tears pricked my eyes. Not because of the pain from Bones's wound; that was already healed. It was because I finally understood what he was doing. Bones wasn't trying to train Tammy. He was showing my mother how to defend herself, something she never would have allowed him to do under normal circumstances. But thinking it was for Tammy's benefit made her follow his instructions, learning how to jab a knife in the right place front and back, then how to deflect some standard defensive maneuvers.

Fabian caught my eye and winked. The ghost knew what Bones was doing, too.

By the time Bones announced it was Tammy's turn, I'd fallen in love with him all over again. Flowers and jewelry worked for most girls as a romantic gesture, but here I was, misty-eyed at watching him show my mother how to stab the shit out of him.

Tammy was human, so it took her longer to get the gist of things. Still, after an hour, she was sweaty, bloody, and very proud of herself for successfully stabbing Bones several times in the heart.

"Just call me Buffy," she said with a smirk.

"I'm tired," I said, faking a yawn. "I'm heading to bed."

Bones's eyes lit up. Fabian disappeared out the door, saying he wanted to double-check the grounds. My mother gave me a look. Only Tammy didn't seem to realize that no vampire ever yawned for real.

"See you tomorrow," Tammy said. "I've got to shower anyway."

I went up the stairs. Bones stayed below, waiting. By the time I heard Tammy's shower turn on, I also heard light, quick footsteps coming up the stairs.

When Bones entered the bedroom, I'd convinced myself that the noise from Tammy's shower would be sufficient to muffle my mother's hearing. Or that my mom had suddenly gone deaf. And when Bones took me in his arms, I stopped thinking about anything else.

SEVEN

This could be the beginning of a bad joke, I thought as we bypassed the line and strode into Bite. *Three vampires and a human walk into a bar . . .*

If a rogue undead hit man was after Tammy, we were hoping he took the bait and followed us home, because we had a hell of a surprise waiting for him. And here was also hoping that Poppy, the vampire Bones chatted up last weekend, had repeated Bones's tale about the snotty rich human he was guarding. And how he'd be back tonight with her.

My mother refused to dance. She sat at the bar, shutting down every man who approached her, human or otherwise. *She really cared for Rodney,* I thought, my heart squeezing at the memory of the murdered friend my mother had briefly dated. *I hope she finds someone special again.*

We went through the motions of having a good time, dancing, drinking — no alcohol for Tammy, even though she begged — and then dancing again while Bones renewed his acquaintance with Poppy. It didn't escape my notice that Verses stared at us. From his expression, he sensed something was up and didn't want it at his club. Well, neither did we. That's why we had booby traps waiting back at our house and Fabian there on sentry duty. *Come on over, would-be killer. We have treats ready.*

After two A.M., we headed out to the parking lot. Out of habit, I had my hand near my sleeves, where several throwing knives lined my arms. We were three rows away from our Hummer when the air became electrified. Bones and I whirled at the same time, each of us pulling out a knife. My mother grabbed Tammy. Several vampires dropped from the sky to land in a wide circle around us.

Oh fuck, was my thought. We'd left Bite only a few seconds ago. Not nearly enough time to coordinate this kind of attack. I counted, noting the vibe wafting off each of them. *Twelve vampires, several of them Masters.* Too many of them to be just about killing a human heiress. This wasn't about Tammy.

Bones knew it, too. He gave an almost languid look around, but I could feel his tenseness grating across my subconscious. "X, what an unpleasant surprise. This clearly isn't coincidence, so tell me, who betrayed me?"

The black-haired vampire addressed as X stepped forward. "A human hires a hit man to kill his cousin for money, boring. That same hit man botches the job twice, funny. Then the desperate hit man sends a ghoul after the girl to finish things up, my curiosity's piqued. That same ghoul ends up with his head cut off by a mysterious redhead . . . ah. *Now* I'm interested."

"Who's your friend, honey?" I asked

141

Bones, not taking my eyes off X.

"Former coworker, you could say. An overly competitive one who got brassed off when I killed several of his best clients."

Former coworker. X must not have been a small-time hit man for Bones to refer to him that way, which meant the vampires with him had to be badasses, too. Our chances just got downgraded from slim to screwed.

"Could my old friend Bones be involved, I wondered?" X went on. "The young heiress has government connections, it turns out, and so does the Reaper. And the Reaper's supposed to be such a bleeding heart when it comes to humans. When another rumor spread that the human heiress would be here tonight, I took precautions in case I was right about who was protecting her. And lucky me, I was."

Precautions? That was one way to describe the dozen vampires surrounding us, all of whom were armed to the teeth. I glanced back at the nightclub. Would anyone come to our aid? Or would they stick to the whole "no violence on the premises" thing and stay the hell away?

"You're here for me, leave her out of it," Bones said, with a barely perceptible nod at Tammy. "Let her go back inside, and we'll settle this ourselves."

"She may not be why I'm here, but I'll be sure to kill her, too, so I don't risk war."

Clever bastard. If X killed us while we were defending Tammy, he could call it business. Tammy had a contract out on her; otherwise, Bones's people could consider it personal and retaliate for our slaughter. X was covering his bases well.

Tammy began to whimper. X gave her a genial smile. "If it makes you feel better, your cousin's dead. I killed him after I learned what I needed to know about you."

So that's why Don couldn't find Gables, not that it did us any good now.

Bones glanced at me. "Kitten, are you getting angry yet?"

I knew what he meant. Since I found out I'd absorbed fire-starting power from the pyrokinetic vampire I drank from, I'd fought to keep that borrowed ability under control. But now, I let all the repressed anger, determination, fear, and sadness from the past few months roar to the surface. My hands became engulfed in blue flames, sparks shooting onto the ground.

"Kill her!" X shouted.

Knives flew at me in a blur. I rolled to avoid them, concentrating on X. Two months ago, I'd burned an entire property and exploded a Master vampire's head right off his shoulders. *Burn,* I thought, glaring at X. *Burn.*

Except . . . he didn't catch fire. Sparks still shot from my flame-covered hands, but nothing more lethal came out of them. I shook my hands in frustration. *Work, damn you! Flame on, fingers!*

But the previous deadly streams of fire that had scared me with their ferocity seemed to have vanished. The most dangerous thing I could do with my hands now was light someone's cigarette.

"Oh, shit," my mother whispered.

I couldn't agree more.

"Protect Tammy," I yelled, then grabbed for my knives, cursing as I tried to dodge another hail of blades aimed at me. Some of them found their mark, but none in my chest, thank God. Still, that silver burned where it landed, making me fight the urge to yank it out. I flung some of my weapons instead, adding more silver to the barrage Bones had just sent. Then I rolled behind one of the cars for cover, finally getting the chance to snatch out the silver embedded in my shoulders and legs.

Tammy screamed as some of the vampires took to the air. I took two of the knives I'd pulled from my body and sent them winging at the vampire closest to where she was crouched. The blades found their mark, and he crashed into a car instead of Tammy and my mother, who was crouched over her.

The rest of the vampires seemed more concerned with taking on Bones than dealing with Tammy or my mother. I rolled under a truck to get to Bones — and then screamed as my shirt went up in flames.

Goddammit! There must have been oil drops pooled underneath the truck I'd rolled under, and the useless sparks from my hands ignited it.

"Kitten, you all right?" Bones called out.

"Fine!" I yelled back, afraid he'd get killed rushing to check on me.

Stupid, stupid, stupid, I lashed myself. *Oil plus sparks equals* fire, *dumbass!*

I'd just ripped my burning shirt off when a car slammed into me, pinning me to the vehicle behind me. I gasped at the unbelievable pain, paralyzing in its intensity. Tammy screamed. Over that, I heard Bones hoarsely call my name.

Something thudded on the mangled car pinning me. The redheaded vampire. He smiled as he pulled out a silver blade, knowing as I did that I couldn't shove the car off in time to save myself.

But there was something I could do. *Oil plus sparks equals fire,* I thought savagely, and I rammed my fist through the car's fuel tank.

A terrific *boom* went off, combined with the agonizing sensation of being thrown backward, burning, across the parking lot. For a stunned second, I didn't know if I was still alive. Then I realized I wouldn't hurt this much if I were dead.

Move, I told myself, fighting back the lethargy that made me want to curl up wherever I'd landed. *Keep blinking, your vision will come back.*

After a few more blinks, the parking lot was in a double outline, but I could see. *Check for incoming. Do you have any knives left? Two, right, make them count.*

"I'm okay," I called out, my voice almost unrecognizable. I hated giving away my position, but I was more worried about Bones losing it if he was too distracted to feel our connection and thought I'd been blown to bits.

"Christ almighty, Kitten," I heard him mutter, and smiled even though it felt like it cracked my face. I was afraid to look at my skin. Burnt bacon could pass for my twin right now. *You'll heal,* I reminded myself. *Quit worrying about your looks and get back to worrying about your ass.*

I flexed my fingers, relieved that the horrible splitting sensation was gone. Now I could grasp my knives with purpose, and my vision was clearing by the moment. Through the dirty car window in front of me, I saw Bones fighting off four vampires. He whirled and struck in a dizzying display of violence, slicing and hacking whenever they came too close. Now, where were Tammy and my mother?

I'd sneaked around a few dead vampires — one of them crispy, I noticed with satisfaction — and was tiptoeing around a Benz when X sprang out of nowhere. He shoved me, slamming me into yet another car — God, I was so sick of feeling my bones crunch against metal! — but instead of springing forward, I let myself slump as if dazed. X was on me in the next second, knees pinning my torso to the concrete, glowing green gaze victorious as he raised his knife.

My hand shot out, the silver knife clenched in it going straight into his chest. I smiled as I gave it a hard twist. *That's it for you, X.*

But he didn't slump forward like he should have. Instead, the knife he'd raised slammed into my chest without an instant's hesitation.

Pain erupted in me, so hot and fierce it

rivaled what I'd felt when the car exploded on me. That pain grew until I wanted to scream, but I didn't have the energy. Everything seemed to fade out of view except his bright emerald gaze.

"How?" I managed, barely able to croak out the word.

X leaned forward. "Situs inversus," he whispered. His hand tightened on the blade, twisting —

Blue filled my vision. I didn't understand why, and for a second, I wondered if it was even real. Then the blue tilted to the side, X's severed arm still holding the knife in my chest, but the rest of him elsewhere. *Sheet metal,* I thought dazedly. Bones must have ripped it off a car and wielded it like a huge saw.

X was on his back, the stump from his right arm slowly extending out into a new limb as he fought Bones. I wanted to help, but I couldn't get up. The pain had me pinned, gasping and twitching as I tried to escape from it.

"Don't move, Kitten!" Bones shouted. A brutal rip from his knife sliced open X's chest, oddly to the right of X's sternum. Bones twisted the blade so hard it broke off, and then he was next to me, his hand pinning my wrists above my head.

"Kitten."

As soon as I saw his face, I knew how bad it was. That should've occurred to me before, considering I had a silver knife with shriveling hand still attached to it in my chest, but somehow, the pain had blinded me to reality. Now, however, I realized these were my last moments on earth.

I tried to smile. "Love you," I whispered.

A single pink tear rolled down Bones's cheek, but his voice was steady. "Don't move," he repeated, and slowly began to tug on the knife.

My chest felt like it was on fire. I tried not to look at the knife. Tried to focus on Bones's face, but my own gaze was blurred pink, too. *I'll miss you so much.*

The blade shivered a fraction, and a spasm of pain ripped through me. Bones compressed his lips, letting my wrists go to press on my chest with his free hand.

"Don't move . . ."

I couldn't stand it. That burning from my chest felt like it had spread all through me. A scream built in my throat, but I choked it back. *Please, don't let him see me die screaming . . .*

The agony stopped just as abruptly as it started. Bones let out a harsh sound that was followed by a clatter of metal on the ground. I looked down, seeing a slash in my chest that began to close, the skin seaming back together as it healed.

And then Bones spun around. A vampire stood behind him, holding a big knife and wearing the weirdest expression on his face. He dropped to his knees and pitched forward, a silver handle sticking out of his back. My mother was behind the vampire. Her hands were bloody.

"Rough, quick, and thorough, or you won't get a second chance," she mumbled, almost to herself.

Bones stared. "That's right, Justina." Then he began to laugh. "Well done."

I was stunned. Bones swept me up, kissing me so hard I tasted blood when his fangs pierced my lips.

"Don't you *ever* frighten me like that again."

"He didn't die," I said, still stunned by the recent events. "I twisted a blade in his heart, but he didn't *die.*"

"Like he said, situs inversus." At my confused expression, Bones went on. "Means he was born with his organs backward, so his heart was on the right. That's what saved his life before, but he shouldn't have admitted it while I could hear him."

I hadn't known such a condition existed.

Note to self: Learn more about anatomical oddities.

Bones scanned the parking lot, but the only vampires out here were the ones gathered around the side of the nightclub. *Onlookers,* I thought in amazement. *Had they stood there the whole time and just* watched?

Fear leapt in me. "Where's Tammy?"

"I ran her inside after the car blew up," my mother said. "She'd be safe in there, you said."

And then she'd come back outside to face a pack of hit men. Tears pricked my eyes even as Bones smiled at her.

"You saved my life, Justina."

She looked embarrassed, and then scowled. "I didn't know if you were finished getting that knife out of Catherine. I couldn't let him sneak up on you and stab you until my daughter was okay."

Bones laughed. "Of course."

I shook my head. She'd never change, but that was okay. I loved her anyway.

Verses walked out of Bite with Tammy at his side. From her red-rimmed eyes, she'd been crying.

"It's over," I told her.

Tammy ran and hugged me. I wanted to say something profound and comforting, but all I could do was repeat, "It's over."

At least Tammy wouldn't remember any of this. No, her memories would be replaced with one where she'd been sequestered by boring bodyguards provided by her father's former friends. Tammy would go into adulthood without the burden of knowing there were things in the night no average human could stand against. She'd be normal. It was the best birthday present I could give her.

"You fought on the premises," Verses stated.

Bones let out a snort. "You noticed that, did you, mate?"

"Maybe if you hadn't stood there and done *nothing* while we were ambushed, your precious *premises* would still be in one piece!" my mother snapped at Verses. "Don't you have any loyalty? Bones said you were a friend!"

Verses raised his brows at her withering tone, then cast a glance around at the parking lot. Vampire bodies littered the area, one of the cars was still on fire, and various others were smashed, ripped, or dented.

"I am his friend," Verses replied. "Which is why I'll let all of you leave without paying for the damages."

"He doesn't sound like we'll be welcomed back," I murmured to Bones. "So much for coming here during the rest of our vacation to explore all those private areas."

Bones's lips brushed my forehead. "Don't fret, luv. I know another club in Brooklyn I think you'll *really* fancy . . ."

MEANWHILE, FAR ACROSS THE CASPIAN SEA . . .

DANIEL STASHOWER

Daniel Stashower is a two-time Edgar®
Award winner whose most recent nonfiction books are *The Beautiful Cigar Girl* and
(as coeditor) *Arthur Conan Doyle: A Life in
Letters.* Dan is also the author of five
mystery novels and has received the Agatha and Anthony awards. His short stories
have appeared in numerous anthologies,
including *The Best American Mystery Stories* and *The World's Finest Mystery and
Crime Stories.* He lives in Washington,
D.C., with his wife and their two sons.

In those days LifeSpan Books had offices in
a three-story garden atrium building in
Alexandria, Virginia. The building is still
there. Across the street — in the middle of
the street, actually — is a Civil War statue
called *Appomattox,* marking the spot where
seven hundred young soldiers marched off
to join the Confederate cause in 1861. The
statue shows a Confederate soldier with his

hat off, head bowed and arms folded, facing the battlefields to the south where his comrades fell. Originally there was a perimeter of ornamental fencing and gas lamps, but over the years, as South Washington Street grew into a major artery, the fence came down and traffic in both directions simply jogged outward a bit to avoid the base of the statue. Every so often somebody clipped a fender, but the soldier stood his ground.

One night a van plowed into the base of the statue and knocked the soldier facedown into the street, opening the door to a vigorous public debate about whether a busy intersection was really the proper place for a symbol of the Confederacy. The city fathers ultimately fell back on a musty piece of legislation that the Virginia House of Delegates had passed in 1890. It stated, in part, that the monument "shall remain in its present position as a perpetual and lasting testimonial to the courage, fidelity and patriotism of the heroes in whose memory it was erected . . . the permission so given by the said City Council of Alexandria for its erection shall not be repealed, revoked, altered, modified, or changed by any future Council or other municipal power or authority." So the statue went back up. Motorists beware.

I know all this because Thaddeus Palgrave told me. He was a senior editor for LifeSpan Books, and he made a point of knowing such things. Actually, Palgrave didn't tell me directly, he just let it bubble out of him when I happened to be in the room. He had a way of leaning up against the tall window of his office, with his head resting against his forearm, giving impromptu disquisitions on matters of art, commerce, and history. He would usually wrap things up with a pithy moral, sometimes in Latin. *Aquila non captat muscas.* The eagle doesn't capture flies. Don't sweat the small stuff.

It never seemed to matter to Palgrave whether anyone was in the room with him when he made these learned remarks. At first it struck me as a sort of foppish affectation, like an ascot or an ivory-tipped swagger stick, meant to suggest a man of rare breeding set down among the heathens. I imagined him practicing at home, leaning against a bedroom wall, sighing deeply as he tossed off Latin epigrams. But in time I came to realize that he genuinely didn't care what anyone thought of him — didn't even consider it, in fact. There were a lot of people like that at LifeSpan Books.

You may not remember LifeSpan. They

were the people who produced "multi-volume continuity reference works" on various subjects — low-fat cooking, home repair, World War II — and sent them to you in the mail, once every two months. You'd sign up for a series on, say, gardening, and soon the books would begin to arrive, filling you with optimism and resolve. They'd start you off with *Perennials,* followed two months later by *Flowering Houseplants,* then *Vegetables and Fruits.* You'd dip in here and there — do a little aerating, maybe visit a garden center — and congratulate yourself on making such a good start. Perhaps next year, you'd tell yourself, you might even be able to grow your own carrots and tomatoes. And the books would keep coming and coming. *Annuals. Ferns. Lawns and Ground Cover.* You never realized there would be quite so many. Still, some of them look quite interesting. Maybe a little more detail than you bargained for, but it's good. Really, it's good. And besides, you'll be able to get back out to the garden after the Little League season ends. *Bulbs. Herbs. Evergreens.* It begins to dawn on you, at the start of the third year, that perhaps you've bitten off more than you can chew. For one thing, you're running out of shelf space. You start stacking the books up on the worktable in the garage. You'll sort it out in the spring. *Shade Gardens. Orchids. Vines.* One night around ten thirty, during tax season, you try phoning the toll-free number where operators are standing by, in an effort to take them up on the offer of "cancel anytime if not completely satisfied." Your resolve crumbles as you spend forty-five minutes on hold listening to "Gospel Bluegrass Classics," available now from LifeSpan Music. *Pruning and Grafting. Shrubs. Wildflowers.* The last of your children goes off to college. There will be time now for some serious gardening; you might even make a start on a pergola, if only your back weren't giving you so much trouble. *Roses. Miniatures and Bonsai. Rock and Water Gardens.* Over the winter holidays a sudden snowstorm drives your grandchildren indoors. They use the stored cartons of books to build a fort. *Cacti and Succulents. Winter Gardens. Heat-Zone Gardens.* It is a beautiful day in late September and your eldest son is walking a real estate agent through the house. "Yes," he says, "it was very sudden, in the garden. He would have wanted it that way." As they're signing the papers, they hear the soft thump of a package at the door: *Organics.*

■ ■ ■ ■

I applied for an editorial job at LifeSpan straight out of journalism school. They brought me in for an interview with the managing editor, the tenor of which had less to do with my qualifications than with the apparent rarity of the opening. "We haven't had a vacancy here in nearly a decade, Mr. Clarke," he kept saying. "Quite extraordinary, really. So I'm afraid I'm a bit rusty on procedure. We should have coffee, I suppose, yes?"

His name was Peter Albamarle, and he radiated a sense of wary befuddlement, as though someone kept hiding his stapler. "I don't suppose you went to Princeton?" he asked.

"No," I said. "NYU. It's there on my résumé."

Albamarle glanced down at the paper and placed his fingers on it as if it might crawl away. "A very good school. Very good. I only ask because so many of our old boys are Princeton men. With a few Dartmouth types here and there."

He waited a moment as if I might suddenly recall that I had gone to Princeton after all. I shook my head.

159

"Well, that's neither here nor there," he continued. "We were most impressed with your application. With that piece you wrote." He pushed a copy of a small academic journal across the desk at me. It contained an article I'd written: "Connected by Fate: Aspects of Dickensian Happenstance." My debut in print. I nodded and tried to look appropriately modest, like a Princeton man.

"That's how our recruiters found you. We rely heavily on our recruiters. And they were right about you. You have a fine sense of the balance of fact and narrative."

"Thank you."

"And it strikes me as remarkable that your article should have come across my desk just now. We occasionally take on a new photo editor or researcher, of course, but the writing jobs never turn over. Never!" His eyes widened at the wonder of the thing.

"How is it that the job became available, if I might ask?"

"Oh," his face darkened. "Jane Rossmire. She was tremendously competent, really a most extraordinarily good worker, but she left us suddenly. A bit awkward. We won't speak of it. I'm sure she's doing much better now. And no one really blames Thaddeus Palgrave."

"Excuse me?"

"I mean to say, no one really believes — ah! Miss Taylor! Will you take young Mr. Clarke down the hall for his writing trial? Purely a formality, you understand, I'm sure the pashas upstairs will approve my decision, but there it is."

He said nothing more as I was led away to an empty office. I had been warned about this stage of the interview process and had studied up at the library with some old copies of the *Ancient Worlds* series. As I understood the exercise, I was expected to take several bulky packets of material from the research department and turn them into a smooth, lulling sort of prose, in much the same way that blocks of cheddar are emulsified into Cheez Whiz. The tough part was writing transitions, which often marked huge shifts of time or geography. *Despite such intriguing glimpses from prehistory, students of archeology seem time and again drawn to a later period, to the sweep of centuries from about the thirteenth century B.C. up to the Christian era.* This stuff is harder than it looks. According to office legend, one writer had his contract terminated over the phrase: "Meanwhile, far across the Caspian Sea . . ."

Apparently my sample essay on the marriage of Hatshepsut met with general approval. By the end of the week I had signed on as a junior editor on the Civil War series. If all went according to plan, I would serve an apprentice period on the research staff, then ease into some small-scale writing assignments, like captions and sidebars, and finally ascend to the Valhalla where chapters were written.

There are some who would tell you that LifeSpan Books was no place for an ambitious young journalist. I would respectfully disagree. At that time LifeSpan was part of a vast empire of magazines, including *Styles* and *NewsBeat*. The books division was where they sent the career correspondents who needed a tune-up or a drying-out period. I learned a lot from those guys. I remember one afternoon — the day of the *Challenger* shuttle disaster — when I tagged along with a group of them to watch the coverage at the corner saloon. They sat around talking about the ledes they had written nineteen years earlier on the day of *Apollo 1*. It was a three-martini master class. You don't get that in J-school.

At that time there were only two other people in the building who were under age thirty, a pair of photo editors named Brian Frost and Kate Macintyre. They scooped me up on my first day and taught me the rules of the road — the location of the supply closet, the proper operation of the balky Xerox, the kabuki ritual of the time sheets. After work they took me out for beer and nachos, insisting that it was a company tradition. "When you pass your research apprenticeship, you start making real money," Brian explained. "Then the nachos are on you."

"And on that day," Kate added, "an angel gets his wings."

It soon became understood that the three of us would spend our lunch hours together. In good weather, we picked up sandwiches from the cart in the lobby and took them down to a park bench overlooking the Potomac. Kate, a proto-Goth who spent her evenings creating "media collages," felt that it was her duty to bring me up to speed on five years' worth of office gossip. Brian, who played keyboard in a punk-jazz fusion band, did his best to inject a note of moderation.

"You're giving the new guy the wrong idea about this place," Brian said, toward the end of my second week. "You're making it sound like some sort of French bedroom farce. You know, with slamming doors and people running around in their knickers. It's not like that."

"It's not? Hey, New Guy? Am I giving you

the wrong impression?"

"I find your candor refreshing," I said.

"I know, I'm adorable. And did you notice that guy we passed in the elevator? With his glasses on a green cord? That's Allan Stracker. He's been having a sidebar with Eve Taunton for three years. She still thinks he's going to leave his wife."

"Allan writes a column for the *Alexandria Gazette*," Brian added, judiciously. "On public zoning concerns."

"Having a sidebar?" I asked.

Brian raised his eyebrows at me. "In office parlance, it refers to the enjoyment of certain intimacies outside the confines of marriage. The derivation is obscure, but it appears to date to an incident in which a certain managing editor's passionate addresses were interrupted by the sudden arrival of his wife. His explanation, we're told, was that he was merely researching a sidebar for *Healthy Lifestyles*. His wife's response is not recorded."

This is how people talked at LifeSpan. If you asked someone where the coffee filters were kept, the answer was likely to touch on the role of the coffee cherry in Ethiopian religious ceremonies.

"What about you, New Guy?" said Kate, crumpling up an empty bag of potato chips.

164

"Any dirty details we need to know? Is there a string of broken hearts trailing back to Greenwich Village?"

"There was somebody in New York before I moved down here, but she — I got a letter."

"We've all gotten those letters," Brian said. "I keep a file."

"Too bad Jane Rossmire isn't here anymore," Kate said. "She had a thing for anguished writer types. You'd have liked her. You could have been all dark and brooding together."

"I'm not dark and brooding."

"My mistake."

"Hang on," I said. "Jane Rossmire. Isn't she the one who left? Didn't I fill her job? Something to do with Thaddeus Whozits?"

Brian and Kate exchanged a look. "Thaddeus Palgrave," Brian said. "LifeSpan's answer to Heathcliff."

"What's the story there? Mr. Albamarle made it sound as if Palgrave had driven her off the premises with a pitchfork or something."

"Nobody really knows," Kate said. "I mean, considering we've got a building full of researchers, there's surprisingly little in the way of hard data on Palgrave. And nobody's seen or heard from Jane in six months. I've tried calling. The phone is disconnected."

"I liked her a lot," Brian said. "She'd seen the Ramones eight times. I made her a tape of Sham 69."

"They never should have assigned her to Palgrave," Kate said.

"I'm not following this," I said. "What happened? Were they having a sidebar?"

"I don't think so." Kate used her straw to poke at a clot of ice in her Diet Coke. "I think he just drove her insane. It happens to everybody who works with him, to some extent."

"He's that difficult?"

"Actually, he's very polite and occasionally quite charming," Brian said, "but impossible to figure out. He's been here for more than ten years, but he has no friends. It's understood that he has a degree from Oxford, which explains his weird, not-quite-English accent, and he did something at the Sorbonne for a while."

"Which accounts for the icy hauteur," Kate said.

"The man simply does not play well with others," Brian agreed. "Nobody has ever seen him go out for lunch. Not once. He sits at his desk every day eating a tuna and avocado pita pocket, with his nose in a book."

"Maybe he's just —"

"Shy?" Kate gave a snort. "Is that what you were about to say, New Guy? No, Thaddeus Palgrave is not shy. He holds himself apart. He looks down his aquiline nose at the hoi polloi. Has he given you one of his off-the-cuff Latin witticisms yet?"

"No, I haven't even met the man."

Kate glanced at her watch. "Well, the moment is at hand. We have a paste-up at four o'clock. He'll be there." She stood up and brushed some crumbs off her lap.

"What's a paste-up?"

"Just before a book goes to press, we have a meeting to review the galleys. All the pages get pinned up on the walls so everyone can take a last look."

"It's really just an excuse to open a bottle of wine on a Friday," Brian added. "Everyone stands around patting themselves on the back for a job well done."

"Everyone except Palgrave," said Kate.

"Yeah," said Brian. "Everyone except Palgrave."

At four o'clock I trailed into the corner conference room behind George Wegner, a thirty-year man who had started his career on the Russia desk of *NewsBeat*. More than a hundred layout pages were pinned to the cork walls, and as Brian had suggested, the air was heavy with self-congratulation. Wegner spent twenty minutes earnestly telling me about the brief "bill of fare" sections he had written near the front of each chapter, teasing the contents and laying out the themes to come. "If it's done right," he told me, "the reader won't even be aware of it. But it's vital to the structure of the chapter. It gets the reader's mind pointed in the proper direction. So, for instance, in the chapter just before Missionary Ridge, it was important to —"

"*Bluff and genial?* Can you possibly be serious, Mr. Wegner?"

The voice caught me off guard. I turned to find Thaddeus Palgrave hovering at Wegner's elbow, an expression of amused contempt playing over his features. I had never seen him up close before. He had a high, broad forehead and an underslung jaw, giving his head the appearance of an inverted pyramid. His dark blond hair was flecked with gray, but his face was taut and unlined, making his age hard to figure — no younger than forty-five, I would have guessed. His narrow eyes were dull green and — though he would have objected to the cliché — as cold as ice. Sometimes there's no other way to say it.

Wegner recovered more quickly than I did. "Thaddeus, I don't believe you've met our newest member of the staff? May I present —"

Palgrave ignored my outstretched hand. "You are excessively fond of the phrase *bluff and genial,* Mr. Wegner."

"Excuse me, Thaddeus?"

"In *The Deadliest Day,* you informed us that Ambrose Burnside was the 'bluff and genial commander of the right wing of the Army of the Potomac.' In *Second Manassas,* you declared that John Pope, 'though bluff and genial off the battlefield, had gained a reputation as a determined tactician in the western theater of the war.' And now, in *The Road to Chancellorsville,* we learn that General Joseph Hooker, 'a bluff and genial man, took command of the Second Division of the Third Corps at the start of the Peninsula Campaign.'" Palgrave cocked his head toward the galley where the offending phrase appeared. "I could go on."

Wegner tried to laugh it off, but his ears were reddening. "I'll have to watch that," he said. "Still, every writer has his little quirks, wouldn't you agree?"

"If by that you mean most writers are lazy

and inaccurate," Palgrave said, "then of course I am forced to agree. Or have I misunderstood?"

The room had gone silent. Peter Albamarle, the managing editor, stepped forward to try to save the situation. "I'm afraid I do that sort of thing all the time, Thaddeus," he said. "I'd be embarrassed to say how many times I've used the phrase 'fell back under a curtain of flying shot and blue smoke.' No one in my chapters ever makes a strategic retreat. They invariably fall back under a curtain of flying shot and blue smoke. It's become something of a —"

Palgrave waved him off, keeping his eyes fixed on Wegner, pinned and wriggling against the cork wall. "General Hooker was neither bluff nor genial," Palgrave said. "Quite the contrary, in fact. I suggest you review Mr. Daniel Butterfield's seminal biography, *Major-General Joseph Hooker and the Troops from the Army of the Potomac at Wauhatchie, Lookout Mountain and Chattanooga.* You will find it a most bracing corrective. As the ancients might say, *Age quod agis.*"

It was clear that Wegner had stopped listening well before the Latin epigram. He took another sip of wine, scanning the room as if idly looking for his ride home. Then, pretending to be unaware that all eyes were upon him, he set his plastic cup down on top of a light board, glanced at his watch, and fell back under a curtain of flying shot and blue smoke.

"That man is such a prick," Brian said, setting down his pint glass. "I mean, who *does* that? And to George Wegner, of all people?"

We were in the Irish pub on King Street, holding something of a wake over a communal plate of nachos.

"He's not a prick," Kate said. "He's not a prick at all. He's a vampire."

"You think everyone is a vampire," Brian said. "You think Lionel Richie is a vampire."

"Who's to say he's not?"

"And Spandau Ballet."

"I did not say that Spandau Ballet were vampires. I said they were zombies. Not the same thing."

"You've been impossible ever since *Mystic Summonings.*"

I fingered a "Guinness for Strength" beer mat. "Ever since what?" I asked.

"*Mystic Summonings.* Or was it *Cosmic Beings and Haunted Creatures*?"

"I have no clue what you're talking about."

"Sorry, New Guy. Before your time. We used to do a series called *Tales of the Un-*

known. Surely you've heard about it? You must have seen the commercials." Brian cleared his throat. *"A man is about to get on an airplane,"* he intoned. *"Suddenly he has a strange premonition of disaster. He turns and leaves the boarding area. That same airplane —"*

"No," Kate interrupted. "Come on, Brian. That's *Library of Strange Happenings.* I meant *Tales of the Unknown."*

"Oh, right. Right. Let's see. *On a wind-swept hillside in Romania, a strange ritual unfolds far from the prying eyes of frightened villagers. Huddled deep within the folds of a billowing cloak, a lone figure mounts a broken stone altar. In his hands he clasps a bejeweled —"*

"There you go." Kate swirled the dregs of her wineglass. "Palgrave is a vampire. It all fits."

Brian went after a sliver of jalapeño with a tortilla chip. "I once spent twenty minutes with Palgrave getting a lecture on the difference between a slouch hat and a forage cap. He's just a prick. There's nothing supernatural about it. Sometimes a prick is just a prick."

"What about Jane Rossmire?" There was an edge to Kate's voice now. "I'm telling you, she's gone. Without a trace,"

Brian chewed for a moment. "Well, when you put it that way, I guess Palgrave *must* be a vampire. I mean, she couldn't possibly just have moved out of town or gotten a better job. The vampire thing is the only possible explanation. What a fool I've been."

"She would have said good-bye."

"Maybe she was embarrassed," Brian said. "After today, I wouldn't be surprised if we never see George Wegner again."

Kate signaled for another glass of wine. "I'm telling you, Thaddeus Palgrave is a creature of the night. Come on. For one thing, his name is Thaddeus. What kind of a name is that? It's like he signed the Declaration of Independence or something."

"I'm not sure I follow your reasoning," Brian said. "There's a guy in accounting named H. Basil Worthington. Is he a vampire, too?"

"Um, look," I said. "I get it that I'm the new guy and maybe I should stay out of this, but are you serious? A vampire? With fangs and a black cape?"

Kate rolled her eyes. "We're not talking about the *Hammer House of Horror*. Get a grip. I'm talking about vampires. Real vampires."

"You're kidding me."

"They walk among us, dude," said Brian.

"My grandfather eats black pudding. It's not a huge leap."

"As creatures of the night go, they're actually pretty interesting," Kate said. "Did you know that Mexican vampires have bare skulls instead of heads?"

Brian snorted. "Always the researcher. The curse of LifeSpan Books."

"Really, though. Can you imagine what that would look like? A bare skull?"

"Like the cover of a Grateful Dead album?"

"I just think it's interesting, that's all. And supposedly there are vampires in the Rockies that suck blood through their noses. They stick their noses into the victim's ear. How cool is that?"

"I vant to sneef your bluh-ud." Brian was on his third beer now.

Kate ignored him and barreled ahead. "In early folklore they're often described as ruddy and bloated, probably from gorging on blood. I did a sidebar once on *strigoi* — you know, the Romanian vampires? Did you know that they have red hair, blue eyes, and two hearts?"

"Like Mick Hucknall," said Brian. "Plenty of heart. No soul."

I looked at him. "So if Thaddeus Palgrave suddenly starts singing 'Holding Back the

174

Years,' I should run away?"

"First, unplug his amp," said Brian. "That's just common sense."

"Well," I said, "it's been an interesting start to the new job. Just to be clear, when my mother calls to ask how things are going, I should tell her that everything's fine, I did some really good research on the Spotsylvania Courthouse, I found an apartment, one of my coworkers is a vampire, and I'm trying out for the office softball team?"

"That's about the size of it," said Kate.

"I wouldn't mention the softball team," said Brian. "You don't want to get her hopes up."

Kate was fingering the rim of her wineglass. "I just can't believe that Jane Rossmire never even said good-bye." She turned to me. "Hey, New Guy, we're getting to be friends, right? Brian and I have warmed your heart with our zany banter and all, right? Do me a favor. If you ever decide to disappear for no reason, take a minute to say good-bye. Just slip a note under my door or something. One word. *Good-bye. Thanks for the nachos,* maybe."

I finished my beer. "It's a promise," I said.

Several weeks passed before I realized that I had unwittingly drifted into Thaddeus Palgrave's crosshairs. My job at that time was to fact-check finished copy against the original research material, making sure that every fact and quote had a proper annotation. If there was anything in a chapter or sidebar that I couldn't verify from the research packets, I was supposed to put a red check in the margin. The chapter couldn't go to the production department until the red checks had been removed.

At first, while I was learning the ropes, I often had to go back to the writers when I couldn't confirm a particular factoid. Invariably they'd say something to the effect of, "Oh, sorry, I got that out of the *Boatner's* I keep here on my desk." As I got the hang of things, I did the checking from my own sources and rarely had to touch base with the writers. In time I no longer bothered to take note of which writer had actually written the pages. That being the case, I hadn't realized that I'd been working on one of Palgrave's chapters until he appeared suddenly in the door of my office. It was four fifteen on a rainy Friday afternoon. I had been looking forward to the weekend.

"Worm castles," he said.

I swear the temperature dropped by ten or fifteen degrees. He had a purple file folder in his hand and was tapping it against the door frame.

"Worm castles," he repeated.

"Excuse me?" I said.

He opened the folder and turned it so that I could see the page of text inside. There was a single red check mark in the margin. He sighed heavily. "You have queried the term *worm castles* in my sidebar on dwindling Union rations."

"Ah. So I did. Please, Mr. Palgrave, sit down." I tipped my gym bag off the folding chair in the corner.

He stayed where he was. "Mr. Clarke —" he began.

"Jeff," I said. "Please call me Jeff."

He looked at me with what appeared to be genuine curiosity. "Whatever for?"

"Well, it's just — if we're going to be working together, I thought it would be nice to be on a first-name basis."

"Do you imagine that we're going to become friends, Mr. Clarke?"

I tried to read his eyes. "I just thought —" I broke off and tried again. "It's casual Friday."

The answer appeared to satisfy him. "Yes, of course. Jeff." He somehow broke it into two syllables, as if translating from Old English. "Let us review the offending section of my description of food rations during the Chattanooga campaign."

"Look, I was simply checking the sources. I didn't mean —"

"As always, a staple of the Union fighting man's diet was hardtack, a hard, simple cracker made of flour, water, and salt. Hardtack — a term derived from *tack,* a slang term common among British sailors as a descriptive of food — offered many advantages to an army on the move. Cheap to produce and virtually imperishable, hardtack easily withstood the extremes of temperature and rough handling to which it was subjected in the average soldier's kit. Indeed, the thick wafer proved so indestructible that soldiers were obliged to soften it in their morning coffee before it could be eaten. This extra step offered an additional advantage — at a time when improper storage conditions meant that many of the army's foodstuffs were infested with insects, a good soaking in coffee allowed any unwanted maggots or weevil larvae to float to the top of the soldier's cup, where they could easily be skimmed off. As a result, the soldiers often referred to their hardtack rations as *worm castles.*"

Palgrave stopped reading and looked at me expectantly. "Well? This did not meet with your approval?"

"It's perfect," I said. "Very concise and informative. But I need a source for the phrase *worm castles*."

"A source?"

"I've checked every source in the packets you were given. Furgurson, Foote, Livermore — all of them. I've found any number of slang terms for hardtack. *Tooth dullers. Dog biscuits. Sheet iron. Jaw breakers. Ammo reserves.* But I can't find *worm castles*."

"I don't see the problem."

"I need a citation. It may be just a formality, but I need it. My job, as I understand it, is to check the facts — even the trivial ones. If somebody says that Grant's first name was Ulysses, I have to check it. You can't just say that Civil War soldiers walked around using the phrase *worm castles* without a source. What if they didn't?"

"They did."

"I'm sure they did. I just need you to tell me where you got it."

He narrowed his eyes. "Mr. Clarke, I have worked here for thirteen years."

"I appreciate that. And I've only worked here for a few weeks. So I'm asking you to help me do my job."

"You may rest assured that my facts are in order."

"With respect, I can't take it on faith. I

need a source."

"I am the source."

"But how do you know it's right?"

"It just is." He closed the folder and stared at me for a long moment. *"Per aspera ad astra,"* he said, walking away.

I recognized that one. Through hardship to the stars.

Palgrave began weaving a single unverifiable fact into every page of his work. Again and again I went to him asking for sources. Each time he looked me square in the face and said, "It just is." The red check marks continued to bloom in the margins of his copy, creating a logjam in the production chain. The burden of breaking the jam rested entirely with me.

One day Peter Albamarle appeared in the doorway of my office. It was rare to see him moving among the drones, so I had a pretty good idea of what was coming. "I understand you and Thaddeus have been at odds," he said.

I looked at his face and knew my job was on the line. My first job. The job that was supposed to be my entrée into big-time journalism. "Not at all, Mr. Albamarle," I said.

He folded his hands. "Thaddeus . . . can

be something of a challenge," he said slowly.

"I'm sure we'll iron this out. I'm still learning the lay of the land."

"Perhaps." Albemarle stepped into my office and closed the door. This can't be good, I thought. "It's no reflection on you," he said, "but not everyone is cut out for this job. If you like, we can reassign you to *Imagination Station* and pass Thaddeus off to a more seasoned researcher."

Imagination Station. The kiddie series. The Siberia of LifeSpan Books. "I'm sure that won't be necessary," I said.

"It's not a reflection on you," Albamarle repeated. "Thaddeus takes a certain pleasure in being difficult. This office is his entire world. He has never once in thirteen years taken a vacation. Not once. I've tried to speak with him, but . . ." He raised his palms and shrugged.

"I understand," I said. Actually, I had no clue, but I understood that he was prepared to throw me under the bus.

"It's just — it's just that if you can't resolve your issues, we won't be able to meet the drop date. That's ten days from now."

"So I have to find a source for each of the red checks in Mr. Palgrave's work."

Albamarle gave a tight nod. "Exactly," he said.

"Without his cooperation."

"I'm afraid so."

"Somewhere among all the tens of thousands of books and references we have available on the Civil War." I flipped the pages of the book I was holding. "A needle in a haystack — only the haystack is the Library of Congress."

Albamarle had the decency to look abashed. "I'm afraid that's the situation precisely," he said.

And the strange thing was, I began to think I could do it. I wanted to prove to Palgrave that I could take whatever he threw at me. It became my only goal in life to erase every single red check. I came in early to get first crack at the 128 volumes of *The Official Records of the War of the Rebellion.* I dipped into the memoirs of officers and enlisted men — *Company Aytch* by Sam Watkins and *Following the Greek Cross* by Thomas Worcester Hyde. I made a special study of Major General John D. Sedgwick, the highest-ranking Union casualty of the war, who fell to a sharpshooter's bullet at Spotsylvania. His last words: "They couldn't hit an elephant at this distance."

Brian and Kate watched with mounting horror. "You can't learn everything there is to know about the Civil War in ten days," Brian told me. "It takes three weeks, minimum." But I wouldn't be deterred. I began refusing to go out for lunch, preferring to stay at my desk with a tuna and avocado pita pocket, skimming through regimental histories. If a call of nature pulled me away from my desk, I hummed "I Cannot Mind My Wheel, Mother" on my way down the hall. After five days, I had erased seven check marks. By the eighth day only three remained. And by the last day I had whittled the list down to a single red check mark — the one that had started it all. Worm castles.

On the night before my deadline, Brian and Kate returned to the office after dinner and found me dozing over a copy of *Advance and Retreat.* "Right," Brian said. "This is not healthy. We're going out for a drink."

They pulled me out of the building, all but dragging me by the ear, and hustled me to the Irish pub. Kate refused to speak until we were settled in a corner booth with beer and nachos. "This has to stop," she said at last. "You're turning into him."

"Look, I'm the newest member of the staff. I'm just trying to save my job. If I have

183

to put in a little extra time, so be it."

"Extra time? You no longer leave your office. You no longer sleep. You have become careless in certain areas of dress and personal hygiene."

"My hygiene is fine, thank you."

"Why are you doing this, exactly?"

"I told you. I want to —"

"No," Kate said firmly. "It's not about your job. You're doing it because you think you're going to crack the big mystery."

"What mystery?

"The mystery of Thaddeus Palgrave. You think there's some kind of pot of gold waiting at the end of the rainbow. You think he's going to take you under his wing or something. You want him to sponsor you for membership in the League of Pompous Dickwads."

"Mr. Clarke," said Brian, imitating Palgrave's vaguely British accent, "the packet of clippings and scrap material you have gathered on the Union fortifications at City Point has been deemed sufficiently anal by our board of directors. It is my pleasure to present you with a Pompous Dickwad badge and decoder ring."

"*Asinus asinum fricat,*" Kate said. "The ass rubs the ass."

I sipped my beer. "You two have issues," I said.

"Yeah," said Brian. "We're the problem."

"Look, I appreciate that you're looking out for me, but the deadline is tomorrow and I have to get back."

"Not a chance, New Guy. This is an intervention. We're deprogramming you."

"But tomorrow —"

Kate reached across the table and grabbed both of my hands. "I'm going to tell you a story," she said. "Three years ago, I took my sister's kids off her hands for a weekend. By Sunday afternoon, I'm going nuts. I'm desperate. So I take them to a Renaissance fair in Wheaton. It's pretty grim. Jesters. Minstrels. Guys in funny hats playing flutes. So there I am, drinking a flagon of Diet Coke and watching a beanbag toss, and who do I see standing nearby, waiting for the royal joust to begin? None other than Thaddeus Palgrave. Wearing a white shirt and a bow tie. Holding a tankard of mead. And that, New Guy, is the road you're on. One day you, too, will be a man who attends Renaissance fairs in his work clothes."

I considered this. "I have a life outside the office, you know. I have other things going on. Maybe I'm just gathering material." I regretted it as soon as I said it.

"Ah! The novel!" Kate clasped her hands together. "How's that going? Does it feature a recent college graduate nursing a broken heart? Does he struggle, with quiet dignity, to build his life anew?"

"No," said Brian. "It's about a promising young journalist learning his craft, with quiet dignity, as he makes his way in a cold, unfeeling world."

I reached for the pitcher and refilled my glass. "How did the two of you manage to fill your time before I got here?"

Brian leaned back. "In later years, it was recalled that young Jeff Clarke never spoke of his novel, giving no hint of the epic struggle playing out in the fiery crucible of his genius. Whenever the topic was raised, he gave a boyish grin and pushed the subject aside."

"With quiet dignity," Kate added.

I never made it back to the office. We ordered another pitcher of beer and just talked. Brian talked about his band. Kate talked about her family. I talked about my romantic woes and had the good grace to laugh at myself just a bit. At one point Kate reached across and ran her fingers along Brian's arm, answering a question that had been in my mind for some time.

We closed down the bar at two A.M. I left them outside the parking garage on Cameron Street, pretending not to take an interest in whether they left in one car or two. There was a light dusting of snow on the cobblestones, and I had my hands in my pockets as I trudged toward my apartment, occasionally turning my face up to the falling snow.

I'm still not sure what made me turn up Prince Street to walk past the LifeSpan building, but as I looked up at the third-floor windows, I was only mildly surprised to see a light in Palgrave's office. As I drew nearer, I could see a shadow move across the window.

I kept walking. That wasn't me anymore, working away in the middle of the night. I was a young man who knew how to enjoy life. I was a man with friends and ambitions and a half-written manuscript. I glanced up again. The light flickered as the shadow passed again.

The guard at the security desk was sleeping, and I took care not to wake him. I rode the elevator to the third floor and buzzed myself in with my entry card. Everything felt dim and empty. My shoes made a peculiar crackling sound on the industrial carpet.

It's important to understand that I never intended to speak to Palgrave. I just wanted to spend a few minutes in my office. I knew now that I wasn't going to be able to erase that last check mark. I think I may have been planning to write a note of explanation to Mr. Albamarle. If Palgrave happened to see me and register that I was working every bit as hard as he was, well, so be it. I settled behind my desk and took the cover off my typewriter, leaning back in the chair to compose my thoughts.

When I woke up three hours later, Palgrave was sitting opposite me in the folding chair. It took a few moments for it to sink in. I can't say I was startled — somehow his presence struck me as familiar and almost reassuring — but I knew at once that we had turned a strange corner. For one thing, he was smiling.

He waited a few moments while I came around. "You sleep here?" he asked.

"No," I said. "No, I just came in to do a little work. I didn't mean —"

He waved it off. "I sleep here. Most of the time. I have an apartment, but it's just for show."

"What?"

He was rubbing his chin, staring at me appraisingly as if trying to guess my age and weight. "You're very persistent, Mr. Clarke," he said.

"It's the job."

"The job, yes, but more than that. You're curious. Always asking people about their hobbies, their interests."

"Look, I never meant to be nosy, I just —"

"No, it's good. I should do more of that sort of thing. I forget to do it. There's so little point, in the circumstances. The time is so short, it scarcely seems worth the trouble. People like you are gone in the blink of an eye."

I bristled. "No, you're wrong. I'm committed to this job. I'm going to stay at least five years. If you drive me off this series, I'll do my time on *Imagination Station* and work my way back. I'm in for the long haul."

"The long haul!" he cried. "Five years!" He clapped his hands. I had never seen him so animated. "Five whole years! As long as that? Do you know how long I've been here?"

"Thirteen years."

"Well, yes, I suppose. Thirteen years in this particular building. But do you know

189

how long I've been . . . *here?* In the larger sense?"

"I'm not quite sure I —"

"Twelve hundred and sixty-seven years. But my relationship to time isn't quite linear."

"Pardon me?"

"So you'll forgive me if your five-year commitment fails to impress. You must excuse me if I haven't troubled to get to know you, to stand at the water cooler and make inquiries about your life and your interests and your football team. Would you take the trouble to get to know a fruit fly? Would you pause to exchange pleasantries with a falling leaf or a raindrop running down a windowpane?"

I struggled for a foothold. "I have no idea —"

"Shall I tell you my source for that troublesome information in my latest chapter? Worm castles? Mr. Clarke, I was there. At Chancellorsville. In 1863. I heard it firsthand. I tried to tell you: I'm the source." He reached past me to a bookshelf and pulled down one of the early volumes of the series. *Mustering the Troops.* He flipped it open to a section of regimental photographs, showing rows and rows of grim-faced young men posing with their units before they mobilized. "There I am in the third row, Second Connecticut Light Artillery. No one could understand why I insisted on using this particular photo in the book. Just my idea of a little joke. And they say I have no sense of humor."

I peered down at the face he had indicated. It was grainy and nondescript. "Mr. Palgrave . . . Thaddeus . . . I don't understand any of this. You're telling me that you're some sort of supernatural creature? Is that what you're trying to say?" I thought about Kate and her Mexican bare skulls and *strigoi.* "You're a vampire of some kind?"

He shook his head, even pursing his lips as if disappointed by my pedestrian line of thinking. "Not a vampire, not a werewolf, not a zombie. We're not at all like those people, though we have no objection to them. In fact, they can be quite useful. But we don't drink blood or howl at the moon. Nothing so colorful. We simply observe. We are researchers, like yourself. When all this is gone, there must be some record."

Even now, I still clung to the notion — or perhaps the hope — that this was all an elaborate joke. "You — you're a researcher," I said. My voice had gone flat. "A researcher who's lived for hundreds of years. And of all the places in the world where you might go — of all the fascinating, *important* places where you might go — you've chosen to spend thirteen years in an office at LifeSpan Books?"

He appeared delighted by the question. "Isn't it wonderful?" he cried. "As I mentioned, our relationship with time is not quite linear in the way you might be thinking. But these past thirteen years have been a wonderful break."

"A break?"

"Don't you see? I'm on vacation! All of this is just another Renaissance fair to me!" He sighed fondly. "But it's time to be getting back."

"Getting back. To your research job."

"Actually, Jeff, I'm no longer in research."

"No?"

"No. I'm in recruiting. And we're all terribly impressed with you. With your application. And so soon after Miss Rossmire! Do you know Miss Rossmire, by the way? I'm sure you'll like her."

I lurched to my feet. "You — you're impressed with me? But all those red checks. All those missing citations. All that —"

"Just a formality during the apprentice period. Nothing to worry about now. I'm really quite charming when you get to know me, as you'll discover in the fullness of

192

time." He extended his hand. "What do you say?"

I simply stared at him.

"Do you need some time to think about it? Of course you're perfectly welcome to stay here and carry on as before. I will be moving on, and there will be no further obstacles to your advancement. Should you elect to remain, however, I should perhaps mention that matters will not proceed as you might wish." He leaned up against the window, resting his head against his forearm. "If you and I part company tonight, you will continue here for another twelve years. It's all a bit conventional, I'm afraid. After four years you move into a small town house in Shirlington, telling yourself that you need space for an office in which to write your novel. Two years later you fall behind on the mortgage, and your new girlfriend — Cheryl, from copyediting — seizes upon the opening to move in with you, in the interests of sharing expenses. What had been a casual, halfhearted romance on your part now becomes fraught with the expectation of marriage. You resist for two more years, finally bowing to the inevitable two days before Cheryl's thirtieth birthday. Within three years you begin an affair with a woman you meet at Gilpin

Books, which becomes public just as your wife discovers a lump in her left breast. Her bravery and fortitude as she battles with cancer is thrown into brilliant relief by your disgrace; she is a martyr in the eyes of everyone you have ever known. Though you tend to your dying wife with saintly devotion, it is too late for redemption. At her funeral fourteen months later you sob inconsolably and no one makes a move to comfort you, not even Kate and Brian. In time you turn to drink, and after many warnings and probation periods, you finally lose your job at LifeSpan. For a while you cobble together a living of freelance writing and editing, but the loneliness weighs heavily. One rainy night, driving home from a strip club in the District, you slam your car into the base of the *Appomattox* statue at the corner of Washington and Duke. You are not hurt — indeed, in your drunken state you find the accident to be the very last word in hilarity. You climb out of your car, spread your arms to the heavens, and roar with laughter as the rain drenches your face. At that moment, you are struck and killed by a dairy van."

I couldn't speak. He reached past me for the list of missing citations on my desk.

"I don't understand," I said at last. "Why

is it — how do you —"

"Don't you see?" He spread the page across his knee and erased the last of the red check marks, brushing away the crumbs with a flick of his hand. "It just is. You'll see. It just is."

Everything started to happen very quickly then, but I found time for a final piece of business. Before we left, I slipped a note and a five-dollar bill under the door of Kate's office:

Aeternum vale. Farewell forever. Next time, the nachos are on me.

The Innsmouth Nook

A. LEE MARTINEZ

A. Lee Martinez has published six novels, most of which involve either monsters or armchair metaphysics. Usually both. He has a reputation as a "humorous fantasy" writer that he's not always comfortable with, but as long as the checks keep coming, he'll keep cashing them. If you see him on the street, please, don't call him zany. His first name is Alex, but he sometimes goes by Lee (presumably) to confuse and beguile his many enemies.

The box held horrors beyond imagining, papers inscribed with hopelessness and pain. All men faced it on a daily basis, praying to whatever gods might be, cruel and indifferent to the suffering of mortals, that it would not be the end that they found when they reached into its darkened interior. That ever-present box, haunting every house, every apartment, every place where civilized men dwelt, reminding all that they

196

were not masters of their fate, that no matter how much a man might want to deny it, the universe demanded its pound of flesh and would never be satisfied, would never stop sucking the life from a man, would feed on misery and sweat and blood until a man's death. Sometimes, even beyond that.

Philip, like all civilized men, had learned to live with the box. Even become somewhat expectant of its demands. Lately, though, he'd realized just how much it had enslaved him. How he trudged to it every morning and bowed before it like a puppet without a will of his own. But even knowing that didn't free him from its tyranny.

So this morning, like always, he walked to the box, that maddening box, and reached into its shadowy depths and withdrew its unholy commandments.

"Shit," he groaned. "Bills."

He slammed the mailbox shut ruefully. He thought about getting an ax and chopping the damned thing down. But you couldn't kill the thing. The box wasn't the beast, not even the head of the beast. It was just a tentacle, reaching out from the great unknown, from that horrible place where credit card bills, junk mail, and despair were spawned.

A chill wind swept up from the ocean

below. The clouds parted to allow a glimpse of sunshine. But it was only a glimpse before the sky became that endless broiling gray.

Philip ran inside. Vance was making breakfast. The smell of eggs and bacon was the first encouraging moment of the day.

"It's the last of the eggs," said Vance, ruining the moment. "Anything good in the mail?"

Philip grunted, unable to articulate in words what Vance already knew. It was easier for Vance, though. He'd just come along with Philip on this venture, but it was Philip who'd thought of it.

Why the hell did he think anyone would want to visit a bed-and-breakfast in this chilly cultural wasteland? There were areas in New England, plenty of them, with quaintness to spare, with color-changing leaves and folksy folks full of folksy homespun wisdom accompanied by folksy accents.

And then there was Clam Bay. Cold even when sunny, gloomy even during the four weeks of "summer," trees without leaves all year long, and full of weird people. And not in the quirky way. No, these were just weird. Quiet, not unfriendly, but wary of strangers. And anyone whose family hadn't lived in the town for at least five generations was a stranger. It didn't help any that Philip's great-great-grandfather had been one of Clam Bay's citizens. And that the house Philip had inherited had been a literal ruin until he'd invested thousands of dollars into fixing it up in hopes of attracting tourists. He was still an outsider.

It was kind of hard to hide. Not just because everyone in Clam Bay had a tendency to wear gray, shuffle slowly as if dragging themselves reluctantly across the land, and speak in a slow, halting, decidedly nonquaint, nonfolksy way. They also looked alike. It was a small gene pool in this town, and it hadn't really worked out that well for any of the citizens of Clam Bay.

Also, the clamming was lousy in Clam Bay.

Philip and Vance ate breakfast in near silence. There was no need to remark on their growing pile of bills and the lack of tourists. Without looking at the budget, Philip estimated they had another four months before the all-consuming debt . . . well . . . consumed them.

The bell attached to the front door jingled. Philip and Vance jumped up and ran to greet the visitor. Their hopes were dashed by the sight of the Clam Bay constable.

"Hello," said Philip halfheartedly.

The constable nodded and tipped his gray

hat. "Mornin', fellas. I'm afraid we have us a slight little problem here."

Philip tried to place the accent. It wasn't New Englandish. Not quite. Clam Bay had its own special dialect. It really was a world of itself. Too bad it wasn't in the charming Old World way, but the creepy, skin-crawling fashion. But for all their creepiness, the folks of Clam Bay hadn't done anything to Philip or Vance.

And now there was a problem.

The constable led them outside and pointed to a hanging sign posted by the road. "Want to tell me about this?"

Vance said, "I found it in the attic. Thought it looked Old World. Kind of cool."

The icy wind made the sign swing. The constable steadied it. "We'd like you to take it down, if you could."

"Why?"

The constable made a snorting noise and spat up a wad of green phlegm. "We just would rather if you did."

"Excuse me," said Vance, "but this isn't a police state, is it? We can have anything we want on our house, can't we?"

The constable frowned. It wasn't easy to detect, because the citizens of Clam Bay had mouths bent downward naturally. "Ehyah. It's just, well, we don't like to think about it. About the old town name, huh." He worked his jaw as if testing to see if it still functioned properly.

"You can barely read it," said Vance.

"It's a memory," said the Constable. "A bad memory that we would rather forget."

He gazed out toward the ocean with a strange combination of yearning and dread. Nobody swam in Clam Bay's waters. They were too cold. But sometimes, Philip would catch a citizen or two standing on the beach. Always with that same unsettling expression.

"We'll take it down," said Philip. "No problem."

The constable nodded. "Ehyah." He rubbed his face. "Ehyah." He shuffled away, never taking his eyes off the sea.

"Why'd you agree to that?" asked Vance. "It's a free country."

"Oh, stop it," said Philip. "Who really cares? We gotta live here, right? At least for another few months."

"It's censorship. It's bullshit."

"Yeah, yeah. You can fight the good fight when we go back to New York."

Grumbling, Vance wrestled with the sign, stubbornly trying to uproot it with his bare hands.

■ ■ ■ ■

Clam Bay's general store was large on the outside. But on the inside, it was half empty. The weird thing was that instead of splitting the store down the middle with empty aisles on one side and filled aisles on the other, the arrangement was seemingly random. There was the canned goods aisle, an empty aisle, the cereal aisle, produce, another two empty aisles, frozen foods, one more empty aisle, ethnic foods (which amounted to tortillas and taco shells), several more empty aisles, and at the very end, farthest from the entrance, the meat aisle. Even weirder, the lighting of the store was a murky twilight that refused to venture into the empty aisles, leaving them shadowy regions of darkness. Sometimes, Philip thought he saw something lurking in the aisle between frozen and ethnic. Not exactly saw, but sensed.

There was nobody ever in the store. He was sure that people shopped here. They had to. It was the only place to get groceries. But he never saw anyone other than the raggedy guy by the cash register. So Philip wasn't really paying attention when he nearly plowed into the woman as he turned into the aisle.

They jumped simultaneously.

"Oh, jeez. I'm sorry," he said.

She smiled. It'd been a while since he'd seen a smile like that. And she wasn't wearing standard Clam Bay gray or black. No, she had on a blue sweater and some tan slacks, and Philip realized how cheery tan could be in these circumstances.

"Don't worry about it. I should've been looking. It's just . . . well, I'm just not used to seeing anyone else here." She extended her hand. "I'm Angela."

"Hi, I'm —"

"Philip," she interrupted.

"Have we met?"

"Oh, no. I just arrived in town yesterday. But the village is buzzing with gossip about the two" — she made air quotes — " 'big-city fellows' who moved into the Bay."

He had a hard time imagining Clam Bay buzzing. The cashier was sitting slouched by the front of the store, motionless, staring out the window.

Angela moved past him and headed toward the register. He hadn't finished his shopping, but he followed her. "So what brings you to Clam Bay?" he asked.

"Just visiting my mother."

That surprised him. She didn't have the

look of someone born here. She wasn't gorgeous. Or even especially attractive. In a different place, she might even be on the pretty side of plain. But here, in this place, she was a knockout. How the gene pool worked that one out, he couldn't figure.

"I was adopted," she said. "That's what you were thinking, right?"

He nodded. "Yeah, was it that obvious?"

"No, but it's the first thought any outsider should probably have. So how about you?" she asked. "Why did you and your" — she broke out the air quotes again — " 'life partner' decide to move to Clam Bay?"

"Not really a good reason for it, I guess. Just bad judgment on . . . Wait. What did you call us?"

"Oh, I'm sorry." She blushed. "Was that the wrong term? I didn't mean to offend."

"You think . . . Uh, we're not gay."

She laughed. "Oh, it's all right. Nobody here cares about something like that. We're pretty tolerant of alternative lifestyles."

"We're not gay," he said with a little more force than intended. "We're just friends."

"Are you married?"

"No."

"Girlfriends?"

"Not at the moment."

"Confirmed bachelors?" She raised an

eyebrow.

"Not confirmed," he replied.

"So two single guys from the big city move to our little town and open a bed-and-breakfast. But you're not gay."

"We're just friends," he said.

"Right. Because straight men open bed-and-breakfasts all the time."

"These straight men did."

"Straight men named Philip and Vance."

He wanted to argue, but he was suddenly beginning to question it himself. The thought was so distracting that he barely noticed when she ended the conversation and bid him farewell.

Vance took the news of their "big-city fellows" status better than Philip. Probably because it turned out that he actually was gay.

"You're what?"

"Well, I'm not entirely sure," said Vance, "but I'd say it's seventy-thirty for it."

"But I've seen you with women."

"That would be the thirty part of the equation," said Vance as he sipped his coffee.

"Oh my God. That's why you agreed to do this with me. You think I'm gay, too!"

Vance chuckled. "Dude, you're not gay."

"I know I'm not, but do you know I'm not?"

"I'd say ninety-two-eight on the straight side," said Vance.

"How the hell —"

"They've made some terrific advances in gaydar, dude."

Philip laid his head on the table and thought about it for a while. "So eight percent gay?"

"Remember that week you went around humming 'Hello, Dolly'?"

"That's worth eight percent?"

"That, and the fact that *you* did want to open a bed-and-breakfast. Even I had my doubts when I first heard you mention the idea."

"Bed-and-breakfasts are not an innately gay enterprise," countered Philip.

"Fair enough," said Vance. "But I wouldn't lay odds on many single straight guys who start these things up."

"But —"

"I don't make the rules, dude. I just get them from the website."

"So if you don't think I'm gay, why did you agree to do this with me?"

"For the reason I originally said," replied Vance. "I'd just lost my job, had nothing holding me in the city, and it sounded like something to do."

"And that's it?"

Vance shook his head. "Philly, I love you, buddy. I do. But you're not my type."

"I'm not?"

"What? Are you insulted?"

Philip was pondering that when the front door jingled. He didn't know how he still managed to get excited at the sound. It never meant a tourist looking for a room. It had been raining for the last few hours, a slick, frozen rain that made the roads hard to travel. So maybe someone had to stop, and the Nook was the only place convenient. It was a long shot, but he peeked out into the foyer with a smidgen of hope.

It was Angela. Although she wasn't a tourist, she wasn't an unwelcome sight. He introduced Vance.

"This is my *friend* Vance," he said, hitting the *friend* part hard. "My good *friend* Vance."

Angela and Vance exchanged smirking glances. And he could see their point. Hitting *friend* too hard was a double-edged sword. It could be trouble.

"Don't mind him," said Vance. "He's just discovering he's homophobic, but otherwise, he's a good guy."

They gave her a quick tour. The rain started coming down harder, judging by the increasing beat on the roof. Lightning flashed, too. Lightning without thunder. Philip couldn't remember hearing thunder once in Clam Bay, even in the heaviest storm.

"You guys did a great job. I hardly recognize the place," remarked Angela when they completed the journey and ended at the kitchen. "Love the decorating."

"That was mostly Vance," said Philip. "I'm more of the carpentry and plumbing guy."

"Yes, and I'm in charge of flower arranging and doilies," said Vance with a perfectly straight face.

She reached out and put her hand on Philip's. "I believe you."

He breathed a sigh of relief.

"Actually, I believe Vance. We had a talk when you were making the espressos." She took a drink of hers. "You make a great espresso, by the way."

Things were looking up in Clam Bay just then.

The front door jingled again, just as the lights flickered on and off. It wasn't uncommon during a fierce storm.

"You two stay put," said Vance. "I'll check who it is."

"Thanks," said Philip.

Vance left as the lights continued to flicker.

"Wiring," said Philip to Angela. "We're still working on it. So I'm glad you stopped by."

"Yeah. Me, too."

They shared a smile.

The lights went out. Given the darkness of Clam Bay nights, he expected nothing but black. But there was a soft green light coming from the foyer.

Vance screamed, but the sound was cut short. Philip and Angela ran to see what had happened.

It was hard to discern details. Vance was on the floor, groaning. And something stood over him. Something with large eyes that radiated an unearthly emerald glow.

"What the —" started Philip.

Silent lightning flashed, and the person, the *creature* because there was no other word for it, was illuminated, just for a moment. The thing was hunched, gray-skinned. It had a huge head with a gaping mouth. And frills on the side of that head extended as a strangled hiss rose out of its throat. Philip didn't hear the sound, though. He was too busy looking out the windows, where shadows lurched. At least four or five of them. And each one sported those same unearthly eyes.

He stood transfixed, unable to move. It

wasn't terror that held him. Terror was too tangible. Terror was overwhelming. But this strange creature, even mostly hidden in shadow, was simply the unknowable. It was the intangible made real, and there was no easy way to absorb it. So he just stood there and gaped, even as the creature menaced Vance.

Angela rushed forward. The monster lurched at her. She seized it by the hand, spun into it, and did some kind of kung fu move that happened so fast, the creature was thrown to the ground before Philip even knew it happened. The fish creature shrieked, flopping around on its back. The creatures outside joined in on the gruesome dirge.

She yanked Vance off the ground and dragged him back to Philip.

The front door pushed open, and the bell jingled as several more creatures entered.

"Is there a back door?" asked Angela.

When neither Philip or Vance replied, she grabbed Philip by the shirt and shook him. "Your back door, Phil!"

"Uh . . . in the back," he replied.

She pulled both the men with her as she moved toward the exit. They didn't get far. Three other creatures must have slipped in the back and blocked the way. There was no way out. The creatures' raspy breathing and eerie green glow alerted them in time to avoid stumbling into an ambush. In the foyer, something was smashed to the floor.

"My vases," said Vance.

But he said it the fancy way, the way Europeans did. Philip wondered why it had taken him so long to figure out Vance was gay. Then he wondered about the stereotyping and how absurd it was. Then he realized how absurd it was to think about this while the creatures from the Black Lagoon were about to eat him alive. But that was kind of the point. It was easier to think about something stupid than about the alternative, pressing as it might be.

"The cellar," whispered Vance. "We can hide in the cellar."

Philip had always hated the cellar. It was musty and dank. But it was the only choice as the creatures closed in on the kitchen. They went down. Angela had the good sense not to let the trap door slam. Vance had spent a week organizing the cellar, so even though it was dark, there was little to trip over. Vance moved like a cat. At least, Philip assumed Vance did. It was hard to tell in the darkened cellar. But Vance managed to retrieve a flashlight without making a lot of noise. He flicked it on, covering it with his hand to keep the light low.

They said nothing as the creatures trod over their heads. They watched the trap door, waiting for it to open, waiting for the monsters to come down and devour them. But after a few minutes, the creaking stopped and the raspy breathing faded.

They still didn't speak for another five minutes after that.

"What the hell are those?" Vance finally asked, so softly Philip almost didn't hear him. "Are those monsters?" His voice rose. "Are those fucking monsters?"

"Deep ones," said Angela.

"What the hell is a —"

"Just a story," she said. "Not even that."

"What's that supposed to mean?"

She wiped her brow. "It's hard to explain. You know how every small town has a story? Clam Bay is no different."

"I'd say it's different," whispered Philip through clenched teeth. "I'd say it's very goddamn different."

The floor creaked, and they were quiet again.

Angela leaned forward, the flashlight casting eerie shadows on her face, making this seem like a ghost story told around a campfire. Except the ghosts were real, and it wasn't some dumb kid ready to jump out

212

and yell "Boo" when you got to the scary part. No, it was an actual monster that was going to jump out.

"A long time ago," she said in a low, low voice, "back before Clam Bay was Clam Bay. Back when it went by another name, the people made a pact with the ancient god who waits in the depths of the ocean."

"What's he waiting for?" asked Vance.

"Nobody knows," replied Angela.

"Then how do they know he's waiting?"

"That's hardly important at this moment," said Philip.

"Well, she brought it up," said Vance.

"Will you just shut up about the waiting?"

Vance glared. "You don't have to raise your voice at me like I'm the asshole."

"You're right. Sorry."

"If anything, you're the asshole. If you hadn't come up with this B-and-B idea in the first place —"

"I know," said Philip.

"I'm just asking a question, trying to get a handle on the situation —"

"Holy hell, Vance. I've already apologized. What the hell more do you want from me?"

"Are you sure you two aren't a couple?" asked Angela.

"Just finish your story," said Philip.

"There's not much more to tell. The deep

ones came as servants of the sea god. They offered secrets of power and immortality, and the people took them up on it. I'd rather not get into the details."

"What details?" asked Vance.

Angela paused. "They're not important."

"Maybe there's a clue to what these things want," said Philip.

"I hope not," she mumbled to herself, though they both heard. Caught, she was overpowered by their intent stares. "Okay, but you aren't going to like it. They . . . uh . . . I believe the term used is *mingled their blood.*"

"You mean, they cut themselves?" asked Philip. "Like when kids make themselves blood brothers?"

"Uh . . . no."

"Oh my God. Don't tell me that they ate people."

She shook her head.

"Then how did they . . ."

"They fucked the fish monsters."

"They what?" asked Philip.

"Yeah, how does that even work?" added Vance.

"I don't know," she replied, "but they figured it out. And the deep one DNA eventually started turning people into fish monsters, too, and more and more citizens swam out to sea, never to return. Probably would've happened to everyone, except at some point the government got wise and stepped in. Raided the town, using Prohibition as a pretense, killed everyone who had too much fish in them.

"But they left some behind, people who were still more human than not. The town renounced the deep ones, and everyone tried to forget about it. Most of the citizens left. But there were still some who had enough deep one in them that they couldn't leave the bay, couldn't abandon the sea. They stayed behind, trying to move on as best they could. Waiting for the deep ones to return. Anticipating their return, but dreading it at the same time."

"And now they're back," said Philip.

"To have sex with us," said Vance.

An ominous silence filled the cellar.

"We were all thinking it," said Vance.

"That didn't mean you had to say it," said Philip.

The cellar door creaked as it slowly opened. They searched for a place to hide, but there was none. A pair of deep ones lumbered down the stairs. They moved with the same shuffling gait the citizens of Clam Bay possessed. The flashlight and their glowing eyes mixed to form a putrid illumination, allowing Philip his first clear glimpse of the monsters. The resemblance to the citizens of Clam Bay was rather obvious. From the walk to the slack-jawed expression to the only slightly more scaly skin. If anything, the deep ones seemed less monstrous because they were fully monsters, not caught in some halfway genetic dead end.

Despite his best efforts, his glance fell across the lead creature's groin. They seemed to lack the necessary equipment for blood mingling, but maybe they were more fish than human. He was no expert, but he thought fish reproduce by laying eggs and then the male would come along and deposit his contribution. If that was the way this was going to work, he supposed he could handle it.

A thunderclap rattled the house. The first thunderclap Philip had heard in Clam Bay. And possibly the last. The lights flicked back on, revealing the deep ones, in all their briny, mottled-green glory.

Vance seized a wine bottle and smashed it over the leader's head. The bottle shattered. Red dripped down the deep one's body, but it was wine, not blood. The creature itself appeared unharmed. It didn't even move with the blow. But it did turn its fish head slowly, degree by degree, in Vance's direction.

He smiled and laughed nervously, as if trying to pass the whole thing off as a bad joke.

The deep one opened its mouth. A horrible gurgle bubbled up from its throat. Its body twitched in a spasm. Its gills throbbed. It retched, spewing a black stew of seaweed and fish bones all over Vance.

Philip hoped this wasn't foreplay. The last time he'd been willing to have sex while covered in vomit, he'd been in college. He wasn't nearly drunk enough tonight.

"Excuse me." The deep one pounded its chest while clearing its throat. It was a horrible scraping sound.

The humans all took a moment to analyze the creature's apology. There was an accent. The same not-quaint, vaguely New Englandish accent as the good citizens of Clam Bay. The voice was raspy but decipherable. It had less to do with what the deep one said and more to do with that it said anything at all.

A fit of coughs racked the creature. Seawater dripped from its open mouth. It wiped its lips and sucked in a scraping breath.

"By Dagon, the air is dry. Could we

trouble you for something to drink?"

Philip sat on the porch overlooking the beach. The rain came down in a fine mist. His beach umbrella protected him from the worst of it, but he zipped up his jacket as a stiff breeze swept across Clam Bay.

"Hey," said Angela. "Vance said I'd find you here."

She leaned over and gave him a kiss, then sat in the chair beside him.

"They're coming," he said.

"How do you know?"

"The beach," replied Philip, taking her hand. "When the sand turns to a light brown mud, that's when you know."

"How's the remodel coming?"

"Good. We finally got the bigger bathtubs installed. Now we just have to rip out the rest of the carpeting." He took a sip of his soda. "They drip. A lot. Easier to mop up hardwood than fight a never-ending battle against mildew."

They watched the tides go in and out for a few minutes until the deep ones appeared. Strange how quickly Philip had gotten used to the sight of fish monsters lumbering from the ocean. Sometimes, there was just one or two. Never more than five. They trudged up the beach, toward Philip and Angela, and the lead creature spoke.

"Is this the Innsmouth Nook?"

"Yes, sir." Philip could tell by the gills that this was a male. The females had a more elaborate fringe.

"We have a reservation for three," said the deep one.

"Just follow this trail up to the house. My partner, Vance, is ready to check you folks in." Philip jumped to his feet and saluted casually. The deep ones didn't shake hands, and he didn't mind that.

They deposited a mound of fresh fish at Philip's feet. Rusty bits of dull metal were mixed within. Philip spotted a couple of doubloons and several jewels. The deep ones shambled away.

Tourism had come to Clam Bay. Cold even when sunny, gloomy even during the four weeks of "summer," trees without leaves all year long, and full of weird people. But for the right kind of people, creatures from the depths looking for a chance to revisit the old country, there was a certain charm to the place.

A customer was a customer. And aside from the dripping and the rasping, the deep ones were polite and easy to please. They brought their own food, and cooking was easy. Just throw a raw tuna on a plate, garnish with seaweed, and serve with a tall glass of seawater. For the most part, the deep ones were quiet and undemanding. The only danger was getting caught in an extended conversation with the more fervent fish folk. They could talk for hours upon hours about the glory of R'lyeh and the beautiful oblivion destined to sweep up from the ocean's depths to consume the surface world. But that was more tolerable than when that Scientologist guy spent the night.

Things were looking up at the Nook. It wasn't what Philip had in mind when first embarking on this endeavor, but life called for flexibility. He was making a tidy profit, and Clam Bay, still dreary, wet, and cold, had more to offer than he'd ever imagined.

He took Angela in his arms and gave her a long, deep kiss.

"Okay," she said. "I get it. You're not gay."

They shared a chuckle.

"So up for a little . . . mingling?" he asked.

"I thought you'd never ask."

Smiling, she took him by the hand and led him toward the Nook.

SAFE AND SOUND
JEFF ABBOTT

Jeff Abbott was once involved in a taxicab race with Charlaine Harris in North Carolina (he did not win). He is the internationally bestselling author of twelve suspense novels, including *Trust Me, Panic, Fear,* and *Collision.* He is published in more than twenty languages. He is a three-time Edgar® Award nominee, a two-time Anthony Award nominee, a Thriller Award and Barry Award nominee, and a past winner of the Agatha and Macavity awards. He lives in Austin with his family. You can read more about Jeff and his work at www.jeff abbott.com.

If Jason Kirk was still alive on the tiny island of Sint Pieter, that happy news would boost Nora Dare's ratings to a level that made media presidents tremble, rewrote the rules of news coverage, and produced new business case studies at journalism school.

Nora Dare sat at her Constant News

Channel (CNC) desk, lacquered talons skimming the notes on the most recent police report. Her cameramen readied themselves in the gleaming studio, the sound checks ringing in her ears. She put her carefully mascaraed gaze on the computer screen buried in her desk, scanning for any breaking updates. The interview had to be played carefully — to make the story last longer, without seeming exploitative of a missing young man's tragedy. But, Nora knew, no one walked that line better than she did.

Of course during those treasured moments when she interviewed Jason's family — which was roughly every other night on her cable-news show, *Dare to Fight Back* — she pleaded for Jason's safe return, and she meant every word. Because if the young man turned up safe and sound, well, then, that was ratings gold. Not gold: better, platinum. Maybe even uranium. For three months, college student Jason Kirk's disappearance while on vacation with his family had made for a deliciously high market share.

Stories as long-legged as Jason Kirk's did not happen every day. It had all the elements Nora considered key to a ratings grabber: a highly attractive, sympathetic victim with an easy-to-remember name; a photogenic mourning family stunned by tragedy's random sideswipe; an exotic locale; incompetent local police; a mysterious, exotic woman who had last been seen with the missing young man.

The theories had come up, and Nora had dissected them with the care of a coroner. Jason had been kidnapped (an early favorite and still the feeling of the Kirk family); Jason had been sold into slavery (popular for two weeks); Jason had been murdered by the mysterious woman, robbed, his body dumped into the ocean (more likely); Jason had drowned, drunk, in a swim off a Sint Pieter beach and the woman had simply fled the scene (the preferred theory of the local police); or Jason had committed suicide (Nora quickly slaughtered that theory; it would savage her ratings).

But now, everything had changed, and the story had fresh life. A witness from a small town on the far north tip of the island claimed that a young man fitting Jason's description had been spotted near her house. The eyewitness was a young woman who could have been a little more photogenic (didn't they, Nora wondered, have dentists in Sint Pieter?) but was earnest and heartfelt in her sureness that she'd seen Jason.

The makeup director tended to Nora's eyebrows with the gentlest of touches while Nora's director, Molly, slipped an update onto Nora's interview pages.

"Um, Nora, I'm not really comfortable with your headline theme tonight."

" 'Hope or Hoax' is perfectly accurate." Nora didn't flinch as a stray hair was plucked away from her near-immaculate brow. It was a point of honor for Nora that she never flinched. She made other people flinch. It had been a rocky road on the climb to ratings glory and the multimillion-dollar book deals. There'd been that suspect in one case who'd killed himself after Nora grilled him (could his guilt then be clearer? Nora had saved the taxpayers the cost of a trial, in her mind), and the other one where the man she'd proclaimed guilty for five months for killing his wife had, well, been found innocent via DNA evidence. Nora still had her doubts, as did any right-minded viewer. " 'Hope or Hoax' is what tonight is about," she said with an air of irritation.

Molly raised an eyebrow. "I see your point, but I think it's a bit cruel to the Kirks to call this hope."

"If it's hope," Nora explained with a smile

of infinite patience, "then the viewers have a reason to tune in tomorrow. If it's hoax, then they get to see me rip this little lying bitch to shreds."

"It just seems a bit . . ."

"What?"

Nora thought for a minute Molly's mouth was forming the fatal word *tasteless,* but Molly crossed her arms. "Opportunistic. We're walking a very fine line here, Nora."

"The only opportunistic person here might be this witness, this" — she glanced at her notes — "hotel worker, Annie Van Dorn. She could just be an attention seeker, a publicity hound. You know how I despise those loathsome people."

"I know, feeding on tragedy. The vultures."

Nora thought she detected sarcasm lurking in the vicinity of Molly's tone but decided Molly wasn't that stupid. "The intro stands."

"All right, Nora." Molly turned and walked back to the director's seat in the control room.

Nora watched her go. She'd have to keep an eye on Molly. That girl was an unappealing mix of judgmental and ambitious. Most unbecoming. Opportunistic? No one was a greater friend or advocate to the Kirk family than Nora was. And poor lost Jason. She was truly his only friend, the person doing the most to keep his face in front of millions each day. She waved away the makeup artist.

They went live thirty minutes later, and Nora, after her standard setup on the missing Jason's history, cut straight to the satellite interview with the young woman who'd *supposedly* (Nora wove this knotty word into every sentence; it was her second favorite, after *allegedly*) seen Jason on the far side of the island.

Annie Van Dorn's skin was a caramel color; her voice lightly accented, her English excellent. Slightly crooked teeth, but otherwise a nice face. She'd put on what Nora surmised was her Sunday best for the interview: a neat white blouse, three years out of fashion. Annie stood in front of a gnarled, wind-bent divi-divi tree in her yard that, to Nora, evoked an air of mystery and danger and Caribbean intrigue. The tree looked like a hand, reaching to clutch the young woman.

"Annie, tell our viewers about yourself," Nora said. Her voice was bright, open, and friendly.

"I work at a hotel on Sint Pieter, in housekeeping." Annie had a quiet, mild voice. A servant's voice, Nora thought.

"But not the hotel from which Jason vanished?"

"No, ma'am, another one." Annie wisely did not try to work the hotel's name into her answer. Nora frowned on free advertising.

"And what exactly do you claim you saw last night?"

"Well." Annie swallowed. "It was close to midnight, and I was at home in Marysville, on the other side of the island from where young Mr. Kirk vanished. I was getting ready for bed — and I thought I heard a noise in the yard. I live with my sister, but she was asleep already. I went to the window, and I saw, in the moonlight, a young man standing in the yard. Close to this tree."

"Describe him to me." And at these words, a picture of Jason appeared on the split screen: blondish, handsome enough to be a model, six three, with a wide grin and broad shoulders, dressed in a T-shirt and baggy shorts. Smiling the smile of a man who has his entire and likely quite-happy life before him, and is savoring a particular moment of fun.

"I couldn't see him well in the shadows. I thought maybe it was an old boyfriend of mine, at first. He was sticking close to the trees, not drawing closer, not really stepping out into the moonlight." The camera panned across Annie's yard: The viewers could see a dense growth of the divi-divi trees, dark and close; a neighbor's fenced yard; a clothesline with athletic jerseys, jeans, and a checkered tablecloth snapping in the twilight air. Rustic, Nora thought, yet ever so mildly forbidding.

"Do your old boyfriends often stop by late at night?"

"Only one. Who might need money now and then and doesn't understand I won't loan him any," Annie said with a little more spine in her tone, and Nora nodded. Her viewers would like Annie for her moral stance.

Annie continued: "So I went outside and called out 'Who's there?' then the moonlight broke from the clouds, and I saw it wasn't my old boyfriend. This man was tall, he was white, with blond hair, wearing a dark shirt, baseball cap, and muddy jeans. I thought he was a prowler then, and I stepped back toward my house."

"Were you afraid?" Nora pounced.

"Not exactly. When I could see him, I just felt this . . . sadness. I can't describe it; it was strange. He looked lost, like he needed help. Like he was confused. I wanted to comfort him. It's like I could sense his need

— like when you see a lost child."

Nora's voice sharpened into a needle. "And then what happened?"

"Well, my neighbor's dog got roused; it started barking really loud, and the neighbor's porch lights switched on, and the man just sort of vanished into the divi-divi trees."

"He ran off?"

"I guess. I didn't hear him. He stepped back into the shadows and then he was gone. I ran to where he had stood and there was no sign of him." Annie swallowed.

"And you're sure this was Jason Kirk?"

"At first, ma'am, I wasn't. Then when I saw his face in the moonlight, clear as day — I knew it was him. He's been all over the TV here, and the newspapers. I am sure it was him."

Nora took a moment to let that grab her viewers by the collective throat. "And how did he — this man you thought was Jason — look to you?" Nora said, leaning forward.

"Heartbroken. Pale, like he was ill. Lost, I thought. Strange that he seemed lost when a whole island is looking for him."

"Did you see anyone else with him?"

"No, ma'am, but it was very dark, cloudy; the moonlight kept coming and going."

Nora let the words sink in. "Annie" — and here she knew it was important at this single

229

moment to be kind and understanding — "are you sure about what you saw? Because you can understand" — dramatic pause, Nora gave her most sympathetic head tilt (patent pending) — "how very cruel it would be to give Jason's family false hope."

"Yes, ma'am, I do understand. It was him. I'm as sure of it as I can be."

"Have you talked to any tabloids or other papers about what you saw?"

"No. I wouldn't. I'm not selling a story, Ms. Dare. I only wanted to help . . ." Annie bit her lip. "I called the police, and I called your people, because you've been the one talking about him every night on the TV."

Nora allowed herself a satisfied smile. Her efforts, as always, were for the public good. "But you see how hard it is to believe that if Jason was in trouble, and you were willing to help, that he ran away simply because the neighbor's dog started barking."

"I can't explain it."

"And how did the Sint Pieter police respond?"

"They did come out to the house. But I don't think they believed me, at least not at first."

"Thank you, Annie." Nora switched to act two now: Inspector Abraham Peert. He was the third head of the Kirk investigation in three months; Nora's reports had made it clear that his predecessors either were incompetent or actively wished the Kirk family — and by implication all tourists — ill. Peert had a lean, angular face that looked like he was always biting hard into a lemon. This would be only his second appearance on the show. He'd been her guest right after his assignment to the case but had refused Nora's demands (*requests* was entirely too soft a word) for further interviews.

Nora gave Peert a quick introduction and said, "Is it possible that this young woman's story is true?"

"I suppose that it is, but we can find no supporting evidence." He kept his tone carefully neutral.

Oh, Nora thought, *I shall enjoy this. He's done nothing to follow this lead. Get me my cross and nails, boys, it's hammering time.*

"Is it possible that Jason Kirk is alive? Perhaps ill, perhaps wandering in the wilderness on the north side of Sint Pieter?" Nora said.

"Again, we can only postulate," Inspector Peert said. "Ill and wandering freely for three months seems most unlikely. Surely there would have been other reports of him; our search crews would have found him if he were rambling insensate. If he is alive and roaming the hills, then that suggests that he does not want to be found."

Nora had to decide whether to play that comment as a hurtful blow to the Kirk family or as an exciting, intriguing new twist in the story's worn fabric. She tilted her head again — she was *known* for the beauty and forcefulness of the head tilt — and decided the audience was hungry for a bit of the inspector's flesh. "Why would Jason Kirk be in hiding? Nothing in this boy's past suggests a desire to be away from his family. They are an absolutely wonderful, upstanding family, Inspector." She said this with a convincing thunder, as if Peert held the opposite view.

"No one knows what goes on in the human heart," Peert said quietly. "But I will say that I believe Annie Van Dorn believes she is telling the truth. We administered a lie detector test; she passed it."

That was a news bomb. Nora was speechless for a minute; Molly should have known that tidbit and warned her about it.

Peert pressed on: "If she saw him, then Jason Kirk is not in trouble; he is hiding from us."

It was not fair. It was not what Nora was expecting. It was not a dodge. And if Jason Kirk was simply hiding out on the island —

well, then, he was simply a spoiled brat who'd driven his parents nearly mad with grief. And made Nora look like a fool in front of millions.

This could not be. All of this emotional calculus played out in Nora's mind in less than five seconds. "If he is hiding, then why?"

"I do not know. We cannot know his reasons. If he has been kidnapped, there is no reason for his abductors to wait three months and not ask for a ransom."

Nora went back on the attack. "How soon will you expand the search in that area?"

Now she heard the steel in Peert's voice — even through the distance of the satellite hookup — and it infuriated her. "What choice do we have? You have turned American opinion against our entire nation. We have searched for this young man as if he were one of our own. We have followed every slim lead, and we have allowed your federal agents to comb our sovereign territory. We have endured your abuse and your innuendo as to our competence" — here Nora tightened her lips and straightened her papers, which was Nora's signal to Molly to cut to commercial now — "and in short, we have done everything possible. You cannot hurt us more, Ms. Dare, but if we do not pursue a lead, we will have to live with ourselves. So every lead will be pursued."

"I would hope so, and I think it's a shame that you have not already expanded the search."

Peert made his tone as sharp as hers. "We did search the area around Miss Van Dorn's house; there was no sign of an intruder. None. No footprints, no broken grass, nothing." Now his voice was rising. "So. She believes what she saw, but we can find no evidence."

Nora thought Peert didn't know his place; he was ruining the story's next phase of life. "Or you simply can't find what might be right in front of your eyes. What police academy did you attend again, sir?" One useful weapon in her arsenal was to make people justify themselves. It never failed.

"What journalism school did you attend, madame?"

Nora blinked, and for a moment the head tilt wavered. She'd never experienced anyone successfully biting back. Her lips narrowed into a slash. "I attended law school, which makes me uniquely qualified to report on cases regarding justice." The cameras were still live; that idiot Molly hadn't cut off Peert. "I will hold you to that promise to expand the search, Inspector. Let's go to Jason's parents . . ."

In her earpiece she heard Molly hiss: "They backed out. They're too upset. They want you to quit hammering Peert."

"I'm told we've got satellite difficulties in Los Angeles, where the Kirks live, so we'll wrap it up for this evening." And then she ended the Jason Kirk segments as she always did: "Jason, I will never stop searching for the truth, and I hope we can bring you home, safe and sound." And she held her noble, dignified stance — she was justice without the blindfold — letting the viewers drink her in as they cut to her theme song and logo.

The post-broadcast tantrum was a thing of beauty: Nora raged at the ingratitude of the Kirks, at the unwelcome (and unprofessional) steeliness of Peert, at the stupid hotel maid who probably hadn't seen anything at all and now had thrown Nora's show into a tailspin, at the fates. When she was done, Molly got her a glass of water and a sedative. Nora gulped both.

"Peert wasn't supposed to be all uppity," Nora said.

"He got tired of being your whipping boy," Molly crossed her arms. "Did you

235

think he'd dance to your tune forever? He's fighting back. He's tired of the abuse."

"Abuse? I think you meant to say *my investigation.*"

"Nora, maybe it's time to find a new case for you to . . . investigate. Maybe Jason didn't vanish on vacation." That phrase had been Nora's lead for the first two months of Jason's disappearance. "He could be in hiding. He could be shacked up with a woman. He could have been smoking weed in the mountains of Sint Pieter for the past three months, watching his face on the news. This one is getting ugly."

"No. This one is getting good. Maybe this is all, like, you know, *The Bourne Identity,*" Nora said.

"What?" Molly said.

"Maybe he got hurt and he doesn't know who he is," Nora said. She sounded like a woman awakening from a dream. "Oh, yes. Wouldn't that be great? That would be a story. Then I could bring him home. Get me a doctor who knows a lot about amnesia."

"Amnesia. Please be kidding."

"I don't kid. Humor and justice are not friends, Molly." She crossed her arms. She was going to get control of this story back; November sweeps were imminent. "We're going to Sint Pieter. Make the arrangements."

"Sint Pieter?" Molly stared at her.

Honestly, Nora thought, she did see two ears on the sides of Molly's head. If only a brain nestled between them. "Yes, hon. Peert's dragging his feet; we have a legitimate witness, it seems. And the day after tomorrow is the three-month anniversary of the night Jason vanished. I feel the story demands my presence. Go get the travel booked. Me, the film crew, makeup, and" — feeling magnanimous, and realizing someone would have to deal with the front desk and the security escorts and the autograph seekers — "you for director."

"Should we let Jason's family know you're doing this broadcast?"

Nora's eyes glittered. "I want them there. Get them in the same room they stayed in when Jason vanished. And me the penthouse."

"Um, I know the Kirks are having money problems. They've been away from work, you know, spending so much time in Sint Pieter looking for their son . . . I don't know if they can afford another trip back."

"They told you this?" It had not occurred to Nora that anyone on her staff might have developed a friendship with the Kirks. Nora thought Molly simply told them when and where to be for their satellite interviews with Nora.

"Yes."

"Hmmm. All right. Given that it's the anniversary, we can pay for them to go. Book coach for all but you and me. We'll have work to do on the way down. I want every bit of dirt we can find on the good Inspector Peert and on this Annie Van Dorn."

"All right, Nora. But if you can spare me during the flight, I think I'll sit in coach with the Kirks."

"No. It's not appropriate for you to get too close, too emotionally involved with the story."

Molly stared at her. "I just feel so sorry for them."

"And I don't?"

Molly's face paled. "Of course not. I never meant to suggest . . ."

Nora's voice was a drip of acid. "On second thought, put the Kirks in first class with me. We can talk. You can ride in coach with the film crew." Nora waved fingers at Molly. "Go. Book tickets; find an amnesia expert who wants a little attention. Maybe one with a book to promote?"

Sint Pieter was, to Nora's mind, a strip of

lousy dirt that South America had hawked up from its throat and spat out its mouth. A hundred miles off the continent's northeast coast, Sint Pieter was narrow and twenty miles long. It had achieved independence from the Netherlands in 1970 and, in Nora's view, had done little since then except misplace Jason Kirk. It was warm and wooded with stubby trees and studded with stunted little towns. The main town, called Willemstadt, boasted a half dozen luxury hotels, sparkling beaches, and fine restaurants. Tourism had made Sint Pieter rich until it lost Jason Kirk. Now that the island had been branded by Nora as dangerous, business was down fifty percent.

They were staying at the same Willemstadt hotel that Jason and his parents had been staying in when he vanished. Molly had pulled strings to get the Kirks the same room they'd had before, and they'd reluctantly agreed.

"Welcome, Ms. Dare," the Hotel Sint Pieter's manager said through a tight smile.

"Thank you. I sincerely hope you have beefed up your security since Jason Kirk vanished," she said. The first two weeks of the disappearance she'd regularly suggested the hotel had inadequate security, before it became a boring drumbeat and she could blame the Sint Pieter police.

"We have," the manager said. "We certainly want to keep you safe."

"Naturally," Nora said. She grew conscious of the simmering stares from the staff. The nerve of these people, she thought. She begrudgingly waited for Molly to finish the check-in and then bolted halfway across the lobby, heading for the elevators. Molly followed, rushing, tossing multicolored Sint Pieter currency at the bellhop.

"I have a real vision for tonight's show, Molly," Nora said. "We start with the family in the suite where they stayed . . . Are they here yet?" The Kirks had decided not to fly with Nora and the news crew, much to Nora's annoyance.

"Yes. They arrived yesterday. They went and scoured the countryside near Annie Van Dorn's house," Molly said quietly.

"Hmmmm," Nora said. "Without me? How odd. Did they find anything?"

"No."

"I wish you'd sent a local camera crew with them."

"Nora, they want their privacy sometimes."

"Privacy doesn't find the missing." Honestly, she thought, she was doing everything to find Jason; couldn't his parents just cooperate? "Okay, for tonight's show, we retrace the steps Jason made on that fateful night."

"I would suggest you not call it by that term in front of his parents."

"Someone went shopping at the unsolicited opinion store."

"I've expressed only one opinion," Molly said mildly. "I guess my second one is that you seem on edge."

"Do I? What an odd thing to say. I'm not nervous. I'm motivated."

"Nora," Molly said. "It will be fine. Do the story, remember this boy. But I think it would be best if we moved on to a new case for you to focus on. I think you've done all the good you can do for Jason Kirk."

"If I'd found him, I would have done all the good. I need to find him, Molly." Nora's voice went low, and Molly looked surprised at the grit in her boss's voice. "That girl who vanished hiking in Vancouver, well, we never found her. That couple from Illinois who went missing in Hungary. Never found them. This is a small island; I should be able to find out what happened to Jason Kirk."

Molly opened her mouth to point out that the small island was surrounded by a vast ocean, and that the police were actually in charge of searches, not Nora Dare, but instead she simply closed her mouth and nodded.

The suite. Then the nightclub where the mysterious and beautiful woman no one on Sint Pieter seemed to know had spirited Jason away, and then the beach where his torn shirt, the buttons ripped free as though in a fit of passion, had been found in the sand. The shirt was the only physical evidence of his disappearance.

Gary and Hope Kirk — Nora loved the appropriateness of the mother's name — sat in the suite where they had been staying when their only child vanished. Nora's eyebrow arched when the Kirks gave Molly a hug. She didn't believe in getting close to the subjects. Both were pale and wan, as though grief were a disease slowly claiming them. They did not spend much time looking at each other.

But when the cameras started, Mr. and Mrs. Kirk joined hands, presenting their united face to the world.

"So let's recall the night that Jason vanished. You'd spent a wonderful family day on the beach, yes?" Nora said.

It was the prologue to tragedy, and the Kirks did not disappoint. "Yes," Hope Kirk said. "I didn't feel well — I'd gotten sunburned and we decided to take it easy. We ate here at the hotel and then came back up to the room."

"But Jason got restless, as young men will," Nora prodded.

"Yes," Hope said. "He wanted to go out to a bar and have a beer. I mean, you understand, he was on vacation with his parents. How rare is that? A college kid, and he was happy to be with us. We'd had a great time. We enjoyed each other's company. He invited my husband to go with him . . . but Gary said no."

Four little words, each an explosion of accusation. Gary glanced at his wife, and even though they were holding hands, Nora sensed a foggy coldness rising between them. *An unmet blame,* Nora thought, liking the phrase, wondering how she could work it into a question or her summary at the end of the show. "I wanted to stay here and take care of you," Gary said.

"A sunburn's not fatal," Hope said. "I would have been fine."

Gary stopped looking at Hope. "So. I didn't want to cramp Jason's style. Maybe he wanted to meet a girl. He can't do that with his old man in tow."

And Hope opened her mouth, as if to say, *And he can't vanish with his old man in tow.*

243

Instead she just said: "So Jason kissed me on the forehead and told me to feel better, and he left. Gary and I stayed in and watched movies."

"And . . ." Nora began, but Hope wasn't done.

"So, while our son vanished off the face of the earth, Nora, we watched movies. A movie we'd seen in the theater and parts of on cable. I mean, when he needed us, we were watching this stupid, stupid movie." Her voice cracked like glass. "He was being kidnapped, or killed, or drugged, and we were sitting in this room, watching a movie." Her voice, usually calm, rose toward a scream.

"I think . . . I think being back in the suite is a bad idea, Nora," Gary said. "This isn't helping anyone . . ."

Hope pulled her hand free of his and pounded her chest with the flat of her hand. "He comes to me in my dreams. He says, 'Mom, I'm trapped. I can't get where I'm supposed to be. I'm trapped here and no one can help me.' He begs me to help him escape."

This was new, Nora thought. Interesting. Because if Hope was cracking up, it was a whole new twist and angle to the story.

"Cut," Molly said to the cameraman.

"Don't you dare," Nora hissed.

"I can't help him, I don't know how." Hope Kirk's words broke into a howl, face in hands, ruined in grief.

Three bars stood down the street from the Hotel Sint Pieter, and Jason Kirk had visited them all. Nora and a quiet Molly and an utterly silent cameraman had followed his tracks.

The bartender at the Beer Pig crossed his thick arms. "Well, I only remember him because of the woman. Gorgeous she was, like a Halle Berry type. Very elegant, well dressed, sexy. I was surprised she was talking to an American college boy."

"Did you see them meet?" Nora asked.

The bartender squirmed slightly under the hard, bright lights set up by the crew. "Well, yes. I saw her come in. She came to the bar, ordered a glass of pinot noir. Every guy in the room noticed her. Two other guys tried to buy her a drink. She said no, she was waiting for someone."

"Waiting for someone," Nora said, with portent.

"Yes, ma'am, waiting for someone. I heard her clearly, and I thought, well, who's the lucky guy. But so this blond American kid comes in, and he comes to the bar, and the hottie, she locks her gaze on him. She wasn't much older than he was, but she had a maturity. A woman of the world, but I mean in a classy way. But . . . he came over to her. He bought her another glass of wine. He must have felt confident in himself."

Nora tilted her head. "And they talked."

The bartender nodded. "Yes . . . but for her to have said she was waiting on someone, it implies she knew him. I don't think she knew that boy before he arrived."

Nora said, "So maybe she was waiting on a *type* of someone."

The bartender shrugged. "I guess. She was ravishing. You couldn't take your eyes off her."

"You never heard him call her by her name?"

"No, ma'am."

They moved on to the Glass House Pub. The waitress said, "Jason Kirk and this very pretty woman shared a bottle of pinot noir. She paid with cash and she tipped very well. I thought they were on a date. I'd never seen her in here before, and I would have remembered her, I think. He was drunk. Not obnoxious, but not in full control of himself."

"Maybe she drugged him?"

"I think the bottle of wine drugged him. I

mean, I never saw her slip anything into his wine." The waitress shrugged at Nora. "She steadied him as they walked out, her hand on his back as they walked out. I see it all the time. He looked besotted by her. Any man would have been."

"Have you seen this woman before or since?"

"No." And that had been the answer of all Sint Pieter: No one knew this remarkably lovely woman.

The bouncer at Jake's Tallboy, who wore a suit for the occasion of his interview, said, "I might not have let the kid in; he'd been drinking a bit too much, not loud but walking unsteadily. But no way I could keep her out. The boss would kill me. It's a bar for people on vacation; we're supposed to accommodate beautiful women. She thanked me for letting him in."

"You heard her speak?"

"Yes. Slight accent, a Caribbean/British mix. Elegant. But . . ."

The pause was an opening. "Yes."

"She gave me a cold chill. Listen, I could see she was a stunning beauty, but I'm gay. I wasn't seduced by her charms, you understand? I looked in her eyes and there was no *there* there, if you know what I mean."

"No," Nora said, "tell us."

"The old saying is the eyes are windows to the soul. That soul was blank. I don't know how to say it. Blank. But not like drunk blank. Just unsettling. Empty wrapped up in pretty, you see?" The bouncer cleared his throat.

"Fascinating," Nora said.

"I would say she gave me a chill, the kind you get from having to deal with an extremely unkind person. I remembered her immediately after the story about this boy broke. She gave me the creeps, and I'm sticking by my story."

"You saw them leave."

"Yes. He staggered a bit; she held him. I asked if they needed a cab, and she shot me a rather nasty glare. She said she was fine. She. Not they. A bit cold toward the boy, I thought."

While the bouncer spoke, the police sketch of the mysterious woman came up, with the caption *Last seen with Jason Kirk*.

"And the security tape, did it show her?" Nora asked. She already knew the answer.

"Um, we didn't put cameras in until after all the attention you gave us from Mr. Kirk disappearing." A bit of anger colored the bouncer's tone. "There was no tape. But when they were leaving, I heard him say he was at the Hotel Sint Pieter but in a room adjoining his folks', and I laughed a bit, because I thought, *Dude, you will have to find another bed for you and that lady.*"

Nora thanked him, turned back to the camera, and said, "Next, the final stop on Jason Kirk's tragic night."

The bar at the hotel where Jason Kirk stayed was called the Eclipse, for no good reason. But Nora, touring it with the camera following, pointed out that eclipses had once been seen as portents of doom and approaching evil. The bar was not busy, and people cleared out when the cameras started rolling. As if the tragedy might be contagious.

The hotel manager stiffly told Nora that several people saw the couple having a quiet drink in the corner, locked in conversation, heads close together. Jason charged a bottle of pinot noir to his parents' room account. They drank half the bottle, then headed out the rear of the hotel toward the private beach.

"And no one has seen him since?"

"No, ma'am."

"And the hotel security cameras at the entrance and exits?" Again she knew the answer, but the facts bore repeating.

"The tape malfunctioned . . . It showed

mostly white static."

"Bizarre timing," Nora said, and while they spoke, the hotel's mangled footage of Jason Kirk and the woman, flooded with digital snow, played on the screen. "You can make out Jason, and the outline of the tall woman, Jason leaning close to her as they stumbled out the back door."

"Yes. Then the static clears up a few minutes later. We can't explain it."

Nora thanked him and turned to her final guest, who had joined them at the last stop. "The recent alleged sighting of Jason Kirk near Marysville, on the northern tip of the island, has suggested one theory: that Jason is hurt, suffering from amnesia. I'm here with Dr. Kevin Bayless, an expert on amnesia and author of *Still Here But Not Sure,* an exposé on amnesia that argues memory loss is actually quite common." The camera panned to a tall, thin man in a suit with a blood-red tie. "Doctor, from what you've heard, is it possible that Jason Kirk could have suffered an injury that blocked his memory?"

"It certainly can't be discounted as a possibility. If he was intoxicated and suffered a blow to the head, he might not know at all where he was, who he was." Bayless had a breathy voice that reminded Nora of the soft hiss a radio made, not quite tuned to a station.

"How long could the amnesia last?"

"Anywhere from minutes to hours to weeks," Dr. Bayless said, as though giving Nora a gift.

"We know his torn shirt was found on the beach. He might have been attacked. Describe to me and our viewers what kind of injury could induce amnesia."

"Well, there are several, and as I point out in my book, just out last week, amnesia is far more common or likely than we know . . ."

Nora saw Molly waving frantically at her, the cut sign. Molly had never gestured so wildly during a broadcast.

"We have a breaking situation, ladies and gentlemen, we'll be right back."

"Um, will I get to mention my book again?" Dr. Bayless asked.

Molly ignored him and looked stricken. "Annie Van Dorn is on the line. She said Jason Kirk is standing in her backyard again."

They rushed to the cars, drove the fifteen minutes to Annie's side of the island, Nora swearing at Molly: "Don't call the police, let us handle this, don't call. No one gets there before we do. If it's him, we have to get him on tape."

"I'm not calling, I'm staying on the line with Annie, but the Kirks will call Peert . . ."

Nora cursed. She'd forgotten about the Kirks. Oh well, but the police might well bundle up Jason and haul him off to the hospital. Surely not before the happy re-union. A strange flood of emotion coursed through Nora: anticipation of the greatest story in her career, and a sincere relief that he was okay. That a story of hers could have a happy ending. It was so rare.

"Uh-huh, Annie, yes, I'm here," Molly said. The cameraman drove like a maniac, blasting through a red light at the edge of town, barreling the car into the blackness. No streetlights out beyond the tourist zones; Sint Pieter suddenly felt to Nora like a much more ancient, lost world, a back corner of reality. The only light was the wash of the headlights of the Kirks' car behind them.

"Is he still there?" Nora screeched.

"Yes, well . . ." Molly started, and Nora seized the phone.

"Annie? This is Nora Dare."

"Yes." Annie sounded frightened. Eight minutes had passed since her phone call.

"Is Jason still in your yard?"

"Yes. Standing by the trees. I'm not sure

he knows I saw him. My outside light's off. But I saw him, in the moonlight, I can tell it's him again. What should I do?"

"Leave the lights off; I don't want the neighbor's dog to frighten him off again. He may not be well. He might be confused. Don't approach him."

"I'm afraid," Annie said. Her voice — calm and sturdy in the first interview — seemed to fold and crumple. "My sister's not here. I'm alone."

"We'll be there in just a few minutes."

"I'm going to hang up and call the police," Annie said.

"No, sweetheart, stay on the phone with me," Nora said. A dread touched her heart. "We're handling calling the police, okay? We'll be there in just a few minutes." Then she added: "You don't happen to have a camera, do you? I suppose the flash might send him running if he's panicked . . ."

Annie gave off a choked sob. "I'm afraid of him."

"We'll cut off our lights before we get there so he doesn't run," Nora said.

Annie made a soft little whispery mewl. "He is walking toward the house. Slowly." Annie's voice cracked with anxiety. "Oh my God, he's coming here."

"Annie. Don't scare him."

253

"Don't scare *him?*" Annie said. "Why is he here?"

"Annie," Nora said, and she said this with the firmness of tone that made her a star, "Don't let him see you're frightened. He has to be reassured so he doesn't run again. You're going to be a hero, Annie, to his family, to Sint Pieter."

"He's at the door," Annie said, and she didn't sound afraid anymore. More just surprised. "He's just standing at the door."

"Annie, you have to help that boy. You have to help him as much as I have," Nora said. "He must need help."

"Help him," Annie said. Sounding a little sleepy. "He's . . . he's better looking than his picture." Nora could hear the door swinging open. And Annie saying, "Hello."

The phone clicked off.

Three minutes later, they were at the small bungalow. The clouds had scudded to the south. Bright moonlight spilled across the eaves, the flat glass of the windows, the bent shadows made by the divi-divi trees. Nora was out of the car before it stopped, heading around to the backyard.

The car with the Kirks screeched to a stop, and she heard Hope screaming, "Jason! Jason!"

Nora ignored her and ran into the scrubby backyard. No lights on in the yard. A dim light burned in the kitchen. The back door — where Jason had come to — stood open.

"Annie?" Nora called. "Jason? Jason, it's all right. I've brought you your parents, sweetheart. Just come on out." She glanced behind her; the cameraman was struggling to get his gear squared on his shoulder.

She stepped inside. A small, modest back entry, then a kitchen. The tile was worn and peeling but the room was spotless. A dinner on the plate — noodles and salad and sliced tomato, a glass of soda next to it — lay half eaten. The window by the table fronted the backyard. She must have been eating a late meal, feet tired from cleaning hotel rooms all day, when she saw him.

Nora walked quickly through the house. No sign of Annie. No sign of anyone else. No sign of a struggle.

No Jason.

Gary and Hope Kirk tore through the house, and in the still distance Nora heard the rising cry of police sirens.

"He's not here."

"Was he ever?" Hope Kirk screamed at her. "My God. Is this a trick?"

"She said he was here."

"Well, she's not and he's not. This is just

a sick prank. I can't — I cannot keep doing this, Gary. I can't. I can't. I can't." Hope fell to her knees on the wooden floor. Gary Kirk knelt by his wife, put his arm over her shaking shoulders.

"We are done with you," he said to Nora. "I mean, what was this stunt? Invented drama for the ratings? An exclamation point on the whole awful evening of revisiting our loss? Did you put this young woman up to this? Did you just need some damn footage, Nora?" His voice rose into a roar.

"No, of course not . . ." Nora's voice trailed off. "She said he was here. She said he was." And now she saw in the doorway Inspector Peert, with his lemon-sucking scowl. She turned back to Gary Kirk.

"We counted on you. You wouldn't let go. You said you wouldn't forget him. But this . . . tricking us, this is too much," Gary hissed.

"I had nothing to do with this," Nora said.

"Yeah, this drama just happens the night you're filming."

"Blame Annie Van Dorn, not me." Nora's voice shook, and she glanced; the cameras were rolling. *Oh, Molly, damn you,* she thought. Molly stared at her. "Ask Molly, she took the call."

Peert folded his arms. "Did you hear this

woman say she saw Jason?"

"I heard her say she *thought* it was Jason. But then Nora took the phone . . ."

"Oh, this is too much. Too much!" Nora whirled on Gary Kirk. "You listen to me. I could have helped any missing person anywhere in the world, and I helped your son. I kept this entire island looking for him, and I kept the whole U.S. of A. thinking about him and praying for him to come home safe and sound. Without me, everyone would have forgotten him, just a kid who got drunk and probably drowned in the ocean." She stopped, slammed a hand over her mouth.

"It was never about him, was it?" Hope Kirk said in a small voice. "It was about you. Always you."

"Molly, tell them. Tell them what Annie said!"

"I didn't hear, Nora, you did." Molly turned to Peert. "Annie Van Dorn did call, did say that she thought Jason was standing in her backyard. We rushed over. I heard nothing else."

"You're fired, you backstabbing bitch," Nora said.

"I work for the network, not you," Molly said in her usual calm voice.

"Find Annie Van Dorn," Nora said to

Peert. "She saw Jason, identified him at her back door. I heard her say hello to him."

"Then what?"

"Nothing. She hung up. But find her, she'll confirm what I said."

"I'll confirm what?" Annie said. She stood in the open back door, a bit breathless. She blinked at the crowd.

Nora lurched toward her, clutched her arm. "You said . . . you said Jason was here."

Annie blinked again. "Oh. Yes. I did. I went outside to see after I called you, but there was no one there. Someone was playing a trick on me."

A long, low moan from Hope Kirk.

"You didn't speak with Ms. Dare?" Peert said.

"Well, she kept insisting the man must be Jason Kirk, and I got tired of hearing her say that and I hung up." Annie's voice was dreamy-raw, as though she'd just woken from sleep.

"Oh my God, this is insane!" Nora said. "In-freaking-sane. I had an entire conversation with her. She said he came to the door, she was afraid of him, she could see him at the door, she said hello to him . . ."

Annie shook her head.

Nora grabbed her, shook her. Annie seemed limp, like a cast-aside rag doll. Peert pulled Nora's hands from Annie's throat.

Four in the morning. Nora lay dozing. The echoes of the past hours: the real fear in Annie's voice, the blame in the Kirks' accusations, the staring disbelief of that traitor Molly, the dazed surprise of Annie in real life. There were talks of charges to be brought, of a lawsuit by the Kirks. The network brass fumed; Nora knew, in her lawyer's readiness, that she was going to be burned by this, very badly.

And all she'd tried to do was to bring a boy home, safe and sound.

A breeze poured in from the open balcony window. She was on the top floor of the Hotel Sint Pieter, where she belonged, and having drunk half the minibar when she got back to her room, her body felt feverish from the alcohol. She got up; the cooling ocean breeze was a relief. She was groping toward the bathroom when Jason Kirk said, behind her, "You made it very hard for me."

She froze. She shook her head, as if to settle her imagination back into its distant corner of her brain. Then he said the words again, and she spun in stark terror.

Jason Kirk stood on the balcony, kissed by moonlight. The wind ruffled his light hair slightly.

She tried to scream and she couldn't. Oddest thing. She sank to her knees.

He said, in a voice barely louder than the ocean wind, "You keep telling people you will never forget, you will never stop looking. Safe and sound, right?" He shook his head. "I needed you to stop looking. Do you know how hard it's been?"

Nora's mouth worked. How had he gotten here? It wasn't possible. Not possible.

He looked better than his photos and his videos. Handsome face, high cheekbones. Even in the broken moonlight he had dark eyes, pools of black that could let you fall into their depths.

"May we talk?"

Nora nodded, and he stepped into the room.

"You're alive," she said. "Oh my God. Jason, the *story* this will be."

"There is no story. You would let it go on forever, or as long as you could use me. There is no story. I need for there to be no story."

She hardly heard him, her mind spinning with possibilities and ramifications. "Listen, you have to come with me. Now. Let your parents see you . . ."

"You don't see how cruel that would be? I have to be . . . dead to my mom and dad. I

260

have to stay that way."

"I don't understand." She groped for the lamp, clicked it on. "Were you at Annie's house tonight?"

"The tasty little maid? Yes. She only remembers what I want her to. I won't bother her again." He took a step toward her. He wore old jeans, a worn soccer jersey, and a long low cap favored by Sint Pieter toughs. Like clothes she'd seen on the neighbor's clothesline at Annie's house. "She played her part."

"I don't understand . . ."

"I wanted to draw you here, bait you with what you couldn't resist. Me, on the verge of safe and sound. To bring you to me. Because you put my face everywhere, I couldn't come to you to stop you. I couldn't get near a boat or a plane or anything else. I needed you to come to me so we could have our chat." He crossed his arms. "I need you to shut up about me, Nora."

"I can . . . now that you're found." She nearly felt giddy. That little bitch Molly would be gone. The Kirks would see that she'd only meant the best. And having broken this case open, having *personally* brought their son home, she would be the undisputed queen of cable news.

"I'm not found. It's time for the world to

261

forget about me. Move on to the next tragedy."

"But I don't understand."

Jason smiled; there was something wrong with two of his teeth. Small, pointed, in the lush curve of his mouth.

Nora said, "Oh."

"The woman who made me — she left me. She didn't like the sudden attention. She came to Sint Pieter to feed. She liked me so she left me . . . like she is. Not just dead. But you put my picture everywhere, you talked about me nonstop, I had to hide in the hills, far away. Live on rats, stray cats, rabbits. It doesn't quite do, Nora. I've nearly starved to death because of you. I want to go where there are beautiful young things pulsing with life. Las Vegas. London. New York. Which means you have to let me go."

Nora's mouth worked. This was an even better story. This would change human history. Agree to whatever he wanted but get a photo, get his voice on tape. Her own camera was on the desk. Her gaze flicked to it. "Sure. Okay. Whatever you want. I'll stop. I'll never talk about you again."

Jason said, "Let's have everyone talk about you for a change."

"Tonight, on *The Molly Belisle Show* — the

262

one-month anniversary of the death of Nora Dare." Molly gave her best steely-gazed look to the camera. "Nora Dare plunged to her death from her hotel suite in Sint Pieter while pursuing answers in a missing-person case. Now she is the story. Was it suicide, driven by an insane need to keep covering a story? Was she murdered by an islander who blamed her for the drop in tourism? Where are the police in their investigation — and are they dragging their feet to find the killer of a brave journalist? Stay tuned!" The music boomed; the opening credits showed Molly standing before her logo with a confident head tilt.

In Las Vegas, the hunter that was once Jason Kirk clicked off the television with a smile and headed down to the casino. He'd managed to stow onto a boat from Willemstadt to Panama, drink a bit from the crew without drawing attention, and hunt his way quietly up to America. His picture wasn't on the news anymore, and now he had dark hair. Life — or afterlife, to be exact — was good. People never looked at him too closely, unless he was looking hard at them, and then they forgot. Or they died.

In Marysville, Sint Pieter, Annie Van Dorn watched her television and fought a little shudder. That Dare woman had been crazy.

She rubbed at the little raw patch on her throat that had taken forever to heal. She was tired but not as exhausted as she used to be, and she no longer saw beckoning backyard shadows that both frightened and thrilled her.

In Los Angeles, Hope Kirk got up from the couch and thumbed off the television. She opened a beer — Jason's favorite brand — and went to his room, sat on his bed, drank half her beer. She stared at the frat party photos and the track awards and the science fair ribbons, the remnants of her lost boy's life. She felt drained of tears. She finished the beer and went to her own bed. Gary was already asleep. She curled close to her husband and wondered if she would dream of Jason tonight. Her nightmares, where he pleaded for her help to escape a trap, had vanished the night Nora Dare died. Hope didn't dream of Jason anymore, and she could not decide if that was comfort or curse.

SEEING IS BELIEVING

L. A. BANKS

L. A. Banks, recipient of the 2008 Essence Storyteller of the Year Award, has written more than thirty-five novels and twelve novellas in multiple genres under various pseudonyms. She mysteriously shape-shifts between the genres of romance, women's fiction, crime/suspense thrillers, and of course, paranormal lore. She is a graduate of the University of Pennsylvania Wharton undergraduate program with a master's in fine arts from Temple University, and she is a full-time writer living and working in Philadelphia. Visit her website at www.vampirehuntress.com.

ONE

Port Arthur, TX . . . Current Day

"I think you all need a break . . . maybe a vacation?" Sheriff Moore said, nervously fingering the brim of his hat. He dangled it between his legs as he sat forward on the small sofa, suffering the unbearable summer heat in the tiny trailer. "That's what your momma woulda wanted, sugah. I knew her that well as her friend."

The pretty young woman before him didn't answer, just sat Indian style on the floral-patterned armchair wearing flip-flops, a tank top, and shorts, with her head in her hands, massaging her temples with her eyes tightly shut. The sight of her distress wore on him. Emma Atwater's child shouldn't have to be living like this. Her long braids created a curtain over her lovely face, but he didn't have to actually see her expression to know that she'd probably taken offense. It was in the way she'd become eerily still for a few seconds, her shoulders tightening, before she'd blown out a long sigh.

A large fan in the window provided the only sound for a few awkward moments and seemed to invite in mosquitoes through the torn screen as it circulated humid, thick air in the cramped space. Ice cubes melted in his exhausted glass of lemonade and then chimed as they slid against one another. Texas heat was a bitch in August, and it was painfully obvious that if she couldn't afford the electric bill going up from running the air conditioner, then a vacation was out of the question.

Sheriff Moore glanced around and then bit his bottom lip with an apology in his eyes. He was getting too old for all of this; his nerves couldn't take it. But things being what they were, retiring at age seventy wasn't an option. Everybody had bills to pay . . . Still, this girl didn't even seem to have a chance. Other young girls would be on summer break from college, going to the beaches. Emma's baby girl hadn't ever done anything like that, not that he could remember.

Exasperated, he dragged his fingers through his gray hair, hating how what was left of it felt like it was plastered to his head with sweat. "I know times are rough for everybody," he added, self-correcting his previous suggestion. "I just was thinking that if you and your brother got away for a little while, maybe changed your environment, you'd . . . uh . . . feel better, *then* we could talk."

"Ralph is working, can't take off, even if I could afford to go away."

"But maybe your brother, he could help you . . . Even though he moved away from here, I know he loves you . . . and could be there to make sure you were all right, wherever you decide to go."

Jessica looked up and just stared at the

man for a moment, too weary to be pissed off. Constant patrolling had clearly been the culprit that weathered his skin to a ruddy light brown hue. His elderly blue eyes were clouded with worry and heat. The poor man looked like he was about to keel over. Sweat stained his uniform, especially under his arms and where his beer belly pressed against the tight buttons of his shirt.

He was right, everybody had bills to pay — so he didn't need to feel sorry for her. Shame was, he was just as trapped in his life as she was in hers. Besides, not that it was any of the sheriff's business, Ralph had changed his name to Raphael when their mother died and had moved to Houston — albeit, why her brother thought the woman hadn't known things was beyond Jessica. It didn't matter anyway. Although the sheriff was right, her brother loved her and she loved him dearly . . . Raph just found it hard to live his life around somebody that could see so much. Ordinary people wouldn't understand.

"I really don't think you should go away all by yourself, if you do get even a day away," Sheriff Moore said in a tender voice.

"So, now I'm crazy?" Jessica lifted her chin and adjusted her yellow tank top that was sticking to her torso. "Okay." She hadn't meant to sound annoyed, but she was. The man wasn't listening to a word she'd said.

"Aw, now, darlin' . . . crazy is *not* the word I was using. I said *tired.* That's *all.*"

Sheriff Moore leaned in closer, imploring Jessica in a conciliatory tone of voice when she simply sucked her teeth and looked out the screen door. "You know I respect what your mother used to do, and you seem to have picked right up on her gift, too. She could see things. The whole department relied on her to help solve murders, since as long as I can remember . . . Why you know, the boys in Beaumont, Galveston, even as far as Houston would come see her when they couldn't crack a case — and you've got her vision. That's why I came to you for this one, especially after you helped us find that little girl before something even worse happened to her. You've got the gift, no arguing that. So, I wasn't casting aspersions . . . but you've also been through a lot. Losing your job at the store in town, losing your momma . . . brother moving away just a year ago . . . I just thought —"

"That I was also losing my mind?"

"No, I didn't say all that. You keep putting words in my mouth."

"It was *werewolves,* Sheriff Moore. Plural," Jessica said as calmly as possible. She stared at him and held him with her gaze. Thoughts of the way her father had been found years ago danced at the edges of her mind and caught fire, but she pushed the old haunting memory aside. "Those bodies you keep finding in West Port Arthur right off Sabine Lake are not all chewed up because of Mexican drug wars and gators feeding off of what's left. Mark my words," she added, standing and stretching, "if you comb down the Sabine Pass and the Sabine River, you'll find more."

The sheriff's shoulders slumped for a moment, and then he finally pushed himself to stand. "Jess, honey, what am I gonna tell them federal agents, huh? They've been finding bodies up and down the Gulf of Mexico — that's why they have FBI all over it with them boys from Homeland Security. They said drug warlords did it; I said fine by me, let's bring 'em in. This is the U.S. of A."

"It's not that simple, Sheriff," Jessica said quietly, hating to ruin the elderly man's sanity with the truth.

He let out a hard breath and then carefully placed his hat back on his head, his eyes never leaving hers. "I was frankly trying to lay low and stay out of all this drug business, but when folks from the area started showing up missing, I had no choice but to report what we found. But facts being what they are, I can't go telling them boys from up north about werewolves eating good townsfolk in the bayou and then dragging them across state lines to dump them in West Port Arthur, Jess! They'd have me committed."

They stared at each other for a moment, both seeming to know that he hadn't meant to raise his voice. He was in a ridiculous dilemma where the plain truth was totally unacceptable.

Still, Emma Atwater was many things, a whole mess of contradictions, but she didn't lie to her children. Jessica remembered clearly that her mother had told her that Jessica's gift was pressed down and overflowing compared to her momma's own — no doubt an expression Momma had gotten from scripture readings on the rare occasion that she went to church. The one thing her momma couldn't countenance was hypocrites, and since her momma could sense feelings and thoughts, church gave her the hives. Jess sent her gaze out the window, remembering how her mother would get so mad at the whisperers that said nasty things about her and her children behind their backs.

"I do miss her," Jessica finally said in a quiet voice, trying to shift the subject to let the troubled officer off the hook. "Maybe that's part of it?"

"I didn't mean to holler at you, sugah . . . I'm just in a delicate position. I think you should maybe take a drive to get away for a few days. When you come back, then, we'll talk . . . all right?"

Jessica nodded but placed her hand on Sheriff Moore's forearm to stay his leave. "I want you to look at the pattern of the killings . . . the phase of the moon when they happened. Get a farmer's almanac and just do that for me. You don't have to tell anybody. Then, I want you to go to the Navajo reservation and ask the shaman there for two things . . . See if they can make some silver bullets for you and your men, and a potion bag filled with silver shavings, wolfsbane —"

"Jess, honey, please . . ." He closed his eyes and let out a weary exhale.

"Just do that for me in secret, okay? Wear the bag the shaman gives you. You were one of my mother's oldest friends. She really liked you, and you all trusted each other. So trust me and her now."

He opened his eyes and nodded, becoming misty at the memory. "She was good to me and my wife when we lost our boy . . . That's how I came to know her. She helped me find his body and who killed him. So I feel like I should be looking out for her baby girl, too . . . and this just hurts my soul to hear you talking out of your head like this, honey."

"Well, my momma is standing right beside you," Jessica said quietly, briefly nodding toward his left.

He glanced around quickly and spoke in a nervous voice. "She used to do that . . . would go see the other side and ask questions."

"Yeah, I know. It was really a trip growing up with her." Jessica let go of his arm. "Then again, I used to freak her out, too." Inclining her head to Sheriff Moore's left, Jessica spoke to what appeared to be thin air. "So he'll believe me, Momma, tell me what he had for dinner last night?" After a few moments passed, Jessica shook her head. "Bourbon ain't no dinner. At your age you need to be taking better care of yourself."

"You think I should really get the silver bullets?"

Jessica nodded. "*And* the bag . . . And don't go hunting for these suckers without those bullets when it's a full moon."

TWO

It was clear that Sheriff Moore wasn't going to listen to her, clear as a bell rung in church at high noon. The old man was gonna get himself killed for sure. Better stated, he was gonna get eaten. Her conscience wouldn't allow for that; her mother had brought her up right, after all. Plus, these beasts were encroaching on her hometown. Had taken a couple of young kids in high school that were making out after dark by the lake. Wrong place, wrong time, and tore 'em up so badly, according to the sheriff, that their families didn't have much left to put in a casket. Now that was just *wrong.*

Jessica walked to the refrigerator and opened it, looking for more lemonade. Her cell phone was pressed to her ear, and she glanced up at the clock. At two in the afternoon, Raph wouldn't be up yet. When it rolled over to voice mail, she muttered a curse under her breath and hit redial. "Answer the danged phone!"

"What?" Raphael said in a sleepy, irritated tone. "I was working till four."

"I'm sorry," Jessica said, squeezing her eyes shut. True, her brother had been working at the strip club until four, but he hadn't gotten to sleep until eight and still had company in his bed. "I . . . I . . . just need to ask you a favor."

She heard Raphael get up and start moving.

"Stay out of my business, boo. You might see what you ain't ready to deal with, calling me all early . . . You supposed to be psychic, so you just oughta check if —"

"My bad, but I need to ask you for —"

"Some money."

Quiet settled on the line between them.

"Never mind," she said, hurt, about to hang up.

"Now there you go, all proud. I have been waiting for the last two years for you to just call me up and let me help you, boo. What's the matter with you? You're my baby sister, so why you feel like you can't ask me for help? That hurts me, Jess."

"I'm trying to hold on to Momma's trailer," she said as her voice cracked. "I'm trying to hold on to everything she was and did, and I'm not able . . . Then I gave the sheriff a tip, like she used to, and he thinks I'm crazy."

"You ain't hardly crazy," her brother said, soothing her with his voice. "You was so good you used to scare Momma. I know that to be a fact."

Jessica nodded, sniffed hard, and wiped

275

her nose. "I'm sorry. I don't know where all that came from." The tears came from a deep-down pain, something she'd shoved down so far that she hadn't remembered where she'd even buried it.

"I do," Raphael said bluntly, but his tone was still gentle. "You're twenty-two years old, ain't had no fun, been living like an old lady; that's what's wrong with you."

"Yeah, well, I lost my job . . . Nobody around here is hiring, really. Can't even put up my college money anymore, much less —"

"I been done *told* you, girl, that if you just fill out the application to where you wanna go, I got you semester by semester — we family!"

"But that's not right," she said, squaring her shoulders. "You have things you wanna do with your life . . . like go to Paris and —"

"I work these poles like my ass is greased lightning, honey chile, I'll have you know. I am going to Paris again, this weekend, and will be there until fashion week, so I *am* living my dreams. You worry about living yours, boo."

Jessica smiled and wiped her face, and then chuckled. "You are such a hot mess."

"I am hot to death 'cause I drop it like it's

hot . . . So what you need?"

She couldn't answer him for a moment. She really hadn't thought out what she would do or what she needed. All she was sure of was that she wanted to go to New Orleans to help people survive what was hunting in their bayou.

"I honestly don't know," she murmured, staring out the window. "I wanted to get away . . . go to New Orleans for the week-end, but —"

"Only on two conditions," Raphael said.

"What?" Jessica said, a new smile tugging at her cheek.

"You go to the bank and take some of that money that's gathering dust in your college savings account . . . Get it before that sucker crashes and I have to go down there and hurt somebody — and you tell me how much you took out to go to New Orleans. I'ma send you a replacement check that you can cash when you get back. That's the logistics — but I want you to promise me that when you come back, you'll register for college, at least the local community college, for the fall semester."

"But, I —"

"Uh-uh, Miss Thang. I've been listening to excuses for the last four years. You take your pretty little behind down there and register, since you're jobless and all now. Go to school!"

"But how am I gonna keep the lights on and pay for food, Raph? Be serious."

"You get you some student aid or whatever, and you let me worry about lights and food — you can work on campus; you're below the poverty line. Anyway, that's condition one . . . My help comes with love-strings attached. You're too smart and got too much going for you to be wasting time like this," he added with emphasis.

Jessica leaned against the refrigerator and smiled. "Okay. I'll go to school, but I'll be looking for a job."

"Fine by me, drive yourself crazy, if you wanna, but the registering for classes in September is not up for negotiation, girl-friend."

She closed her eyes and tried to modulate the amusement in her voice. She loved it when her big brother fussed at her . . . It was pure love that reminded her of her mother's tough-love tactics.

"Any more conditions?" Jessica asked, then took a slow sip of her lemonade.

"No, just the one I've been on you about for too long. I want you to get laid while you're in the Big Easy; just be sure to use a condom — don't need no babies or STD

278

drama while you're trying to get an education."

Jessica spit out her lemonade and began coughing.

"That's right, I said it," Raphael said, now laughing. "Tell the truth and shame the devil. I may not be as good as you and Momma on the second sight, but I ain't blind. When's the last time you got some, girl?"

"Why you all up in my business, Raphael!" Jessica squeaked. "I don't do that to you."

"Huh . . . Oh, so now I'm *Raphael,* not Raph. Uhmmm-hmmm . . . and yes you *do* do that to me. See, I have to use words; you just bust into my room and look around with your third eye. Same difference."

"I do not!" Jessica shouted, laughing. Her face burned, and she pushed away from the refrigerator and began walking through the trailer.

"Yes, you do — don't lie. But we ain't talking about me; we happen to be talking about you. Last boyfriend I remember was in high school, senior prom. Then a few fly-by-night dates, and I could tell you didn't give any of those half-thug-wannabe knuckleheads any. Then you even stopped going to the clubs looking . . . Last I heard you'd

stopped going to church, too, like Momma
— most of them in there was either already
married, old, or would like me better, tell
the truth."

"You ain't never lied," she said, stopping
by her favorite chair and flopping down in
it.

"I want you to enjoy life, boo," Raphael
said in a gentler tone.

"I'm doing okay."

"No, you're not," he said softly.

Jessica held the phone close to her ear and
swallowed hard.

"You want what we all want . . . a prince."
He let out a long breath and then allowed
his voice to dip down low. "That sure ain't
what I dragged home with me last night . . .
but in a tight spot, he'll do."

She chuckled sadly and just shook her
head.

"But you want the full package — the
three Hs . . . somebody who's gonna be
honest, honorable, and *hetero* . . ."

"Yeah, I do," she murmured, allowing her
shoulders to sag.

"You don't want to give it away and then
find out he lied . . . or some other mess,
right?"

Jessica just nodded and released a sad sigh.

"But since you see so much . . ."

"I see the drama coming before they open their mouths." She sprawled out in the chair with her eyes closed, needing to hear her brother's comforting wisdom. "The older I get, Raph, the more I can see — the more I can see in advance, the lonelier it is."

"That's why you need to get out of Port Arthur. Ain't nobody there for you . . . That's why I had to leave."

"But I don't know if I can do the third thing you asked me to do while just on a weekend, you know?"

"I love you, too, boo . . . I know you ain't like me . . . and I appreciate the delicate way you tried to put that. I was just messing with you — you are definitely not a booty-call kinda girl."

"It's not like I haven't thought about it over the last four years, trust me."

"Say what!"

Jessica cringed. The last thing she'd meant to tell Raphael was that! "I mean —"

"Don't even try to clean it up; you cannot take that back. I at least hope you've got a pocket rocket or something that takes batteries!"

"Raph, don't start, okay . . . I'm embarrassed enough as it is." Jessica let out a hard breath, opened her eyes, and stood. "I've gotta go."

He laughed gently into the phone. "All right — I'll mind my business, but I don't want my sister losing her mind or becoming some old, dried-up prune. You go have fun in New Orleans and register for class. Maybe some tall, fine hunk who's trying to get educated might find his way to school with you, who knows?"

"That would be a hopeful thought," Jessica said, smiling, glad that her brother wasn't going to continue to rant. "But, seriously," she added in a quiet voice, "I don't know how to thank you enough."

"That's what family is for," Raphael said, his tone somber and holding a tinge of wistfulness in it. "You *always* had my back, sis . . . You *never* outed me, never judged me, and *always* loved me — no matter what. If people talked about me, you'd come home with your nose bloody and knees all scraped up from fighting for me. Hair all wild . . . Remember those days?"

"Yeah, I do," Jessica said, blinking back fresh tears.

"Well, that was what *I* needed, somebody who loved me regardless . . . so now helping you with what you need is the very least I can do."

"But —"

"Jess, no *but*s. Let somebody give you

282

something, for once."

"All right," she finally said, knowing her brother would not be moved.

"I love you," he told her and then made a kiss sound against the cell phone.

"I love you right back."

THREE

He tried not to stare when she walked up to his spiritual paraphernalia store window and stopped. Her gaze was fastened to the silver objects that glittered in the late-afternoon sun. Golden-rose light spilled over her warm brown skin and caught in her freefall of shoulder-length braids. Her yellow tank top clung, giving his imagination help as his gaze slid down her curvy frame . . . He just wished she would step back so he could also see her legs. But he didn't dare move, lest he frighten her away. Maybe, if God was listening to quick prayers, she'd come into the store.

He'd never seen her around New Orleans before, and she didn't have the carefree look of a college student on break or the relaxed vibration of a tourist. Her pretty face was cast over with anxiety, her eyes holding a hungry quality of someone hunting for something but not sure what.

"Justin," his grandmother called out from

the back of the store just as the pretty woman in the window looked up.

He hadn't realized that he'd nearly been in a trance until he heard his name. But now as a pair of gorgeous, intense dark brown eyes studied him, he couldn't move or speak.

"Justin! Do you hear me calling you, son?"

"Yeah, Grand . . ."

But the moment he turned his head to answer and looked back, the girl was gone. Panic shot through him, although he wasn't sure why. He'd seen beautiful women before, but this one . . . There was something he couldn't place his finger on, something surreal about her. Justin rounded the counter and raced across the floor, glad that at this late hour all his usual customers were gone.

The mystery woman had just gone down the block a little ways, and he jogged to catch up to her, admiring how her shorts hugged her round, tight butt from behind. Her legs were killer, too. Although she couldn't have been more than five foot six, her legs seemed like they belonged to a much taller woman.

He didn't want to be rude or offend her by just calling out to her; his intention was to get close enough to speak. But she rounded on him so fast and with so much attitude that for a second he was at a loss for words.

"Get out of my face," she said with a frown. "I did not come to New Orleans for no mess."

He held his hands up in front of his chest. "I just saw you looking in the store window for something that we mighta had, then you walked away. All I wanted to do was see if I could help you. Dang . . . my bad."

"Oh," she said with a lot less venom. "I'm sorry. I just don't like guys I don't know running up on me in the street . . . and I've been looking all over for a shop that my momma used to come to when she was alive, but I can't find it. She never came back after the storm, but I was hoping I could remember where it was."

Justin nodded. "A lot of places didn't reopen after Katrina . . . and sorry about your momma."

"Thanks," Jessica said quietly. "It's cool. It's been a couple of years."

"But you never get used to losing your momma," he said, looking at her and studying her face. "Justin," he said in a gentle tone. "The name's Justin." He extended his hand for Jessica and she took it, shaking it quickly and then letting it go.

"I'm Jessica, but my friends call me Jess." She hugged herself.

He had a strange feeling as he stared at her. She seemed disoriented and a little confused, the same way people look when they're trying too hard to remember a name or to recall something they've forgotten.

"You know, this heat out here ain't no joke," he said after a moment. "Why don't you come back down the street and soak up some air-conditioning while I see if we have the stuff you would've gotten in the other store."

"Okay, thanks," she said quietly, tilting her head as she spoke. "Yeah, maybe the heat is throwing me off."

She'd never felt like this in her life, had never been so blind to another person's thoughts. He gave her an inquisitive look along with a brilliant smile, then turned to head back toward his store. She kept her arms hugging her midsection, nursing the mild current of excitement that flowed from his hand into hers from just a touch. He was talking to her but she was only half listening, her mind trying desperately to sort out a hundred random thoughts at once.

Lost in her own thoughts, she tuned in to the slightly musty male scent that wafted off his body. His skin was the coppery hue that told her he had to be Creole. Beneath his bright white T-shirt she could see an extensive network of toned muscles. He was not too bulky . . . Lanky was how she'd describe him — and utterly delicious. The guy easily loping beside her was a full head taller than she was, maybe more, which made him approximately six two. However, what really captured her attention were his eyes.

They were golden amber brown, as though someone had splashed fine gold glitter into the dark hazel of them. He was clean shaven and had a beautiful, full mouth — a mesmerizing one that made her stare at it from the corner of her eye. He'd locked his hair and had it tied back in a long ponytail, but ringlets of silky black curls had escaped the stylistic invasion. The tone of his voice was a melodic alto, and before long she realized that tiny butterflies had escaped to flutter around in her belly. But it disturbed her that she couldn't hear his thoughts.

Jessica forced her gaze to the ground as he opened the store's front door. Cool air assaulted her, and she had to admit that it felt really good.

"Okay, so, what are you looking for that you couldn't see from out there?"

"Uhmmm . . . you're going to think I'm

crazy," she began slowly, hoisting her crocheted handbag higher up on her shoulder.

"No judgments when people ask for stuff in my store. Just tell me what you want, and if I have it, you've got it. If not, I can get it."

It was hard to look at him and make words come out of her mouth at the same time. He didn't seem that much older than she was, and he owned a store?

"This must take a lot of work," she said, changing the subject until she could work up the nerve to explain why she was really there. She'd expected to find an old crone minding the occult shop, not some hunk with a gorgeous smile.

"It does," he said with a casual shrug. "But I have to do something to keep the bills paid while I go to school at night — I'm taking up business marketing and management, entrepreneurship track. Tuition over at Xavier is hefty, but I'm not complaining."

"That's really cool . . . being able to run your own business, even in this economy, and still go to school. I've been saving for four years to try to go . . . but I'm definitely going to register this fall."

Her honest comment seemed to make him stand up taller. "That's good, real good.

Don't give up on your dreams. I only got a leg up with a store because Mom and Grand used to do psychic readings in here . . . but after Mom passed, Grand didn't wanna see no more, so she gave me her part and said sell it. I couldn't bear to do that, so I rebuilt it."

Jessica opened and closed her mouth. "Your mom was a psychic, too."

"Wait . . . your mom had the gift?" Justin just stared at her, gaping.

Jessica nodded as he laughed and walked in a tight circle with his hands on top of his head.

"That is too deep," he said, laughing.

She smiled and nodded. "Yeah — ain't it just?"

"Are you gonna fill that young lady's order, son, or spend an hour telling her all our family bizness?"

Jessica and Justin turned at the sound of the elderly woman's voice, and after a moment, a bent figure parted the green-glass beaded curtains that led to the back rooms. The short brown-skinned matron was draped in a multicolored crocheted shawl. Deep lines were etched into sagging, leathery skin, but her eyes still sparkled with a mysterious golden amber hue that seemed to take years off her age.

"This is Grand," Justin said with a patient smile.

"Ma'am," Jessica said, giving the older woman respect in the way that would have done her mother proud.

Justin's grandmother gave a little snort of annoyance and came up to Jessica, peering at her with suspicion. "You's pretty enough," she said with a half smile that could have easily been mistaken for a scowl.

"Thank you, ma'am," Jessica said shyly, not sure why this old woman made her so nervous.

"Don't need ta thank me — thank the Good Lord for the way He blessed ya. Now whatchu want with my Justin?"

"Grand, please don't start," Justin said quickly. "The young lady didn't come in here for all of that, she just came in here to —"

"I know what she came in here fer," Grand said in a peevish tone, folding her arms over her bony chest.

"Maybe I should go," Jessica mumbled and then turned to leave. "It was nice to meet y'all."

"See, that's the problem with young folks." Grand let out a little grunt. "You's too fast to jump to conclusions. I said I know why you came in here, sugah. Open up that bag of yours and let's talk plain."

Jessica turned around to look at the old lady.

"I know you got some serious hardware in there. Gonna take a coupla days to get bullets made for it. But'chu gonna need more than that to go after what's down in Johnson's Bayou."

Jessica remained very, very still. She and Justin stared at Justin's grandmother, slack-jawed.

"After what happened to my Lula, I didn't wanna see no mo', but that don't mean I *cain't* see." Grand lifted her chin and narrowed her gaze on Jessica. "But you too young to be throwing your gift away by trying to go git yo'self kilt."

Moving to the store counter, Jessica set her crocheted bag down on it and slowly extracted her father's old service revolver. Justin looked at the gun; Grand just shook her head.

"So, you's fixin' to go into the bayou . . . all by your lonesome and handle up a whole pack of lukegaroos? Girl, you plum lost your natural mind."

"Whoa, whoa, whoa." Justin rounded the counter and stared at the gun for a few seconds, then looked at Jessica. "Tell me that isn't the plan, because if it is, I'm not

291

making you silver anything, let alone bullets."

"Okay, fine," Jessica said, growing annoyed. What business was it of theirs what she'd planned to do? But the old lady had said *pack,* as in more than a few like she'd imagined — that was her idea of a pack, but the old lady made it sound as though there were way more than that . . . She'd also acknowledged that there were werewolves out there.

Grand scoffed, picking up on Jessica's thoughts. "You ain't crazy, chile — not for knowing what ate up them people on the news. What makes you crazy as a bedbug is trying to go after what kilt my Lula all by yourself."

"Grand, we are not going into that," Justin said, frowning.

"Boy, I used to change your diapers, so don't you sass me!" Grand fussed as she pointed a gnarled finger at Jessica. "Baby girl, lemme tell you . . . There's a lot of mess up in that bayou that ya need to leave be. My daughter was carrying him," she added with a quick jerk of her head toward Justin. "I tol' her not to do no readings while she was carrying that boy . . . but money was funny and my daughter didn't listen. She took a client — a man. His wife was a hussy, was cheatin' on him, and my daughter didn't have the sense she was born with not to tell him so."

Justin let out a groan and walked away. "Grand, would you *please* stop."

"No, 'cause this chile fixin' to do somethin' that don't make sense, so I'm gonna tell her how mess goes 'round and comes 'round."

Grand squared her shoulders and walked up to Jessica. But Justin seemed so uncomfortable that Jessica glanced at him, torn. Part of her wanted to know what had happened, and the other part wanted to stop the story that seemed to be causing Justin so much pain.

"Don't look at him," Grand said. "He's closed-mouthed about everything, always been that way. So you need to give me your undivided."

Grand nodded as Jessica's attention was wrested back to her. "Now, like I was sayin' . . . My daughter told and that husband went home as mad as a caught thief. Lef' his no-good wife. After gettin' caught in two-timing ways, the wife blamed my daughter. Have you ever?" Grand sucked her teeth and let another grunt of disgust pass her lips. "But you know hell hath no fury like a woman scorned." Grand's gaze softened, and then she looked at her grand-son. "Sooner or later you gonna haf'ta tell somebody . . . maybe somebody who got a good heart and who can accept you for who you is."

"If you violate my privacy, Grand, I swear, I'm out." Justin stared at his grandmother, his eyes holding a promise to never forgive the offense.

"This girl here got a good heart and it involves her, you know?"

"How?" Justin shouted, spinning on his grandmother and talking with his hands. "Don't do this, Grand!"

"Wasn't till she walked in here and I got up close that I could see . . . but her daddy was the one messing with that swamp witch."

"What?" Jessica shrieked and then tried to adjust her tone. "Ma'am . . . ?"

"Spells and counterspells — they was gun-slinging juju like it was the wild, wild West," Grand said, waving an arthritic hand for emphasis. "First bad dose came when the wife hit my pregnant daughter . . . tried to make her have a monster — but as you can see, Justin is fine." Grand raised an eyebrow and stared at him hard. "Satisfied?"

"Thank you," he muttered.

"You just gifted, is all," Grand said with a

dismissive wave toward Justin before turning her focus back to Jessica. "But then, once my daughter realized what that hussy had tried to do, she did a reverse double-deadbolt spell on that cheating wife . . . sent that hatred right back where it came from. And you do know that a mother trying to protect her baby is stronger than a she-devil trying to do dirt, right?"

Grand waited for Jessica to nod and then squinted and pointed at her, vindicated. "Uh-huh, you know I'm tellin' it right. Word is, that swamp witch, who by the way was quite a Jezebel, had a lot of bad IOUs out there, jus' nobody would challenge her. But when my daughter did, the Lord worked in mysterious ways . . . All that bad she had out in the world came fer her all at one time. Turned her into what she was trying to make Justin. Your momma had a hand in it, too," Grand said, nodding. "Uh-huh. That woman had worked roots on your daddy to get him to leave y'all . . . He was a lawman, had morals and principles, but once that she-devil got her hooks in him, it was all she wrote. So whatever your momma sent back her way added a little topspin on my Lula's spell, and probably everybody else's, too. It's bad business to start root-slinging down here in New Orleans — never know how the juju is gonna ricochet."

Jessica turned slowly and slumped against the counter, hugging herself.

"Your daddy loved your momma dearly, baby . . . loved you and your brother. But that bayou witch . . ." Grand shook her head. "She was built the way that'd make even a churchgoing man turn a blind eye to the Lord. Big bosom," Grand added, using her hands to demonstrate. "Long legs, big ole Creole backside, tiny waist, pretty face, long black hair . . . and them green eyes — pure evil in 'em, though."

"They said my daddy run off when we was young and they found him dead, tore up by gators. Sheriff Moore found him on the Louisiana side of Sabine Lake." Jessica looked into Grand's ancient eyes and blinked back moisture.

"Wasn't no gators, baby," Grand said gently. "Just like it ain't been no gators eating people like they say on the news, and it sure wasn't no hurricane that kilt my girl, no more than it was feral dogs that ravaged her body." Grand lifted her chin. "For all them years, she couldn't get to my daughter, because Lula had put down protections and barriers . . . but the storm, oh, Lawd, that storm washed it all away."

"My momma got sick around then, but

she passed two years ago," Jessica murmured, her gaze going from Grand to Justin. "The doctors could never tell why she was getting weaker and weaker . . . never found out exactly what it was. They just said she was sick."

"Uh-huh . . . that's an old-time spell. Jus' make a person waste away for no good reason. *Mean.* Your momma probably put something down here to keep that Jezebel and her evil ways kept here and away from her young'uns . . . just like my Lula did. Even evil got an uphill battle when going against a mother's love." Grand let out an angry sigh. "She prob'ly just sent evil your momma's direction, seeing as how your momma died from sickness, not from gettin' ate."

Jessica's hand flew to her mouth. "This witch cast spells so bad that she *made* werewolves?" Her eyes darted between Justin and Grand, and yet she couldn't read Justin's frown.

"No, baby," Grand said gently. "She didn't cast no spell, she became her own spell."

Jessica's body slumped against the counter again as though someone had punched her. "But you said there was a whole den of them now . . ."

"Uhmmm-hmmm . . . all them men she

297

does her dirt with. All it takes is a scratch, a nip, sharing some spit. By now, who knows how many men she done swapped spit with? If I was younger, I'd go out there and spell-battle her myself!"

FOUR

Although Grand sometimes got on his last nerve, he had to admit that she was very, very wise. Talking frankly had loosened Jessica up enough that she agreed to come home with them for a real down-home meal.

Crawfish over grits with gravy was Grand's specialty, but she didn't pull out all the stops for just any ole body. He could tell that Grand had taken a shine to Jessica . . . So had he. If she passed Grand's tough inspection, then what else was there — the problem was, nobody had ever come this close to finding out his secret.

But he couldn't worry about all of that now while listening to the wonderful sound of Jessica's voice. Plus she smelled so good, a light citrus mixed with baby oil coming off her legs mixed with a little perspiration. Add in Grand's kitchen magic and he was done.

"So, if this witch is a werewolf, how in the heck do we get to her?" Jessica asked, leaning closer to him and dropping her voice to a conspiratorial whisper. "She did your momma, mine, my daddy . . . and now she's got a bunch of lovers-turned-wolves out eating people? She's gotta be stopped."

The challenge was in Jessica's eyes, the unasked question lingering there — *Why haven't you tried to shut this bitch down a long time ago yourself, especially when you have all the tools and a grandma that can see?* Guilt stabbed him; what could he say? There was no way to explain that without exposing what he was.

"The only way to get to her is during the day when the moon isn't in full phase," Justin said quietly, now allowing his knee to brush hers. He loved the way she leaned in, the way her eyes lit with passion. Loved the urgency in her voice and the way she hung on his every word.

"Then . . . we can do that." Jessica took a quick sip from her lemonade and then clasped her hands together tightly in her lap.

"If you shoot her while in human form, you'll go to jail for murder one, Jess."

Jessica sat back and blew out a long breath. "Maaaan . . ."

"Lock her in her house with brick dust," Grand hollered from the kitchen. "Silver shavings go down next, and then bar all her windows and doors with holy water, pour it over her threshold. Follow up with salt."

"Grand, I thought you was cookin'," Justin called out.

"I am," Grand fussed back. "I can walk and chew gum!"

Jessica smiled and then leaned forward and touched his arm. "Ever since I was little, I always felt so strange . . . Do you know what I mean?"

All he could do was nod; her touch had dried the saliva in his mouth.

"I knew I wasn't like other kids, knew my momma wasn't like other mommas. Until today, I haven't run across anybody that made me feel like I was home, like I was with family. Like it was okay to be different. Even extended family shunned us."

He knew exactly how she felt and exactly what she meant. Without even thinking about it, he gathered her hands within his, as though that were the most natural thing to do in the whole world.

"I think your difference is beautiful, Jess," he said quietly, hoping his grandmother would mind her beeswax for a while. "I'll help you trap that swamp witch and her pack in her house, if you want . . . They can't keep killing innocent people."

A warm, soft palm slid out of his to touch

his cheek. He almost closed his eyes at the sensation that it sent through his body.

"Why can't I see you?" she murmured, studying his face with her liquid brown gaze.

"Ya needs ta answer that girl!" Grand called out from the kitchen, making them both laugh. "And ya best go home to be taking care of your dog."

Jessica hid a giggle behind her hand. "You have a dog?"

"Kinda," Justin hedged. "But this is why I don't live here," he said, shaking his head. "No privacy." He took her hands within his again and let out a heavy sigh. "You know how old folks can be."

Jessica sat back, extracting her hands from his with a smile, glancing around. "I hear you . . . I thought you lived here?"

"With Grand . . . Oh, noooo. Got my own apartment close to Xavier."

They both laughed, and he was glad that his grandmother's intrusion had broken Jessica's spell. Two seconds more and he would have told her all that she wanted to know.

"Then since you all find me so funny," Grand said in a peevish tone, "y'all go wash up and come eat and stop sitting on the sofa making goo-goo eyes at each other."

For the first time in a long time, Jess felt

her sexuality awaken with a roar. What had always been a dull ache or a dream-state want was now a beast.

Justin stood in the hotel lobby, stalling, the same way she was. They'd long since sopped up grits and gravy with Grand's buttermilk biscuits, done dishes, and talked strategy and laughed together. She felt like she'd known Justin Cambridge all her born days, and the short walk in the humid evening air from Grand's apartment over the shop to the hotel made her feel like she was floating on air.

Drawing on everything her momma had taught her, she finally dredged up the strength to say good night. This one was a keeper and was old school, like her. It wouldn't do to just ask him up to her room and be brazenly bold. But dang, he was so fine, so kind . . . just sexy as hell.

"I'd better go," she said with a slight smile.

"Yeah . . . you'd better," he murmured, but he didn't move.

"I have to come by the shop tomorrow to get all that stuff Grand was saying I'd need."

"*We'd* need," Justin corrected.

"I hadn't realized I said that," Jessica said, covering her mouth. "I —"

"It was fine," Justin said, placing both hands on her upper arms.

302

Warmth soaked into Jessica's skin and practically melted her bones. Her breath hitched when she tried to speak.

"I'd better go," he said with a widening smile. "I want you to think I'm a gentleman."

She smiled and arched an eyebrow. "Want me to *think* that you're a gentleman?"

He gave her a dashingly sexy grin. "Uh-huh."

She couldn't help laughing at the mischief she saw in his eyes. "So, what changed your normal ungentlemanly behavior?"

"You," he said, his smile fading. "Gotta be a gentleman around a true lady." He leaned in, kissed her forehead, and stepped back. "So, I'ma go, okay?" He made the hand gesture that said he'd call her on her cell and left her with a wink.

"Yeah," she murmured, and gave him a little wave as he turned slowly, looked back once, and loped away.

She woke up with the sun, tangled in the sheets. All she could think about was Justin's voice, his sexy smile, his body . . . his beautiful locks . . . And then oddly she could suddenly envision his huge black dog. For some strange reason, the big, lovable animal made her smile and made her want to hug it like a big teddy bear.

A chime on her cell phone practically made her fall out of her bed. She quickly grabbed it off the nightstand and opened it, then smiled. The message was brief, but she read it over and over again before answering.

Know it's early — couldn't sleep. Wanna get breakfast?

Jessica laughed and sent back a smiley face with one word, *OK*.

She greeted Justin with a big smile as he walked across the hotel lobby.

"Good morning."

"Good morning yourself," she said with a chuckle, then yawned.

"Couldn't sleep, either?" He waggled his eyebrows and she looked away.

"I slept all right." Her wide grin told on her.

"Yeah, okay . . . I didn't."

"Then you need some coffee," she said, laughing, skirting the subject he was fixated on.

"That ain't all, but I'm a patient man."

She whirled on him and opened her mouth. "You did not go there."

"My bad, my bad," he said, laughing, leaning away from her. "I thought women appreciated honesty, especially those who could see."

"We do, but dang."

Jessica began walking again, peeping at him over her shoulder as he bounded toward her and then loped a few paces behind her, smiling. There was just something about him that she couldn't define — something very primal and different yet honest and dear.

After they'd settled at a table and ordered, Justin's expression sobered.

"I brought you something, but not to be used here. This is a going-away present for when you head back to Port Arthur, all right?"

She didn't know what to say as he dug into his jeans pocket and produced a handful of silver bullets. "Justin . . ."

"You take these home, you hear," he said in an urgent rush. "I can lay the brick dust and all of that . . . If I would have done what I was supposed to years ago, maybe your momma would still be here. But I don't want you in harm's way."

"But if this woman killed my momma and my daddy —"

Justin held up his hand. "I've got Grand on my side," he said with a mischievous smile.

There was no arguing that Grand was a formidable force, no less than she could argue about the way Justin made her feel.

"Believe me, I'm not trying to send you home . . . far from it," Justin said quietly, leaning even closer. "But I want you safe. Cool?"

She nodded but didn't answer; that's as much as she could commit to right now. The full moon was a few days away, and she wanted closure. But her money was only going to hold out long enough to keep her around for the balance of the weekend. Tuesday night was when she'd predicted to Sheriff Moore that all hell would break loose . . . and now the last person she wanted caught up in that madness was Justin.

"You be careful, too," she finally said over a sip of coffee.

"I'm cool," he said, then chugged his orange juice.

"I want you to be more than cool. I want you to be safe, Justin."

Her voice had come out soft like a tender brush against his cheek. He stared at her for a moment and then reached across the table to take up her hand. Sure, he'd had a lot of girls, mostly booty calls — nothing serious. But he was so tired of hiding, tired of the double life he was leading. Tired of not being able to share his heart and soul.

"Tell me what she did to you," Jessica said quietly. "That witch. Did she make a spell against you that closed you off from the spirit realm?"

Justin looked down and studied Jessica's hands. How did one even begin to describe what she'd done to him, in terms that wouldn't make her run?

"You've lost so much . . ." Jessica whispered, shaking her head. "Even your dog; how could she attack an innocent animal?"

Justin pulled away and sat back, then raked his fingers through his locks.

"What's wrong?" Confused, Jessica sat forward.

"Nothing . . . It's just a real raw subject, is all." He looked out the window, hoping she'd believe him.

"I'm sorry. I shouldn't have pried . . . It's just that I get the sense that this woman really damaged you — taking everything from you. It had to be a joy-stealing spell."

His shoulders slumped two inches from relief. "Yeah . . . it was something like that."

Saying good-bye got harder and harder to do. All day Saturday he'd taken her around town and then got her to relent and hang out at the movies. Sunday morning he skipped church, instead going to breakfast with her and trying to get her to come back to Grand's for dinner, but wisely she said no. He knew the inevitable was near — sooner or later Jessica had to go back to Port Arthur. But he'd made her a bag of protection and had loaded her down with everything she could want or need to keep her safe at home. Still, standing by her old rusted-out Jeep Wrangler, the last thing he wanted to do was tell her good-bye.

"I'ma call you, all right?" he said, giving her a hug and opening the door.

"You'd better." She beamed up at him and melted his soul.

"I will." He touched the edge of her jaw with the pad of his thumb. "Did you have a good time in New Orleans?"

She nodded, her smile fading a bit as her eyes took on that open gaze that was always his undoing. "This is the best vacation I've ever had."

"Good, then I did my job," he said, trying to make jokes to cover his nervousness.

"Oh, so now I'm work, huh?"

He laughed. "Yeah, you are. Silver bullets, half a storeroom of supplies, and a crazy mission . . . Yeah, girl, you're work."

She touched his chest and became serious. "You be careful."

He couldn't stand it. Maybe it was the heat, the way she looked at him, or the sound of her voice, but one moment he was thinking of what to say and the next he'd lowered his face to hers to brush her lips. She deepened the kiss, much to his surprise and completely to his pleasure. The next thing he knew, he'd backed her up against the car.

"You sure you don't want me to drive behind you to Port Arthur?" he said, breaking the kiss on a quiet gasp. "Like . . . I could come over and help you put down all the protective barriers, make sure the place was tight — then I could come back."

She didn't answer fast enough, seemed semidazed, and before she could change her mind, he was out.

"Get in, I'll follow you."

"But —"

"No . . . it's cool. I'll be right behind you."

"It ain't much, but it's mine," Jessica announced, wishing she'd thoroughly cleaned her trailer before special company came by.

"That's all that matters," Justin said in good nature, looking around.

She studied him; the hair was literally bristling on his neck and he seemed nervous. It was odd, but he kept turning his head, tilting it like a hunting dog might.

"I need to get these barriers down fast," he finally said, reaching for her bag. "My gut is never wrong, and something doesn't feel right."

"But it's not a true full moon . . . I thought you said we had a few days."

He looked up at the night sky. "Some say it doesn't have to be exactly full . . . just waxing near, if the entity is strong — and I'm assuming by now, after all these years, she is."

"Then what about Grand!" Jessica said, rushing to help Justin put a brick-dust circle around her small trailer.

"Grand got the shop and her apartment ridiculously barriered. My grandmother never, ever, ever goes out when it's near a full moon, during the full moon, or a few days after."

Jessica allowed her shoulders to slump with relief. "Okay, but you should check on her before the night's up."

"I will," Justin said, focused on the task. "Hand me your dad's revolver. This needs to be loaded and you need to know how to shoot it."

She watched him manage the task, then accepted the weapon back from him. For

310

the sake of his male pride, now didn't seem like the time to inform him that she already knew how to use it.

"We'll seal up your windows, your threshold . . . This trailer is like an aluminum can to those things without it. Easy access."

His comment didn't make her feel better, but his confident presence did.

"How come you didn't go after her before?" Jessica stood on her steps holding the gun, watching Justin work.

"Long story."

"Last I checked, we got time." She smiled, but it was a tense smile like his.

"You know," he said, after a moment. "When a witch casts a spell on you, sometimes only she can break it. I guess I was holding out stupid hope that one day I could reason with her. But now I don't care anymore."

"I care," Jessica murmured. "You're going to all this trouble for me and throwing away your chance to get whatever evil she put on you lifted."

He shrugged. "It's worth it." Then he looked at her without blinking. "You're worth it . . . and I never felt like this before."

Jessica opened her front door, but the second she did a low growl paralyzed her.

"Get inside!" Justin shouted.

Jessica couldn't move for a second, and what met her eyes didn't sync up with her brain. A huge wolf with massive saliva-dripping jaws and red glowing eyes barreled right toward Justin. But as her arm lifted to fire the weapon, he shed his clothes and turned into the huge black dog she'd seen in her mini morning vision.

Justin didn't have a huge dog . . . Justin was *the huge dog?* Now it all made sense . . . This explained so much.

Brain numb, her outstretched arm held its aim. Somewhere in her gut she knew if she didn't hit the charging beast before it collided with the protective Newfoundland, the infection from the one would surely ruin the other. It all happened in slow motion; it all happened in seconds. Her arm came up, she pulled the trigger. Her shot tore into the beast's shoulder, which knocked it back and only made it angrier. Justin leapt out of the way of a vicious claw swipe and made the beast charge again, and just before impact, Justin dodged out of the way to allow the beast to hurtle into the large oak tree in the front yard.

The weight of the centuries-old oak crashed down on the monster and temporarily pinned it. Jagged branches dug into its fetid flesh, making it howl in agony as it struggled to free itself. Roars of fury cut into the night as the Newfoundland circled his quarry, forcing the beast to expend both energy and blood.

Justin was a shape-shifter? That reality alone would have been enough to make her pass out, if their lives weren't on the line. She squeezed hard on the trigger, and this time the slug caught the beast in its side. But there was no telling how many bullets she'd need to finally put the creature down. In one angry toss, it flung the tree off itself and was getting up. The only saving grace was that the wounded thing in her front yard was obviously having trouble deciding who to go after first. That bought them maybe two seconds, as it quickly made up its mind and whirled on Justin.

A patrol car screeched up as Jessica continued to fire. A shotgun blast hit the beast right between the eyes when it turned toward the new sound, and then the sheriff aimed at the fleeing dog.

"No, Sheriff! That's my guard dog!" Jessica shouted as the sheriff whirled around and Justin bounded off between the trailers.

"Jesus Christ in heaven, what the hell was that thing, Jess?" Sheriff Moore scratched his head, still shaken. Sweat poured down his face as he watched the beast turn into a naked, voluptuous woman. The poor man seemed dangerously close to a coronary.

"You know what it was," Jessica said quietly.

"Where'd the dog go?" Sheriff Moore stammered, looking around. "I got to thinking about what you said, some things your momma used to tell me . . . then I got worried because you were gone — and you never go anywhere. Thought maybe —"

"You told me to go on vacation, remember?" Jessica's gaze remained fixed on the body that was slowly turning to ash. "Damn, she must have been really old."

"But that killer dog . . ."

"Sheriff, he's loyal and brave, and I love him," she said loud enough for Justin to hear. "I went to New Orleans to find him . . . No doubt he fled back there, so he wouldn't be shot. Given what was out here, I guess I needed him more than I realized." Emotionally spent, Jessica started back up the trailer steps. "But I told you I wasn't crazy."

She shut the screen door and listened as the stricken sheriff drove off. Raphael came to her mind and, without waiting to process any other thought, she called her brother.

A very sleepy voice entered the receiver, and Jessica pressed her cell phone to her ear. "You up?"

"Do you know what time it is, boo?"

"I met somebody while on vacation," she said, ignoring his cross tone. She needed to talk, needed to hear encouragement in the form of a friendly voice that understood the strange life that lived side by side with the supernatural.

"Get out — divulge all," Raphael said, sounding as though he was waking up.

"Well, for starters, he's a shape-shifter."

Raphael sucked his teeth. "Boo, don't be so judgmental, we've all got issues."

EPILOGUE

One Month Later

"I told you she'd be back," Grand said in a triumphant tone. "Mark my words. You jes' lucky you was able to get back in your car real sneaky and come home after she went to sleep. But you mighta made both of you all sleep better if you would have trusted her to not hold your condition against you, especially after saving her life. She would have let you stay, but what do I know? I'm an old lady."

"Grand!"

"I'm not telling tales out of school, she really has taken a shine to you." Grand raised her eyebrows and continued working on her peach cobbler. "Some things are jus'

315

natchel at y'all's age."

"She's bringing her brother . . . and I wanna pass his inspection," Justin said, changing the subject. "I don't want him to think I'm dogging his sister."

"So now you're making jokes at your own expense," Grand said, chuckling and shaking her head.

"You know what I mean, Grand . . . C'mon."

"All right, all right," she said, waving him away. "You'll do fine — you don't judge him, he won't judge you . . . and he knows what you are. She told him."

Justin closed his eyes with a groan.

"Everything is fine . . . Ain't been no killings lately here this last month."

He stopped and stared at his grandmother. "Why not, Grand?"

"Oh, I forgot to mention that I locked them other wolves up in their swamp shack, the whole den . . . By now, they probably turned on each other. Serves 'em right. Sorry I didn't get that she-devil, too . . . Woulda saved you kids the trouble."

THE PERILS OF EFFRIJIM

KATIE MACALISTER

For as long as she can remember, Katie MacAlister has loved reading. Growing up in a family where a weekly visit to the library was a given, Katie spent much of her time with her nose buried in a book. Two years after she started writing novels, Katie sold her first romance. More than thirty books later, her novels have been translated into numerous languages, received several awards, and been placed on the *New York Times, USA Today,* and *Publishers Weekly* bestseller lists. Katie lives in the Pacific Northwest with her husband and dogs, and can often be found lurking around online.

ONE

"Now remember, this is a vacation, not carte blanche for you to run amok and be obnoxious."

I made a little pout, which let me tell you,

ain't easy when your face is shaped like a Newfoundland dog's muzzle. Which mine was by dint of the fact that my most magnificent form to date was that of an extremely handsome, debonair, and utterly fabulous Newfie. "Have I ever run amok and been obnoxious?" I asked my demon lord, a kinda clueless Guardian by the name of Aisling Grey.

She lifted her hand and prepared to tick items off her fingers.

"Yeah, yeah, whatever," I interrupted before she could get going on what may or may not have been a few unfortunate incidents in my past. "Kiss kiss. Have a nice time on Drake's yacht. Don't let the door hit you on the ass on the way out."

"It's not too late to send it to the Akasha," Drake said as he walked past me, a baby carrier in each hand. "You would be able to enjoy our vacation without worrying about whether the demon was causing trouble."

"Hello! 'The demon,' as you so rudely referred to me, is standin' right here!" I gave Drake a look, but he missed it entirely. You'd think that a guy who just happened to be a wyvern, leader of a group of dragons who marched around the earth in human form, would be a little more aware of things, but Drake was like that, always missing my pithy comments and witty repartee. "And Aisling wouldn't send me to the Akasha. That's the cruelest thing a demon lord can do to her charming, adorable, and entirely innocent demon, one who, it might be pointed out, was recently praised for actions above and beyond the call of duty with regards to the birthing of the spawn."

Drake muttered something extremely rude in Hungarian under his breath as he took the spawns out to the car.

"One," Aisling said, doing that finger-ticking-off thing again. She made mean eyes at me as she did it. "You will cease referring to the twins as 'the spawn.' They have names; use them. Two, yes, you were of great assistance when it came to their birth, especially since you had to don human form to do so."

I made a face. "Man, that was totally sucky. You should have seen the size of my package in human form. It lacked, babe. It just lacked."

"Two and a half — you will not tell me, in any terms whatsoever, about your genitalia, be it in doggy or human form."

I rolled my eyes. "Sheesh, Ash, loosen up a bit. I didn't go into actual measurements or set up a website devoted to it."

"For which the world is truly grateful."

"Yeah, well, I'm still peeved at May for making me take that form. Human form is just so boring."

"May was doing the best she could given a bad situation," Aisling said, pointing to a suitcase sitting near the door when István, one of Drake's elite guard, came in from where the car was waiting to take Aisling and Drake to a yacht he'd hired for a couple of weeks' vacation. "Just that one is left, István. Are you and Suzanne set for your trip to New York?"

"Yes, we will leave as soon as Jim is picked up."

"You make it sound like I have a baby-sitter," I grumbled, a bit annoyed. "You know, I'm over a thousand years old — I think I can take care of myself for ten days. Just leave me a credit card and the number of the local pizza place, and I'll have a Mrs. Peel–athon while you're gone. And maybe a Morgan Fairchild–athon. Rawr."

"Now there's a recipe for disaster." Aisling's lips thinned as she continued. "Three: You will obey Anastasia. I have formally given her the right to give you orders, and you will respect that and do as she commands."

"She just better not let that creepy apprentice of hers around me," I said, scratching an itchy spot behind my ear. "During that lunch when you dragged me to meet Anastasia, that Margarine Chip chick looked like she wanted to gut me."

"*Buttercup* is Anastasia's apprentice and unused to demons," she said, her nostrils flaring in that nostril-flaring way she had. "You will be polite and courteous to both of them, do you understand?"

"Yeah, yeah, keep my nose clean, gotcha," I said, wandering over to my favorite British newspaper, the one with the girls flaunting their bare boobies. "So long as Anastasia takes me to Paris to be with my darling Cecile, we're all good."

"Four: While you are visiting Cecile, you will do anything that Amelie asks you, and you will leave when Anastasia says it's time to leave. You are not to beg Amelie to stay with Cecile. She is a Welsh Corgi. She can survive the nights without you."

"I don't see why I have to spend the nights at a hotel with Anastasia," I said, tapping my toes on the picture of a particularly busty chick. "It would be easier for everyone if she just dumped me off at Amelie's and let me have my vacation there, with Cecile, rather than picking me up every night like it was some sort of day care or something."

"Five," Aisling said as Drake reappeared

at the door, giving her a raised eyebrow. "You will remember that if you step out of line, the Akasha awaits."

"You wouldn't really let anyone send me there," I said, rubbing my head on her leg just to let her know I'd miss her. "There's no way out of the Akasha unless you're summoned out or get a special dispensation from the Sovereign. You don't know 'cause you've never been there, but it's hell, Aisling, it's really hell. Worse, 'cause Abaddon ain't that bad once you figure out how to avoid the torture seminars. But the Akasha? Brrr. Bad mojo all around."

"Just you remember that when Anastasia gets here. Are you all packed?"

I nodded toward the doggy backpack she got me for the visits I made to Paris to hang out with my lovely Cecile, she of the tailless butt and oh-so-suckable ears. Corgis may be low to the ground, but they are the sexiest things on four legs, and my Cecile was particularly snuffleworthy, even if she did get a bit grumpy now and then. "Eh? What?" I realized suddenly Aisling had been droning on about something or other.

"*Kincsem,* we will be late for the train if we do not leave now," Drake said, taking her by the arms and steering her toward the door.

"I asked you if you have your cell phone and the phone book with the emergency numbers in your backpack."

"Yup, all there. And extra drool bibs, that nice bamboo brush, a clean collar, and a two-week supply of *Welsh Corgi Fanciers* for when Cecile is napping."

Drake rolled his eyes and pushed Aisling through the door over her protests.

"Be good!" she bellowed as he shoved her into the car.

"Don't forget to bring me back a present!" I yelled back, and waved good-bye before slamming shut the door and heading straight for Drake's library and the leather couch they always forbade me to sit on.

That's where Suzanne found me almost an hour later. "Your substitute Guardian is here," she said, frowning. "Did Aisling say you could sit on Drake's nice sofa?"

"What Drake doesn't know can't cheese him off," I said, sauntering out, waiting patiently while Suzanne fetched my backpack.

"Hiya, babe," I said, greeting the white-haired Guardian Aisling's mentor Nora had dug up to accompany me on my trip to Paris. Anastasia wasn't really my idea of a babe, her being approximately a million years old (or at least looking like it), but

323

I'm nothing if not Mr. Smooth Moves, and I know how the ladies like a little flattery. I did a quick gender check on her (nose to crotch, just to be polite), then sucked in my gut while Suzanne strapped on the backpack.

"Good afternoon, Effrijim," Anastasia said, smiling vaguely. I was pleased to see that her weirdo apprentice wasn't around. "Are you ready to fly to Paris?"

"Been ready all day," I said, accompanying her to the door. She said good-bye to Suzanne, who waved at me (I gave her hand a quick lick good-bye), and waited for me to go first. "I'm glad to see your uber-creepy assistant isn't here. She really freaks me out, you know? I think she has something against demons in incredibly handsome doggy form . . . Oh, hi, Butterball."

"My *name* is *Buttercup!*" The woman who stood waiting at the limo that Drake had arranged for us (against his will, but Aisling has him wrapped all around her fingers) narrowed her beady little eyes at me. "Can we not just banish the demon, Mistress?"

I snickered, about to make a comment about BDSM, but Anastasia's gentle, elderly voice stopped me. She was a nice old lady, so I didn't feel right about shocking her with references to stuff like bondage.

"Aisling has assured me that Effrijim will be on its very best behavior, and I'm quite sure that it will be so," she said, giving me a kind of vague smile as she got into the limo.

"Absotively," I agreed, shouldering the buttery one aside so I could sit next to Anastasia. "Hey, do you mind if we stop at a McDonald's on the way to the airport? I didn't have much lunch and I'm famished."

"But Mistress —" Buttercup started to protest, but it did no good. I flashed her a charming grin before settling back in the seat.

"No, my dear. I know the demon offends you, but consider this a good learning experience. Aisling claims it is harmless, and after meeting it, I am in complete agreement." She flashed a smile my way. "Effrijim is too much of a gentleman to cause trouble, I'm quite sure."

I straightened up a little, pleased by the *gentleman* comment. "Damn straight. Although ya know, you can just call me Jim rather than Effrijim. I really don't use it much 'cause it's kinda sissy sounding, don't you think?"

"Not at all. I think it's quite distinguished. It suits you," she said nicely. I rubbed my face on her just because she didn't think the name was awful (it is, but she didn't admit that, which wins beaucoup brownie points in my book). "I must admit that I'm a bit curious as to why you chose to adopt the form of a dog when you could have appeared in human form."

"Don't get me started on human form," I said, shaking my head. "It's awful, just awful. When May — she's the silver wyvern's mate and a really nice chick even if she is a doppelganger — when May made me take up human form a few months ago, everyone laughed at me. I don't think I'll ever get over the trauma of that experience."

"How very odd," Anastasia said, looking me over. "I can't imagine preferring a canine form over that of a human, but I'm sure you have your reasons."

Buttercup looked sour and mean at the same time, but she kept her piehole shut for the trip to the airport. Until the plane took off, that is.

"Mistress?" I was curled up on a love seat that sat along one side of the jet when Buttercup unsnapped herself from a big comfy chair and moved forward to where Anastasia was sitting with a book. "Are you all right? Mistress?"

"What's wrong with her?" I asked, hitting pause on the DVD I was watching. I slid off the seat and wandered forward, wondering if the old lady was scared of flying or something. I would reassure her that Drake's pilot was really good, and there was nothing to worry about over a quick trip to Paris.

"Mistress?"

"I think . . . Oh dear, I don't feel well. Don't feel well at all," Anastasia said groggily. "I can't seem to keep . . . eyes . . ."

"You're having some sort of an attack," Buttercup said briskly, shaking the old lady by the shoulders. "We will get you to a doctor immediately, but Mistress, the demon! If you are unable to command it, it will do who knows what heinous acts!"

"Hey!" I said, allowing a little blop of slobber to hit her shoe nearest me. "I don't do heinous! Not when I'm on vacation, anyway!"

"Mistress, you must make an effort!" Buttercup demanded.

Anastasia's eyes fluttered open, the faded blue of them cognizant but obviously sedated. A horrible, nasty suspicion filled me at the sight of her dilated pupils. "The demon . . . You must take charge."

"Now, wait a sec," I said, shoving my head in between them to try to sniff at Anastasia's breath. It looked to me like she'd been slipped a mickey. "No one needs to take charge of me. I'm a sixth-class demon. I'm not really bad. Besides, Aisling would skin me if she found out I did anything bad —"

"I am yours to command, Mistress," Buttercup said, grabbing me by the collar and hauling me back. "Tell me what you want."

"No, listen to me —" I started to say, but the old lady's eyes rolled back in her head as she said softly, "I grant you the authority given to me."

I stared in horror first at her, then at Buttercup as she straightened up, a victorious smile on her face.

"You drugged her!" I gasped, shocked to my toenails.

"You'll have a hard time proving that where you're going," she said, then waved her hands around in a hokey manner and said quickly, "Effrijim, I command you in the name of my mistress, in the name of your Guardian, and in the name of all that is good and right in the world. I banish your unclean being to the Akasha, where you belong!"

"Noooo!" I wailed halfway through her speech, but it did no good. One second I was standing next to a comatose old lady who thought I was distinguished, and the next I was next to a rocky outcropping that jutted up out of a sepia-toned landscape

328

filled with shadows, horror, and endless torment.

TWO

"Welcome to the Akasha. Is this your first time here?" a chirpy voice asked. "Would you like some introductory literature?"

I leaped to my feet and realized right off the bat that something truly horrendous had happened.

"Argh!" I yelled, lifting up my arms and staring with horrified shock at five long fingers at the end of each of the two arms. "I'm in human form again!"

"You certainly are," the perky voice said, a tinge of disapproval sounding as it added, "And you seem to have misplaced your clothes — by the love of the saints! Don't do that again!"

I straightened from where I had bent double to look at my feet, turning around to face the person to whom the voice belonged.

A little woman stood in front of me, one hand clapped over her eyes.

"Fires of Abaddon! I got sent to the midget section of the Akasha? I'm in human form in the midget section?"

An irritated look crossed the woman's face as she lowered her hand. "That term is offensive, and shows archaic and ignorant thinking. We prefer the term *little people,* not that there is a little-person section of the Akasha." She took a deep breath, then slapped another smile on her face, but this one looked awfully brittle. "So long as you promise never to bend over again when I am behind you, I am willing to overlook the fact that you are without clothing. Let's see, where was I? Oh, yes, here is a pamphlet that details the Akasha, including a brief history, notable members, and what you can expect over the centuries. Since you look confused, I'll give you a brief overview of the situation: The Akashic Plain, as it is more formally known, is what mortal beings think of as limbo, although in reality it's much more than that. Beings of both light and dark natures are banished here for eternal punishment without any hope of escape or reprieve."

I took the pamphlet she shoved at me. It was illustrated with faces of various beings in perpetual torment.

"The Akasha is governed by the Hashmallim, who are kind of a form of Otherworld police, although they are not bound by any rules except those of the Court of Divine Blood. Are you familiar with the Court?"

"I can't believe that rotten Butterbutt

changed me into a human when she banished me. She did it on purpose; I just know she did. Of all the double-dealing . . . Now what am I supposed to do? I can't stand around like this," I said, waving my hand toward my torso. A horrible thought struck me. I looked. "Satan's little imps! My package! It's . . . it's . . ."

The tiny little woman gave my package due consideration. "*Unimpressive* is the word that springs immediately to mind, and I use the word *springs* without any innuendo whatsoever."

"Aw, man! I'm human with a shortchanged knapsack!"

"Sir."

"What? Oh, yeah, I used to be a sprite," I said. "I'm familiar with the Court. So when did the Akasha get greeters?"

"A few years ago, when it was noticed that many people arrived here without a clue as to what to do next." She pursed her lips. "Some people appear to be even more clueless than others."

"Since this is the ultimate place of punishment, I figured suffering untold torments was pretty much the plan of the day," I said. "This is horrible. I can't stay like this until Aisling notices that I'm not in Paris. I gotta do something!"

"That is your own concern, sir. I should warn you that there is no way out except through intervention of the Sovereign, and it's not likely that it will bother itself with something like a sixth-class demon, now is it?" She tipped her head to the side as she beamed at me. "Especially not one that insists on prancing about the Akasha in the nude. Enjoy your eternity here. Ta-ta!"

She turned and picked her way through the rocky, jarring landscape until she disappeared behind a particularly jagged piece of rock that thrust upward out of the earth as if it had burst forth by immeasurable forces.

"I'd like to ta your ta, sister," I muttered. "Great. Just great. My first day on vacation, and I end up in the Akasha, naked, and in friggin' human form. Good thing I still have my cell phone. I'll just call Ash up and tell her she has to summon me the h-e-double-hockey-sticks out of here."

I picked up my backpack and had just extricated the cell phone Aisling gave me for my last birthday when a herd of five fur-and-leather-clad phantasms suddenly appeared and plowed right into me.

"Hrolf! Look! A naked demon!" One of them stopped long enough to give me the once-over. "What's it got here, then?"

"Hey!" I yelled when the phantasm snatched the cell phone right out of my hand.

"A demon? 'Ere? Roll 'im, Runolf," another of the phantasms said as they continued to move onward.

"Fires of Abaddon! Give that back! And my backpack! *Hey!*"

Runolf the phantasm — a ghost that's been banished and has no hope of ever regaining his or her ghostly self back — stopped long enough to jeer at me. "We're Vikings, demon. We stop for no man! Or . . . er . . . demon. Yar!"

"That's pirate-speak, not Viking-speak, you idiot!" I yelled as I started after him. Here's the thing, though — phantasms come from ghosts, right? So they aren't big in the corporeal department to begin with, and once they've been phantasmed, they're even less on the whole "can touch things in the plain of reality" scale. So while they could zoom around the place like a ghostly Viking blight, those of us bound to physical forms had to fight our way through a landscape that brought new meaning to the phrase *cut your feet to ribbons*. They were out of sight in a matter of a couple of seconds.

"Ow. Ow ow ow. Ow. Son of a sinner!

Now I have a rock shard stuck between my toes!"

I sat down and yelped, leaping up immediately. "What the — ass skewers? This is worse than Abaddon!" I moved over to a spot that was mostly free of sharp, rocky spikes and plopped down to suck on my sore toes. "Man, this is supposed to be my vacation. Not having fun! I wanna go home."

"At least you have a vacation," a voice spoke behind me. "I haven't had any such thing in . . . Oh, it must be seventy years now."

I peered over my shoulder, eyeing the woman who perched on a rock behind me. "It ain't much of a vacation, sister. Who're you?"

"My name is Titania," the woman said, giving me one of those sultry-eyed once-overs that nymphs were so known for. "You're naked. You're a demon and you're naked."

"Yeah, and you're a nymph. I didn't know they sent you guys to the Akasha. I thought they just ripped off your wings or beat you with your halo if you did something bad."

She made a face. "You're thinking of faeries. They are the wicked ones. If I ever catch that bastard, lying, two-timing

Oberon, I shall show him that he can't just throw me away like this. I have rights, too, you know!"

"Titania, huh? What do your friends call you for short? Titty?" I snickered to myself.

She straightened up and gave me a look that would have melted my guts if I weren't a demon. "They call me Titania!"

"Gotcha. Wait a sec . . . Oberon? Titania?" I kicked my brain into high and dug through some old memories. "*Midsummer's Night Dream?*"

"Pfft." She examined a rose-tipped fingernail. "That Will Shakespeare got it all wrong. He said I was a faery. As if! He totally dissed us nymphs, and let me tell you, the nymphood was not happy about that."

"Yeah, I heard you guys can be kind of . . . eh . . . militant," I said, wondering if she wanted to use those long nails to hit all my scritchy spots. Then I remembered I didn't have scritchy spots. At least, not in this repulsive form. I glared at my package.

"What on earth are you doing?" she asked.

"Glaring at my crotch. A Guardian did this to me," I said, mourning the loss of my fabulous doggy form.

She, too, stared at my groin. "She has a lot to answer for."

"You said it. I wish I could do something to pay her back. Hey! Nymphs! You guys are all militant and badass, right? I could have some of your buddies beat up the Guardian who screwed me over."

"We prefer the term *proactive* to *militant*." Titania pulled out a nail file and tended to a fingernail. "And if you had spent your life as underestimated and overlooked as we have been, you'd be proactive about making sure people got their facts right, too."

"I'm a demon," I answered, carefully sitting down and examining my abused foot. "I am all over underestimated."

"Anyway, Shakespeare got it all wrong," she continued. "Oberon isn't king of the faeries at all. He's just an advocate for the Court of Divine Blood."

"Advocate? Like a lawyer?"

"An obscenely vile one, yes."

"Yeah? So what did you do that you got tossed in here?" I asked.

"Oberon, my former lover and disgusting lint in the underbelly of the worst sort of beings, decided to dump me, a priestess in the house of Artemis, for a naiad. Can you believe it? He dumped me for a water trollop!" Her expression went from outraged to calculating in a split second. "But he'd just better watch out, because the minute I'm out of here, I'm going to get my pound of flesh."

"Ew," I said, wrinkling my nose. "Wait — a human pound of flesh or meat from, oh, say, the rump of a corn-fed Black Angus cow? Because the latter sounds really good right about now. Especially with a whisky barbecue sauce."

"If I could just find a way out, I could rally the sisters and we'd have our revenge!"

"On who, Shakespeare? Got news for you, babe. He's dead."

"No, not him. Oberon."

I thought. I always think better sitting down. "Not that I want to rush you, since I've got at least ten days before Aisling comes back from her cruise and finds out that witch on two legs drugged her boss just so she could banish me, but I'm a bit confused. I get that boy toy dumped you in here when he was hooking up with a naiad, but how does that translate to you nymphs going to war against him?"

"He's Oberon," she said, just like that made sense. When I scrunched up my face in an attempt to figure that out, she added, "He didn't just have *me* banished to the Akasha — he had *all* nymphs banished from the Court in order to curry favor for his own kind."

"Oh, yeah," I said, dredging up a memory. "I think I remember reading something about that. You guys got run out of town because you were causing all sorts of trouble."

"We did nothing of the sort. Oberon just made it look like we did," she said, leaping to her feet and shaking her fist at the air. "He will pay for that! He will pay for —" Her words suddenly stopped.

I lifted an eyebrow in a move just as smooth as the one Drake makes whenever Aisling says something outrageous.

"You're a demon," she said.

"You got that right, baby cakes. Sixth class," I said, winking. "But if you are interested in hooking up with me, I gotta tell you that I'm in a relationship right now with a Welsh Corgi named Cecile. She has the cutest little fuzzy butt you ever did see."

She stared at me just like I said something weird.

"You're a demon," she repeated. "Thus, you can get me out of here."

"If I could get anyone out of here, it would be me, because I have a score to settle with a conniving apprentice Guardian, but I can't, so I won't."

"Yes, you can. You're a creature of Abaddon. You can't be dictated to by the Court.

That means you can get out."

"The Court doesn't have any say over me, but I've been sent here, in a roundabout way, by my demon lord. I can only get out if she summons me, and she's not going to know what that witch Butterfat did until she gets back and finds out I'm not with Amelie or Anastasia."

"There has to be another way!"

"Well, yeah, the Hashmallim guarding the door could let me out, but that's never happened, so it's not worth thinking about."

"Oh!" she said, stamping her foot and pointing to a spot in the distance. "Don't you dare cross me, demon! I will make your life a living hell if you don't get me out of here!"

"Look, sister, I just said —"

"Do it!" she bellowed.

Thirty hours later I gave in to her gigantic ongoing hissy fit and headed over to the circle of Akasha, the center of the whole place, where three Hashmallim stood guard over the entrance. It was an ugly spot, like the rest of the Akasha, nothing but sharp jagged rocks with dead-looking scrubby plants that were the same shade of sepia as the dirt.

"Hi, guys," I said as I got up to the nearest Hashmallim. If you've never seen one of these guys, they're Freak City with a capital Freak. They look like something that Jim Henson would have dreamed up after a night of hitting the opium pipe: tall and gaunt figures draped in black, but not really black, some sort of living black that moved and shifted, and oh yeah — they had no faces. Seriously freaky. "How they hangin'? Er . . . that's assuming you have any to hang. So, this nymph named Titania and I were wondering if we could get out of Dodge. She's got some vengeance thing, and I want to give a trainee Guardian what for."

The Hashmallim didn't say anything. He just stood there and stared at me. Kind of. If he'd had eyes, he would have been staring me down. Then again, maybe he was looking at my package. "Now, I know you guys have rules and everything, so Titty and I —"

"Don't call me Titty!" came the echo of a roar that rolled down from a nearby rocky hilltop.

"We are happy to make it worth your while, if you know what I mean," I said, dropping my voice so the other Hashmallim couldn't hear. "I've got a credit card. Well, OK, it's actually Aisling's that she lets me use on TV shopping channels, but still, I know her PIN — I can pull out a wad of cash big enough to choke a behemoth. So whatcha say? Shall we talk turkey?"

The Hashmallim stood there and said nothing. The bastard.

By the time I ran through everything that Titania and I could think of to offer as a bribe — up to and including her sexual favors, and a sweater woven from hair brushed from my gorgeous coat — two hours had passed, and we were still no closer to getting out.

"Look, I don't want to get tough with you. I will if I have to, but you can trust me on this, it won't be pretty."

The Hashmallim remained silent, but it was a mocking kind of silence, the kind that just dared me to try him.

So I did.

It took three days, but eventually, the Hashmallim cried mercy, and opened a rend in the fabric of time and space, shoving Titania and me through it.

"Do not return," it said in its creepy, wheezy voice, then slammed shut the rend. "And do not ever sing that song again!"

"That was brilliant," Titania said, her eyes giving me a long, considering look. "I would have never thought that singing the same song for seventy hours straight would be enough to break a Hashmallim, but you did it. What exactly *was* that song?"

" 'My Humps.' Effective, huh?"

"Extremely so. I thought the last time when you wiggled your butt on the Hashmallim and asked him what he was going to do with his junk that he was going to scream. Well done, demon. Very well done." She rubbed her hands and looked around the busy city street we had been dumped out on. It was Helsinki (per Titania's request), and although it was close to midnight, there were a surprising number of people wandering around. Several of them gave me an odd look.

"What's wrong, you never seen a naked demon?" I asked a woman who stopped and stared.

She looked startled and hurried off.

"OK, I fulfilled my part of our bargain — now it's your turn. You gotta get me to Paris pronto so I can salvage something of my vacation before Aisling gets back."

"A nymph always honors her promises," Titania said, grabbing my wrist and hauling me after her down the sidewalk. "But first, revenge!"

THREE

It turns out they have laws in Helsinki about people walking around the city buck naked. Twenty-four hours after I was arrested, Titania bailed me out of jail, and shortly after that we were on a train headed for a small town in the countryside where she assured me her ex would be celebrating.

"He always loved this area for *juhannus*," she explained as the countryside whizzed past us. It was night, but because of the midnight sun thing that happened in the far north, it wasn't dark out at all. "We celebrated it here for centuries, so I'm certain he'll be here. The nymphood is on their way, so we'll — what's wrong?"

I squirmed in the seat. "It's my codpiece. I don't think it fits."

She rolled her eyes. "Look, you said you wanted some clothes so you wouldn't be arrested again, and I got you some clothes. I'm sorry if it's not what you like, but there's no time to go shopping for you. We have to get out to the *juhannus* so we can smite Oberon."

"Did you have to go shopping at a leather fetish store?" I asked, squirming again so I could adjust the leather thong, that, along with a fishnet tank top and the metal studded codpiece, made up what Titania referred to as clothing. "You couldn't have gotten me something from the Gap? There wasn't a Polo store around?"

The look she gave me resembled ones Aisling had been known to send my way. "If you have quite finished, demon, I am trying to explain to you what will happen."

"You don't have to; I was eavesdropping when you were on the phone in that leather shop. You called up your nymph buddies, and you intend to blow into your ex's party and beat the crap out of him. It's not very complicated."

"Perhaps not, but it will be delicious," she said, almost purring. Kind of like how a tiger purrs before it pounces.

"So where does the part come in where you get me to Paris?" I asked, trying to adjust the codpiece. "Man, it's bad enough I have a substandard package. This thing is squashing everything together into one blob. Here, take a look and see if the blood has been cut off to it."

She held up a hand to stop me from unstrapping the codpiece. "I do not have time to examine your genital blobs. Oberon is a master of manipulation. We must plan our attack down to the smallest detail."

I sighed and slumped back in the seat, listening with only half my attention as she detailed her plans.

Two hours later we met up in a park with the local nymphs that she had rallied, ready to set off on motorbikes to a campsite located on a small lake in a northern region of Finland.

"Let the world hear of the Nymph Offensive of 2010!" one of them called, donning a pair of brass knuckles.

"Nymphs unite! Together we shall challenge Oberon and his fae followers, and show them that we are a force to be reckoned with!" Titania yelled, standing on a box. "We will have vengeance for all those centuries of abuse! At long last, we shall prove our worth! Let there be no quarter for the faeries! They will know once and for all the true glory that is the nymphhood!"

The thirty or so nymphs who had managed to get to Finland on a day's notice yelled their support, shaking their fists and various weapons they had acquired. Some of the nymphs slapped on wrist guards and knuckle protectors; others brandished heavy-duty walking sticks. One waved what looked like a toilet plunger.

"But . . ." One of the nymphs, the one nearest me, looked at me doubtfully. "But we are not all nymphs."

All thirty women considered me. If I'd

been in my normal form, I would have asked for belly scritches. But somehow, I had a feeling these babes wouldn't take that request well. I'm perceptive that way.

"Jim is just here because I owe him a boon for my release," Titania said slowly. "He is not really one of us."

"The Titster speaks the truth," I said, nodding. "I'm just here to hang out until she's creamed her ex, then she's going to get me to Paris."

The nymphs frowned at me. I started to edge away. One nymph frowning wasn't much to think about — thirty of them, armed and annoyed at men in general, were another matter. "Sorry, did I say Titster? I meant her high and gracious nymphness, Titania the Uber."

"We cannot have a non-nymph in a Nymph Offensive," one of the chicks said, frowning some more at me.

"Hey, I'm happy to stay back and let you guys kick serious faery butt," I said, plopping down on the grass. "I'll just stay here and wait for you guys to get done, 'K?"

"You must come with us," Titania said in a huffy voice. "We had a deal. You said you would help me seek my revenge on Oberon. You must do that, or I will not aid you in returning to Paris."

"Yeah, well" — I twanged my codpiece — "I ain't no nymph, and if you have a rule that only nymphs can go along to whoop-ass, then it's not gonna happen."

"We can make him an honorary nymph," the frowny chick said.

Titania looked thoughtful as all the other women voiced their approval of this plan. "I don't see why that wouldn't work. Although he must change his form into that of a female."

"No way, sister," I said, backing up. "I don't even like human form, but there's no way in Abaddon you're going to get me to change into a girl."

"Why not?" Titania asked, narrowing her eyes as she stalked toward me. "Do you have something against women?"

"Like that's even possible? It's just not a good idea for me to take on girl form. 'Cause if I did, all I'd do is jump up and down and watch my boobs bounce."

The nymphs stared at me with accusation in their eyes.

"Not like I've ever done that or anything," I added quickly, then cleared my throat. "So! Men. They're scum, right? Let's go beat up Ti-Ti's boyfriend."

Titania made me ride on her motorcycle after that, in order, she said, to save the nymphs from my lust. They made me an honorary nymph, however, which I hope Aisling never hears about, because my life will be one long pun if she does.

We got to the campsite where the faeries were celebrating midsummer an hour or so later. I knew it had to be the right place because not only were there a bunch of bonfires, there were also Renaissance-faire-ish chicks wandering around in long, gauzy dresses, with garlands of flowers in their hair. That, and everyone present was a faery.

"Look at them," snarled Titania from where the Nymph Offensive was hidden behind several trees circling the lakeside camp spot. "Just look at how they fling themselves around the bonfires as if they, and not we, were beings of the earth!"

"They really do bring new meaning to the word *frolic,* don't they?" I asked, watching the faeries dance like monkeys on crack around the bonfires. "Hey, you can see right through those gauzy dresses when the light is behind them. Hoobah."

"They think they are chosen because Oberon has had us cast out of grace," Titania sneered, "but we will not stand for this anymore!"

"We are of the earth! We will take back what is ours!" Frowny Nymph said. "We will rule midsummer as we were meant to rule it!"

"There will be no quarter for faeries!" Titania said, accepting a long, thin sword from one of the other nymphs. She held it aloft as if it were a beacon. "We will take no prisoners! We will have no mercy!"

"Babe, just between you and me, I think you've seen *Lord of the Rings* one too many times," I said, leaning toward her so everyone wouldn't overhear. "Viggo you ain't. If you want my advice —"

She didn't. "This is war, my sisters!" she interrupted me, waving her sword toward the innocent faeries tripping the firelight fantastic. "It is them or us! All I ask is that you leave that lying traitor Oberon for me! Nymphhood — arise!"

On that battle cry, the group of women charged forward, causing immediate panic in the frolicking faeries. They ran screaming away from us, hands waving in the air as they raced around like winged Ren-faire-clad chickens, bumping into each other, the air thick with spurts of faery dust.

It was chaos, sheer chaos, and although one of the nymphs shoved a rake in my hand before she charged off, wielding a chunk of garden hose like it was nunchuks, I stayed in the back and tried to keep out of the way of maddened nymphs.

"Nice . . . er . . . wings," I said as one flower-bedecked faery in a translucent gown ran past me screaming at the top of her lungs, a nymph in hot pursuit. I wandered over to where two other nymphs had a male faery pinned and were taking turns beating him over the head with a bouquet of flowers he'd evidently strapped to his hip (male faeries aren't, as a rule, the Otherworld's most manliest men). "Two against one — I like your style," I told the nymphs, giving them a thumbs-up as I moved past.

It didn't take long for the nymphs to wreak complete havoc among the fae folk. Ten minutes after they charged in, the whole motley gang of faeries were huddled together in one glittery, gauzy group. Muffled sobs and murmurs of comfort were periodically heard, but they gave the nymphs who stood over them, brandishing their weapons, no further problem.

None of them did except the head faery, that is. Titania had squared off with her ex next to the biggest bonfire. He was a big blond dude with feathered hair and a garland of ivy leaves on his head. "There you are!"

"Titania! My love! My darling! My one

true . . . er . . . one! How I have missed you!"

"You lying bastard!" Titania said as she marched around him. Two of the nymphs held his arms while she circled him, the sword pointed right at him. He looked worried. "You missed me? You're the one who had me banished to the Akasha, just so you could screw some watery naiad!"

"That was all a mistake. It was a glamour! Nothing more! She temporarily deranged my mind, but as soon as I came out of it and realized what she had forced me to do, I moved heaven and earth to get you out and back to my arms, my dearest, loveliest Titania."

"Which explains why you had all nymphs cast out of the Court, eh?" Titania asked, making another circuit around him. This time she poked him here and there with the tip of the sword. She didn't actually draw blood, but he jumped each time the point touched him.

"It was the glamour!" he said, starting to sweat. "I swear to you, I would never have done anything to harm you or your girls —"

The sword poked deep enough into his skin to leave a drop of blood glowing on its tip.

Oberon squawked. "Ladies, I mean ladies!

I would never do anything to harm you or your ladies! You know that, my dearest darling. I live for you, my love. My heart beats for you, only for you. Take my crown, take my wings, take everything away from me — everything but your love."

"Aw, man, I feel that chili dog I had for dinner coming back on me," I said, rubbing my belly. "You don't think you could lay it on a little more thick, do you, bud? I bet another round of you telling Tittles how much you love her would have me refunding."

Oberon's eyes flashed at me for a second before he made puppy-dog eyes at Titania.

"A glamour, you say." Titania stopped in front of him, her eyes assessing what she saw.

"It had to be that, my darling, my beauteous one. You know I have devoted my whole life to you."

I didn't believe it, but evidently Titania fell for it. She lowered her sword and allowed Oberon to scoop her up in his arms, murmuring all sorts of lovey-dovey crap that anyone with half a mind could tell was total bull.

"I think I really may ralph," I told the nearest nymph, the one who frowned so much. She looked a bit green around the gills, too. "Hey, Ti! You gonna get me to Paris before you and the Obster there go off to the land of Boinksville?"

"Certainly. Cobs, take the demon to the portal in Helsinki and see that it's sent to Paris. Now, Oberon, about the repeal on the ban of nymphs at the Court . . ."

The pair of them wandered off. "How long do you give that?" I asked the nymph named Cobs as she gestured for me to follow her. The other nymphs were releasing the wad of damp faeries, all of whom twitched whenever one of the nymphs came too close.

"Oberon is a smart man. I doubt if he'll cross Titania again. Especially after he sees what she's brought with her," she said, nodding as another nymph carrying a box ran past us toward Titania.

"Really? Why, what's in the box?"

She smiled as she swung a leg over her motorcycle. "Wing clippers."

FOUR

"Paris at last!" I said as I got to my feet. Portalling is never easy on the bones, although most portal companies have wised up and put a stack of padding at the recipient portal, so at least you don't actually break anything when you arrive. "Ow. Think

353

I pulled my spleen or something. Still, Paris at last! Hold on, Cecile, daddy is on his way!"

The chick at the portal company's desk barely even looked up from her magazine as I gave her a cheery grin before I headed out the door. I stopped on the doorstep, breathing deeply of the diesel-laden, slightly smoggy, damp, and mildew-smelling air of Paris that I knew and loved. "Paris at last," I repeated happily, then took one step down to the street, and was promptly grabbed by a couple of strong-armed thugs and tossed into the back of an unmarked black van.

"Fires of Abaddon!" I shouted into someone's armpit. I didn't see whose until I was rudely shoved backward with a word that the speaker should have been ashamed of. "What the . . . Hey! Don't I know you?"

"Get off me!" The woman who was on the floor of the van kicked out at me as she got to her feet and took a seat on the bench that ran along one side of the van. "Effrijim! I thought I detected the stench of a demon."

"Ow! No kicking the codpiece! Until I get put back into my normal form, this package is all I have. Anyen? What in the name of Bael's ten toes are you doing here? I thought you ghedes only hung out in the Caribbean.

What are you doing in Paris?"

"What do you think I am doing?" Anyen answered. She was tall and thin, her skin as black as midnight, dressed in a long black coat and wearing black glasses, and possessing a very cool Haitian accent. "I'm here to collect revenants, of course. We're building an undead army, and it's impossible to do that in Haiti anymore. Ever since that damned Internet became popular, everyone knows how to protect themselves from us. It's almost more than a decent, hardworking soul-stealer can bear, let me tell you!"

She sniffled just like she was going to cry, but everyone knew ghedes couldn't cry. It had something to do with their origins.

"Yeah, well, life's tough all over. Take mine, for instance," I said, pulling myself up to the opposite bench. The van we were in had a solid wall between the cargo and driver's area, but judging by the motion, I gathered we were en route to somewhere. "One minute I'm on vacation, about to see the love of my life, and the next — whammo. It all goes to Abaddon. Who nabbed us, do you know?"

She spat out a word that I figured wasn't very nice. "That new Venediger. I heard that she was cleaning up Paris, kidnapping innocent beings just because we have dark origins. She has squads of her minions watching the portal shops, abducting anyone she doesn't deem fit to be in the mortal world. It is outrageous, a violation of my rights, and I shall most definitely be complaining to the Akashic League about it! Only they have the right to hold a ghede, and they would not be so foolish to do so."

"Oh, the Venediger," I said, relaxing. "Jovana. No sweat, then. We're old buds, we are. My demon lord helped put her in power. I'm sure once she knows it's me her goon squad picked up, she'll have me released."

Anyen made a face like she didn't believe me at all, and said nothing more till we arrived at a hoppin' nightclub named Goety and Theurgy.

"Ah, G&T," I said as the two guys who nabbed me hauled me inside the club. Two others emerged to bring Anyen. "Brings back old memories. Hey, there's a buffet here now? Can we swing by it? I'm starving."

The bully boys didn't stop. They just hauled me past the buffet, past the dance floor, and down a dimly lit flight of stairs to an equally dimly lit basement.

"Guys? The V is an old buddy of mine. You might want to tell her that it's me you have, so she doesn't get too pissed with you when she finds out you're doing this."

Neither man said anything.

"Name's Jim. Well, Effrijim, really, but that's kinda girly, so I just go with Jim. Jovana knows me."

They still didn't say anything. They hauled me across the basement and, without one single word, dumped me into a small room, tossed Anyen in after me, and slammed the door shut.

"I will have your heads for this!" she bellowed as they locked the door. She pounded on it, making all sorts of threats, but eventually she stopped and glared at me.

"Why are you looking at me like that?" I asked, kicking aside a cardboard box and plopping down on a dirty-looking cot that sat in the corner. "I didn't lock us in here."

"The Venediger is your friend. You said she was."

"Maybe they're going up to tell her who I am," I said, rubbing my sore toes. Box-kicking while you're barefoot isn't the best of ideas. "Maybe they'll be back all groveling and with plates of buffet food in an attempt to curry favor with me. Oooh, curry. Devils and demons, am I hungry."

"That doesn't help me any," she said in a rather surly tone. "It is your duty to get me out of here."

"Sorry, sister, not again. I just went through one big escape scene — I'm not going to do another. Not for a really long time. I don't think I could stand to sing about my lady lumps one more time."

Anyen turned her back on me, but only after she lit me up one side and down another. It's a good thing I'm immortal, or those curses she'd been flinging at me might have done some damage.

"I'm going to die of hunger. I'm going to starve to death. When Aisling finally tracks me down, she's going to find nothing but a skeleton left," I complained a good eighteen hours later. "You think this mattress is edible?"

Anyen, who had kicked me off the mattress and claimed it for her own, rolled over just long enough to glare at me. I was about to point out that I would share it with her when the noise of a key in the lock had me leaping to my feet. "Yay, Jovana finally heard I was here, and she's going to let me out! That or they're going to bring us some food. Either works for me."

"The Venediger wishes to see you," one of the bully boys said as he opened the door.

I blinked in the relatively bright light. "Yeah, I figured she'd want to make her

apologies to me in person," I said, sauntering nonchalantly out of the room. "Can we
stop by the buffet first? I'm about to faint
with hunger."

"Effrijim!" Anyen belted out my name so
it had the force to send me reeling a few
steps. "I will not be left here! You must take
me with you!"

I thought for a moment about telling her
to suck it up — I am a demon, after all —
but I was feeling generous, so I nodded
toward her and asked the nearest guard,
"Anyen wants to come with. You don't
mind, do you?"

The guard shrugged. "She may come as
well, although the Venediger will not be
ready for her until tomorrow."

"Told ya the V was my good friend," I said
to Anyen as she shoved me out of the way,
jerking her arm out of the guard's hand.
She stalked in front of me, tossing her head
once and saying merely, "We shall see."

We weren't led into the bar proper —
which was closed, since it was now early
morning — but into one of the back rooms.
It was some sort of a conference room, with
a long table that had been draped with a
black cloth, and three people who stood
talking quietly in a small clutch.

"Hey, nice to see ya again," I said, waving

359

at the woman to whom the other two looked the second I stepped in the door. She was small and well dressed and had a pageboy haircut that always made Aisling giggle. "I see you're still going in for those power suits, huh?"

Jovana, once a mage and now the person in charge of the Otherworld in Europe, aka the Venediger, stared at me as if I had an extra testicle.

"Oh, man, you don't recognize me, do you? Yeah, the human form is a bit awkward, huh? But it's really me, Jim. Aisling's demon. You probably remember me in Newfie form. Big black dog, luxurious coat, package that would do a pony proud. Remember now?"

"Take the sacrifice to the table," she said, waving toward me before turning her back on me to fuss over something behind her.

"Oooh, breffies?" I said, hurrying forward. "I'm starved . . . Hey! *Sacrifice?*"

The two burly dudes grabbed me by either arm and jerked me up onto the table. When Jovana turned back toward me, she held a wavy-bladed silver dagger in her hand. I had a really awful feeling I knew just what she was planning on doing with it. "Fires of Abaddon! You're nuts, lady!"

"Silence!" she commanded, and gestured

toward one of the flunkies standing against the wall.

A man came forward, pulled out a scroll, and read. "Demon of unknown origins found arriving via portal in the Latin Quarter on Tuesday afternoon."

"Jim," I said quickly, eyeing that nasty dagger. "My name is Jim!"

"You are charged with violation of the Roaming Demon Ordinance of 2008."

"What?" I squawked, trying to squirm out of the two thugs' grip. "What Roaming Demon Ordinance?"

"In accordance with the laws sanctified by the Venediger, your mortal form will be destroyed, and your being sent back to Abaddon where you belong."

"You can't do that!" I yelled, watching as the Venediger nodded and a Guardian came forward, pulling out a gold stick and beginning to scribe a circle around me. "Aisling is going to be really pissed!"

The Guardian paused, looking up. I'd never seen her before, but evidently she'd heard of Ash. "Aisling? Aisling Grey?" she asked.

"Yeah, that's her. Aisling is my boss." I craned my neck to glare up at Jovana. "The same person who gave you your job!"

Jovana narrowed her eyes on me for a few

seconds. "It is true that Aisling Grey has a demon under her control. But I have heard that the demon's preferred form is that of a dog."

"Man alive, doesn't anyone listen to me?" I complained, trying to pull my arm free.

Jovana nodded to the guard, who let go of me. I yanked my hand free from the other one and sat up, rubbing my wrists. "I just got done telling you that I'm normally in dog form, but another Guardian ordered me into human form because she knew it would tick me off."

Six pairs of eyes considered me as I slid off the table to my feet. I straightened my codpiece, dusted off my leather thong, and raised an eyebrow while I waited for the apologies to flow.

The Guardian rose from where she'd been kneeling. "If this demon speaks the truth —"

"I may be a lot of things, but I've never been a liar," I said grumpily.

"If it speaks the truth, then I want no part of this," she continued, putting away her gold stick. "Aisling Grey is one of the most powerful Guardians in the Guardians' Guild. She is a savant, especially gifted, and someone I do not wish to cross."

"Anyen will tell you who I am," I said,

waving at the ghede.

She glared back at me.

"Hey, I helped you, now it's time for you to repay me," I told her.

"Oh, very well. The demon does not lie. It is Effrijim. I have known it for several centuries," she said, albeit kinda grudgingly.

"There, see? All's well," I said, heading for the door. "I'll tell Ash you send her love, 'K? See ya round."

"Halt!" the Venediger said, and instantly the two guards were in front of the door, their eyes narrow little slits as they frowned at me. "I do not accept this foul thing's statement."

"Foul thing!" Anyen said, starting forward. I grabbed her before she could jump the Venediger. "I am not a —"

"Hackles down," I said softly. "Now isn't the time unless you want to get us both tossed back into that cell in the basement."

"That is exactly where you are going," the Venediger said, putting down the dagger. She looked at it regretfully for a moment before pinning me back with a glare that stripped the hair from my toes. "You will remain there until I can speak with the Guardian Aisling Grey to verify your identity."

"No way!" I protested. "I've got . . . Let

me count . . . Man, I've only got one day left of my vacation. I'm not going to spend it sitting in that room with a pissed-off ghede!"

"Nor will I go back to that squalid little room!" Anyen declared.

"Fine." Jovana shrugged. "Then we will perform your release ceremony now. There will be no Guardian to object to you being sent back to Abaddon, I trust."

Anyen's eyes opened up really wide when the Venediger picked up the dagger again.

"You know what?" I asked Anyen, taking a deep breath and thinking about Cecile's warm, furry little ears.

"What?" she asked.

"We're immortal."

She blinked at me for a second, but that's all I gave her. I grabbed her arm, lowered my head, and charged the Venediger. She sprang to the side, out of the way, just as I figured she would. Anyen and I kept going through, right past the Venediger, the two others staring at us in surprise, and on through the window that opened onto a small garden.

Anyen was fast on her feet, luckily, and although my chest and arms and legs were cut by the glass as I went through the window, we both landed on our feet and took off running.

The Venediger's guards, however, were mortal, and they were less than thrilled about leaping into a mass of broken glass. They were slower getting through the window, and by the time they got to the garden, we were racing down the back alley to freedom.

We split up not long after, Anyen making a snarky remark about me slowing her down.

"You're welcome," I yelled after her as she disappeared into the Tuilleries. "Hope you don't get a really nasty case of zombie rot while you're raising the dead!"

It took me a couple more hours before I finally lost the guard who persisted in following me, so it wasn't until afternoon that I staggered exhausted, bleeding, and dirty from a fall into the Seine through the door of a familiar shop. "Cecile! Baby! I'm here!"

The woman behind the counter at the shop stared at me in stark surprise. "Jim? Is that you?"

"Hiya, Amelie. Yeah, it's me. Where's Cecile?"

"She . . . she . . ." Amelie seemed to be struck speechless, because she simply pointed upstairs.

"Thanks. Mind if I use your shower? I had

a run-in with the Venediger, and I'm all ooky with blood and stuff. See you later," I called as I dashed through the back room, then up the stairs that led to the apartment in which Amelie and Cecile lived.

Cecile was also a bit taken aback by my appearance, her eyes going even more bug-eyed than they normally were when I scooped her up in my arms and kissed her all over her adorable pointy little snout. "My darling, my adorable one! We might only have one day left together, but I will make it a day you won't forget. I promise I'll get back to my normal form as soon as possible," I told her when she tried to squirm out of my hold, her little stubby legs kicking wildly. "This one sucks big-time, huh? Don't worry, my beloved. I'll soon be your big, handsome Jim again. But first, a shower."

The sound of voices drifted in to me when I stepped out of the shower, drying myself on one of Amelie's soft towels. I looked at the codpiece and thong, but decided I just couldn't wear them any longer. By the time I headed out of Amelie's bedroom, I realized that I knew the voices.

"— came back early because Drake insisted on seeing the doctor. It turned out to be nothing, of course, just a case of the sniffles."

"Any illness in infants can be serious," Drake's voice rumbled in response. "I was not easy in my mind until the children had been seen by a proper doctor."

"Anyway, we decided it wasn't worth hauling the babies back to the yacht, so we figured we'd just swing by and pick up Jim and head back to London. Is it here?"

"Aw, man!" I said, marching in to the room. "You're early? Fine! Just ruin my plans!"

The silence that greeted my arrival in Amelie's sunny living room was thick enough to cut with a butter knife.

"Er . . ." Amelie said, her expression kind of shocked.

"Jim! What on earth are you doing in that form!" Aisling demand, her hands on her hips. "And naked!"

Drake narrowed his green eyes at me and muttered something about knowing better than to leave me on my own.

"It's not my fault," I told them both. "You can ask that no-good, conniving Guardian why I'm like this."

"I certainly will," Aisling said, staring.

Drake slapped his hand over her eyes and glared at me. "Put some clothing on, or I'll see to it you have nothing left with which to shock Aisling."

She giggled.

"I don't want to wear clothing! I want my old form back. Let me change back, Ash. Please."

"All right, you can change into your normal form," she said, giggling again. "But I want to hear everything that happened. Only not right now — we had a message from Nora when we got to Drake's house."

I sighed with relief as I shifted back to my fabulous Newfoundland form, making a quick check to be sure everything was the way I had left it. "Boy, did I miss you, tail. And package. And four paws. And —"

"Enough," Drake said, bowing to Amelie. "You will excuse us if we leave in haste. Aisling is anxious to get back to London."

"Yes, I am. Come on, Jim! There's work to be done," Aisling said in her chipper voice as she took Drake's hand. "Nora said there's been a huge outbreak of kobolds and imps and all sorts of nasties in the last few days, and she's overwhelmed and needs our help in cleaning everything up. It'll be like old times tackling them together, huh?"

"Oh, man," I said, covering my face with my paws. "Can't I just sleep here for a couple of days? Cecile and I —"

"Don't be silly," she said, cuffing me on

the shoulder. "You've had ten days together; that's long enough. Besides, there's nothing like a bit of action after a nice, long, relaxing vacation to get your blood pumping again, now is there?"

THIN WALLS

CHRISTOPHER GOLDEN

Christopher Golden is the author of such novels as *The Myth Hunters, The Boys Are Back in Town, Of Saints and Shadows,* and (with Tim Lebbon) *The Map of Moments.* He has also written books for teens and young adults, including *Poison Ink, Soulless,* and the thriller series Body of Evidence. He cowrote the lavishly illustrated novel *Baltimore, or, The Steadfast Tin Soldier and the Vampire* with Mike Mignola. Golden was born and raised in Massachusetts, where he still lives with his family. His original novels have been published in more than fourteen languages in countries around the world. Please visit him at www.christophergolden.com.

Tim Graham woke slowly, the sounds of raucous sex drawing him up into the waking world. He frowned sleepily and looked around in the darkness of his hotel room, as though he expected to find the perpetrators of the disturbance screwing acrobatically on one of the floral-patterned chairs near the balcony slider. He liked to keep a room as dark as possible for sleeping — something he'd picked up from Jenny — so the heavy curtains were drawn and the only light came from the ghostly glow of numbers on the alarm clock. If someone *had* been screwing in his room, he would barely have been able to see them.

But the sounds, he quickly realized, came from the room next door. The bed in there must have been head to head with his own, for he heard the lovers far too well, their grunts and moans and exhortations, the slap of flesh on flesh, the rhythmic tap of the headboard against the wall. Most hotel chains had long since learned to attach the headboards to the wall so they wouldn't knock against it when guests got busy, but apparently that bit of logic had been over-looked here.

At first, Tim smiled. Half asleep, he felt a mixture of envy and arousal.

"Yes, like that!" the woman sighed, repeating it several times, making it her mantra. Then she started to plead, almost whining, urging him on.

After several minutes of this, Tim's erection brought him fully awake. He closed his eyes and put a pillow over his head, trying to force himself back to sleep, but he could not drown out the sounds. His pulse quickened. He wondered how long they could go on. Unless the guy was young — or old and using Viagra to regain his youth — it shouldn't take that long.

He had heard people having sex in hotel rooms before. More than once, he and Jenny had *been* the people making too much noise. One time an angry old woman had banged on the wall and shouted at them to keep it down, and they had laughed and made love even more vocally. Tim had never banged on the wall himself. He didn't like the idea of interrupting, and he had always felt a little thrill at overhearing.

So he listened, his erection painfully in need of attention. Jenny had been gone for just over a year. He was tempted to masturbate, but the image of a sad little pervert jerking off on the other side of the wall disturbed him, so instead he got up and went to the bathroom. With the light on, the bathroom fan drowned out most of the noise from next door. He splashed water on his face and looked in the mirror at the dark circles under his eyes. He had to wait for his erection to subside before he could aim for the toilet, but at last he managed to piss, then washed his hands and returned to bed.

The fucking continued.

"Christ," he muttered.

He wanted sleep more than cheap thrills. The voyeur inside him seemed to have given up and gone to sleep, because though his cock stirred and rose once more, it only achieved half mast, apparently tempered by his growing irritation.

He laid his head back on the pillow and stared up at the darkness of the ceiling. Had they heard him go to the bathroom? The sound of the fan and the flush of the toilet? If so, it had not troubled them at all. If anything, the lovers had gotten louder. The man started to call her filthy names, making her his slut, his whore, his bitch, and she rose to what she seemed to consider a challenge, agreeing with him at every turn. If he'd ever tried that with Jenny, he would never have had sex again, but for these two it seemed a huge turn-on.

Long minutes passed. Tim's throat was dry, his breath coming a little quicker as his erection returned, more painful than ever. He could not help but start to imagine the scene taking place next door, picturing positions and stiletto heels. In his mind the guy was a blur, but the woman had a body sculpted by desire, with round, heavy, real breasts and hip bones perfect for gripping.

He rolled his eyes and shook his head, not daring to look at the clock, though he felt sure he had been awake at least half an hour by now, and had no idea how long they had been going at it before they had woken him.

And still they went on.

Tim lay on his side, listening closely. There was no alternative except leaving the room or hiding in the bathroom, and so he surrendered to eavesdropping, trying to pick out each word. Mostly it was repetition, dirty talk, and baby-oh-baby-come-on from him and give-it-to-me from her. *The classics,* he thought, chuckling tiredly. *Unoriginal but much beloved the world over.*

And then a break in the rhythm, a pause.

"Can I?" the man asked.

The answer, when it came, sounded clear and intimate and close, as if she had whispered the words into Tim's ear.

"You can put it anywhere you want."

Jesus, he thought, breath catching in his throat. It really had sounded like she was there in bed next to him. He listened as the sounds started up again, but soon the man lapsed into silence broken only by wordless grunts. His lover continued to urge him on — demanding, pleading for him not to stop.

Then the man let out an almost sorrowful

groan and the woman cried out in triumphant pleasure and, at last, the thumping of the headboard subsided.

Tim's heart was still thudding in his chest and his face felt flushed, but he figured if he just lay there in bed, he would calm down enough to go back to sleep. He closed his eyes and took a breath.

And she spoke again, there on the other side of the wall.

"Thank you, baby," she said, and he heard it as though she were whispering it right into his ear. "That was exactly what I needed."

The hunger and the pleasure in her voice did him in. He threw back the sheets and went back into the bathroom, where it took only seconds for him to get himself off.

Afterward he lay in bed, ashamed and frustrated and missing Jenny so hard he felt ripped open inside.

Eventually, he slept.

Room service brought his breakfast at nine o'clock on the dot. Tim figured that most people who had their morning meal brought to their rooms were up and out of the hotel for meetings by nine A.M., which explained their being so timely. He signed for his breakfast, giving the thin Mexican guy who'd delivered it a decent tip. In his visits to Los Angeles over the past few years, he had been consistently amazed by how much more effort Mexican immigrants seemed to put into their jobs than native-born Los Angelenos. And not just more effort, but more hustle and greater civility. There was a lesson to be learned in the great immigration battle, but he had lost too much sleep last night to give it very much thought.

Sunlight splashed into the room through the sliding glass door that led out onto the balcony. He liked to sleep in the dark, but during the day he wanted as much sunshine as he could get, and if there was any place in the world to find it, it was right here.

In light cotton shorts and a blue T-shirt Jenny had bought him two years back in Kennebunkport, Maine, he carried the tray out onto the balcony and set it on a little round table. First order of business, he poured himself a cup of coffee — cream, no sugar — and sipped it as he looked down at the beach below, the waves crashing on the sand. The surf made a gentle shushing noise that comforted him.

The hotel backed right up to the ocean. From the balcony he could see the Santa Monica Pier. At night, the lights from the pier provided their own kind of beauty, but during the day the view was truly spectacular. Tim breathed in the salty ocean air and felt cleansed, refreshed. The coffee relit the pilot light in his brain, and he started to feel awake for the first time this morning.

Jenny had loved the view. They had stayed here during both of their visits to L.A. together, the first time only months after they had started dating — it had been that weekend, Tim believed, that they had fallen in love — and the second as a special getaway for their fifth wedding anniversary. Not in the same room each time, of course. Jenny might have remembered the room numbers — he had never asked her — but guys just didn't pay attention to that sort of thing.

And, anyway, it was the view that she had loved, not the room.

With another deep breath, he sipped at his coffee and then set it down, settling into a chair beside the small table. He removed the metal cover over his breakfast plate to reveal a western omelet accompanied by a small portion of breakfast potatoes and half a dozen slices of fresh melon. Sliding the table over in front of him, he tucked into his breakfast. The omelet was delicious, but halfway through, his appetite failed him and he wondered why he hadn't just ordered juice and toast. He ate the melon because it was sweet and good for him, and drank the small glass of OJ that had come alongside the coffeepot, and then he settled back to digest.

Already the day had grown warmer. The weatherman had said it would reach the mid-eighties by noon, and Tim had no trouble believing that. He planned to go to Universal Studios in the afternoon, just for a few hours — it was what he and Jenny had done the last time they were here together — but this morning he intended to take it easy. He got up and went into his room, fetching the James Lee Burke novel he'd bought to read on the plane. Then he shifted the chair to keep the sun out of his eyes, poured himself another cup of java, and sat reading and enjoying his coffee with the sound of the ocean enveloping him.

Twenty or so pages later, he was pulled from the book by the sound of a slider rattling open. He looked up to see a woman stepping out onto the balcony of the room next door. Instantly his mind went back to the night before and the sounds that had come from that room, and he felt both embarrassed and aroused at the same time. This had to be the same woman whose voice he had heard so clearly. It was too early for her to have checked out and a new guest to have arrived.

"Good morning," she said, raising a coffee mug in a toast to him.

Her smile was brilliant. His throat went dry just looking at her — five feet nine or ten, lean and limber like those Olympic volleyball girls, long blond hair back in a ponytail, bright blue eyes — and the pictures he had painted in his mind of last night's acrobatics became that much more vivid. She wore a black and gold bikini that nearly gave him a heart attack.

"Morning," he said, wondering if she would notice the flush in his cheeks — was he actually blushing? God, he felt awkward.

He forced himself back to his book, desperate to look at anything but her. The words blurred on the page. The balconies were open-post style, and he had gotten a fantastic look at her stunning legs.

Just read, he thought, trying to focus. Should he get up and go into his room, or would that be even more awkward?

"I'm sorry," she said. "Am I disturbing you?"

God, he thought, *you have no idea.*

"Not at all. Just enjoying the morning."

"I know what you mean," she replied, sinking into a chair and stretching her legs out, propping her feet up on the railing of her balcony. "I don't have to be anywhere until after lunch and wanted to get a little sun while I have some downtime. It's quiet out here this morning."

She stretched out to maximize her body's exposure to the sun and, consequently, to Tim as well. He held his place in the book with one finger and turned to smile politely at her.

"It's a weekday. People are off at business meetings, I guess."

She shielded her eyes from the sun to look at him. Her lips were full and red and perfect. "No meetings for you?"

"Fortunately not."

He shifted uneasily, not sure he wanted to have this conversation but also not wanting to be rude. And God, she was beautiful. The sounds from the previous night returned as he stared at her, and he could not help imagining those lips saying those things, pleading, moaning, and then . . . *You can put it anywhere you want.* Shit, he'd almost forgotten about that, and now that he'd remembered he could barely even pay attention to what she was saying.

"I'm sorry," he said. "What was that?"

She smiled, a sparkle of mischief in her eyes, as if she knew exactly what had distracted him.

"I asked what brought you to Santa Monica, if not business."

Tim ran though possible answers in his mind, but they all came down to a choice between lying and telling the truth, and he had given up lying years before. He and Jenny had been going through a rough patch, distance growing between them because he had been traveling for work so often, and he had been unfaithful. It had nearly ruined his life, nearly destroyed their life together when he confessed to her, but they had gotten through it. He had vowed that he would never stray again, but it had taken years before she actually seemed to believe him. Forgiving him, though, was something else. She had said she did, but he had always wondered, and wondered even still.

"Honestly, it's sort of a sad story for such a beautiful morning," he said. "What about you?"

She cocked her head curiously, maybe intrigued by the tragic air about him. Tim had seen it before. Maybe someday he would take advantage of the way some women reacted to sad stories, but he had not yet reached a place where he could do that.

"Just sightseeing. A little California dreaming, you know? Started in Napa and made my way down with . . . Well, Kirk's no longer with me."

So his name had been Kirk.

"Kirk?"

She arched her eyebrow suggestively. "I guess I was a little too much for him."

Tim could have taken that any number of ways, but the eyebrow made it clear what she meant. In his mind he could practically hear Kirk's voice even now, calling her every filthy thing he could think of. When he had imagined the woman on the receiving end of those words, she had been nothing like this lovely creature on the balcony. As beautiful as she was, she seemed sweet, even charming.

"I'm sorry to hear that," Tim said.

"It's a morning for sad stories, I guess," she said. "My name is Diana, by the way."

"Tim," he said.

"Sorry if we kept you up last night, Tim."

He grinned, feeling himself flush even more deeply, and glanced away. If he had seen the comment coming, he could have prepared, pretended to have slept through it all, but her directness had sneaked up on him.

"Nah, it's fine. I mean, not for long —"

Diana pouted. "I think I might be insulted."

"— no, no, that came out wrong," he stammered. Then he laughed at his own embarrassment. "I'm a pretty sound sleeper. And who hasn't been on the other side of thin walls at least once, right?"

Her eyes seemed to dance with merriment. "Exactly. That's so true."

She sat up to take a sip of her coffee, her breasts straining against the thin fabric of her bikini top, a single strand of her blond hair — loose from the ponytail — hanging across her face.

"So, are you going to tell me why you're in Santa Monica?"

Her boldness impressed and entranced him. As he thought about it, he could see this woman being the honest, passionate, carnal lover whose voice he had heard through the wall the night before. Yet Diana had many facets, and he saw one of them now, as a kind of sorrow filled her eyes.

"I don't mind sad stories. I've got a whole catalog of them myself. Go ahead. I'm a big girl. I can take it."

Something in that last line made him wonder if she had said it to tease him, but he might have imagined it, added a pouty, sexy insouciance to it that was really only an echo of the night before.

"You might think it's a little strange," he ventured.

Diana turned her chair slightly, basking in the sun even as she transformed their two balconies into a strangely intimate confessional.

"I like strange."

Tim thought about Kirk, the idiot who had apparently left this woman after a night like they'd shared last night. What kind of fool must he be?

"All right," Tim said. He turned down the page in his book and laid it across his chest, staring out at the ocean for a moment before returning his focus to Diana's curious gaze. "I'm on a kind of tour, I guess. I've been to New Orleans and Montreal and to Martha's Vineyard, off Cape Cod. I even went down to this little village on the Gulf of Mexico. They're all places that were important to my wife, Jenny, and me during the years we had together."

The kindness in Diana's eyes broke his heart all over again. "She's gone?"

"Just over a year ago. Pancreatic cancer. It was agony for her, so it was probably good that she went quickly, but I didn't have time, you know? No time to get used to the idea of life without her. It's taken me this long to accept that I've got to live my life. I know she'd have wanted that for me. I'm only thirty-seven. There are a lot of days ahead, if I'm lucky. So I'm on vacation, but it's also kind of our farewell tour."

"Wow," Diana whispered, almost wistful. "That may be the most romantic thing I've ever heard. You're, like, the perfect husband."

A familiar guilt filled him. It had grown like rust on his heart over the years. After he had betrayed Jenny, he had spent every day trying to make it up to her. He doubted he would ever have been able to, really, no matter how much time they had been given together. But he had wanted more time to try.

"Far from perfect," Tim said, staring out at the Pacific.

"No, you're a good guy. I can sense those things," Diana said. "And you're lucky, too."

He frowned. "Lucky?"

The mischief returned to her eyes, and she stood, adjusting the strap of her bikini top.

"You said you were a sound sleeper," she reminded him. With one hand on the handle of the slider, ready to go inside, she glanced over her shoulder at him in a pose so sexy it was painful to behold. "I always have trouble falling asleep. I need someone to tire me out. The only way I can really sleep well is if I'm so exhausted that I'm a quivering mass of jelly. And with Kirk gone . . ."

Diana glanced away, almost shyly, before looking back at him with renewed boldness. "I don't know what I'll do tonight."

Tim could not speak. He dared not move for fear that she would notice the effect she had had on him, if she hadn't already.

Obviously pleased by his speechlessness, Diana opened the sliding door into her room. "Enjoy your day, Timothy."

He managed to croak, "You, too," before her door slid shut.

Shaking his head in amazement, he went back to his book, the erection Diana had caused — the second in a very short time — slowly subsiding. After a few minutes he realized that his thoughts were straying and he had not understood a word he'd read, and he laughed softly at himself. Had that really been an invitation? Did she mean it?

Not that it mattered. As arousing as it was just being in the presence of this woman, Tim knew that any sexual trysts were still in the future for him. In another life he would have climbed mountains for an opportunity to sleep with a woman like Diana, and he knew that he would remember what he had overheard last night for years, maybe forever. Maybe someday he would even regret being faithful to a woman who was now only a memory, but this trip was about him and Jenny, and he would honor that, no matter what. He wanted to start a new life, but not quite yet.

He laughed again, thinking of Jenny. If she were alive for him to tell her the tale, she would have mocked him with love but without mercy. Men, she had often said, were pitifully simple and predictable creatures. Pavlov had used dogs to test his theories about programmed responses, but all he would have had to do was put a man in a room with Diana, and there would have been no need to experiment further.

This final stop on his farewell tour was by far the strangest.

How Jenny would have teased him. God, he missed her.

The phone woke him. In the darkness he searched for it, fingers scrabbling on the nightstand, and only managed to find it when it rang a second time. As he pressed the receiver to his ear, he saw the faint glow of the alarm clock.

Twelve seventeen A.M. After midnight. *Who the hell . . .*

"Hello?" he said, voice full of gravel.

"I can't sleep," she whispered.

It took him a moment, and when the pieces clicked together, his breath caught in his throat.

"Diana?"

"Hey," she said in a sleepy voice.

Tim had come back to the hotel around eight P.M. and eaten a late dinner alone in the restaurant downstairs. Afterward he had held his breath walking past her room, heart racing. Their conversation on the balcony that morning had stayed with him all day, and he had caught himself fantasizing about her, wondering if her thinly veiled invitation for tonight had been more than just flirting.

It hurt his heart. This whole strange vacation had been meant to be about Jenny, and his not being able to get Diana out of his mind seemed a dark stain on pure intentions. But, Christ, he was only human.

"Did you have a nice day?" she asked, when he didn't reply.

"Yeah. I guess. Do you . . . do you know what time it is?"

Even her laugh had that soft, sleepy intimacy about it.

"I do. I'm sorry. I told you I have trouble falling asleep."

They both let that hang in the air for a

bit. Lying in bed in the dark, hearing her voice in his ear, Tim found his memory of the previous night returning with perfect clarity. He could practically hear the thump of the headboard against the wall behind his head, and now that he knew what she looked like, the images in his mind were more than imagination.

"Listen, Diana, I enjoyed talking to you this morning —"

"Can I come over there?"

Tim squeezed his eyes shut. How come this couldn't have happened to him before he met Jenny, or sometime in the future? Six months — hell, one month — from now, maybe his mind would have been in a different place.

"I'm sorry, I just . . ."

You can put it anywhere you want.

Holy God, how was he supposed to handle this? His heart slammed in his chest. His face felt flushed, and once again this woman had given him a painful erection, this time with nothing but a whisper. He felt like a fool for having so little control of his body.

"Tim, hush," she said. "Think about this. You're trying to forget, right? I can give you that. We can help each other. I can make you forget, and you can help me get to sleep."

"It isn't that simple."

"But it is." She laughed that sweet, soft laugh again. "Honey, trust me, I'll make you forget your own name."

There in the dark, he felt himself grin. "I have no doubt you would. And you have no idea how tempting it is — or, actually, you probably do. But this isn't about forgetting Jenny . . . I never want to forget her. It's about making peace with the fact that she's gone, and . . ."

He trailed off. The rest was too personal. He didn't know Diana.

"And?" she whispered.

Tim took a breath and turned onto his side, phone pressed between his cheek and the pillow.

"I betrayed her once. This would feel too much like doing that again."

"She's been dead over a year, you said."

"Not to me. I need to finish saying good-bye. Whatever life has in store for me after, I'll embrace it, but not here. This place was part of us."

"Please?" she said in a little-girl sort of voice. "I can't sleep."

His words dried up in his throat as the reality of the conversation struck him hard. *Please,* she'd said, and now that he reminded himself what she was pleading for, what she wanted from him, he could barely think. It could be the night of his life.

But he would never be able to enjoy the memory of it.

"I'm sorry," he said. "Good night, Diana."

As he reached out to return the phone to its cradle, his hand hesitated involuntarily for just a moment. But if she said anything more, he did not hear it. He hung up and laid his head back down with a mixture of relief and regret.

His arousal subsided and a peaceful sort of contentment filled him. Though he half expected the phone to ring, it did not. He closed his eyes and burrowed down into the bed. Sleep had fled, but only for a while, and soon enough it began to envelop him again.

"Tim."

He came half awake, lost somewhere in a dream.

"Tim."

Now he blinked and opened his eyes. In the darkness he reached out to search the rest of the huge hotel bed to make absolutely certain he was alone there. She sounded so close.

"Are you awake?"

She wasn't in the room; her voice came through the thin wall, a lover's whisper, though she must have been speaking up in order for him to hear her.

He considered replying but then thought better of it.

"Think of something you've always wanted to do but never dared to ask of a woman," she said. *"You don't have to ask me. You could do whatever you want, and I won't stop you. I won't say no. Better than that, I'll ask for more."*

Scenarios played out in his mind instantly, and once again she had him captivated.

"Please," she said. *"I need you."*

She began to tell him in great detail every little thing she would be willing to do, and have done to her, and how much she would enjoy it. How she would moan, even scream.

Then, at last, when he did not reply, she sighed.

"All right. I'll just have to call room service. But you're to blame for what happens."

You're to blame? What the hell was that supposed to mean?

Tim pulled a pillow over his head to block out her voice, but it seemed she had surrendered at last. Yet still her promises echoed inside his head. He lay curled on his side, unable to make his erection go away, unable to deny his arousal, and yet filled with more sorrow and missing Jenny more

392

than he had since the day he had lost her.

At some point he drifted off, temptation still burning in him.

A sharp rap at the door snapped him awake. His eyes burned and his head felt full of cotton. What little sleep he'd had tonight had been shallow and restless. In the blackness of the room he threw back the covers and started to climb out of bed.

Gotta be her. Crazy woman, Tim thought. *I've got myself a stalker.*

"Who is it?" Diana called.

Tim froze, brow furrowed. Had the knock been at his door or at hers? With the walls so thin, it was difficult to know.

A muffled voice replied. He heard Diana unlocking her door and, out of curiosity, pressed his ear to the wall again. The rattle of a room service cart was followed by a murmur of voices. Tim fancied he could smell food — a burger, maybe?

He glanced at the nightstand. In the pitch dark of his room he could barely make out the glow of the alarm clock, which he'd turned away from him. Now he felt his way onto the bed and crawled over to it, turning the clock around to read the time.

Room service at two thirteen A.M.? Did this hotel even have twenty-four-hour room service? Or had Diana persuaded someone to break the rules for her? Tim had a feeling Diana had spent her entire life tempting and cajoling and getting exactly the result she desired.

A spark of irritation ignited within him. Though he felt a now-familiar stirring at the thought of her, his frustration at this long night of broken sleep trumped any lingering arousal.

From next door he heard the sound of a door closing, and he assumed the room service guy had left. But a moment later the murmur of voices began again, both hers and a man's, and then they moved nearer and he heard the creak of weight upon the bed.

"Trust me," he heard Diana say, "this is going to be the best tip you've ever gotten."

Tim couldn't help himself. He laughed softly, falling back onto the bed. "You've got to be fucking kidding me."

But he should not have been surprised. Diana had told him that if he wouldn't come over and have sex with her, she would call room service. He supposed things like this must happen fairly often in the real world, but to him it seemed like something out of the *Penthouse* letters page or some porn film.

Already the noises had begun. How fast had she stripped the guy? Tim lay there staring at the ceiling in the dark and listened to the grunts and moans quickening. Diana urged the room service delivery guy in words almost identical to those she had used with her lover of the previous night. Tim began to get an erection, and he felt a ripple of anger at himself. Tired and frayed and amused, he should not find any of this arousing, but he could not help himself. Men were pitifully predictable creatures.

Not so predictable, he thought. *You didn't go over there.*

But he knew that meant little. Under other circumstances, he would have jumped at the chance to be with a woman like Diana and been just as grateful as, no doubt, the room service guy felt at that very moment.

The noises in the next room reached an initial crescendo, with Diana crying out in a throaty, shuddery orgasm followed almost immediately by the groan of a man stunned by his own good fortune. If last night was any indication, though, Diana would not let it go at that. As soon as the guy had a few minutes' rest . . .

The groan had not stopped. The man's voice began to rise and fall, perhaps with each spasm of his own orgasm. It sounded like he was still coming, like she had brought him to the height of ecstasy and somehow managed to keep him there. The guy cried out to God, but even those words were barely more than grunts.

The headboard slammed the wall in quick rhythm, punctuating each spasm. Diana talked to him, urged him on, and Tim wondered what kind of woman this was, what tantric magic she had that could keep a man locked in ecstasy, and suddenly he knew that although he would always know he had done the right thing, he would also forever regret not having felt what the lucky son of a bitch next door was feeling in that moment.

And then the room service guy began to cry.

In the midst of his climactic groaning, he sobbed and began to say "please" every few seconds. The tone alone told Tim that the man wanted it to end. That he had had enough.

Diana laughed.

"Come on, baby," she said. "Fuck me harder."

Then it was her turn to moan, sounding the way some lovers did when they were locked in a deep kiss, or during oral sex. Tim's erection had returned full force even as he listened with growing unease. The room service guy's cries sounded full of pain now, even fear.

Tim reached out and turned on the light. Sitting up in bed, he stared at the wall, trying to decide what exactly he was hearing.

You're to blame for what happens, Diana had said.

But what, exactly, was happening? This did not sound like sex anymore, not like ecstasy. And now that he thought about it, some of the groans the previous night had sounded full of pain to him as well. What the hell was the woman doing to this guy?

He picked up the phone and reached out to punch the button for the front desk, but hesitated. What the hell would he say? Instead, he put the phone back in its cradle and climbed from the bed. Tugging on the pants he had worn that day, he ran the whole thing over in his mind. He could bang on the wall or go out into the hall and knock on the door, but if he was wrong . . . if this was just extraordinary sex or some S&M thing he was too naïve to understand, he would feel foolish. And to Diana he would appear jealous and full of regret, and he did not want to give her that satisfaction.

Diana's muffled moaning grew louder. The headboard kept banging, although if he was correct the rhythm seemed to have slowed. But in the midst of the man's groaning, Tim felt certain now that he heard sobs and weeping.

That's not pleasure.

Fully awake now, he went to the slider, unlocked it, and drew it open as quietly as possible. Hesitating only a moment, he went to the railing that separated his balcony from Diana's and carefully threw his leg over, settling his weight on the railing a moment in order to shift his weight from one balcony to the next.

You'll be arrested, he thought. *Peeping Tom. Pervert. She'll think you just wanted to see.*

But such reservations did not stop him. Something was wrong. He could feel it in the rising of the small hairs on the back of his neck and the icy dread that raced through him as he crept across Diana's balcony.

Her slider was open halfway. The crash of the surf on Santa Monica Beach, just behind him, covered any noise his bare feet might have made. He paused just outside the slider, hidden from within by the curtain hanging on the other side of the glass. But where the slider was open, the curtain had been drawn back to let moonlight into the room. Tim took a deep breath and held it, then carefully leaned in so that he could get a glimpse into the room.

Diana knelt astride an olive-skinned man, rocking herself back and forth on him, riding him hard enough to keep the headboard slamming the wall. The sensual curves of her body in the interplay between moonlight and shadows made Tim catch his breath. But then he noticed the way the man's body bucked beneath her, the way his hips seemed to come up off the bed with her, not as if he were thrusting into her but as though with each motion she dragged him up with her, as though her sex had clamped onto him and tugged again and again, milking him, attached in some unfathomable way.

So entranced was he by the strangeness of that, and by the swaying of breasts, that at first he did not notice the strange wrongness of the shadows around her face. The man continued to cry out, his eyes rolled back to the whites, his cheeks looking sunken — Jesus, he looked sickly, how old was this guy? Diana had her mouth against his chest and at first Tim thought she must be licking his nipples or his skin, but then Diana shifted in the moonlight, drew her head back a bit, and Tim's heart seized in his chest.

His mind tried to make sense of what he saw. He stared, breathless, as denial tried to fight back the horror and disgust and fear that filled him. Chills rippled across his body and his stomach churned. Bile roared up the back of his throat, and he had to force himself not to vomit.

Diana's mouth was distended, stretched into a pale, blue-veined funnel attached to the man's chest, right above his heart. Her lips trembled with a quiet suction, the skin around them glistening wetly, but he could hardly tear his eyes away from the disgusting proboscis that her face had become.

The man's cheeks were streaked with tears.

As Tim watched in mounting horror, the other man's face seemed to become thinner. His entire body had begun to wrinkle, even to wither, and Tim wondered what he had looked like before he had crawled into that bed. *Kirk's no longer with me,* Diana had said of her previous night's lover. So where the hell was Kirk now?

The room service guy's head tossed to one side, and for just a second, his eyes were on Tim. That was enough.

He swept the screen open and burst into the room. Diana glanced up but did not

400

slow the thrust of her hips, the slam of the headboard, the suction of her hideous mouth.

"Get off him!" Tim shouted.

He grabbed her with both hands, gripped her upper arms from behind, and used his momentum to drag her off the bed, straining with the effort. *Too heavy. What the . . .*

As Diana flopped to the carpet, Tim watched the room service guy dragged along with her, her pussy and that grotesque, distended mouth suctioned to his flesh. Her hips continued to piston onto him and he kept groaning, but his voice had become weaker now and his skin had begun to turn a hideous coal gray. Smoke rose from his open mouth, as if he were on fire inside.

"Jesus!" Tim cried. He wanted to bolt from the room, to pretend he'd never seen this thing, but he knew he would never erase it from his mind.

He reached down and tried to separate them, but Diana flailed at him, fingernails dragging furrows in his neck. She and her prey were on their sides on the carpet. The stretched funnel of her mouth still adhered to his chest, but now Tim saw the lips crawling caterpillar-like, trying to keep hold of the flesh.

"No. No way," he said.

Clutching at his bleeding neck, he stomped a bare foot onto that thin, pale flesh. Her mouth came free with a pop and he saw a black tongue, needle-thin and long — so long — slip from the man's chest before she sucked it back between her lips and spun on Tim.

"What the hell *are* you?" Tim rasped.

Diana hissed, tore herself from the man, and leaped up at Tim. She attacked with her fingers hooked into claws, and now panic raced like poison through his veins. What the hell had he done? Why had he intervened? He grabbed her by the wrists, but she was strong. She spun him around and slammed him into the wall, and that long mouth thrust at him, long black tongue darting out, and now Tim saw that it had a glistening stinger on the tip. He shoved her backward, clenched his fist, and struck her in the temple. He punched her again and again, drove her against the mirrored closet door, which shattered into hundreds of shards that cut their feet as they grappled.

Tim caught only a glimpse of the room service guy out of the corner of his eye before the guy smashed him in the head with the telephone. He spun backward and crashed into the wall, sliding to the carpet even as blood trickled down into his right eye and pain clutched viselike at his skull. Darkness danced around the edges of his vision, and for several seconds he blacked out.

He opened his eyes again to the room service guy's voice. Full of desperation, pitiful and withered, half the life already leeched from him, the poor bastard's cock was still hard.

"Please. Finish," he pleaded.

The hideously disfigured mouth on the creature Tim knew as Diana twitched, then smiled. She reached out and took the lost soul's hand and led him back to bed, mounting him again, reattaching her lamprey mouth to his heart and her sex to his.

Amid the tortured music of the headboard and their moans, Tim managed to stagger to his bloodied feet. He nearly tripped over the guy's uniform as he shoved the room service cart out of the way. Through the wreckage of the closet door he saw a body laid out on the floor inside. The shriveled thing between its legs had once been a penis. The skin was like shrunken leather, split in several places to reveal dry pink meat inside, and the cheeks had torn badly enough to show bone. It looked as though all of the moisture had been sucked out of him, along with all of his youth and vigor, and his life.

Kirk. And now this guy.

Tim had tried. Whatever Diana had done to Kirk, and who knew how many guys before him, she was now doing to the room service guy, and like some kind of junkie, he needed it now, needed her to finish the job. The hook was in deep. The things that made him *him* had already been taken away.

Kirk's no longer with me.

I guess I was a little too much for him.

Tim opened the door and staggered out of the room and down the corridor on bloodied feet. He banged the elevator call button and then ran on to the stairwell door and slammed it open. Ever since Jenny's death, the people who loved him had told him that she would be watching over him. He had never quite believed it — she had gone from this world, a wall thrown up between them — but after this night he was not so sure. It seemed that even those walls could be thin at times.

As he raced down the steps to the lobby, he wondered again if Jenny had ever forgiven him for what he had done. Yet for the first time, it was an idle curiosity. He had loved her as well as he was able and knew she had loved him in return, but she was gone now and would never be able to give him the forgiveness he sought. He would have to claim it for himself. And he would. Tim had done his penance.

Tonight most of all.

THE HEART IS ALWAYS RIGHT

LILITH SAINTCROW

Lilith Saintcrow is the author of the Dante
Valentine, Jill Kismet, and Strange Angels
series. She lives in Vancouver, Washington, with her two children and assorted
other strays.

Most gargoyles go to Paris. It's ridiculous.
When you spend all your time hanging on
the sides of buildings, why go to a place
where you just do more of the same? Even
if the Heart is there beating under the
streets. Even if it is, for pretty much any
stoneskin, *home.*

No, I didn't want to spend two weeks of
vacation hanging on to the side of a building. I was gonna go to Bermuda. Had my
plane tickets and everything. I was even
packing. Suntan lotion, BluBlocker sunglasses, flip-flops. It was an adventure buying the flip-flops at EvilMart. I was thinking
about how in my trueform I only had three
toes, and flip-flops are built wrong for that

kind of foot. Then I figured I wasn't going to be fighting any evil on the beach, so it didn't matter that there aren't three-toe flip-flops out there. It's too bad there aren't. Someone could make a killing.

I guess I shouldn't say things like that, should I?

I got to the front of the EvilMart, wincing at the bright fluorescent light, and for once the Heart was kind to me. She was there.

Blond. The kind of blond that looks dishwater under tubes of buzzing EvilMart light but lights up in island sunlight. Blue eyes, usually tired and bloodshot, and an aristocratic nose under them. She's got a pretty mouth, too, though it's always pulled tight with something like pain. I think if she ever relaxed, she'd be a knockout.

Who am I kidding? Even in a blue polyester EvilMart vest that does nothing for her va-va-vooms, she's a knockout. I like 'em juicy. Give me a girl with real hips any day, not a stick with mosquito bites.

As if I've ever gotten close enough to smell a girl. But I can still look, right?

I'm not dead. Just gargoyle.

Her nametag says *Kate.* And there are always dark circles under her eyes.

She was just reaching up to turn off the light over her register when I shambled up.

It was about two A.M., quitting time. She hesitated, one hand in the air, and I wished I were shorter. Or at least less broad in the shoulders. We stoneskin are built like linebackers — wide and stupid. The sloppy brown hair, hat pulled down to hide my ears, stubble to hide my gnarled skin, and the smell of concrete and rain on me probably isn't very pretty either.

A tendril of that blond hair was falling in her face, and I stopped dead, planting my cheap canvas shoes. My heart made a funny jumping noise inside my ribs, knocking at the cathedral arches.

Then she smiled. It was her usual pained smile, the mouth pulled tight, but her eyes lit up and my heart not only banged on the old ribs, but splashed in my guts. My skin felt too tingling-small, and I had to take a deep breath, reminding myself that my real form wasn't something anyone here would want to see.

"Come on up," she said, and flipped her light off. "I'm just about to go, but I can fit in one more."

"Oh. I . . . Gee. Thanks." Yeah, I actually said *gee*. Her smile widened a bit, and I had to make my feet move. They were tingling, too, just like the rest of me.

I stumped up to her checkout stand and

started unloading the carrying basket. Two beach towels, both printed in big block colors. Two pairs of orange flip-flops, size fourteen wide. White socks — you can't ever have too many socks. Two family-size bags of CornNuts. Sunblock. A two-liter of Coke. A pair of ragg-wool gloves. And three jumbo tins of Bag Balm.

Hey, when your skin rasps against rock and concrete all the time, it gets cracked and stuff. Bag Balm is the *best.*

Her hands sorted the items without any real effort on her part, the checkstand beeping and booping. Her nails were bitten down, and she wore a thin gold necklace. It looked cheap but it smelled real — I've got a nose for metal. The small gold ball earrings she wore were real, too. And this close her skin was dewy even under the glare.

I bulged shapelessly, like a balloon without quite enough air. I've got a boxer's face, including pointed cauliflower ears — not that boxers have pointed ears, you know. I've got a mushroom nose that looks like it's been broken one too many times, and the scarred, pitted skin of any gargoyle past puberty. My eyes are too small, and they're yellow. And my hair is okay — thick and dark — but I must be the only curly-headed stoneskin on the continent.

I'm even ugly to my own Heartkin.

"You must like CornNuts." A quick flutter of a glance from under her long blond-brown lashes. Her hands kept working, bagging everything. "I see you getting them all the time."

She was *talking to me.*

My brain went absolutely fucking blank. "Um," I managed. "Yeah. Like 'em a lot."

Her smile widened a bit. The tips of her two front teeth showed, very white. "I could never eat them. They make my teeth hurt."

It's real fun when you spit 'em at pigeons. Knock 'em right on their little heads; you can feed yourself that way for a while if you're awful poor. You can even spit a CornNut right through them if you get it going fast enough. "You can just suck on 'em until they're soft," I mumbled, and blushed when her eyebrows went up a little. Her smile hovered between genuine and embarrassed for a half second, and a round of cursing went off inside my head.

"Maybe I'll give that a try," she finally said. Uncomfortable silence bloomed between us.

She took the cash, her skin brushing mine. "Is it still raining out there?"

So soft and warm. They don't feel hard and cold like us. No, they're soft and pink

410

and perfect. Especially her. "Pouring." It was raining as if it wanted to drown the city, in fact.

"Well, you've got towels." She grinned, but I only caught the very beginning of her smile because I had to look down in a hurry or I might've grinned back, and a crooked yellow picket fence of teeth is not something she'd want to see. "All right, there you go. You always have exact change. It's nice."

Because I have to. Any gargoyle does; it's a compulsion. Once a gargoyle gets a hoard, we like counting exact change. Each penny is taken from muggers or other Bad People. But that's no reason to waste it, and the count makes us irrationally happy.

Plus, you have to pay in cash when you don't have a real name or a social security number.

My pulse was pounding so hard. Was I going to have an attack right here? Heart, I hoped not. I muttered something and took my bag, almost tripped in my hurry to get out. I left her standing there in the glare, and it wasn't until I got outside that I realized I wasn't having a cardiac arrest or a reaction. I was just stupid.

I loitered outside under the awning for a little while, breathing deep lungfuls of wet, smog-laden air. The cars all hunched their

411

shoulders and turned their backs to the storm, wet metal and rubber moving only under protest. I hung around near the end of the covered section, waiting to see if the rain would slacken. It probably wouldn't until I was halfway home no matter *how* long I waited, that's just my luck.

Besides, about ten minutes after, Kate came out through the sighing automatic doors. She walked straight out into the rain, her thin denim jacket completely inadequate for the weather, and I saw that one of her sneaker soles was flapping a little at the heel.

The sight of the heel rubber sticking to the wet ground, then flopping as she lifted her foot, made something inside my chest hurt. I guess they didn't pay her enough to buy a new pair, even at EvilMart prices. She hunched her shoulders and hurried.

Who was I kidding? I followed her, drifting behind and staying on a parallel course as if I were looking for my own car. I'd done it every night I'd come in for the past month. She had a rusted-down blue Chevy Caprice, and I usually made sure she got in and it started before I faded into the shadows.

Hey, it's a dangerous world. If there's not the Big Bad out stalking, there's other bad waiting right around the corner. Sometimes it's Evil with a capital E. Other times it's grim luck, predators, accident, or just plain human foulness.

I swung my bag a little as I walked, kept her in my peripheral vision. She parked way the hell out in the farthest regions of the lot — I guess EvilMart doesn't want the employees snuggling up to the store.

Kate walked with her head down, her steps slowing as she got out near her car. She looked nervous, and I wasn't sure but I thought she was shaking. It was certainly cold enough. Even I was a bit chilled, and stoneskin don't feel it the way the soft pink ones do. She jangled her keys slightly, sweet music.

The lights were out here in the corner of the lot. That was the first wrong thing. The next was the thickness in the rainy air, like rancid soup. Last was the shadows crowding around, and the red pinprick lamps of eyes blinking on and off.

What the hell? I dropped my plastic bags and my trueform shredded out through the mask of disguise. There went another cheap pair of canvas shoes — my real feet tore out through them, claws spreading lightly on concrete. My legs burned a little as I crouched, gathering myself. The darkness reached down from the sky to touch the ground in a thick, wet curtain.

The Big Bad likes to take its victims in the dark. So Heartkin have infrared and other ways of seeing. She was like a lamp, heat and life shining along my skin, and for a moment it was so bright I was confused but already committed to my leap.

The thing after her was a *kolthulu*. I hit in the middle of the nest of rubbery, snakelike tentacles. They're lined with dry hairy suckers that can strip flesh off bone, but that's no match for gargoyle skin. They give reluctantly under claws, so just brute force is needed to tear the things apart. There was Kate screaming, but I wasn't worried about that just yet because it was a terror sound, not a pain sound. And who wouldn't be terrified in the dark with the sounds of ripping and crunching all around?

The kind of light she was giving off didn't cast shadows, so it was a type of blindness all over me. My coat flapped; I dug my hind claws into concrete that gave like butter and *pulled.* The heartstring of the beast ripped out with a sound of gristle tearing from bone, and the screaming didn't diminish as the tentacles lost their will and life, and became just twitching meat.

There were other sounds, too. Soft sliding sounds, and her voice choked off hard.

Where there's *kolthulu,* there's always bloodsuckers, too. I whirled, the battlefield drenched with directionless illumination that didn't come in through the regular visual spectrum. The Heart in me gave a single loud knock against my meat and bone, thrilling up into hypersonic, and I tore through their hard, thin bodies. They were clustered around her, and the not-light of her dimmed and faltered.

Holy shit. It was only then I realized what was happening.

They were clustering her, and a soft sucking sound echoed against wet pavement and the dark curtain holding the world away. The not-light dimmed even further, infrared taking up the slack in a deep crimson haze. Six of them, one of me, bad odds when I could smell coppery blood.

But bad odds aren't something that worries a gargoyle. *The Heart always wins,* that's what we say. Even if I fell here, others of my kin would get these things. I'd go into the Heart and come back stronger and better.

Or so they said. I didn't want to put it to the test.

Metal crunched as I flung one of them. A car alarm went off, the sound knifing through the other din that I ignored because it wasn't the screaming. The screaming had stopped, and that was a bad sign. A snap of greenstick neck-breaking, and the three remaining bloodsuckers fled, one of them limping badly and hissing in their weird piping tongue. They can't talk right when their teeth are out, the little idiots.

The darkness fled with them, the Big Bad picking up its toys and going home. I stood, half snarling, stone flexing over my skin and the strength of the Heart thudding underneath it. Regular sight returned, and I looked down.

Kate lay sprawled on the wet concrete, rain beading on her pale skin. One of them had ripped her shirt open, and there were her breasts in a cheap black-lace bra.

Hey, I looked. I might be ugly, but I'm not *dead*.

"Oh, shit," I said. My ears tingled, and I stared at her chest. There on the pale slope of her left breast, a sinuous fleur-de-lis curved. The lines were sharp black, as if they'd been inked by a master. But it wasn't a tattoo. It ran with its own odd light, a dark fluorescence human eyes wouldn't see.

She was a Heart candidate.

And I heard running feet and shouts behind me, as black-looking blood mixed with rain and threaded down from the puncture wounds in her throat. She was bleeding. She was a candidate, and she'd been bitten with a gargoyle right next to her, and there were people coming.

It was a moment's work to scoop her up and cradle her close. Her purse fell free, its patent-leather strap broken, and her jacket was in shreds. The sole of her sneaker had been almost torn off. Her sharp chin tipped back, the blood on her skin doing funny things to the inside of my head.

"Jesus!" someone yelled, and I compressed myself like a spring, ready to leap. Situation: One parking lot, people beginning to cluster now that the excitement was over and the cloaking darkness was worn away. One gargoyle, shifted fully into stoneskin and hulking inside his raincoat, his hat knocked off and his hair unraveling away from high-pointed ears. One mortal woman, bleeding from a vampire bite. Her car was a shattered hulk of metal and glass, and just before I sprang I heard sirens in the distance.

Wow, someone actually called the cops this once? Figures.

The world turned underneath me. There was a scream as I vaulted over the heads of the gathering crowd, a sound of effort like grinding boulders escaping me, muscles and bone working overtime. I bounded like a springheel jack, Kate's unconscious head bouncing against my shoulder, and all I could think of was that she might get a concussion if she hit her head on me too hard.

I've never claimed to be the smartest gargoyle in the world. But just that once, maybe I did the right thing.

On the other hand, she was bitten. And things were about to get even more interesting.

My flight left for Bermuda at five the next morning.

Instead of sitting uncomfortably in a business-class seat, pouring down the drinks so I wouldn't think of the empty air between me and the ground, I was crouched in the belfry of Immaculate Conception downtown. The rain beat steadily against the bell tower as I watched the clouds lighten by imperceptible degrees toward dawn.

Yep. I was at home when my vacation started. Lucky me.

Once dawn had a good grip on the city, I climbed down the rickety stairs. This particular church was built in 1911, and it's got the standard architecture — and the winding little stairway behind a painted panel of Saint Stephen in a small side chapel, going down to my cell.

It's actually a comfortable little place. I've got my hot plate and my little fridge — the gargoyle before me wired the place for electricity. I do all my laundry down the street at the Kleen Kloze Washateria, and I've got a toilet and a shower. It's damp, kind of, since it's all underground. But that doesn't matter much to a gargoyle.

And there, on my barely-big-enough bed, Kate lay. Her chest rose and fell with regular breaths, her thin gold necklace gone but her earrings still there. She hadn't moved since I'd laid her down and checked her clumsily for concussion. I tried to repair her sneaker with duct tape, too, because it hurt me to see it all torn up like that.

Now, I touched the supple lines of the fleur-de-lis and felt them quiver against the calluses on my fingertips. The Heart under my skin banged into life, blinding me for a moment, and when vision returned, I caught the lines *shifting* just the tiniest fraction, settling into the familiar circled fleur — the mark all stoneskin spend their nights fighting the Big Bad for. It means a lot of things. Light. Blessing. Beauty.

Those things we're denied, or the things we're too ugly to be comfortable with.

The messy double puncture wounds on

her throat had finally sealed up, since I'd painted them carefully with the coagulant that works best — gargoyle spit and garlic paste. Chewing that stuff up raw makes my eyes water.

I pulled my hand back, and not a moment too soon. The mark twitched, her breathing changed, and she sat right up and screamed.

"Jesus!" I almost went over backward. She scrambled back, producing an amazing kettle whistle of sound, and hit the wall. Tried to keep going, her eyes bugged out of her head and her hands flailing.

I wasn't so worried about the sound getting out. The painted panel of Saint Stephen is over a thick shell of rock that only a stoneskin could whisper aside, and there's the stairs and the other oak door, too. But the sound of her scream burrowed into my head, tugged at the Heart under my skin, and I had to fight against my trueform hulking out and making things interesting.

She stopped for breath, the scream hitching into sharp little sucking sounds as she tried to get in something to breathe and push out the yelling at the same time. I backed up, my heel hitting an empty energy-drink can and sending it rattling. I had both hands up, trying to look harmless, but it's so hard to do when you're built like a weightlifter. Another can crunched underfoot; I stumbled. We stared at each other, Kate and I, and the screaming petered out.

We both took a deep breath, and then we spoke at the same time.

"Please don't hurt me —"

I was a little more on the ball. "I'm not gonna hurt you —" *Boy, is that a lie.*

We stared at each other some more. I tried again. "Hi." The word was totally inadequate. "How do you feel?"

Her hand flew to her throat, and her eyes got very round. Then she noticed her shirt was torn open, and a flush rose up the curve of her neck, exploding in her cheeks like New Year's fireworks. She gulped audibly, and my heart made a funny bursting movement. It was like the movement of the other Heart under my skin, the stone that makes the change into stoneskin possible. If both hearts decided to go wiggy on me, I would be gasping and blushing myself.

She snatched her ruined shirt together. "If you have to rape me," she managed in a queer little choked voice, "please, please use a condom."

Uh, what? "Um." My jaw worked soundlessly for a moment. "I, uh. I'm not gonna rape you, ma'am. I just, um, I thought this was the safest place for you." I swallowed hard, trying not to think that her shirt really wasn't covering much and that I'd seen what she was trying to hide — the shells of the bra, cheap black lace cupping white skin, and the mark shifting against itself. "Since they're trying to kill you. Because you're . . . That mark on you. You've had a near-death experience lately, haven't you?"

Her eyes were full of welling water, washing out the blue and trickling down one smooth cheek. "Oh, shit," she whispered, like she'd been punched. "You . . . you're one of *them.*"

Well, that answered that question. She'd brushed up against the Big Bad recently.

"I ain't one of *them.* They're the Big Bad, and I'm stoneskin. I fight them." Swallowed hard again. Suddenly I was very conscious of my ears poking up — I don't wear my hat at home — and the stone walls and cans on the floor were probably weird to someone who worked at a reasonable dead-end job. "Uh, you got bit. I think you're okay, though."

"Bit?" She shook her head. Her hair wasn't dishwater under the energy-efficient bulbs I have down here. No, it was gold. Spun gold. "I . . . You . . ."

Well, this is going pretty okay. "You had a near-death experience, right? Six months to a year ago, I'd reckon. Right?"

"How did you —" She was having trouble getting whole sentences out. I didn't blame her. EvilMart probably didn't prepare her for this. "Look, is this some kind of joke?"

Not even close. "I'll explain everything. That mark on your chest showed up after your nearly dying. It's changed again because it's been triggered. You're a Heart, and I've got to take you to Paris."

Tense, ticking silence stretched between us like a high wire between buildings, bowing under the weight of a daredevil's feet. Finally, she gulped audibly again. "Say *what?*"

All things considered, it was probably the only response she *could* make. I tried not to stare at her hands, loosening on what was left of her shirt. "The Heart of Hearts is in Paris. I've got to take you there. We'll fly first class, probably." I ran out of words.

She stared at me for another fifteen seconds, then began to laugh. When she finished with that, she burst into tears while I stood there uselessly staring. Even with her skin all blotchy and her nose all full, she was . . . Well. I didn't even think to get her any tissues until she was covered in tears and full of snot.

It wasn't a good beginning. She finally

calmed down, and I wondered if she was going to be any trouble.

Because I was lying to her. I was going to take her to Paris. But I didn't think she'd like what happened when we got there. Of all the jokes life's played on me, this one had to be the most sadistic.

There was a phone box up the street. I stood outside it for a long time in the fine midday misting rain, my hat dripping all around the brim and my shoulders soaked. It wasn't until a stray gleam of sun broke through under the rolled edges of cloud that I realized I was standing in a puddle and it had soaked through my sneakers.

All things considered, she'd taken it really well. Six months ago she'd been married and in a car crash — in that order. The husband was buried, the job at EvilMart all she could get with no experience after being a housewife for five years. The car crash had left her in a hospital emergency room, miraculously healed of a collage of broken bones and bloody bruising between one breath and the next after they'd applied the shock pads. *It was like white light,* she told me. *But not real white light — it was like being blind.*

I knew what she was talking about. It's

the Heart choosing its victim. We stoneskin feel the Heart's pull, but sometimes it pulls the soft pink ones, too.

The Tiend takes a few so the rest of us can go on. Or at least, that's what we're told.

I stepped closer to the phone booth. Its edges were beaded, pearled with rain that was still falling. There was going to be a rainbow soon. Beautiful weather, the type you don't often see in a city where it rains all the time.

Instead of dialing, I took two steps back from the phone booth. Sooner or later the Heart would take her. I didn't have to speed the process up.

But what the hell was I going to do? She was my problem. I was stoneskin. Serving the Heart is what we *do.* Indecision warred with duty, ending in a burp of exasperated indigestion tasting of CornNuts. I'd eaten the whole damn bag on the way here.

It don't matter. The Heart takes its own. And she's so pretty.

The indigestion turned into sourness. I'd left her with an awkward suggestion that she might want to take a shower and that I'd bring her some clothes for the trip. *But why Paris?* she'd wanted to know. *What's there?*

All I could do was mumble that it was

425

what I was supposed to do, that she would want for nothing, that she would . . . be happy. And safe. And the shell-shocked look in her swollen red-rimmed eyes was enough to make me feel as if I'd stepped on a fluffy little helpless kitten. Or two. Or a hundred.

I forced myself back to the phone booth. Put my hand on the receiver. It probably wasn't working, anyway. If it was out of order, that would be a sign that I didn't have to make this call.

It seemed too heavy to lift. I did it anyway and put it gingerly to my ear.

The dial tone was really, really loud. I went to hang it up, and duty caught my hand halfway.

You know what happens if you don't call in. Come on.

The CornNuts tried to crawl free again. The dial tone mocked me. I held my stomach down with sheer force of will and punched the number I never thought I'd call.

'Cause what are the chances of finding a Heart candidate if you never get close to the pinks? Only this time I had, and it figures.

Two rings, and it was picked up. The click of relays punched through my temple; I swallowed a shapeless sound.

426

The voice was even, well modulated, with a hint of tenor sweetness. "Report."

I gave my control phrase and my district. Then the seven little words. "I have a Heart candidate. Request transit."

That was the only thing this number was ever used for.

A slight pause. "Congratulations." He said it like he meant it. "You'll have the tickets and requisitions in six hours."

No point in messing around. "Okay." There was nothing left to say, so I hung up. I thought I caught a muffled "Good luck" before the receiver hit the rest of the phone so hard it shattered. My claws were out, slicing through plastic, metal, and the innards of the phone.

My stomach curdled afresh. *Shit. That's public property.* But what did it matter? After I brought the Heart its candidate, I would stay at the Sanctum and become one of the Inners, keepers of the Mystery and honored servants of the Heart. Any gargoyle in his right mind wants to be part of the Sanctum. From the moment we're hatched or brought in, we're told it's the place to be.

The phone died with a gurgle. Quarters spilled out, and the LED screen on the debit-card reader up top flashed wildly twice.

That's the trouble with the world. It isn't built strong enough to withstand anything.

I turned on my heel. My sneakers were squeaking, since my feet were spreading, toes fusing together and the hind claw jabbing at cheap material. When you shred your shoes all the time, you learn not to buy anything high-end.

When I had everything all back together and human-sized again, I trudged back up the block toward home. I suppose I should've been ready for what happened next.

When I got back into my cell, it was empty. Maybe I should've locked the door. Or thought the stone panel would obey a candidate as well as a Heartkin.

Her car was already hauled out of the EvilMart parking lot. I guess they don't believe in waiting around. There were stars and glittering cascades of pebbly broken safety glass, the damp noxious perfume of the Big Bad, and a lighter gray smell of rain and daylight.

The broken purse had already been swept up and taken away somewhere, too. Midday shoppers didn't glance at me — I was too far out in the lot. After a few moments of standing with my eyes closed, sniffing a little, I found what I was after.

The thin thread of gold necklace almost burned my fingers. My nose twitched as I turned its supple length over and over. Waiting for the little tingle.

A nose for metal is a nose for tracking, that's what the older gargoyles say. Me, I just wait for the tingle. Often as not — even oftener than that — it leads me right to what I'm looking for.

This time it ran along my nerves like burning gasoline and almost pulled me out of my human skin. It was hard work, keeping my shambling shape in some modicum of normalcy as I whipped around, the pull hard and close.

That's when the cop cars arrived, and the smell of the Big Bad wasn't being rubbed out by the rain. It was fresh and fuming from the EvilMart.

"Shit," I whispered, and lunged into a clumsy run.

The cops had their guns out. A SWAT van pulled up, and people started screaming and running because there was a *pocka-pocka-pocka* of automatic fire from inside the building.

Somebody was taking their shopping a little too personally. Or they were trying to kill my Heart candidate.

They kill them wherever they find them,

and I'd made a lot of noise and fuss last night alerting them to the fact that there was a stoneskin around and a Heart candidate to kill.

Stupid me.

I leapt on two cars because of the clots of people spilling out in the parking lot. They crunched under my feet, sloping away as I jumped. It was chaos. The cars crumpled because I had blurred out into trueform. Who cared what they saw? The screaming inside was taking on a more panicked, desperate quality, and for once I was glad I'm not imaginative. Imagination just gets in the way when you have a job to do.

The automatic doors didn't open, so I busted through. Glass tinkled, shattered, and flew. I was moving almost too fast for human eyes to track, and all that mass moving so quickly means it's hard to slow down or stop. My claws dug huge furrows in the flooring as I bounded into the store and had to twist to avoid smooshing some of the pinks who were running around.

Oh, great. Just great.

Harpies.

There were four of them. EvilMarts are built so warehouse-high, the feathered bitches could even skim the tops of aisles. They were circling, looking for something.

430

And there were a bunch of little gray gneevil-gnomes with AK-47s.

Heart have mercy, it's an invasion! I squashed one gneevil by landing on him, spun and leapt, and my nose tingled. Good luck finding Kate in all this — but I had to find her, and the Heart inside me told me she was here.

Well, best way is the most direct way. The Heart in me pulled, and I followed it, building up every iota of speed I could. One of the nice things about being stoneskin: Walls don't hold up to us. Stone we can whisper aside. Steel struts? They break. And drywall? Don't make me laugh.

One of the harpies let out a chilling scream. It'd seen me. The sound shattered glass, and one of the aisles exploded. Dish soap, laundry soap, cleaning products spilled out in a tide. I was going fast enough it didn't matter, claws ground into the flooring as I uncoiled and flew, wind whistling in my ears and bullets spattering behind me.

The wall crumpled like paper. I blew through it and landed in something that looked like a conference room, a long table and a wall with a whiteboard and sheets of fluttering paper tacked to it. Chairs spun as I cracked right through the cheap-ass table. I skidded through another wall and found a break room. The impact broke the coffeepot, hurling it across the room, and the Heart in me sent a ringing thrill through every inch of nerve and meat I owned.

There was a group of screaming pinks cowering in the break room. Drywall dust filled the air. I coughed, digging my hind claws in, and jolted to a stop.

Kate wasn't screaming. She stood in the middle of them, mouth ajar and eyes wide, staring at me. She clutched her broken purse to her chest. She also wore one of my hooded sweatshirt jackets, zipped up to the very top and absurdly big on her. Her hair, long and loose, fluttered on the breeze from me busting through the wall. I opened my mouth to say something right before one of the harpies plowed through the hole I'd made and things got interesting.

I hate harpies. They smell horrible. When you rip 'em apart, they screech so bad it makes your ears want to bleed. They aren't that bad if they're grounded, though. And then there was just Kate to worry about — grabbing her and getting her away from the gnomes with guns.

The packet was delivered — fake ID for both of us; I got the sensitized filmstrip on the picture ID to look like her with just a little rearranging. Plane tickets and a wad of cash for supplies I didn't have enough time to buy. We just barely made the flight, and Kate was still in jeans and my sweatshirt jacket. We'd stopped for ten minutes we couldn't afford in the airport; I bought a handful of clothes in a size that looked like it might fit her and stowed the bag in the overhead compartment. The flight attendant wanted to do it, but I mumbled something and Kate just dropped into the seat near the window. The attendant gave me a dark look and left.

Kate was still trying to process everything, and there was drywall dust in her hair. Air France has really nice first-class cabins.

They spare no expense when bringing in a Heart candidate.

So we had a space all to ourselves, and the attendants fussed over her right before takeoff. Me they just looked nervously at.

I buckled her seatbelt. *"Bienvenue à Air France!"* the intercom chirped brightly, and I didn't let out a breath until the doors had closed and the plane started making its getting-ready-to-go sounds. The seat was wide and deep, and she wasn't even scratched. Just that drywall, and glassy-eyed shock.

"Thank God," I finally muttered. "You

want a drink?"

Color flooded her cheeks again. She hunched her shoulders, darted me a mistrustful glance. "Christ, yes."

"What'll you have?"

"Vodka." Her throat moved as she swallowed. The two little punctures were fully healed now. Gargoyle spit and garlic works wonders. She blinked at me like she was trying to get dust out of her eyes. "What the hell."

"Got it."

We didn't have to wait long. The stews come around a lot in first class. She got a vodka with cranberry juice; I decided a Jack Daniels was in order. As soon as the attendant had finished pouring mine, Kate asked for another. The attendant gave her a weird look, but I palmed up a tenner and she ended up leaving us two vodka and cranberries, visibly hoping we weren't going to be trouble.

"Just don't get drunk," I cautioned.

"Why the hell *not?*" She laughed, a bitter little sound. The seats around us were empty; I'd bet the Sanctum had bought them, too, just to give us some privacy. "What the hell is going on? What the fuck *are* you?"

I winced. "I'm a gargoyle. Stoneskin. We

serve the Heart."

"Gargoyle. Okay. Got that. What were those . . . those *other things?*" She took down another vodka with remarkable aplomb. I doubted she even tasted it, she tossed it so far back.

"Well, there was a *kolthulu*. And some suckmonkeys. And harpies — those were the red and green flying bird things. And —"

"The things with guns? What about those?"

"I'm getting to those. Those were gneevil-gnomes."

"Gnomes. Okay." She eyed the third vodka. "This is so *Twilight Zone*. It has something to do with that scar, doesn't it?" Her right hand made a furtive little movement toward her chest. She put it back down.

"The mark? Kind of. Sometimes people come back . . . special." I sipped at my whiskey. At least in first class they don't water your drinks. "I'm taking you to Paris, to the Heart. You'll be safe there."

And boy, it was my day to lie with a straight face.

"Since the . . . the accident, I've been seeing things. All sorts of things. You're the first thing that hasn't tried to eat me or scared me so bad I wanted to pee myself." Her fingers played with the glass. "I'm sorry."

She was sorry? I closed my lips over a laugh and hunched my shoulders. When I could talk without wanting to spill the truth out, I took a deep breath. "Been seeing things, huh? Weird lights?"

"Yeah. Around people, and sometimes plants. Living things. And sometimes the lights will go out wherever I am, and — what are those things, anyway? Those things after me?"

"They're all part of the Big Bad. They're predators, and sometimes just outright evil. See, the Big Bad is in rebellion against the Heart of All Things. There was a war, back before humans came around, and —"

"Never mind." She picked up the third vodka and poured it down. Set the cup down, and the flight attendant came through to pick things up before takeoff. The plane started moving. "I don't really want to know."

"Fair enough. Just . . . Kate . . ."

She flinched as if I'd tried to hit her. It was the first time I'd said her name out loud. I tried again. "I'm not gonna hurt you. I'm here to protect you." *At least until we get to the Source. And then . . .* I couldn't think about it.

"Great." She let out a short, chopped-up sigh. "Why is this happening to me?"

"I don't know how the Heart chooses." *I wish I did. Maybe then I could've stayed away from you.* Just looking at her hair and her sweet, aristocratic profile made both hearts inside me quiver. Why did she have to be so — "I'm sorry. You want something to eat?"

"You don't have any CornNuts on you, do you?" It was a weak attempt at humor, and it hurt me way down deep inside.

See, I'm stone. I'm hard to hurt and pretty impossible to kill unless you know what you're doing and you're damn lucky. I was hatched and brought up in a stoneskin-only orphanage and sent out to make my way after they trained me and made me tough.

She wasn't. She was soft and smooth and vulnerable. Fragile, even. It don't cost me anything to be brave.

Oh, shit. Heart have mercy.

And here I was carrying her toward doom.

"Nope." I felt about as tall as a runt gneevil-gnome.

"Well, damn." She was still trying. "They were trying to kill me, those things?"

"Yeah."

"And you saved my life." It wasn't a question.

The plane accelerated. It made the sharp

turn to set itself up for the runway. I rubbed one of the soles of my cheap canvas shoes on the top of the other shoe. "Yeah."

"Thank you." She paused. "Do you have a name?"

"Uh, no. Don't get one." *Got a control number and a smell and a territory, but no name. Called me Curly at school.* I'd probably die if she ever called me that.

"You don't even have a name? Jesus."

I tried not to feel even smaller. "Sorry."

"Me, too," she said, and closed her eyes. The plane accelerated toward takeoff. She gripped her armrests, her knuckles turning white.

It was gonna be a long flight.

Eight hours and some change later, we landed in Paris. The jeans I'd bought her didn't fit, but the red sweater did, and I guess she was probably happy to get out of my jacket. It was raining here, too, so she kept the sweatshirt jacket anyway and zipped it up over the sweater. She was still in her beaten-up, heel-flapping sneakers, too. One of them was still shredded, just barely held together by the duct tape I'd applied.

It was enough to hurt the Heart itself to see. We were ushered into a VIP lounge, and another stoneskin met us — one of the In-ners. He had a fedora on, a long coat covered in raindrops, boots, gloves, and long dark hair that looked shiny and clean, hid-ing his face. A glitter of eyes deep under the brim of the hat passed over her, over me, and then winked out briefly before return-ing. "Well, hello. You must be the candi-date." He didn't offer his hand, but he did bow a little. His hair swung. "I hope your flight was pleasant?"

A muted announcement in French came through the lounge speakers. Kate stared at the Inner like he'd just asked her to take her own head off. She clutched her broken purse to her chest.

I cleared my throat. "I brought her. I, uh, hope —"

"You're to come along." His voice was actually pleasant and smooth. Not like my gravel-rasp.

Well, the Inners. What can I say? They're blessed.

"Oh, I . . . Gee." I actually floundered.

"Come along, we shouldn't linger." He made a quick movement and turned on his heel. Kate actually glanced at me, like she was looking for directions.

Oh, hell. "It's okay," I lied, awkwardly. Through the wall of glass all along one side of the first-class lounge came foggy Paris light. I swear I could feel the Heart — *the* Heart, the big one — throbbing behind each little droplet in the mist, singing to the sun even through the rain and mist. "We'll go together."

She gave me the same tight smile she'd given me each time I walked up to her checkout line. Now I wondered how much of that smile was seeing under the mask of my human seeming. She hadn't even asked about my claws or the ears or the way I'd fought us both free of the gnomes and harpies.

"Okay," she said quietly. "If you're going, too, I guess it's all right."

My heart tolled like a bell inside my ribs, and then it fell with a sick splash to somewhere around my toes. Or even deeper.

I was doomed.

What can I say about the Sanctum? Well, it's green and it's quiet. Heartlight bathes everything, and during the day it's easiest to get to if you stand where the glow of the north rose window of the most famous cathedral in the world *should* be . . . and step *sideways*. It's not a step you can take physically. I offered my arm to Kate as the Inner stood watching us from the edge of

440

the glow.

Kate put her hand through it and her tight smile didn't waver. I stepped, she came with me, and the light burst over us.

"Oh." She sounded shocked.

I didn't blame her.

No matter where you step *from,* the Sanctum always starts you in the same place: a quiet garden full of golden light and the cloaked and hooded forms of the Inners gliding around. One of them approached us, and Kate clutched hard at my arm. "Oh," she said again.

"It's a bit much the first time," our guide said. He'd stepped through right after us and crowded us forward. "If you'll come this way, miss. Brother, Jean-Michel will show you your quarters. We'll meet at nightfall."

She didn't want to let go. "Jesus — please, no —"

Smart girl. I loosened her fingers from my arm, gently. Very gently, because her bones could break before I squeezed hard. "Kate. Please. Go with him. It'll be fine."

"How come they get names and you don't?" She looked up at me. "And they're so *bright.*"

"You'll get used to it." The lie was ashes in my mouth. "They get names because

441

they're Inners. They've brought Heart candidates in. Like you." *And they get the beauty and the name.*

"So —" She still didn't want to let go. "You're coming back, right?"

"Yeah." I tried to sound reassuring. "Just go with him, Kate. Please."

"Okay." She squared her shoulders and lifted her chin, and stepped away. "Okay."

God, that hurt, too. I watched as the guide took her away. Her hair lit up in the Heartlight, pure spun gold. She wasn't walking like it hurt anymore, and I hoped the first thing they'd do was give her new shoes. You don't have to wear them in the Sanctum, it's warm and springtime there always . . . but that flapping heel, my Heart.

My chest was full of lava. It was a struggle to keep my ugly face impassive. Jean-Michel, cloaked in gray with his hood drawn up and shadowing his face, sighed. His gloved hands folded together. "That's the hardest part, isn't it?" His voice was just as musical as the guide's. "Don't worry, brother. It will all be well."

"Yeah," I mumbled. "Sure. What am I supposed to do?"

"Now you come with me. You bathe." He paused for the briefest of moments. "And you choose your knife."

442

■ ■ ■ ■

They left me alone in a pretty, open suite that glowed with Heartlight, falling with the sunlight through the open spaces that passed for windows here. There's no need for glass when it's always balmy. I don't think I've scrubbed behind my ears that hard since the orphanage.

So all that afternoon I sat in the window, looked out on yet another garden, and turned the obsidian knife in my hands.

They've got all kinds — kukris and daggers and diver's knives and even butcher knives. Hilts of every description. But the metal all reminded me of that thin thread of gold — the broken necklace that even now I had in my other fist. My hands were wide and blunt, and as soon as I saw the rock knives — flint, obsidian, bloodstone, you name it — my fingers tingled.

What are you thinking?

This was the Sanctum. It was green and perfect, and it smelled sweet, and the Inners didn't move with that lurching awkwardness that shouts *gargoyle*. They'd all made their tithe and Tiend, and the Heart had taken their candidates, and they were here to serve. They got to bathe in

Heartlight every day.

They had names. The thing every gargoyle wants, a name of his very own.

But dammit, Kate. *Kate.*

I tipped my head back, bonked it gently on the window frame behind me. The frame was pure stone.

There was an Inner at my door. A guard. I wondered how many gargoyles considered something stupid when they brought their Heart candidate here. All of them? Just me? There wouldn't be a guard if none of them did. Or was he there because I might need something? Like a good pep talk?

Like a reminder of why we did this? The Heart must feed. It fights the Big Bad; it powers all of us, gives us pieces of itself that grant us the stoneskin trueform. It even gives us names. True names, ones that don't fade. None of that comes cheap.

But . . . Kate.

I had my feet outside the window before I thought of it. Pulled them back in.

What was I thinking? I was still damp from my bath, tingling from the Heartlight, and in a gray robe and cloak with a big, deep hood. I would still shamble, though. I couldn't move gracefully at all. And I would have to keep my hands hidden. They all wear gloves.

Kate. She had a name. She probably took it for granted, too.

Where would they have her? If I had to guess . . .

I didn't have to guess. The entire Sanctum was ablaze with expectation, the Heart's singing to one of its own. I could just follow it to find her. Or I could follow the ringing pull from the necklace in my fingers.

Or I could just sit here until they came to get me. I could do what I had to and get a name. I could be beautiful.

Kate.

I slipped the obsidian knife up my sleeve, pushed my feet out the window, and landed on garden loam.

The door was wide, and old, oak bound with scarred iron pulsing with life. I put my hand on it and the iron zinged, singing in a high carbon whine. It creaked a little as it opened, and I peeked in.

The chapel was long and narrow. At the very end the stone rose like a wave, shaping itself into an altar draped with crimson velvet and pillows. I pushed my hood back. It fell away from my ears and I could breathe again.

Kate lay there, very still. The walls throbbed. It was deep down and close to the Heart. The beats were a melody the Heart inside me echoed. It was hard to keep everything human-sized and inside. The trueform just kept wanting to bust out.

The corridors had been sleepy and deserted. I'd done my best to glide and managed not to lurch too much. The necklace quivered in my aching fist. I'd wrapped it around the leather-wrapped hilt of the obsidian knife and pulled both up inside my sleeves.

They'd put her in a red dress. It was beautiful. *She* was beautiful, in a way I'd never be. Her arm was over her eyes and her hair spread out over the pillows.

God and Heart both forgive me. I pulled the door shut behind me as quietly as I could. My whisper boomed against the walls. "Kate?"

She stirred a little. Her arm moved.

"Kate. Wake up." What if they'd drugged her?

This was a fine time to start changing my mind. I'd done my duty all my life. But this . . .

Being in the Heartlight makes you think about things a little differently, I guess. Or maybe it was the way she'd clutched at my arm. Maybe it was the way she'd looked when she asked me why they got names and

I didn't.

Maybe it was because no matter how many times I made an excuse to stand in her checkout line for a pack of gum, she always smiled at me. Or because . . .

Oh, *hell* and damnation. I would rather be ugly on the outside than ugly all the way through.

"Kate?" I whispered again, more urgently. The chapel floor was carved with fleur-de-lis, all circled, all tangled together. I stepped on them without mercy as I lurched toward the altar. They dug into my feet, sharp sliding edges. "Heart and Hell, Kate, wake up. Please."

Her arm slid away from her face. She blinked, and the chapel walls resounded with a gong-struck quivering. I made it to the altar as the stone whispered away between fan vaulting, the Inners appearing in the leaf-shaped doorways.

Had they just been here, waiting for me?

"Shit." I reached the altar and my human form shredded away. I whirled, my back to Kate, who let out a high whistling scream. The Heart thudded, and its light drenched us all with crystal clarity.

The Inners moved forward, and they each had their own knives. Their hoods covered their faces, but their eyes gleamed from the darkness underneath.

"The Heart demands," one intoned, in a deep, beautiful bell-voice.

"The Heart demands!" the others answered, in chorus.

Kate screamed again. It was a lonely, despairing sound.

I put my feet down, dug my claws in. *"Stay back!"* I yelled. The harsh note cut across their singing, a blot on their beauty.

I should have never brought her here. Too late now.

They drew closer. They didn't pay any attention to my warning, and both hearts inside my skin stopped beating.

Everything grew still. And I made up my mind. Too little too late, but I did it. I decided, and everything inside me fell into place.

I set the point of the obsidian knife against my chest. *Oh, my Heart. Kate. I'm sorry.*

They wouldn't hurt her if the Heart received its tithe. That was the Tiend — the payment of a heart.

They were almost close enough to spring. I knew that even though they were in robes, they were still gargoyles. I knew their strength and speed because I knew my own. Kate grabbed at my shoulders. She was shouting something. I couldn't hear her through the noise of my heart and my Heart crashing in my ears.

The Heart spoke to me.

And I shoved the knife in hard, piercing both Heart and heart. It's not that difficult if you know where to press. If you're determined, and if you can hit one of us when we're flesh and not stone. Or flesh in just one vulnerable place.

The Heartlight dimmed.

And my hearts . . . stopped.

It felt like I'd been dropped in broken glass, rolled around, then dipped in acid and pulled apart. My head pounded. Everything seemed put together wrong.

Oh, shit. Didn't I die?

There was a blurry light. Silvery and cool. Something warm stroking my forehead. It felt good.

"I think he's coming around," she whispered.

My eyes opened slowly. "Kate?" I croaked.

Behind her was stone ribbing. It was the same room I'd been in all afternoon. No sunlight, though. This was pure Heartlight, and the pulse in the walls was soft and satisfied.

"I'm here." She touched my cheek. Smiling. She was smiling. "Hey."

"Welcome back." This was from our guide. He'd pushed his hood back, and I stared at him in wonderment.

Smooth skin. Regular nose, low wide cheekbones, blue eyes. He wouldn't win any prizes, but he wasn't a squashed-together linebacker with pitted skin and picket-fence teeth.

He was unquestionably gargoyle, though. His ears came up to points and I could sense the Heart in him, echoing the beat in the walls.

"What the . . . ?" It was the best I could manage.

"Congratulations." He pushed his long, straight dark hair back behind one ear. "You passed the test. You're an Inner now. You can stay here, or you can go out into the world and do the same kind of work you did before. With your Heart." He glanced at Kate, who was still in the same red dress. It was satin, and my God but her va-va-vooms looked even . . . well, voomier.

"Huh?" I blinked. Kate stroked my cheek again.

"They told me you wouldn't hurt me." Her smile was a little less tired now. The dress was cut low enough that I could see the upper edge of the mark on her left breast, running with its dark fluorescence.

"All I had to do was scream. No big deal, I've done a lot of that lately."

"I'll leave you two to get acquainted." Our guide nodded smartly. "Brother. Miss Katherine."

"What the *hell?*" I still sounded lost. Everything hurt, but the hurt was receding. "The Heart —"

"The Heart has had its tithe." The guide nodded, once. "You fulfilled the Tiend. Rest."

And with that, he swept out the door. It closed softly, and I stared up at Kate. I stared at her so long she shrugged, defensively.

"This is all weird as fuck." Her shoulders hunched. "But it's better than checking at EvilMart."

"He looks . . ."

"Not so bad, huh? You're much better." Her grin lit up her entire face. "They explained everything. Well, mostly everything. You did what you were supposed to do, and now you're free."

"I thought I was dead." The weakness retreated. I pushed myself up on my elbows and lifted my hand.

The fingers were still callused and strong, but they weren't gray and gnarled. And when I touched my own face I didn't find craters. I found smooth skin and stubble, and my nose wasn't a squashed mushroom. My tongue ran over my teeth, and the familiar geography inside my mouth was different. If I looked in a mirror, I probably wouldn't see yellowed picket-fence teeth. I'd see straight white pearls.

I was in a stranger's body.

"I kind of figured you had a crush on me." Kate sat back on a low stool. There was a mirror across the room, and I wasn't sure if I wanted to look in it. Outside the window, the garden drowsed under gentle silver Heartlight. The smell of jasmine smoked in through the window. "I mean, all those CornNuts."

"I'm not ugly?" I sounded about five years old.

"You never *were*." She folded her arms. "But we've got to work on our communication. And what do I call you, anyway? Didn't you ever give yourself a name?"

I stared at her fish-mouthed for a while until she broke up laughing. It was a nice sound, and the smile that cracked over my disbelieving alien face felt like sunshine.

"Call me what you want," I mumbled, and that broke her up all over again. I settled back into the bed and stared at her. It was like waking up Christmas all over. "I'm not ugly?"

"You never were ugly. Ever." She moved as if she were going to get up, and I flung out a hand to stop her.

A stranger's hand. "Please. Kate. I'm sorry, I —"

She sank back down and stared at me. We looked at each other for a long time. "You mean you're sorry for bringing me here, when you thought I was going to be a human sacrifice?"

My neck felt like rusted metal when I nodded. My hair moved on the pillow.

She nodded, golden hair falling in her eyes. She looked very solemn, and the Heart inside me — it was still there, ticking along as if I hadn't shoved a knife in it — turned over. If I could have torn it out and given it to her, I would have.

Because it had been hers all along, hadn't it?

"Yeah." She settled back down on the stool. "It's still better than checking at Evil-Mart. Just relax, for now. We'll have to think up a name for you, they say. And they say we can go wherever we want, that you've got a vacation you didn't go on."

My throat refused to work right for a few

seconds. Then I got the words out.
"How do you feel about Bermuda?"

THE DEMON IN THE DUNES
CHRIS GRABENSTEIN

Chris Grabenstein did improvisational comedy in New York City with Bruce Willis before James Patterson hired him to write advertising copy. He is the Anthony and Agatha award–winning author of the John Ceepak/Jersey Shore mysteries, *Tilt-A-Whirl, Mad Mouse, Whack-A-Mole, Hell Hole, Mind Scrambler,* and *Rolling Thunder;* the thrillers *Slay Ride* and *Hell for the Holidays;* and the middle-grades chillers *The Crossroads* and *The Hanging Hill.* His dog Fred has even better credits: Fred starred on Broadway in *Chitty Chitty Bang Bang.* With five brothers, most of his summer vacations growing up were pretty scary, but the only paranormal creatures Chris encountered were the mermaids at Webb's City Drug Store in St. Petersburg, Florida, where the whole family went every August to visit his grandparents. The humidity was pretty monstrous, too. You can visit Chris (and Fred) on the Web at www.chrisgrabenstein.com.

I don't know why I'm lying here dreaming about 1975 and the demon in the dunes.

It's summer. Seaside Heights, New Jersey. Saturday. August sixteenth. 1975. The night I first saw the demon lurking in the shadows at the dark edge of the sand.

Kevin Corman and I are running down a moonlit street away from the Royal Flamingo Motel and our families.

"You score?" Kevin asked.

"Yeah." I held up two warm beer cans. "Schlitz."

"Your old man won't notice?"

"I don't think so," I answered — nervously as I recall. I wasn't a big rule breaker when I was a teenager. I usually stayed quiet. Stayed out of trouble.

"Far out," said Kevin, taking my two Schlitz cans and stuffing them up underneath the flapping coat of his leisure suit. He was dressed to score that night. Dressed like John Travolta would dress a few years later when he had the same sort of Saturday night fever.

Kevin and I were on our annual two-week family vacations down the shore. We were neighbors back home in Verona, New Jersey, went to the same high school.

"Uhm, were you able to get any, you know, booze?" I stammered as we tried not to look too conspicuous: two teens — one nervous, the other cocky — skulking down Ocean Avenue at 9:30 at night. When we were younger and on vacation, this is the time of night when we would've badgered our parents into taking us up to the boulevard for swirled soft-serve ice cream cones. Now, our mothers and fathers stayed by the motel pool to play cards, smoke cigarettes, and drink highballs out of indestructible plastic cocktail glasses while we lied about heading over to Funtown Pier so we could go out drinking ourselves.

"My parents drink whiskey, Dave," said Kevin. "Extremely hard to rip off, man. Doesn't come in a can."

"Yeah."

"Sometimes, my dad snags miniature bottles off airplanes. Doesn't bring 'em on vacation, though."

"Cool."

"Hey, you ever even drink whiskey?"

"No. Not really."

"Word to the wise: Beer and wine, mighty fine. Beer and whiskey? Mighty risky."

I nodded as if I knew.

"So, where's Jerry?" I asked.

"Said to meet him over on K Street."

"Cool." We had two more blocks to go. "What about, you know — the girls?"

"Relax, dude. They're college girls. Means they'll have their own wheels."

"Yeah."

"And Dave?"

"Yeah?"

"Chicks this hot? They definitely know how to find the dunes, bro. Probably been going down there to make out since we were like in junior high."

I shuddered to think about all the things the curvy college freshmen we had met eight hours earlier might know. They were both nineteen. Kevin and I were infants: sixteen-year-olds with pimples when we ate too much pizza. Our buddy Jerry McMillan was a little older. Seventeen. He'd been "held back" a year. Always said he liked second grade so much, he took it twice.

We reached K Street.

"I did score these." Kevin flashed me a half-empty pack of Kent cigarettes he had undoubtedly stolen out of his old man's Windbreaker. "Want one?"

"No, thanks."

"You ever try one?"

"Nope."

He shook the pack. "More taste, fine to-bacco."

I waved him off.

Kevin shrugged and lit up. He smacked down a long drag and let it out in a series of billowing smoke rings. I remember I was impressed.

"We are looo-king goooood," Kevin said between deep tokes, doing a pretty good Chico from *Chico and the Man.* A lot of guys did the same imitation back in the seventies, but Kevin had the shaggy Freddy Prinze hairdo to go with it.

We waited. Kevin smoked. He looked pretty damn cool doing it, and that made me wonder if I could ever look cool enough for the night's coming attraction: my first blind date.

The two girls we had met on the beach had a friend.

That's why I had splashed on some of my father's Hai Karate cologne. Found it in his Dopp kit along with some foil-wrapped condoms. My parents having sex. That was something I definitely didn't want to think about when I was sixteen and being fixed up with a college coed who probably had sex several times a day between classes.

"Where the hell is Jerry?" Kevin said as he ground out his cigarette butt in the sand at the crackled edge of the asphalt. "College chicks this hot won't wait forever. They're from Philly, man!"

My heart beat faster.

We'd first met the two Philly girls when they were half naked on the beach and Jerry McMillan had had the balls to stroll over to their blanket and talk like a letter straight out of *Penthouse* magazine: "Is it hot out here or is it just you two?"

They should've laughed or groaned or even puked at Jerry's lame pickup line. But, no. They both thought our somewhat older friend was cute. Most girls did. Jerry McMillan was lean and lanky with droopy eyes that made it look like he was half asleep at all times. He kept his shiny helmet of hair sleekly combed over his ears, its slanting divide always parked directly over an ironically arched eyebrow.

As it turned out, the girls Jerry had randomly decided to hit on were looking to get down and boogie. They eagerly volunteered their names (Donna and Kimberly) and local phone numbers. They were staying at the Bay Breeze Motel with another friend, Brenda. Three college girls in a single room. No parents. They were all probably on the pill. A lot of girls were popping birth control pills in 1975 because

460

"makin' love with you is all I wanna do," at least according to Minnie Riperton's big hit single on the radio. Everybody who was sixteen or over that summer had already lost their virginity.

Everybody except me.

"We've already done the Boardwalk," sighed the girl named Donna, arching her back, stretching her double-D cups to the max. If Jerry McMillan was a *Penthouse Forum* letter, this Donna was the Pet of the Month without the staples.

"So," said Jerry, "I take it you two are *bored* with the *Board*walk?"

Incredibly, the girls laughed at that lousy line, too!

"Yeah," said Donna, who had Farrah Fawcett's winged hairstyle from the pinup poster. "We want to have some real fun, you know? We are ready to feel the funk and party hearty!"

"Then, ladies, you came to the right beach," said Kevin, who had been pumping iron on a bench in his garage all winter and spring so his chest and stomach would be ready for just this moment. I hung in the background. When you're a timid teen, it pays to have brazen friends like Kevin and Jerry.

"So, Sunshine," said Jerry, crouching

down so the girls could gaze dreamily at his droopy eyes. "You ever heard about the dunes down south? In the state park?"

"Sure," said the other girl, Kimberly, as she rolled over to tan her back. She was wearing a very small bikini spotted with Wonder-Bread-wrapper-colored polka dots. The bottom was actually two tiny triangles held together by white plastic rings at her hips. She reached around to unsnap the hook holding her skimpy top in place so she wouldn't have an unsightly tan line racing across her back to add to the white dough-nuts the sun-blocking circles would defi-nitely be leaving on her flanks.

"Meet us down there," said Kevin. "Ten P.M. We'll bring the liquid refreshments."

"We'll find some driftwood, too," added Jerry. "Rub a couple stiff sticks together and see if we can start a fire." Every cheesy thing the guy said made these girls giggle.

I said nothing.

When I was sixteen, girls terrified me.

"Can we bring Brenda?" asked Donna, whose bikini was full of burnt-orange and harvest-gold flowers. Reminded me of the coffee percolator back in our motel kitchen-ette. "Brenda's different. Likes to read books and junk."

"No problemo. She can hang with Dave.

He reads books, too. Finished the summer reading list like back in June."

It was true. In books, I could be cool like Jerry and Kevin.

"You sure?" giggled Kimberly. "What if Brenda is like a total dog?"

"Doesn't matter," said Kevin. "Dave will bring his leash and walk her while the rest of us get down and get funky!"

So at nine thirty that night, Kevin Corman and I stood underneath a hazy street lamp waiting for Jerry McMillan, more booze, the two horny college chicks, and my blind date with the bookish Brenda.

Like I said, Jerry was seventeen but looked even older, so he was always the one in charge of procuring the adult beverages for any party, be it a kegger or a spontaneous bonfire on the beach in Island State Park. He had headed over to Barnegat Bay Bottles, the scuzziest package store in all of Seaside Heights, maybe New Jersey, to procure a couple cases of beer and several bottles of Boone's Farm wine: Apple and Strawberry. Both flavors tasted like Kool-Aid laced with malt liquor. Maybe gasoline.

It's amazing how much I'm remembering now about that summer night in 1975. How vivid it all seems — especially when I realize I haven't thought about any of this for decades. I grew up. Went to college. Became rich and famous. Locked my summers down the Jersey Shore inside a mental shoebox with the rest of my long-forgotten memories.

But tonight, as I lie in bed, fitfully drifting in and out of sleep, crisp details fill my head.

The swimming pool at the Royal Flamingo Motel with a curving slide lubricated with a trickle of water so you slid down even faster.

The Funtown Pier, home to all sorts of rickety thrill rides — including Dr. Shallowgrave's Haunted Manor.

The swarm of suntanned bodies bopping up the beach with their radios on. All of them, in my memory, swaying to the blare of a Tijuana Brass soundtrack, the theme from *The Dating Game.*

But, most of all, I remember Brenda Narramore.

Please don't tell my wife, who is snuggled up beside me now, cradled against my back, but I am dreaming about a girl I met one summer nearly three and a half decades ago.

Brenda Narramore.

My first summer love.

My muse and inspiration.

How many times have I redrawn her body, first as a leather-clad warrior in my comic books, then as an indestructible street fighter in a ripped and slashed flight suit as the heroine in my graphic novels? How many hours have I spent retracing her curves and lines? In fact, I made my fortune transforming my memories of Brenda Narramore into pen-and-ink drawings of Belinda Nightingale, superheroine of the post-apocalyptic world.

The critics always label my impossibly busty Amazon in her tight, revealing costume as "nothing more than an adolescent sexual fantasy."

They're right.

She is.

She is Brenda Narramore.

The girl I once feared I'd let the cloaked demon snatch away.

Jerry's car finally crunched across the seashells on the shoulder of the road.

I could hear "Love Will Keep Us Together" leaking out of his car stereo. Captain and Tennille. It had to be on the radio. No way would Jerry buy a cassette that bogus.

Jerry — who actually possessed a legal New Jersey driver's license in addition to his fake one from New York State that made him officially eighteen and therefore old enough to buy booze — had his own car. A

Starsky and Hutch Gran Torino with a modified V-8 and a Cruise-O-Matic transmission. I can still see the scooped manifold jutting up over the hood. His "ex-dad" had given the car to Jerry just after the divorce.

"What it is, what it is," he said as he scrolled down his window. "You bring your bread?"

I dug into my shorts. "Five bucks, right?"

Jerry snatched the wrinkled bill out of my fist. "Funkadelic. You steal it from your old man?"

"Nah. I mowed lawns last month."

"Dyno-mite." He turned to Kevin. "Don't leave me hangin', bro!"

Kevin passed off his cash with a slap to Jerry's palm.

"What it is, what it is," said Jerry. I forget why. We all said that in 1975, I guess. "Hop in, brothas!"

Kevin called shotgun. I climbed into the backseat with the two cardboard flats filled with beer cans — one slightly refrigerated case of Schlitz, another of Falstaff. A wrinkled grocery sack stuffed with twist-cap bottles of what Boone's Farm called wine clattered every time Jerry hit a pothole.

"Didn't even need to hire Squeegie tonight," Jerry bragged. "The blind doofus with the Coke-bottle glasses was working behind the counter."

If Jerry couldn't score our adult beverages with his fake ID, Squeegie was always his fallback plan: a burned-out World War II vet who slept in the Dumpster out back behind the liquor store. Squeegie would do just about anything for two bucks. Of course, back in 1975 gas cost forty-four cents a gallon, a stamp ten, and a whole pack of cigarettes only thirty-five.

The last time someone sneaked me a pack here in New York City, it cost him nine dollars, and I only got to smoke one before my wife caught me, started crying, and flushed about eight dollars and fifty-five cents' worth of tobacco down the toilet.

I had told her I'd quit.

I had lied.

We met the Philly girls at the state park.

Brenda Narramore was beautiful.

A dark pyramid of wavy hair tumbled over her shoulders in a cascade of kinky corkscrews. Her body was perfectly proportioned, up top and down below. She even wore sexy librarian glasses before they became fashionable. That's why Belinda Nightingale always accents her skintight leather breastplate with horn-rimmed reading glasses.

That first night, however, the real Brenda was not costumed as an Amazon princess. I remember she wore an embroidered peasant blouse tied off with a sash, the shirttails barely covering her bikini bottom. It looked like she was wearing the tiniest miniskirt ever sewn. She also carried a canvas flower-power beach bag.

"Hi, guys," said Donna. "This is Brenda."

Donna more or less said that to me, officially pairing us up for the evening.

"Hey," I said.

Brenda Narramore smirked. Her raven-black eyes sized me up. I don't think they liked what they saw.

"Shall we?" said Jerry, who was lugging the clinking bag of Boone's Farm bottles under his arm. He held out his free hand and Kimberly, the lanky girl who tottered like she was already wasted on cheap wine, took it.

"Need a hand?" Donna said to Kevin, who carried the case of Schlitz.

"I'm good."

She squeezed his bulging upper arm. "Strong, too."

He shrugged. "I work out a little."

"A little?" She was kneading his arm like some Italian women work over cantaloupes in the produce aisle.

"C'mon," said Kevin with a well-practiced shake of his shaggy hair. "Let's boogie."

They headed down to the beach.

Brenda Narramore looked at me. I never felt so scrawny or childish, standing there soaked in Hai Karate, wearing my best Orange Sunkist "Good Vibrations" T-shirt and denim cut-offs, straining to hold on to that case of Schlitz without all the cans tumbling out because, somehow, maybe from the condensation dripping down the sides of the aluminum tallboys, the cardboard bottom had become sopping wet.

Brenda pulled a pack of Doral Menthol cigarettes out of her beach bag. Stuck one between her plump lips. Flicked her Bic and lit up.

I guess I was gawking at her.

"Dream on," she sneered on the exhale.

She ambled down to the beach.

I followed. A safe distance behind her.

We scraped up some driftwood and used the brown paper wine bag to start a small beach fire.

Not a raging bonfire, just enough extra warmth to help the beer and wine make everybody feel good 'n' toasty. Intoxicated after chugging three tepid cans of Falstaff (the beer that promised "man size pleasure"), I became hypnotized by the fire. I saw chattering mouths and contorted faces dancing in the flickering flames, not to mention a flock of shadowy witch doctors leaping across the sand, furiously stretching out their twitching limbs to reach the not-too-distant dunes where, it seemed to me, more nefarious shadow friends might lie in wait.

Remembering Kevin's sage words about beer and wine being considered mighty fine, I unscrewed the cap off a bottle of Boone's Farm Strawberry Hill and started guzzling.

It's no wonder, not much later, I started seeing real phantoms. The demon in the dunes.

I gulped the wine, because I was nervous, sitting scant inches from Brenda Narramore, who kept lighting up Doral Menthol cigarettes while exhaling her own hazy cloud of specters, adding them to the mustering swarm of ghosts sent swirling skyward by our smoky campfire. One time, when I shifted in the sand, our thighs actually brushed. I don't think Brenda Narramore felt it, but I was extremely glad I had worn the tight cotton cutoffs instead of my J.C. Penney polyester shorts, which would not have done a very good job concealing that night's rising adolescent fantasies.

Then, believe it or not, Brenda actually

turned, pushed a few bouncy hair coils out of her eyes, and smiled at me like she knew every secret I had ever had.

"Ciggy-boo?" she said, holding out her crinkled Doral pack.

"He's a wimp," sniggered Kevin, who was bogarting one of his dad's Kents on the other side of the fire circle, letting the cigarette dangle limply off his lips. "Dave doesn't smoke."

I reached out for Brenda's proffered pack. "Hey, there's a first time for everything, bro."

"What it is, what it is," said Jerry, admiring my sense of adventure.

I pulled a white, filtered tube of tobacco out of its wrinkled cellophane container. "Dorals, huh?"

Brenda nodded. "They're menthol," she whispered, her voice husky and helpful.

"Cool."

For some reason, that made Brenda laugh. Maybe she thought I'd said, "Kool."

"Need a light?" she asked.

"Yeah. Thanks."

She found her Bic in the breast pocket of that gossamer peasant blouse, which, when backlit by the fire, was basically see-through. I could see she was round and firm and perfect.

"Thanks." I took the lighter. Rolled the little ribbed wheel with my thumb a few times. It sparked against the flint.

"Smooth move, Ex-Lax," said Kevin, my buddy the expert smoker. "Hold down the button, spaz."

I did as suggested. Heard butane gas hiss up from the tiny plastic tank.

"Now flick it."

I flicked.

The flame torched up six inches and scorched my nasal hairs.

"Here," said Brenda. She braced a warm hand on my thigh and plucked the unlit cigarette out of my mouth. "I'll light it for you."

She smacked hard on the Doral she had already had going in her mouth until its tip glowed as bright as the dashboard cigarette lighter when it popped out of its hole in my dad's Buick. Red hot, she plucked her cigarette from her lips, put mine in its place, and lit it off the end of the glowing one.

This wasn't just my first cigarette — it was also my first lesson in chain smoking.

"Since it's your first, just puff it," Brenda said as she handed the smoldering ciggy-boo back to me. "Don't inhale right away."

"Cool."

But I did.

Hacking and coughing and choking, I ignored Kevin's laughs and took another sip of that horrible strawberry wine, grimaced, and tried again.

This time, the smoke filled my lungs a little easier. Slid down my windpipe a little smoother. Maybe it was the menthol. It felt like I was sucking on a hot candy cane. And man, did I feel good. Something powerful shot through my veins, made me feel as funny and clever as Jerry and Kevin combined.

"Taste me, taste me." I raised my cigarette and recited Doral's famous TV jingle as if it were Shakespearean verse. "Come on and taste me!"

Everybody laughed. The three girls. My two buddies. Jerry McMillan even winked at me just to let me know I was finally catching on to how to play the game, finally growing up.

Finally joining the fraternity of the tight and the cool.

So I smacked down some more smoke. Stifled some more coughs. Felt a rush of nicotine that made me feel like a jolly genius with superhuman powers. I jumped up and did my best to impersonate the jazz chanteuse voice of the singing cigarette pack in Doral's cheesiest TV commercial: *"Taste me, taste me. C'mon and taste me! Take a puff and let me do my stuff!"*

Everybody was doubled up, laughing, holding their sides.

Brenda Narramore included.

Blurry from beer and wine, dizzy from tar and nicotine, I stumbled sideways and accidentally dropped my "ciggy-boo" in the sand.

"Here," said Brenda. She was already firing up its replacement for me.

I plopped down next to her. Took my second smoldering stick. I coughed like I had bronchitis. Felt dizzy. My brain was all kind of fuzzy, but I think Brenda Narramore had moved closer to me. Our thighs kissed.

I couldn't follow up on whatever that might mean because Kevin wanted to tell ghost stories.

Understandable.

We were sitting around a hypnotic driftwood fire under a full moon. The three girls were giddy and loose thanks to the beer and wine. In fact, Kimberly had already crawled into Jerry's lap wearing nothing but her bikini.

A good ghost story would force the other ladies to leap into the first available pair of strong, manly arms they could find (such as the ones Kevin had spent the winter and spring sculpting in his garage).

And so Kevin started spinning his tale.

"My uncle Rocco works for the Verona Volunteer Rescue Squad. One night, they get this call from over in Montclair. Now, Montclair is a bigger town, has a professional ambulance crew, firefighters, the whole nine yards. But, last March, there was this *huge* accident. A horrible wreck. Seven girls in a station wagon, cheerleaders on their way home from a basketball game, wrap themselves around a telephone pole."

Donna gasped. It was all the encouragement Kevin needed.

"Anyway, my uncle Rocco and his partner hit the siren and lights because it's all-hands-on-deck time, you know? There's only one problem: They're from Verona and don't know the roads over in Montclair too good. So they pull over to the side of the road. Whip out a map. Can't figure out where the hell they are. All of a sudden, Uncle Rocco senses somebody staring at him through his window. It's freaking him out, but he turns around and sees this old black dude standing right outside his door."

"What'd he do?"

"He rolled down his window."

Donna gasped again.

"Remember, it's early March. Technically

still winter. So when Uncle Rocco rolls down that window, he's hit with a blast of cold air. He can see his breath steaming out of his mouth, it's so frigging chilly out. Anyways, he sizes up the old black dude. The guy doesn't look like trouble. Kind of dapper, a college professor type, you know? Wire-rimmed glasses, tweedy sport coat with the patches on the sleeves, neatly trimmed goatee. The works. Anyways, the professor standing outside their vehicle asks Uncle Rocco if he's looking for the car wreck. 'Yeah,' he says. The old black guy nods. 'It's about a mile east of here.' "

When he was doing the black man's voice, Kevin made him sound all warbly and spooky. The girls moved closer to their guys. Well, Donna and Kimberly. Brenda just sat there smoking Dorals, staring into the fire.

" 'You sure?' my uncle Rocco asks. 'Yes,' says the black man. 'Take the next right, then turn left at the second traffic light. The second, mind you. Not the first. The second!' "

"So what happened?" Even Jerry Mc-Millan was mesmerized.

"They take off. Siren wailing. Lights spinning. They do the right, hit a major highway, count the traffic lights. Long story short, they find the wreck right where the old man

476

said it would be. They set to work. The station wagon is totaled. Buckled up on itself like an accordion. So they get out their power saws and pry bars. Work off the doors. Cut open the roof."

"Are the girls all dead?" asked Kimberly.

"No, they're rushed to the hospital. All seven of them."

"They didn't die and turn into ghosts?" Kimberly whined. "I thought this was supposed to be a ghost story."

"It is. Hang on."

Donna scooched closer to Kevin. Kimberly wrapped her arms around Jerry's neck. Brenda fired up two fresh Dorals at the same time. A double-barreled shotgun. Offered one to me.

"Thanks." I took it. They were getting easier and easier, milder and milder. I took a puff and let the Doral do its stuff.

"Anyways," Kevin continues, "after they run the girls to the hospital, all the ambulance crews are hanging out in the ER parking lot, shooting the breeze. Uncle Rocco asks some guys from the other volunteer squads how they found the wreck. Most bust his chops; say they used a frigging map. One or two, though, one or two say this old black dude walked out of the shadows and told them where to go. Black guy in glasses with a goatee. 'We couldn't see his breath,' says this one paramedic from another town near Montclair. 'What?' my uncle asks. 'It's freaking cold out,' says the other rescue worker. 'My breath was steaming out of my mouth, but this black guy? You couldn't see no breath.' My uncle suddenly remembers: He couldn't see the black dude's breath, either!"

Donna is too scared to gasp again. So she shivers. Her teeth chatter.

"A week later," Kevin continues, "Uncle Rocco goes to visit the girls in the hospital, wants to see how they're doing. They're all fine. One of the girls, though, is black, and she's got stuffed animals and flowers and a couple of framed pictures propped up on her bedside table there. 'Who's that?' my uncle asks, pointing at one of the pictures. 'My grandpa,' says the girl. 'He died last November.' And the guy in the picture? Dig this: He's wearing wire-rimmed glasses, a goatee, and a tweed sport coat. Just like the black dude with the invisible breath. To this day, Uncle Rocco swears it was the girl's grandfather who told them how to find that wreck! The old man came back from the dead so his granddaughter wouldn't have to die, too! He was like her guardian angel!"

Nobody said anything for about ten seconds.

The fire popped and crackled.

"That's freaky," whispered Donna. She hugged herself. I could see whole patches of goose bumps sprouting on her arms.

"You cold?" Kevin, ever the gentleman, offered her his leisure suit jacket.

"I know a better way to warm up." She took Kevin's hand. "You ever done it in the dunes?"

"Not with a fox like you!" Kevin grabbed a fresh six-pack and a beach blanket. The two of them headed for the privacy on the other side of the sand mounds.

Meanwhile, the totally trashed Kimberly, teetering in Jerry's lap, was so stoned she had become fixated on the glowing tracers trailing behind the bright red embers drifting up inside the fire's curling smoke.

"You know," said Jerry, seizing the moment, "if you were the new burger at McDonald's, you'd be the McGorgeous."

"Shut up," said Kimberly, stumbling up, noisily slapping some sand off her bikini-bottomed butt. Then she burped. "Let's go screw."

And they left us, too.

Brenda Narramore and I were all alone.

We silently smoked more of her Dorals.

She twirled off the plastic wrap on a second pack. The sand around us started to resemble one of those ashtrays near the elevators at a fancy hotel. Stubbed-out butts stood at attention like tiny tombstones all around us. My chest ached.

About two cigarettes later, I heard soft moans rise over the dunes to the east.

I gestured toward her beach bag. "You bring a good book? We might be stuck here awhile."

She dug into the canvas sack. "Yeah."

I recognized the burgundy cover: *The Catcher in the Rye.*

"Good book," I said.

"You've read it?"

"Hasn't everybody?"

"Not Donna and Kim."

I nodded. Fiddled with the label on the Boone's Farm wine bottle. "I read it when I was like twelve, I think."

Brenda slid her glasses up her nose. "I actually like books more than boys. Sorry, David, but, most of the time, there's more going on between the covers of a good book than between most men's ears."

I nodded again. Message received.

I jammed the half-empty bottle of sickly sweet wine into the sand and reached for another can of Falstaff. At least my beer had promised me "man size pleasure" tonight.

I choked down a foamy swig and said, "Cool job."

"What?"

I nodded toward her book. "Being a catcher in the rye. Standing on a cliff in a swaying field of grain, watching out for a bunch of kids playing tag. If they come too close to the edge, I'd catch 'em, too. Save 'em."

"It's not a real job, David."

"Should be."

She cocked a quizzical eyebrow. "Really?"

"Oh, yeah. Way too many people pushing kids off cliffs these days. Making them grow up too fast. Sending them off to die in pointless wars."

Her face softened. "So, tell me, David — exactly how old are you?"

"Sixteen."

"You seem older. Wiser."

"Is that a good thing or a bad thing?"

"Good."

"Far out."

That made her smile grow. Her lips were plump and moist. "You're not like other guys, are you, David?"

I laughed. "Correct-a-mundo. Most of the other guys I know are over there in the dunes making out with the other girls." I drained my Falstaff.

"So, Dave? What do you do?"

"Huh?"

"What. Do. You. Do?"

"I go to school. Verona High. Next year, I'll be a junior."

"Really?"

"Yeah."

She moved closer. So close, I could smell the minty smoke trapped inside her tangled hair.

"That's not who you are, Dave. What do you like to do when you're you being you?"

I had heard college girls were into philosophical discussions about the meaning of life and stuff. Could shoot the bull all night. So I thought for a second. Gave an honest answer: "I like to draw some."

"You're an artist?"

"No. I wouldn't say that. I just like to draw. I did that clown on the matchbook cover for the Famous Artists Correspondence School. Flunked."

She grinned and dipped into her beach bag.

"Show me." She held up a Bic ballpoint pen. "I'll be the judge."

"I usually work with a Flair or a Magic Marker . . ."

"Show me."

Fine.

"You have any paper in there?" I asked.

She handed me her copy of *Catcher in the Rye.* "Draw inside it. On the blank pages up front."

"Aw, I can't do that."

"It's not a library book, Dave. It's mine. I own it. I want you to draw in it."

"You're sure?"

"Yes."

"What if I suck?"

"You won't. Draw."

So I flipped open the paperback cover. Started scribbling on a blank page near the front.

"You have pretty eyes," she said.

"Thanks. They're hazel," I said without looking up from my sketch. "They change color depending on what I wear."

"Fascinating."

She arched up on her knees with both arms pinioned between her thighs so she could lean in and watch me draw.

Her breath was soft and rapid.

I had always had a knack for doodling cartoons. Read a lot of comic books when I was a kid. Really did take that Famous Artist test, only I drew Binky the Skunk, not the clown. Took a couple of their correspondence classes through the mail, too. And every time I hit the mall, I always checked out those humongous Michelangelo and Da Vinci art books at B. Dalton. However, the work of art I created for Brenda Narramore was chiefly inspired by the Bill Gallo School of cartooning as seen in the sports pages of the *New York Daily News.*

I drew her as a baseball catcher with a corked bottle of rye whiskey trapped in his mitt.

"Voilà!"

"Nice," Brenda whispered, her voice as smoky as her ciggy-boo. "Sign it."

I did.

"I was thinking about giving him a loaf of bread," I said as I swirled out what my autograph still looks like to this day, "but the bottle was easier to draw. And how would you know it was *rye* bread? I'd have to dot it with seeds or something . . ."

I was babbling because Brenda Narramore had her warm hand prowling up my right knee, slowly creeping it higher, inching up and down toward my thigh. The front of my cutoffs was a pup tent.

Suddenly, Brenda stood and towered over me like the Colossus of Rhodes if Mr. Colossus had long tawny legs. She peeled her gauzy peasant blouse up over her head. Shook out her scrambled forest of hair.

"Have you ever drawn a nude, David?"

She held out her hand.

And, just like the other boys and girls that Saturday night, we headed off toward the privacy of the dunes.

We slid down behind a protective bunker of sea grass and sand.

"I've never . . ." I mumbled as she unbuttoned my jeans.

"Don't worry. I have."

Her heavy breasts swayed as her fingers worked over my zipper.

"What about . . . ?"

She put a finger to my lips.

"Shhh. You're just nervous."

I nodded. I was.

"Here." She dug into her beach bag. Found the crumpled Doral package. "Have another smoke. It'll calm you down."

"I thought we were supposed to, you know, smoke afterward."

She lit two fresh Dorals.

"We will, Dave. We will."

That's when I saw it. Behind her. Just above her shoulder.

She held out a cigarette. I didn't take it.

"Dave?"

I wasn't paying attention to her anymore.
How could I?

How could anyone?

Ten feet behind Brenda Narramore, lurching out of the shadows, was the demon of the dunes! An ancient, decrepit man — no, the gaunt walking skeleton of an old man, all jagged bone edges and drum-tight skin. He was hunched over in pain as if his spine were fused into a crooked hump. The thing was barefoot and cloaked in a shroud of white that only fluttered down to his knees, fully exposing the dried scabs and weeping blisters tattooing his shins.

I shoved Brenda away. Roughly. The two cigarettes she'd been holding fell like fire-streaking comets to the sand. I fumbled with my zipper.

"It's . . ."

She looked where I was staring, where I pointed.

"What?" She saw nothing.

If only I had been so lucky.

A malevolent cloud moved away from the moon so it could illuminate the demon's monstrously withered face. Under the folds of the hooded cloak, I saw sunken, hollow cheeks. A gaping hole for a mouth. No hair. Not even above his hollow eyes. No eyelashes, either. Just the puffed-open, bulging

486

eyeballs of a startled embryo.

I know I whimpered.

"David?"

My whimpering freaked Brenda out.

I didn't really care.

Panicked, I tried to scrabble backward, to scale the dune wall, to escape over the top of that horrible sand trap and run away from the demon only I could see.

Then I heard the creature's leathery lungs rasping for breath. Snoring backward, its chest expanded like a balloon — causing its shriveled face to be seized with unbearable pain.

That's when Brenda abandoned me.

"You guys?" she screamed as she ran away, covering her breasts as best she could. "You guys?"

I wanted to run away, too, but my legs were paralyzed.

The demon of the dunes staggered forward. It wheezed, and I was hit with the rank odor of death. It raised its right arm and pointed one gruesomely long, bony finger at me.

"Who are you?" I stammered, even though I knew the answer: The demon was my drunken hallucination. My emaciated pink elephant. Apparently beer and wine weren't always fine. Wine and beer could be something to fear. Especially if you polish off a whole six-pack and chase it with a half a bottle of strawberry-flavored rubbing alcohol.

Especially after listening to ghost stories.

This creature had to be a nightmarish manifestation of my latent Catholic guilt. An illusion. A hideous incarnation of my unbridled shame about what Brenda Narramore and I had almost done. This was the thing the nuns had warned us about. Mortal sin manifested in the guise of the Grim Reaper. I wasn't married to Miss Narramore, but I had seen her naked breasts. I had almost done more.

I deserved to be tortured by the devils and demons of my own imagining.

As the beast lurched closer, I could smell the rancid-meat breath seeping out its mouth hole.

"Stop! Now!"

It croaked the words.

"Stop! Now!"

I move uncomfortably in the bed.

Try not to wake my wife.

Why am I remembering Saturday, August sixteenth, 1975?

Am I, for whatever reason, meant to finally

unravel the mystery of the demon in the dunes?

Honestly, it's something I haven't thought about in more than three decades.

Long ago, I feared that my actions that hot summer night had riled up a slumbering spirit bent on punishing those who did not adhere to its stern moral code.

I imagined the wizened old man under the wrinkled robe to be the ghost of one of Brenda Narramore's distant relatives who, like the grandfather in Kevin's tale, had come back from the dead to protect her chastity and, when he couldn't persuade me to stop, turned his wrath on her!

For a time, I was certain that the demon lurking in the dunes was Brenda Narramore's guardian devil.

The next morning, I remember, Kevin and I went out for breakfast at this deli where they made extremely greasy fried-egg and bacon with cheese sandwiches. Hangover food.

"So, dude — you totally freaked that Brenda chick out last night."

"Yeah."

"What'd you do? Pull out your wanker?"

I shook my head. "I saw . . . something."

"What? Her humongous titties?"

I looked up from my sandwich.

"Hey," Kevin said defensively, holding up his hands, "everybody saw her running up the beach, man. She let it *all* hang out."

I didn't know what to say. I couldn't tell Kevin about the demon I thought I had seen in the dunes. We weren't little kids anymore. We weren't allowed to see prowling phantoms in the shadows or bogeymen hiding underneath our beds.

"I guess I acted like a dork," I finally said.

"Don't worry, bro. Plenty of fish on the beach. We'll meet some fresh chicks. Probably today." He held out his Kent pack. Two bent cigarettes were all that were left inside the wrinkled pouch. "Smoke 'em if you got 'em."

"No, thanks."

"I thought you smoked now."

"I'm quitting. My lungs still hurt from last night. Feel like charcoal briquettes."

"You'll get used to it, bro. You just cough up the phlegm and junk in the shower every morning. That clears 'em right out."

I waved him off.

Kevin sighed. Put his Kents back in his pocket. "Bummer."

"Yeah."

One week later, however, Brenda Narramore forgave me.

On the second Saturday of my family's two-week vacation, she strolled boldly up the beach, wearing nothing but a bikini and big sunglasses, her hair as wild as a brown sea of coiled serpents. She headed straight for the rolled-out towels where Kevin, Jerry, and I had set up shop for the day.

She had her beach bag slung over her shoulder and carried a portable radio like a lunch bucket, swinging it alongside her hip, letting it brush against the stretched fabric of her bikini bottom. I think "My Eyes Adored You" was droning out of the solid-state Sanyo's tinny speaker.

"I remember my first drunk," she said softly as my eyes did as the song suggested.

"What was it like?" I asked, my mouth drier than burnt toast.

"I saw giant lizards." She shot out her tongue. Flicked at imaginary flies. Rolled it back to moisten her lips. "Where are your two little buddies?"

I gestured to the left, where Jerry and Kevin were flirting with two bubbly blondes on a nearby beach blanket. High school girls. They had decided to "aim a little lower" after six straight days of crashing and burning with college chicks.

"You want to blow this pop stand?"

Brenda asked.

"Sure."

"You ever do the Haunted House on the Boardwalk?"

"Once. When I was little."

"You ever do it with a girl?"

I could only shake my head.

"It's dark in there, David. Real dark. Nobody can see you doing whatever it is you want to do."

We headed down to the Seaside Heights boardwalk.

"My snobbier friends at school call this Sleaze Side Heights," Brenda remarked as we strolled past buzzing pinball emporiums and the blinking lights of popcorn wagons.

"I take it they've been here before?"

She laughed. Tucked her arm under mine.

"You got any smokes, Dave?"

"Nah."

"You quit already?"

"Sort of. Maybe."

"Too bad."

I pulled a soggy dollar bill out of my swimming trunks. "They sell 'em over there," I said, gesturing to a smoke shop wedged between a French fry stand and a skeeball arcade. "You still doing Dorals?"

She nodded.

"Menthol, right?"

"Right."

"Don't disappear."

"I won't."

And she didn't. Not then, anyway.

It was easy to buy cigarettes when you were sixteen back in 1975. Everybody smoked. Brenda said at her college, you could even smoke in the classrooms. There were disposable ashtrays on every desk.

I handed her two packs of Doral Menthols.

"They were only forty cents each."

"Thanks, Dave." She uncurled the plastic wrapper off a pack, lit up a cigarette fast. I remember her hands were trembling slightly until she huffed down that long first drag. After she finished her smoke, Brenda grabbed my arms and pulled me close. Let me feel her bikinied breasts press against my chest. "Did buying me my ciggy-boos wipe you out?" She exhaled the remnants of stale smoke that had been swirling around inside her gorgeous chest up into my eyes.

"Yeah. I only grabbed like a buck this morning . . ."

She tugged playfully at my swimsuit's elastic waistband. Glanced down at my unambiguous bulge. "Funny, your pockets don't look empty."

My ears went sunburn red. I so wished I had worn blue jeans to the beach. Maybe an athletic cup.

"Don't worry, Dave. I've got cash." She broke our clinch and headed toward a clapboard kiosk. "I'll spring for the tickets."

We had been cuddling up in front of Dr. Shallowgrave's Haunted Manor, the rickety, ride-through spook house on the Funtime Pier. It was the closest thing Seaside Heights had to a genuine Tunnel of Love. Brenda bought five tickets for each of us, and we stepped into the waiting two-seater roller-coaster car. It was shaped like a skull.

"Welcome to the frights of Seaside Heights," said the guy who lowered our safety bar. He was about my age. Had more pimples. He also spent a little too much time eyeballing Brenda, checking out her tight top. When he finally stepped away from our car, he whistled in admiration and gave me a knowing nod: "Looo-king goooood, bro. Looo-king good."

The car jostled forward. I heard the pull chain clanking underneath our feet. Barn doors swung open, and our slow moving love seat was tugged into a dark tunnel filled with hazy smoke, ultraviolet lights, tolling bells, and hokey pipe organ music.

Brenda snuggled closer. I draped my arm over her shoulder.

She moved my hand to her breast.

"Welcome to my Haunted Home!" boomed a sinister recorded voice. "Ride in peace! Mwa-ha-ha!"

I heard a *whoosh-click* of compressed air. Hidden doors sprang open. Two skeletons with tattered clothing flailing off their jangling bones flew out of dark cupboards.

Brenda shrieked. I laughed.

And kept my hand locked on second base.

Next came the mannequin strung up in a noose. Then another dummy puking up bright red blood into a witch's cauldron.

"Gross," mumbled Brenda.

"Yeah. I told him to stay away from the chili."

We rounded a bend and entered the Haunted Library. An automaton — a shriveled old woman who resembled Norman Bates's dearly departed mother after a witch doctor had shrunken her head — was rocking back and forth in a creaky chair in front of a wall of bookcases. A rubber rat popped in and out of a hole in her rib cage. Some of the books shook in the shelves while a gargoyle serving as a bookend flashed its bright red eyes.

That's when the lights went out.

Our car froze.

All the moaning and groaning and spooky music slid to a stop.

The ride had died.

The tunnel was pitch-black.

"Guess they forgot to pay the electric bill this month," I quipped.

"Smoke 'em if you got 'em," said Brenda, fumbling through her canvas bag, crinkling open that pack of Dorals I had bought her.

She flicked and flicked her Bic but the gas didn't catch. The flint just sparked and strobed.

"Damn," she muttered, the white tube stuck to her upper lip.

"Here," I said. "Let me."

I took two cigarettes out of the pack. Stuck them in my lips.

"Use these," said Brenda, handing me a book of matches.

I gazed into her eyes. Flicked a paper match across the strip of sandpaper at the base of the book. Tried to light the cigarettes as suavely as I'd seen tuxedoed rogues light double smokes in the movies.

I inhaled on mine while I handed Brenda hers.

"I thought you quit," she said, taking a puff and snuggling closer.

"I changed my mind."

"Cool," she said.

"Yeah," I said. "It's the menthol."

We laughed and smoked, the glowing hot tips of our cigarettes casting the only light in the darkened tunnel. When the cigarettes were nearly finished, Brenda held hers elegantly off to the side. "Come here, big boy."

I did as instructed.

We French kissed like crazy. It tasted a little like two ashtrays licking each other, but I didn't care. I was alone in the dark with an incredibly sexy woman dressed in a bikini too tiny to fit my two fists. I flicked my cigarette down to the ground, leaned out of the car so I could stomp it out without looking down, then sank my hands into her wild hair to pull her face closer to mine.

Soon, my hands were sliding down across her bare shoulders, down to those barely contained breasts straining to burst free.

"I hope it takes all night for them to fix it," she moaned.

I was heading for third when he showed up again.

The demon from the dunes.

The emaciated man in the rumpled white cloak, his hooded face more horrifyingly gaunt than I remembered, the jawbone clearly visible beneath the skin, the nose a sharp protrusion of jagged cartilage. He was struggling to breathe through his gaping mouth hole. As he hovered in the darkness behind our car, I realized he was luminous, as if he had been irradiated in a nuclear bomb blast. His body was a floating, yellow-green X-ray; his head a skull wrapped in translucent skin.

"Stop!" he hissed at me, turning the air in the tunnel rank. *"Now!"*

I tried to ignore the glowing demon because it was obvious from the darting tongue dancing around inside my mouth and the hand guiding mine southward that Brenda Narramore sure as hell didn't hear her ghostly guardian of sexual abstinence wheezing his words of warning at me!

"Stop!"

I closed my eyes, tried to make the thing disappear.

"Stop!"

I sneaked open an eye and saw the demon once again attempting to raise its rigor-mortised right arm like the Spirit of Christmas Yet to Come from the Dickens tale so it could point a bony finger of condemnation at me.

That's when the lights thumped on. The

audiocassette of scary music slurred back to
life.

Brenda giggled. Pushed my wandering
hand, inches from heaven, aside.

"Just our luck."

"Yeah."

The car lurched forward.

The demon had disappeared.

A day later, Brenda did, too.

"Vacation's almost over," she said when we
kissed good-bye in the parking lot of her
motel that Saturday night.

"I'm here for another week."

"Me, too. But then, I'll be going back to
school."

"I could come visit you. I could take the
bus to Philly."

"No. You can't."

"Why not?" Listening to my own whining, I should have known the answer.

"You're too young, David."

"But . . ."

"This is what it is. Fun. A summertime
fling. Don't get all serious on me."

The transistor radio in my head rolled
through every sad song about summer
romances ever recorded. "See You in September." "Sealed with a Kiss." Chad and
Jeremy's "A Summer Romance." The Beach

Boys wailing about "having fun all summer long."

"But . . ." I stammered again.

"Don't worry, Dave, before letting you go, I want to feel some kind of good-bye." She was paraphrasing Holden Caulfield from *The Catcher in the Rye.* "Sad or bad, I need a good-bye." Her tongue tunneled into my ear again. "We'll head back to the dunes. Tomorrow night. Say our good-byes there. Finish what we started."

"Uh-huh." She was cupping my crotch.

"And David?"

"Huh?"

"It won't be sad or bad. It'll be the best good-bye you've ever had."

I nodded. I had already forgotten about my imagined visitor back in the funhouse. Hell, I had forgotten my own name.

The next night, however, Brenda was gone.

"We thought she was with you," said her roommates when I showed up at their motel for our hot Sunday night date down in the dunes.

"Did she go back to Philly?" I asked.

"No. Her stuff is still here. Don't worry, Davey. She'll show up."

But she never did.

I kept going back to the Bay Breeze Motel.

Her two girlfriends kept telling me they hadn't seen or heard from her since that day she went to the Boardwalk with me. Her beach bag was draped over the headboard of the bed she had been sleeping in. The sheets were rumpled and cold.

On Tuesday, Kimberly and Donna called the Seaside Heights Police.

The cops asked me all sorts of questions.

On Wednesday, my dad came to the police station with me and brought Kevin's father, who was a lawyer.

I answered every question as honestly as I could without embarrassing myself in front of my family. The police didn't need to know about the beer and Boone's Farm. About Brenda and me making out in the haunted house. I stuck to the facts. *Wheres* and *whens.*

"I only hung out with her twice," I said, sounding much younger than sixteen after two hours of interrogation. "I hardly even know her . . ."

"Are you officers finished?" asked Kevin's dad, sounding exactly like *Owen Marshall, Counselor at Law* from TV.

"Yeah," the cop said. "Miss Narramore's family is worried, is all. Nobody's heard from her since Saturday. Not like her not to check in, they say."

"I'm sorry," said my father, "but David here is in no way responsible for any of this. For goodness' sake, officers, Miss Narramore is a college student. Nineteen. She should be able to take care of herself. She sure as hell shouldn't be running up and down the beach playing Mrs. Robinson, seducing high school boys!"

I remember the cop nodding. "They're going through a rough stretch."

"Who?" my dad asked.

"Her family. The girl's grandfather died a couple weeks ago. Now she disappears. They're not thinking straight, you know? Keep pushing us to dig something up. I figure she's just another runaway, like in that new Springsteen song. Guess she was 'Born to Run.' "

The grown-ups all nodded.

I didn't. In fact, I froze.

Because, in my mind, at that moment, I knew exactly what had happened to Brenda Narramore.

It was just like that old man who had come back from the dead to help the rescue squads find his granddaughter.

The demon in the dunes was Brenda Narramore's recently deceased grandfather!

When I wouldn't stop pawing her, groping at her on the beach and in the Board-walk spook house, when I wouldn't listen to his ghostly demands to leave his grand-daughter alone, he had found a way to stop *her!*

That's when I would've totally freaked out if I hadn't started seriously smoking, full-time.

Dorals at first, to honor Brenda's memory, I guess. But Dorals were low in tar and nicotine. Not enough juice to wash away the guilt that came with the weight of know-ing that my actions had caused a beautiful girl to be "disappeared" by a demented dead relative.

I moved on to Marlboros.

Unfiltered Camels.

Cigarettes can numb you out. Erase a lot of mental anguish. Help you stuff down all sorts of feelings of guilt and shame and remorse. I think this is why, when I was a kid, all the priests and nuns smoked. We Catholics needed all the help we could get.

By Halloween 1975, I had forgotten all about Brenda Narramore. Callous of me, maybe, but I just assumed that the police officer was right. She was a runaway. Yes, that first month back home I would sneak down to the corner drugstore on my bicycle to check out the newspapers from Philadelphia and down the shore. I kept searching for a gruesome story like "Missing Girl's Body Found, Flesh Ripped off Her Beautiful Body by Deranged Beast" or "Monster Stalks Jersey Girl." But I never found anything about Brenda Narramore at all. Not even in the tabloids with the stories about Elvis and aliens.

The demon in the dunes was, most likely, what I first supposed it to be: a figment of my overactive imagination. Face it, seeing evil creatures lurking in blank white spaces is what a comic book artist does.

I just started seeing my mythical tormentors earlier than most.

However, after that ride down the tunnel of love with Brenda Narramore, I never saw that particular apparition again. I blocked him out of my waking thoughts. Only let his image seep into my subconscious when it needed an especially hideous creature to haunt the shadows of my graphic novels, like my first *New York Times* bestseller, an early Belinda Nightingale tale called *The Withered Wraith of Westmorland*.

The only thing I can't comprehend: Why am I thinking about all of this again? Why now?

Why today?

Why am I drifting back to Seaside

Heights, August 1975? Surely there are more important places and dates in my life for me to review. Especially now.

I hear a knock on a door.

Remember where I am.

My wife crawls out of the hospital bed.

I creak open an eye. Expect to see a doctor. Maybe a nurse.

It's a middle-aged woman with short-cropped, wiry gray hair.

"May I help you?" my wife asks weakly.

"I'm sorry," says the visitor. "I'm an old friend of David's. When I read in that papers that he . . ."

The visitor holds up a faded paperback book. Burgundy cover.

The Catcher in the Rye.

She opens the front flap. Shows my wife the doodle of the baseball catcher with the bottle of rye in his mitt. My wife nods. Recognizes my signature.

The demon in the dunes didn't kill Brenda Narramore. She grew old and frumpy.

I try to speak. Groan out her name. Can't. Too weak.

Dammit! Why am I thinking about that night we first met?

Saturday. August sixteenth. 1975.

I close my eyes. Race back. Replay it.

The young, topless Brenda Narramore

505

hovers over my trousers.

"Shhh. You're just nervous."

I nod. I am.

"Here." She digs into her beach bag. Finds the crumpled Doral pack. "Have another smoke. It'll calm you down."

"I thought we were supposed to, you know, smoke afterward."

She lights two fresh cigarettes.

It appears. Ten feet behind her, lurching out of the shadows. The gaunt walking skeleton of an old man, all jagged bone edges and drum-tight skin.

A man, maybe not all that old, maybe barely fifty, who only looks like a walking, hairless cadaver because he has been undergoing radiation treatments and chemotherapy for his lung cancer.

The demon wobbles forward; close enough, this time, for me to see his eyes when that cloud drifts away from the moon.

His hazel-green eyes.

My eyes.

"Stop!" he wheezes. *"Now!"*

And I know.

He is my wraith.

The ghost of a person on the verge of death sent forth to haunt himself.

He is me.

I am sixteen years old but staring at my

506

own dying soul, shrouded in a white knit hospital blanket from Memorial Sloan-Kettering Cancer Center in New York City where Brenda Narramore has come to say farewell to her long-ago summer love, where my wife has kept constant vigil, sleeping by my side in the hospital bed, forgiving me when I bribed an orderly to sneak me a pack of Marlboros so I could creep downstairs to the sidewalk with my rolling IV pole of postchemo drips to have one last smoke. My wife, who is weeping now because I am dying while the most crucial events of my life flash before my shuttering eyes.

I force my spirit back in time in an attempt to right the wrongs I did to myself.

"Stop!" I wheeze at my younger self. Me as I was and as I will become. *"Now!"*

I have, mercifully in my final moments, been given the opportunity to go back and warn myself.

On the beach.

In the funhouse.

My first cigarette and the one that got me hooked for good. The one I never quit from again.

Or did I?

I hear my withered lungs rattle. The inside of my chest itches and burns.

Did I heed my wraith's command?

I will never know.

For if I did, I won't be lying here dying while dreaming about 1975 and the demon in the dunes.

HOME FROM AMERICA

SHARAN NEWMAN

Sharan Newman is a medieval historian. That is a constant in her life. As a writer, however, she has published fantasy (the Guinevere trilogy), eleven historical mysteries (the Catherine LeVendeur series), three nonfiction books, and a number of articles and short stories in several genres, including one in the Stephen King issue of *Fantasy & Science Fiction.* For her most recent book, *The Real History of the End of the World* (Berkley, 2010), she was able to use all of these genres to find how people through history have envisioned the end of time. She lives on a mountainside in Oregon.

Patrick Anthony O'Reilly had dark curls, deep blue eyes, and a smile that could bewitch any woman from eight to eighty and beyond. He had the gift of gab, a hollow leg for porter and poteen, a fine tenor, and a cheerful readiness to join in any brawl going. Every St. Paddy's Day he was sure to be found at Biddy McGraw's pub, weeping in homesickness for Galway and cursing the English. In short, he was as fine an Irishman as ever came out of Cleveland.

When his friends pointed out to him that his family had come over to America in 1880, Patrick brushed the fact aside as unimportant.

"That doesn't make me a whit less Irish," he'd brag. "Four generations in America and not one of my family has ever married out."

"Who else would have you?" his friend Kevin once countered. "Might have done you some good if they had. They breed runts in your clan."

That was a low blow. Patrick hadn't spoken to Kevin for a month after that. But what did you expect? Kevin was a typical American mongrel: Polish, Italian, and Irish. The best you could say about his family was that they were all Catholic. But it was the jab at his size that cut Pat so deeply. He was barely five foot two, with hair gel. His parents were even shorter; his mother not even five feet. Pat had had to develop a lot of charm to get himself noticed in a world of hulking football players and long-legged women.

His size and youthful looks also meant that he could never get a pint without his ID being scrutinized with a magnifying glass. And sometimes even then, nervous bartenders shooed him out.

At twenty-five he still lived with his parents and worked at the post office alongside his father, Michael, and his cousins, sorting mail from all over the world while never leaving his own neighborhood. The O'Reillys tended to stay close, enduring the teasing about their size as a unified and slightly daunting group. Over the generations, they had made the local post office their own, and it was rare that anyone over five and a half feet tall was given a job there.

Pat rebelled inwardly at this extreme clannishness, but his secret desire was not to escape to a more varied culture. What he dreamed of most, with all his heart, was to return to the old country, not the Ireland of industry and high tech, but the land it had once been. Patrick O'Reilly really lived in a world of Celtic glory, of valiant battles and ancient adventures. He saw himself as the heir to Cu Chulainn and Niall of the Silver Hand. He was the navigator for St. Brendan, sailing beyond the edge of the horizon. He was one of the Wild Geese, following his king into exile. He was Michael Collins and

Charles Parnell and Eamon de Valera, fighting tyranny.

He was anyone but himself. Anywhere but the post office, watching stamps fly by from places he'd never see.

Since he paid little for his room and board, Pat had spent years squirreling away his paychecks until he had enough to finally make the trip to Ireland in style. But now that there was a tidy sum in his account, he still felt uncomfortable taking anything out, even for the trip of a lifetime. The whole family was like that, not exactly miserly, but reluctant to spend on anything but the necessaries. Pat thought he'd escaped the trait until the time came to make a withdrawal. The only thing any O'Reilly ever spent money on was shoes. Not one of them would dream of appearing in knockoffs. The finest leather and the best construction were essential. Most of the family spent more on shoes than food.

Perhaps he delayed the trip simply because he'd never gone anywhere without at least a few other O'Reillys. He'd tried to suggest to his parents that they make a family pilgrimage back to Ireland, but they always laughed and asked why he'd want to do that, when America had been so good to them all.

"We were driven out of Ireland," his

mother, Eileen, reminded him. "No one wanted us there. We were starving and forced to work for nothing."

"That we were," his father, Michael, nodded sagely over his briar pipe. "Here we've made our own Ireland, one that no one can invade. I wouldn't go back there for all the gold in the world."

Eileen gave him a sharp glance of warning that Pat didn't notice.

"But you've never been there, either of you," he whined. "Nor have your parents or anyone in the family. I just want to see the auld sod. I want to find my roots!"

"Don't be a muggins!" His dad cuffed him gently. "You don't need to look for your roots. The trees are all around you."

Pat didn't ask again, but he never stopped dreaming.

One day in spring, Pat came home from a late shift, eager for the porter stew his mother usually left for him to warm up. Instead of a solitary dinner and a beer, he found the house full to the rafters with cousins, uncles, aunts, and other assorted O'Reilly attachments. No one said a word, a miracle akin to the Second Coming. There was only one reason Pat could imagine for such solemnity.

"Who died?" he asked.

His mother stood slowly. In her hands she gripped a large, bright green envelope, edged with gold. Pat noticed right away that it hadn't gone through the post. There was no stamp, only a pristine blob of sealing wax. It didn't look like a death notice. The gold seemed to shimmer like the Cuyahoga River in flames.

Still no one spoke. This unnerved Patrick most. Normally a family gathering would have put a henhouse to shame, with all the squawks, shouts, bursts of laughter, wails of infants, and, of course, the firmly stated opinions that eventually would lead to blows.

"Mom?" he asked warily.

At last she broke the silence. "It's come," she quavered, clutching the envelope to her chest. "We haven't been asked in fifty years, not since my granddad's time. I thought they'd forgotten all about us."

She searched in her pocket for a tissue, too overwhelmed to continue. Her sister, Teresa, took over.

"It's the invitation to the summer gathering," she told Patrick. "Only a thousand are so honored to be asked, and it happens only once every ten years."

"Imagine that," Pat's father murmured.

"Out of all those millions of O'Reillys. And, when you add us up, that's sixty-odd people right here. I thought we were never invited because they wouldn't ask so many of us. Who'd have ever thought it?"

Patrick was tired, hungry, and out of patience. "Will one of you either tell me what's going on or else let me get to the kitchen for my stew?"

"It's Ireland!" Aunt Teresa looked at Pat as if he were dense. "We're all going to the Beltane Gathering, the O'Reilly *fine* re-union. Now, young man, you'll finally see just how deep your roots go."

Then the storm broke and everyone began to talk at once.

Patrick paid no attention to the babble around him. Ireland! He couldn't take it in. After all the years of denying any interest in it, suddenly everyone was acting as if they'd been given the key to Heaven. Of course, that had always been Pat's attitude, but he was astounded to find that others had been harboring the same longing.

The family immediately passed from chaos to high-gear efficiency. Dentist appointments were canceled, weddings postponed, mail stopped. The post office proved a problem, since their branch was almost totally staffed by O'Reillys or their in-laws.

515

Pat was amazed that his father managed to get them all vacation time at once.

"How did you do it, Dad?"

Michael winked and tapped his nose. "I guess there's a bit of the old craft still in me." He gave Patrick a conspiratorial grin.

Pat had no idea what his dad meant. Many of the things going on in those weeks before the journey bewildered him. The clothes his mother and the other women were packing came from trunks in the back of their closets. The bright colors and wild patterns were startling to him. He'd never seen any of them in anything but jeans or tailored dresses for church and parties. The men were equally odd, packing briar pipes and gnarled walking sticks that had also appeared in the depths of the storerooms.

As the preparations grew more frantic, his confusion became tinged with a sense of dread that made no sense to him, either. He tried to shake it. This was his life's dream. He didn't want it spoiled by irrational worries. But the behavior of his elders gave him a sense that he was walking blindfolded on a staircase with no railing.

"There's something off about this. They're keeping secrets," he complained to his cousin Jerry. "The aunts and uncles, my mom and dad. When I come in, they all stop talking. If the phone rings when I'm home, they ask the caller to ring them later. My parents argue in whispers after they go to bed."

"Don't be daft," Jerry grinned. "You always did think the sun shone out your ass. They aren't keeping anything from you. There hasn't been a secret in this family since Aunt Kate ran off with the milkman. And we found that one out eventually."

"I never believed she'd decided to join the Carmelites and take a vow of silence." Pat was momentarily diverted from his worry. "Aunt Kate even talked in her sleep."

"So, how do you think all of them together could be hiding some great, dark secret?" Jerry shook his head. "We need to celebrate, not mope about. After over a hundred years, we're going home to Ireland! The first thing I'm going to do is have a proper draft Guinness. What about you?"

Pat allowed his cousin to ramble on but couldn't escape the belief that his parents' generation was in a turmoil about the upcoming trip. They were all thrilled and excited, definitely. But there was an undercurrent in their conversations that made him nervous. Something about the gathering, or Gathering, was putting them all on edge.

Eileen had no patience with his prodding.

"We told you," she snapped when he'd been at her about it all during dinner. "It's a sort of family reunion."

"We have *more* family?" Patrick was aghast at the thought. "I suppose O'Reilly is a common name. So what could be so awful about that? Why are you all so jumpy? Is there something wrong with them?"

"Of course not!" She thumped another serving of potatoes onto his plate. "I've never met them, but I've never heard anything bad about them, either."

"Then why haven't I ever heard anything about them at all?" Patrick pushed the plate away. He knew that refusing food was guaranteed to get his mother's attention, and her goat.

Eileen's lips tightened to a thin line. She took a deep breath before answering.

"You're hearing about them now," she said in a dangerously quiet voice. Then she softened. "I'd tell you more, my darling, but the others think it best if you wait until we get there. You'll understand then."

She got up and went to the kitchen for more gravy, but Patrick was sure he heard her mutter, "I hope."

On May twenty-fifth, the day of the flight,

the O'Reillys met in the boarding area at the airport. Patrick had never seen his entire family all in one place outside someone's home or in church. It mortified him to realize what a loud, uncouth bunch they were. The children were running around, squealing with excitement, and Cousin Jerry was egging them on. The others were all hugging and greeting as if they hadn't all been seeing one another every day for most of their lives. His cousin Liz had dyed her black hair a neon green in honor of the occasion. Pat tried to edge away from them, to pretend he was just another businessman for whom a trip across the Atlantic was nothing special.

Of course they wouldn't let him, but dragged him into the mob with jokes and claps on the back, all at eardrum-shattering decibels. Patrick felt the tips of his ears turning bright red. He vowed that as soon as they landed at Shannon, he was going to distance himself from these boorish tourists as soon as possible. They were going to Ireland to drink and party. He was on a sacred quest to find his heritage.

The flight was predictably rowdy. Pat couldn't understand why the other passengers and the flight attendants were so tolerant. They even seemed to enjoy the impromptu rendition of "Galway Bay" from his father, Jerry, and the uncles.

In the gray light of morning the plane slid down through the cloud cover and the O'Reillys got their first glimpse of what for them was the Promised Land.

There was a whoosh as everyone let out their breath at once. Pat's father put an arm around his mother.

"Look at it, my love," he sighed. "Did you ever think there were that many shades of green in the world?"

Eileen smiled and caressed his hand. "I never thought I'd see them. Whatever happens, this is worth it."

"Nothing will happen." He cocked his head in Pat's direction. "This will be the grandest vacation we've ever had. Won't it, son?"

Pat didn't answer. He was staring out the window with the fervor of a pilgrim in sight of Jerusalem.

There was a bus waiting for them with *O'Reilly* painted in big black letters on the side. The clan piled in, exhausted and eager at the same time. Pat realized that he had no idea what kind of place they were going to. He had imagined some sort of manor house, with polished wood wainscoting and stone fireplaces. Or perhaps a nice resort hotel with a golf course.

Instead the bus drove for what seemed like hours into a countryside where there seemed to be nothing but windswept fields and hundreds of sheep wandering freely. Finally, they pulled in to a sort of trailer park, with old-fashioned silver caravans arranged in concentric circles around a couple of large, whitewashed buildings with thatched roofs. There was smoke coming from the chimney of one of them, and Pat got his first whiff of the heady and slightly intoxicating scent of burning peat.

Then they were surrounded by a sea of people, all of them small, with dark hair and skin ranging from deeply tanned to the shade of pale milk. *Jesus, Mary, and Joseph!* Pat thought. *There really are more of us in the world.* The babble of accents was surprising, especially coming from such familiar faces. The English assaulting his ears was broad Australian, British, and Anglo-Indian. He even thought he heard cadences of Spanish and French. How far had the O'Reillys emigrated?

Pat and his family were shown to one of the caravans, which turned out to be nicely appointed in a three-quarter size that was perfect for them, with a small kitchen and a shower in its own stall next to the bathroom. Eileen was delighted.

"My grandmother told me about these, from when she was a little girl," she told Pat. "Isn't it cozy? Just like the ones the Travelers have, although not so colorful."

She seemed disappointed about that, but, for once, Pat was too tired to try to get more information. He wanted a shower and a sleep. Then, he promised himself, he'd rent a car or a bike and strike out on his own.

It was the singing that woke him. Dusk had fallen and the bar must have opened. Pat now saw the sense in having this reunion far away from other people. He pulled on some clean clothes and ventured out.

A huge bonfire had been built in a hollow in front of one of the buildings. Long trestle tables and benches were ranged around it. Lamplight gushed from the open door and all the windows. The tables were full of people happily tucking into shepherd's pie. Every hand held a glass. The smell of the lamb and potatoes was enticing.

Pat picked up a plate and a glass. Perhaps he'd wait until tomorrow to make his getaway.

The fire grew higher, sending out sparks in bursts of blue, red, gold, and green. In a haze of alcohol and peat smoke, Pat thought

522

what a neat trick it was to make it seem as if the fireworks were coming out of the center of the blaze.

There was singing and drinking and dancing and drinking and wrestling matches far into the night. Pat soon realized that he had imbibed more than he could stand. He knew this because he tried to stand and failed. He began to crawl back to the trailer, blaming his lack of stamina on the jet lag.

His eyes must be going, too. He'd hardly gone ten yards when he felt someone fall on top of him.

"Oops-a-daisy!" a lilting feminine voice giggled. "Sorry, mate! I didn't see you down there."

Pat muzzily looked around for the source of the body and the voice, but didn't see anyone. Jerry must have been right. The porter in Ireland was much stronger than the kind they drank in the States. He continued on to the trailer and fell into bed.

He awoke the next morning feeling completely disoriented. The silver curve of the ceiling gave him the impression that he was lying inside a metal ball that was rolling uphill. After several moments spent clutching the edge of his bunk to avoid falling out, he realized that it was only the wind sweeping from the ocean across the treeless land that was rocking the trailer. The door to his parents' cubicle was ajar. Pat peeked in and found they were gone. The clock on the wall said half past ten.

As Pat dressed and boiled water for coffee, he read the program that he found on the table.

"Welcome!!! Welcome!!! Welcome Home!!!" it began.

Pat liked their enthusiasm. He skimmed down the page. It seemed that he had already missed the full Irish breakfast. The morning seemed to be taken up with seminars, not what he had expected. However, if everyone was inside listening to edifying talks, he should have no trouble creeping off.

The kettle whistled and Pat sat down again with his mug. He looked over the program more carefully.

"What the hell . . . ?" he said, reading the titles of the seminars. " 'How to keep your pot of gold in trying times.' 'Invisibility, the best defense.' 'Which end of the rainbow?' 'To jig or not to jig: fighting the stereotypes.' 'Making shoes that last.' What kind of nonsense is this?"

Burning with curiosity and no little annoyance, Pat gulped down his coffee and set out in search of someone who could tell him what this was all about.

The sun was beginning to burn off the morning fog as he crossed the field to the central buildings. Wisps of smoke still rose from the coals of the bonfire. Pat saw no one, although he could hear music coming from the far building. A banner above the door proclaimed this the meeting hall.

Inside, the building was a typical Irish shotgun house, if much larger than most. A long hallway stretched from front to back, with rooms branching out on either side. The subjects of the talks were posted on the doors. Pat first looked into the one on invisibility, but it was empty. The next room was the talk on keeping a pot of gold. This one was packed. He edged into a space near the door. No one noticed him as they were all intent on the speaker, a solemn woman with thick spectacles and a mound of white hair pulled into a bun.

"Of course," she was saying, "apartment living makes subterranean deposits difficult. However, a well-constructed space beneath the floorboards, preferably in a bedroom, can be used in a pinch."

"But what about fire and thieves?" a man in the front row asked.

"We always have to worry about thieves," the speaker told him. "As for fire, don't they teach the protection charms anymore? Really, that should have been explained to you about the time you were weaned, young man. What is this race coming to?"

She gestured to the audience. "How many here never learned the five essential charms?"

Over half of the group raised their hands. The woman sighed. "Eithne, add that to the seminars for tomorrow. Just because you're living away from home doesn't mean you can go native." She looked at the note cards in front of her. "Now, where was I? Oh yes, guarding against fluctuation in the price of gold."

Watching the audience intent on every word, Patrick was certain he had found the secret his parents had been hiding; he came from a family of lunatics. The sooner he was out of here, the better.

He started out the open door, back into the sane sunshine, when he collided with something. He wasn't much hurt, for it was soft.

"We meet again," a voice said in his ear. "Is this the American idea of courtship?"

Very, very slowly, Pat turned his face in the direction of the sound.

In the sunlight something was sparkling. The bits of light gradually coalesced into the form of a woman. When he could make out her face, Pat saw that she was straining in concentration, eyes squeezed shut and her mouth tight with effort. At last she came into focus. He saw that she was about his own age, with black curls, hazel eyes, and the sun-touched skin of the Australians. She laughed at his expression.

"I know I'm not great at reappearing," she said. "But that's no reason to look like a dying mackerel."

Pat closed his mouth. "Excuse me," he said. "I'm going back to my bed until I wake up."

It had to be something in the beer. There was no other explanation. Perhaps this was some sort of CIA experiment. He probably wasn't in Ireland at all, but strapped into a chair with electrodes stuck in his brain. Although why the government would want him to believe that beautiful Irish-Australian women could appear out of thin air was more than he could imagine.

Before he could make a move, the sound of applause signaled the end of the talks. The doors flew open and people came piling out. Patrick grabbed his father as soon as he appeared.

"You have got to tell me what's going on!" he demanded. "Am I hallucinating or crazy? Is any of this really happening?"

Aunt Teresa appeared at his elbow. Had she been there a second before? She shook her head at Pat in disgust.

"That's what you get for being blind drunk last night and missing the breakfast meeting," she told him. "Eileen, it's time you told the boy the truth. I never agreed with the way you and Michael kept him so completely in the dark."

"Mind your own business," Eileen shot back. "It's not like you told your children the whole truth."

"Well, they at least know the five charms." Teresa went nose to nose with her sister. "You just let Patrick stuff his head with all that Celtic nonsense."

"This is not the time," Michael said, gently pushing the women apart. "Come along, Pat. Teresa is right for once. Your mother and I have some explaining to do."

They settled back into the trailer. Eileen fussed with the tea things for a bit, making such a clatter that conversation was impossible. At last she set mugs down for each of them. Michael cleared his throat.

"You see, son," he began. "You seemed so

happy thinking you were a Celt that we didn't want to —"

"Oh my God!" Pat interrupted. "I'm adopted!"

"Of course not," Eileen laughed. "And you with your granddad's nose and his mother's own eyes. Don't be silly."

"It's the O'Reilly name, Pat," Michael continued. "We took that when we came to America. We're Irish, right enough, but not from the Celts. Our ancestors were the *Fir Bolg,* who were here before the *Tuatha* ever landed and long before the Celts appeared."

Patrick waited for the rest of the explanation. He knew the old stories. The *Fir Bolg* were the Irish defeated by the *Tuatha de Danann* at the first battle of *Magh Tuiredh.* They were relegated to the wilds of Connaught, and some were enslaved by the conquerors. Later, Celtic invaders defeated the *Tuatha,* who faded away under the hills and became the *sidh,* the fairies of Ireland. At least, that was the legend. His father had always stressed that the *Fir Bolg* were the first ones, the true Irish. But it was just a story.

Pat searched his parents' faces for signs of suppressed laughter or incipient madness.

"All right," he said carefully, in case they became violent. "Our family is descended from the oldest of the Irish. Interesting. Are you saying that we're part of the *sidh?* Don't you think that's a bit odd, seeing as they're mythical?"

"They're not a myth," Eileen stated. "A legend. There's a big difference."

Michael leaned over and put a hand on Pat's arm. "We should have told you, son, but we've tried so hard to fit in. We put our money in banks, instead of burying it. No one in the family has soled a shoe in decades. America was a new start for us. It's not as though it was easy for our kind here in Ireland, forced to work for the *Tuatha,* hunted by men for our gold, and," he faltered, "and by other things."

Something finally connected in Pat's brain. He leaned back in the chair and started to laugh.

"You had me going there," he told them. "You and that girl with the vanishing trick. You can't be serious. You want me to believe we're leprechauns?"

Michael drew himself up. "And why not?" he asked. "Is there something wrong with that?"

"We taught you to be proud of your heritage," Eileen added. "None of us married out for four generations in America and four hundred in Ireland. Teresa was right; we should have taught you the charms. But

530

we thought you were charming enough on your own."

She smiled fondly and stood up, brushing her hands on her swirling peasant skirt.

"Well, now that you know, shall we get back to the group? There's a seminar on soda bread recipes that I want to go to this afternoon."

"A few of us were going to go down and dig our own turf. It will be too damp for the fire tonight, but we wanted to see what it was like," Michael said. "Want to come with us, son?" He got up, too.

"Whoa!" Pat caught them at the door. "You tell me a boatload of bilge like that and then expect me to just get on with the party?"

"Sure," Michael answered. "You've got your explanation. Now that you know you're not going mad, you can get on with enjoying yourself. Once you've learned the five charms for staying out of trouble, you can take the invisibility class."

"But no cobbling shoes," Eileen warned. "Some of these others have some idiotic idea about tradition and want to go back to the old ways, but I say that's bringing back the bad old days. I'll never be a cobbler to a bunch of airy-fairies who still live in earth mounds."

Pat was too dumbfounded to resist as they took his arms and led him back to the reunion.

"The very first thing you do, my boy," Michael said after lunch was done, "is get to the charm class. I always told your mother that you should have at least been taught that much."

"Right, Dad." Pat could think of nothing to do but go along for now. There were too many of them to fight, and they all seemed to share the same delusion.

He hesitated before going to the charm session, not because he thought it was silly, which he did, but because that Australian girl might be there. And he wanted to find her again. Not because she was attractive, not at all. He was determined to get her to tell him how she had made him think she could turn invisible. Pat grinned to himself. He was sure he already had enough charm to talk that one around. A woman didn't bump against him twice unless she was interested.

Pat did a circle of the camp and the session rooms, but didn't see his quarry. It occurred to him that she might still be invisible, and then he shook himself for even considering such an absurdity.

The charm class had barely started when

he arrived. The teacher, a slim man even shorter than Patrick, spoke with a lilt that seemed more Spanish than Irish. Pat wondered how many O'Reillys there were in the Mexico City phone book.

"The five charms — pay attention now." He glared directly at Pat. "These can save your life and your gold." He held up his hand and counted them off. "You must learn to ward off fire, flood, cave-in, wicked tongues, and most of all, the envy of the ones who stayed behind."

Someone in the front raised a hand.

"Why should we care about the Old Ones?" a boy asked. "They didn't have the courage to get on the boats with the rest of the *Fir Bolg.* There are hardly any left here, my mother says, and they have no power."

"No power?" The teacher made a complicated gesture with his left hand. "You take a dozen steps outside the rings here and see what happens. No power! Do you know how much force there is in a grudge held for two hundred years? They hate us all for escaping while those cowards stayed behind. Now I want you all to know these inside out before you leave this room. No power," he muttered again. "What are they teaching them these days?"

Pat did his best to pick up the chants and

gestures, mostly because he knew his parents would grill him. The rest of the people in the room were practicing as if their lives depended on it. Once again, Pat longed to get out and find the Ireland of his dreams. He wondered if that was the reason this remote site had been chosen. Out in the wilds of Connemara, surrounded by treacherous bog, with no car and a cell phone that only worked in the States, the only way to leave was to walk and hope to find some sort of habitation that would let him call for a taxi.

He was getting close to risking it. Looking around him at all the idiots solemnly waving their hands about while reciting words in a language a thousand years dead, if not entirely made up, Pat felt like a duck in a flock of loons.

That afternoon he spotted his cousin Jerry sitting at a table with a bunch of people from the invisibility seminar. They were on the other side of the bonfire, so Pat was sure that it was a trick of the light that made them fade in and out. Just to be sure, he took his glass and went over to join them.

"Hey, Patrick!" Jerry greeted him heartily. "Isn't this the most amazing holiday ever? Who'd have thought we were magical? Won't they get a laugh out of this at Biddy's when we get back?"

"You aren't going to let our friends know we're leprechauns!" Patrick was aghast. "Don't we get enough guff about our size as it is?"

"But look what I can do." Jerry concentrated on his arm and it slowly vanished, leaving a pint mug floating in midair. "They'll be buying me drinks all night, just to watch."

"And none of this seems strange to you?" Pat asked, gesturing at the happy commotion around them.

Jerry scratched his nose with his perceptible hand. "Not really," he decided. "It feels like family, only with a few twists. I mean, when you think about it, this answers a lot of questions about us. Like why we're so short and can still drink everyone else flat. And why my dad won't even polish his own shoes. If that was your slave job, you wouldn't want to be reminded of it. Although," he added in a conspiratorial whisper, "Sheila told me that Ferragamo's real name is Fergus. What do you think?"

"I think you're all barking mad," Pat thumped his glass down. "Or I am. Either way, I've had enough."

"Pat, what's wrong with you?" Jerry asked. "This is what you've always wanted, isn't it?

535

We're back in our homeland, among our people, and learning really cool tricks. Not to mention really hot cousins distant enough to date. Loosen up!"

"This isn't what I dreamed of." Pat was nearly in tears. "I'm trapped inside a double circle in the middle of nowhere. I've seen nothing of the country. Some old fart tells me my ancestors were shoemaking slaves instead of heroes. I don't know how you do that disappearing thing, and I don't care. I came here to soak up the real Ireland, to come home at last. And you all seem happy to camp out for a while, learn some parlor tricks, and go back home."

"Well, yes, that sums it up," Jerry grinned. "Haven't you been listening? We're proud of what we came from. Real leprechauns, who'd have thought it? But our family had the gumption to get on the boats and get out. We all went places where we could be free, even marry out, like Kate and the milkman. I want to be back in Cleveland in time for baseball season. I love it here, but it's not my home."

Disheartened, Pat went back to the trailer. In the distance he could make out fiddle music that indicated that some people were sticking to the stereotype and dancing a jig.

He had another week before the flight

back. If he left the group now, there was still time for him to do all the proper things that returning Irish did. He wanted to kiss the Blarney Stone and try the holy water at Knock and stop at every pub between Dublin and Galway. There was no reason why he shouldn't. He still had a stack of euros in his wallet. Plenty to have fun on.

He scribbled a note to his parents, telling them he'd meet them at Shannon to catch the plane. Then he tossed some clothes into his backpack along with a toothbrush and razor. He'd hitch a ride to the nearest town and take a bus from there. Maybe he'd even find some real O'Reillys who'd take him in.

There were still a few hours of daylight left. Pat followed the dirt road the bus had taken. As he left the encampment, the fiddle music stopped as if cut off with a knife. Probably taking a whisky break, he thought. If he had turned to look, Pat would have seen the circles of trailers shimmer and slowly vanish in the slanted sunlight.

He hiked about a mile to a paved road. It wasn't long before a car came along, with a middle-aged couple in it. The driver slowed and then stopped. The woman gave him an appraising look.

"You're young to be out on your own," she decided.

"I'm older than I look," Pat smiled.

The woman's eyes lit up. "Oh, an American!" She nudged her husband. "Roddy, the lad's come from America. Are you home to see the family?"

"That I am." Pat climbed into the backseat. He felt oddly crowded, as if there were someone beside him. He must still be affected by invisibility classes and peat fumes. Deliberately, he spread out his arms and announced to the world at large, "I've been waiting for this all my life."

In the camp, Eileen and Michael had just found their son's note.

"Heaven preserve him!" Eileen exclaimed. "Whatever made him do a crazy thing like that? Doesn't he know how dangerous it is?"

"The poor boy." Michael shook his head. "His head's been so stuffed with fairy tales that he couldn't cope with real fairies. I have to go after him."

"You'll never find him in the dark," Eileen clutched her husband's arm. "Especially since he doesn't want to be found. He'll be heading for civilization, anyway. In the city he'll only run into muggers and wanton women. If he can get there, he should be all right until morning."

Her words sounded hollow to Michael, but he saw the sense in them. "We should talk to the organizers," he said. "This must have happened before. They'll have a plan."

"Yes, of course, helicopters or BOLOs or something," Eileen agreed, wringing her hands. "My poor, foolish boy!"

Pat was having the time of his life. The couple, Roddy and Mary O'Connor, had taken him to a pub in Ballyveane for dinner and had invited him to stay the night on their farm. They were full of ideas for places he should visit.

"You should climb the Rock of Cashel and see the Ring of Kerry and of course, Newgrange, where your people buried their dead," Roddy told him.

"Don't you mean *our* people?" Pat asked, as the car turned onto a dark country lane.

"Oh, that was long before our time," Mary laughed as she put on the brake. "Grab him, Roddy, and don't take your eyes off him!"

Before Pat knew what was happening, Roddy had twisted around in the front seat and taken hold of his leg.

"Did you think you'd fool us with that cinema accent?" he crowed. "We knew what you were the minute we laid eyes on you. Now, take us to your pot of gold, or we'll tip you headfirst off the cliffs and into the sea."

"I can't believe this." Pat was more angry than concerned. "Did my cousin Jerry put you up to this? Or those fruitcakes at the fairy ring? You can't believe I'm a leprechaun."

"You won't get us that way, either." Mary said. "You're one of the Little People all right. Who else would wear fine leather shoes to thumb a ride?"

Pat's hand went to the door handle. Mary had started driving again, but they were going slowly enough for him to leap out and not be much hurt. Roddy didn't seem to have a good grip on him, but Pat found it hard to move his legs to break free. It was as if someone else were holding him. Suddenly, he was overcome by a primal panic.

"Look out!" he screamed. "You'll hit that sheep."

For a split second, Roddy let go. Pat took a deep breath, scrunched his eyes shut, and, without even trying, vanished.

He pushed the car door open and rolled out, crawling and then running to get away. Roddy and Mary shouted and stomped after him a few feet before giving up. They were still blaming each other at the top of their lungs when Pat reached a grove of trees and relaxed enough that his body re-appeared.

"Damn." He realized. "I left my backpack in the car."

He still had his wallet and passport, though, and the town couldn't be that far away. If he could get his bearings, he should have only a mile or two to walk. Pat sighed. He supposed it was time that he accepted the truth, however nonsensical it seemed. He wasn't the reincarnation of Brian Boru, but of silly little men with stubby pipes and green trousers who spent their lives making shoes.

His life in America was looking better and better.

The night was chilly, although the drink from the pub was still warming his veins. Pat struck out in the direction of the town. He hoped to bypass the dirt road and hit the main one, just in case Roddy and Mary were still hunting for him. The terrain was rough and pocked with mud puddles. He kept feeling that someone was at his elbow, guiding him. Nevertheless, Pat slipped time and again, falling into the bog and clambering up until he was soaked and filthy.

Just when he had decided to curl up in the first dry spot he came across, Pat caught a scent he recognized, a peat fire. He followed his nose.

In the middle of the gorse was a small house, covered in sod. It reminded Pat of a hobbit hole. The door was low enough that even he would have to stoop. He smiled to himself. Leprechauns. The real *Fir Bolg* must live here, not exiles spending their holiday role-playing. Maybe it was time he embraced his heritage. He knocked.

The door creaked open. A wizened face peered out. "Begorra! If it isn't Cousin Patrick! We heard ye were in the land again."

They knew his name! Now Pat understood the feeling he had had all evening of someone lurking next to him. He grinned. "I've lost my way. May I come in?"

The door opened wide and Patrick entered, feeling that he'd finally found the real Ireland. He couldn't wait to rub Jerry's nose in it.

The inhabitants of the hut were two little men, both looking older than time. They both seemed thrilled to see Patrick.

"You'll be with the tour," the first one assumed correctly. "You people hardly ever come out to find us. We've always been hurt by that. Such a long time for a family to be apart. It's an honor to have you. Look, Seamus, it's Patrick O'Reilly, home from America, and looking to find the family!"

"Is it now?" The other man had been sitting facing the fire, sharpening a knife on a whetstone, but now he turned and smiled.

With a rush of horror, Patrick saw that the man's teeth were shining copper, filed to razor-sharp points. His heart froze as he understood. These weren't relics of mythology, nor were they modern, assimilated leprechauns. The little men were really the Oldest Ones. There was not even a veneer of civilization in them, only ancient, primal needs and hate.

Patrick rolled off his stool and tried to crawl for the door.

They were too quick for him. Each man took one of Pat's arms. As they forced him to the floor, Pat marveled at the strength in their shriveled bodies. They bent over him, cackling in delight.

"Home from America, the renegade bastard," Seamus said, as he raised his knife. "And just in time for supper."

Pirate Dave's Haunted Amusement Park

Toni L. P. Kelner

Toni L. P. Kelner is the author of the "Where Are They Now?" mysteries, featuring Boston-based freelance entertainment reporter Tilda Harper, and the Laura Fleming series, which won a Romantic Times Career Achievement Award. She's also a prolific writer of short stories, many of which have been nominated for awards. Her story "Sleeping with the Plush" won the Agatha Award. This is the third anthology Kelner has coedited with Charlaine Harris, and she looks forward to many more. Kelner lives north of Boston with author/husband Stephen Kelner, two daughters, and two guinea pigs.

From as early as I could remember to the year I turned eighteen, my parents and I spent part of every summer at Bartholomew Lake. We always stayed in a hotel made up of lakeside cabins, which was naturally called Lakeside Cabins, and spent our days swimming in the lake, eating fried fish, and making at least one expedition to the local amusement park.

So when I decided to get out of town to get my head together before making a decision that would affect the rest of my life, it only seemed natural to head for that same lakeside hotel. My psychologist would probably have suggested that I was trying to recapture my lost girlhood, but I hadn't seen my psychologist since the attack that nearly killed me.

While I was in the hospital recovering, a delegation had come to tell me the truth about the thing that had attacked me. After that, I stopped going to therapy. Though my guy had done a great job helping me deal with the loss of my parents, I didn't think he'd have much insight into the loss of my humanity. In fact, he'd probably have tried to put me away if I'd told him I'd become a werewolf.

I spent most of the first part of the week at Lake Bartholomew swimming and sunning and eating ridiculous amounts of food. My days were freakishly normal, something I hadn't felt since the attack. I didn't mind being alone. I hadn't been alone much since the local pack took it upon themselves to start easing me into my new life. Naturally they hadn't wanted to risk me losing control, but since I'd gotten the hang of making the Change, I thought I was entitled to some downtime. Alone.

But by the end of the week, the pack was concerned that I was lonely. In fact, several of the packs in the area were concerned, and they wanted me to know how concerned they were. I'm sure their feelings had nothing to do with the fact that the annual Pack Gathering was to be held on the next full moon or that I'd be choosing my pack affiliation at that Gathering. Surely it was only interest in my welfare that led to the phone calls, cheery letters, and cards with cartoon wolves, plus three flower arrangements, two fruit baskets, one cookie bouquet, and a box of frozen steaks. There were countless e-mails, Facebook messages, and tweets. It was flattering at first, but since the point of the vacation was to get away from it all, the flood of attention got old fast.

It wouldn't have surprised my former psychologist a bit when I decided to retreat further into my past, which is how I found myself at Pirate Dave's Adventure Cove.

The amusement park was as campy as ever, starting at the gate with the ticket taker's red-and-white striped shirt and the jaunty kerchief on his head. The entrance to the park was a giant pirate ship shaped out of concrete, with sails permanently hoisted and a Jolly Roger flying proudly above. The graffiti on the sign was new, though. Though an effort had been made to remove the spray-painted words, it was still easy to see that somebody had X'ed out the word *Adventure* and scrawled *Haunted* instead. I briefly considered texting the woman who'd presented the "Other Supernatural Species" slideshow at Werewolf Orientation to ask if ghosts were real but decided it might lead to a support group rushing to Lake Bartholomew to be there for me.

The posted park rules — no running, no bad language, no cutting in line — were the same as always. Well, nearly the same. For one, they'd added a rule about turning off cell phones during performances and, for another, instead of "Ship's Articles," the list was labeled "Keep to the Code." I wondered how much the *Pirates of the Caribbean* movies had added to the park's popularity.

The influence of the movies was even more obvious when I made it inside the park, where Pirate Dave himself was standing atop an ersatz crow's nest to greet arriving guests. In my day, Pirate Dave had been a dapper Captain Hook type, with a red coat and abundant black curls. This version was an homage to Johnny Depp, complete with guyliner and scruffy braids. He even wobbled a bit as he bowed to the ladies, though that might have been because the platform was getting a bit rickety.

Still, I waved and enjoyed the appreciation in Pirate Dave's eye when he bowed in my direction. After all the diets I'd endured and the exercise regimens I'd abandoned, it had taken being turned into a werewolf to give me the figure I'd always wanted. Though my denim shorts weren't outrageously short and my tank top showed only a modest amount of cleavage, I knew I looked good. So it was gratifying to finally be noticed by Pirate Dave.

I'd had crushes on quite a few Pirate Daves over the years, particularly the one who'd worked the late shift when I was in my teens. Neither a clone of Captain Hook nor of Captain Jack Sparrow, the nighttime Pirate Dave had worn a snowy white shirt with tantalizingly tight breeches. His auburn hair had been just long enough to pull back into a ponytail with a leather thong, and he'd had a way of looking at me that had made my teenaged hormones rise like a stormy tide.

The current Pirate Dave just didn't compare. In fact, as I wandered through the park, I decided that very little in the place compared with my memories. Admittedly it was larger than it had been, with several roller coasters and thrill rides added, but two of the biggest draws were closed for repairs, and most of the others could have used a fresh coat of paint. The crew members were cranky, and the place just looked grubby. No wonder the crowds were smaller than I'd expected at the height of the season.

Still, I enjoyed not having to stand in long lines for rides, and the games were a lot more fun now that I had werewolf strength and speed. Though I didn't particularly need a plush sea monster or mermaid, I couldn't resist the temptation to shock the stuffing out of the pirates manning the games when I repeatedly knocked the milk bottles off the table and hit the gong at the test-your-strength booth seven times in a row. When I got bored, I handed my prizes to the nearest little girls and went in search of junk food.

As the day wore on, I told myself that the only reason I was sticking around was to watch the parade at dusk, with its fanciful floats, appropriately attired musicians and dancers, and cheap plastic doubloons thrown to the crowd. It had nothing to do with a yen to see if the night shift Pirate Dave was as good-looking as the one I remembered.

In years past, the parade had paused in front of the Shiver-Me-Timbers Ice Cream Shoppe, which was about halfway through the route. That's when Pirate Dave would announce that it was time to choose a Sea Queen to join him on his voyage. Candidates would gather in front of the float, and he would toss a bucketful of coins. Most of them would be plastic, but one was supposedly an actual doubloon, and the girl who caught it would be crowned Sea Queen and get to ride on the float with Pirate Dave for the rest of the parade. Though it was supposed to be random, the Sea Queen was invariably a toothsome wench, as Pirate Dave would proclaim, never a gawky teenager in braces like I'd been.

I also told myself that I'd only stationed myself at Shiver-Me-Timbers because it was the best place to see the parade, but I couldn't help noticing that quite a few other women were hanging around nearby. Maybe this meant that Pirate Dave was worth waiting for.

As night fell, the parade started and I got my answer. As I'd remembered, there were elaborate floats, dancing wenches, and a pirate band. Plus they'd added a lively calypso group. I enjoyed it tremendously, despite the delay when one of the floats broke down and a new tractor had to be brought out to tow it for the rest of the route. Finally Pirate Dave arrived in command of a spectacular reproduction of his ship, the *Brazen Mermaid.*

I think my heart actually stopped for a second. Unlike the rest of the park, Pirate Dave was just as gorgeous as ever. Maybe more so — surely he hadn't dared to wear breeches that tight before. When the float stopped and he announced that he was seeking a Sea Queen, I joined the throng of eager women without thinking.

I was watching his every movement, as were all the straight women in the crowd, but now I had werewolf-sharp senses, so when Pirate Dave held up the coveted golden doubloon, I could tell he was only pretending to toss it into a bucket of plastic coins, when he'd actually palmed it. I could also catch the way his eyes scanned the available women, and that tiny hesitation when he chose his target. The lucky gal — a tall, buxom blonde in a halter top — was just behind me. Knowing that, I knew exactly when he threw the doubloon toward the blonde and used my better-than-human reflexes to jump at just the right moment to snatch it before she could.

I held it triumphantly over my head, smiling when I heard the blonde mutter, "Bitch!" After all, it was truer than she knew.

As for Pirate Dave, he was shocked but hid it quickly and said, "Arr, a toothsome wench indeed. Join me, my Sea Queen!"

The crowd cheered as I made my way to the float, where a pirate flunky waited to help me up the rope ladder.

"Permission to come aboard?" I asked.

"Oh, the boardin' will come later," Pirate Dave said with a roguish grin, and the crowd roared.

Once I climbed the ladder, Dave put his arm around my waist and pulled me to the front of the float.

"And what be your name?" he asked.

"Joyce."

"Queen Joyce, then." To the crowd he proclaimed, "All hail Queen Joyce, the fairest maiden to ever sail the seven seas!" The flunkies led the crowd in a chorus of "Arr!" and the float started moving again.

As we waved to the crowd, Pirate Dave said, "That were a worthy catch you made."

"I bet you say that to all the Sea Queens."

He laughed and dropped into the kind of small talk he probably made with all the

Sea Queens. What was my home port? Was I traveling with a crew, or was this a solo voyage? Had I ever seen a port to rival the Adventure Cove? I answered appropriately, but I was finding myself increasingly distracted. It wasn't because Pirate Dave wasn't even better-looking up close — he was, with charisma to burn. But there was something odd about his scent. It wasn't a hygiene issue or overdependence on men's cologne, though I'd halfway expected Old Spice. It was strangely exotic, with a metallic tang. Short of sniffing him openly, I couldn't figure out any more than that.

When we reached the end of the parade, Pirate Dave helped me down from the float, then looked deeply into my eyes. "Join me for the fireworks tonight," he said with no trace of piratical lingo.

I hesitated, put off by the near command. "Actually I'll probably be gone by then."

"No, stay. Come to me at the pavilion." His voice was oddly urgent.

I tried to decide if he was pushy or just extremely intense before finally saying, "I'll try."

He looked as if he intended to attempt to convince me further, when a park employee ran up and gestured wildly. I took that as an opportunity to slip away.

My first instinct was to head directly for the parking lot, but then I reconsidered. How often did I get a chance to spend time with a teenage crush, or at least a new version of him? A little necking with a pirate might be just the thing to wrap up my vacation. If Pirate Dave tried to go further than I wanted to, he'd find out that I was a whole lot stronger than I looked.

I grabbed a jumbo bucket of popcorn, or "parched maize" as it was listed on the menu of the snack bar, and wandered through shops. The crowds had thinned considerably once the parade was over, which was the opposite of the way it used to be, when people would come to the park when it was too dark and cool for swimming. Another one of the big rides had just gone out, and the people who'd been on board when it shimmied to a stop weren't shy about complaining in ways that thoroughly violated the Code.

I had a good mind to talk to management myself. The trash cans were overflowing, the tables at the restaurants were sticky with spilled soda, and if I stepped in one more wad of gum, I was going to Change into something angry. The place had always been immaculate — was it that hard to find good help?

I was scraping gum off my sandals on the curb near the Kraken, the largest of the park's roller coasters, when I saw a shadowy figure sneaking around where it wasn't supposed to be. The Kraken had a long track with plenty of turns and two loop-de-loops, and the whole area was landscaped so there were plenty of places to hide. Some of the lights had gone out, so it was quite dark around there and a human wouldn't have noticed, but I could definitely see somebody.

I probably should have called for a park guard, but I hadn't seen any security people since the parade, and it would have been foolish to make a fuss if it was just somebody retrieving a ball cap that had fallen off during the ride. Besides, I was bored and had nothing better to do. So after making sure nobody was close enough to see me, I jumped over the low fence and followed. At least I tried to, but in between stepping around a bush and dodging a power pole, I managed to lose him and found myself behind the shed that housed the ride's high-tech workings. I looked around for the intruder but decided he'd gone and was about to leave myself when I sensed movement behind me. Before I could turn, there was a sickening pain in my head and I fell.

I woke instantly aware, the way I had since

being Changed. I was lying on a thin pad of some sort, like a futon only considerably mustier, and it did little to protect me from the chill of the concrete floor. It was dark, even to my eyes, so I could see next to nothing, and all I could smell was machinery oil and buttered popcorn. It was the popcorn that convinced me that I was still in the park.

I felt around for my purse but couldn't find it, and the only thing in my pockets was spare change. I started to stand but hit my head on something. When I reached up, I felt some kind of pipe or bar. I scooted around on my butt, feeling around, and realized that I was totally enclosed by bars. I was in a cage! Just for a moment, I felt the wolf inside stirring. I didn't like being in a cage, and it was all I could do to keep from throwing my head back and howling!

I pulled my knees close to my chest and inhaled deeply and slowly, the way I'd been taught by the pack. According to the instructor, I was supposed to gather my chi or find my center or something equally mystical, but for me, the breathing was enough to prevent me from Changing.

Just then I heard footsteps. A door opened, and dim light flowed into what now looked like a basement workroom. There were tools on shelves and tables around the edge of the room, but unfortunately nothing was close enough for me to reach. A moment later, Pirate Dave stepped inside, and his expression was far from friendly.

"I didn't realize you were so adamant about my staying for the fireworks," I said. "Or is this how you treat all your Sea Queens?"

He didn't respond, just came closer.

Once again, I noticed that his scent was wrong. It was like nobody I'd ever encountered, and I finally recognized the metallic tang I'd noticed a hint of before. It was blood.

He stopped just out of my reach, met my eyes, and said, "I want to know why you're here."

"You tell me! You're the one who locked me up in a damned cage."

He seemed taken aback. He went down on one knee, so we were eye to eye. "Why are you here?"

"Hello? Because you put me here!"

Now he was clearly nonplussed. "Tell me who you are."

"I'm Queen Joyce, remember?" Since I could see my purse on a workbench, I added, "You've got my stuff — go check my driver's license."

"Damnation!" he said as he stood. "What are you? Witch? Demon spawn? God, not the fae! Please don't be one of the fae."

"Excuse me?"

"Don't bother to deny it — I should have known from the way you snagged that doubloon. You're not human!"

"Well, neither are you," I said, suddenly convinced that nobody with that scent could be.

"True enough." He smiled, but it wasn't a happy smile. It was, however, toothy. Overly so, with two prominent fangs.

"You're a vampire?" I'd been told about vampires during Werewolf Orientation, but I hadn't really believed it. At that point, it had been hard enough for me to believe in werewolves, let alone all the other horror movie denizens. If the issue of immunity to vampiric influence had been mentioned, I hadn't been paying attention.

He eyed me again. "You move too fast to be a zombie. Not foul enough for a ghoul. Too tall for a leprechaun. Werewolf?"

"We prefer to call ourselves Lupine Americans."

"I knew my troubles had to be supernatural in origin — no human could cause so much chaos. But I hadn't suspected werewolves. What are you after? The park? Or were you hired by some other power?"

"Because the whole supernatural world is dying to own a run-down amusement park. Let me explain this to you slowly. I. Am. On. Vacation."

"I may not be able to glamour you, wolfling, but there are other ways of getting information, ways I don't think you'll enjoy," he said, circling the cage slowly. Then he picked up a power drill from one of the workbenches. "I understand you heal quickly, but I wager that this would still hurt."

"It would if you had an extension cord," I pointed out. "Besides which, if you get close enough to try anything, I'm going to give myself a lesson in vampire anatomy. From the inside."

He put down the drill. "I don't have to get close. All I have to do is wait for you to get hungry. Hungry as a wolf, you might say."

"What makes you think I'm going to stay in this cage?" I deliberately started to undress. Well, not completely — the pack members I'd met were comfortable with public nudity, but I wasn't. I did take off my sandals and shorts and pulled my bra off under my shirt. The panties and shirt would withstand the Change.

"No wolf could tear through those bars," Pirate Dave said smugly.

I concentrated, and the mist of the Change surrounded me, blocking both my view of the vampire and his view of me. One of the first things I'd had to unlearn was the idea that a werewolf had to become a wolf. After all, a wolf is genetically the same as a dog, and there were lots of breeds of dogs. When the mist cleared, I charged through the bars of the cage and leaped at him. Pirate Dave screamed like a little girl as I bit down on his ankle. Admittedly, a chihuahua wasn't the most fearsome of canines, but my teeth were plenty sharp and I definitely had the element of surprise on my side.

He tried to kick me away, but I wasn't nearly so interested in inflicting damage as I was in getting away. The door was still open, and I went for it. Unfortunately the vampire did, too, and I discovered that vampires move awfully fast. He slammed the door before I was even halfway there. I skittered to a stop, then turned to run as he reached for me.

The ensuing chase would have been ludicrous if it hadn't been — Hell, it was just ludicrous. I couldn't stop long enough to Change into something more useful in a fight, and he couldn't catch me unless I slowed down. Finally I dove back into the cage, right back where I'd started from.

"Stalemate," he said, as I scooted back into my shirt and Changed back to human. Of course, I ended up with one arm sticking out of the shirt collar, but eventually I got myself covered, though there was no way I could wriggle back into my bra.

"This is ridiculous," I said. "What's your problem with werewolves anyway?"

"I've got no interest in werewolves as long as you stop trying to ruin my park. I'd always heard your kind were ill-educated thugs, but I never expected a pack to make a move on me."

"For one, I'm neither a thug nor ill-educated. I'm a marketing exec, and I graduated from Harvard. Cum laude. For another, I'm not in a pack."

"A lone wolf?" he said, raising one eyebrow. "How trite."

"And lastly, I don't give a shit about your park. The place is falling apart anyway."

"Because of you!" he snapped. "I caught you red-handed behind the Kraken, which you were undoubtedly about to sabotage."

"I was there because I saw somebody sneaking around."

"Oh, that's original."

"And since I've only been in town a week,

561

I couldn't have caused any of the problems you must have been having all summer, given the lovely condition of this place. I'm surprised the board of health hasn't shut you down." I saw something almost guilty in his expression. "You used that look-deeply-into-my-eyes thing on the inspector, didn't you?"

"I'd do a lot more than that to keep my park open. If you don't start telling me what I want to know, I'll show you just how much."

"Your park? I thought you were just the figurehead." A thought occurred to me. "Oh my God! How long have you been Pirate Dave?"

He actually managed to bow sarcastically. "I am the original Pirate Dave."

"Have you been feeding off Sea Queens all these years?"

He shrugged. "None of them suffered from it. In fact, they quite enjoyed it."

"Ew."

"And how many humans have you murdered as a ravening beast?"

"The only human I've ever bitten was you. Scratch that, since you're not human. Which reminds me. Could I have a glass of water to wash the taste away? Old meat is just rank."

His face reddened, and I thought I might have gone too far, but suddenly a jaunty sea chanty echoed through the room. Pirate Dave reached into his pocket and pulled out a cell phone.

"What is it? . . . How? I was just there! . . . Was anybody injured? . . . I'll be right there!"

He hung up as angrily as it was possible to hang up a cell phone and shoved the phone back into his pocket.

I said, "Whatever it was that just happened, obviously I couldn't have had anything to do with it."

"All part of your plan, no doubt," he said. "You kept me occupied while your littermates committed further acts of vandalism."

"Right, I tricked you into knocking me unconscious. Just admit that I'm not involved, and let me out of here."

"I don't think so, wolfling. I'll be back to deal with you later. Feel free to take any form you like to leave your cage — you still won't be able to get out of this room." In a breathtaking burst of speed, he was gone and through the door, and a second later, I heard the lock turn.

"What an idiot!" I said to the empty room. I waited five minutes to make sure he was really gone before Changing to a teacup poodle to get out of the cage. Next I went human so I could reach through the bars of the cage to get my clothes. Once I was dressed, I rummaged around in the tools on the workbench, found a power screwdriver — and an extension cord — and took the hinges off the door. Then I picked up my purse and left.

I saw plenty of park employees on my way through the building, which was apparently the park's administrative headquarters, but not one said a word. I wondered how many other Sea Queens they'd seen making discreet exits after private visits with Pirate Dave. I'd been prepared to Change and make a dash for freedom if need be, but as it was, I just strolled back to the park's public areas and out to the parking lot. The fireworks started as I got into my car, and I hoped Pirate Dave was going to go to bed hungry.

I considered getting in touch with somebody in one of the packs when I got back to my cabin, just to check out Pirate Dave's powers and the whole vampire/werewolf dynamic, but then I saw the messages shoved under my door. Two more fruit baskets and a balloon bouquet were waiting for me at the front desk. I decided that was enough pack attention for one night. As long as I stayed away from Adventure Cove for the next couple of days, I shouldn't have to worry about Pirate Dave again.

I might have been able to stick with it, too, had it not been for three things. One, when I read the local newspaper over breakfast the next day, I learned that two children had been hurt in the breakdown of the Kraken the night before. Though neither injury had been serious, one was bad enough to keep a little girl out of a softball tournament she'd been practicing for all year. There was also an article about the park's recent troubles, complete with speculation about the number of people who'd be out of work should the park shut down.

Two, there were more pack offerings waiting for me when I went by the front desk to get the deliveries from the previous night: fruit, cookies, and a spa basket.

Three, and possibly the reason that would have convinced me all by itself, I'd spent all night having extremely vivid dreams about a red-haired pirate.

That's why I was the first person in line when Pirate Dave's Adventure Cove opened, and I spent the day looking — and sniffing — for signs of sabotage. I wasn't exactly subtle, but nobody noticed. The news about the park's problems had spread, so there were even fewer guests than there had been the day before, and the employees were clearly demoralized by impending unemployment. I paid particular attention to the area around the Kraken but got nothing.

I'm not sure exactly what I expected to find. Pirate Dave had been sure the threat was supernatural, and unfortunately my experience with the supernatural world was next to nil. At least I could be fairly sure that the saboteur wasn't another werewolf — I knew what we smelled like.

The park was so empty that I wasn't sure if they'd bother with the evening parade, but when night fell, I was at Shiver-Me-Timbers, waiting for the *Brazen Mermaid* to arrive. As soon as the float stopped, I joined the scant half dozen candidates for Sea Queen.

Pirate Dave's reaction upon seeing me was priceless. His face flushed, and he glared at me as he gave his usual invitation in a harsh tone that scared off two teenage girls. When it came time to throw the doubloon, he didn't even pretend to fling it to anybody but me. I walked past the same flunky as before to climb the rope ladder and wasn't a bit surprised when Dave grabbed me before I was halfway up and yanked me the rest of the way.

"All hail Sea Queen Joyce!" he thundered, and motioned for the float to start moving.

"Miss me?" I asked as we waved mechanically to the pitiful excuse for a crowd.

"What the devil is your game, wolfling?"

"Shouldn't that be Queen Wolfling?"

"You should be keelhauled after what you did to those children last night."

"I had nothing to do with that," I snapped. "Which should be clear even to you by now."

"What's clear is that you're playing some kind of game with people's lives."

"How many times do I have to tell you that I'm just here on vacation? I don't want the park to close. Why else would I spend the entire freaking day sniffing around for whoever it is who's trying to ruin you?"

He waved in silence for a moment. "You're telling the truth? You really did that?"

"Can't vampires sense lies?"

"That's witches," he said. "All I can do is glamour humans into telling the truth."

"Oh. Sorry."

"But I do read body language, and yours . . . I believe you."

"Finally!"

"Please accept my apologies for abducting you," he said awkwardly.

"And for hitting me over the head?"

"Yes."

"All right, then," I said magnanimously. "Apology accepted."

We waved more amiably for a minute, and then he said, "You must admit that having a werewolf show up is a remarkable co-incidence."

"I suppose. I don't know how many of us there are."

"None of the supernatural races are nu-merous — most of our numbers are in decline, and naturally women are particu-larly sought after."

That certainly helped explain why all the packs were so interested in me. Fresh blood and all that.

"Well, I didn't find anybody supernatural in the park today. Not that I've met enough to know what they're supposed to smell like, but everybody I sniffed today was normal. Of course, that kind of thing is harder to do when I'm in human form."

"I can imagine."

"Why would somebody be so set on put-ting you out of business anyway? Is it vampire politics? I'd heard the infighting can get pretty nasty." I was basing that more on books I'd read than on the orientation I hadn't paid attention to.

"So I understand, but that doesn't affect me."

"Oh?"

"I have very little contact with my own kind." I didn't have to be an expert in body language to know he didn't want to talk about it.

"Well, I'm pretty sure it's not werewolves — that's the one scent I know well. Witches? Ghouls? Space aliens?"

"Space aliens? This may be a joke to you, but I'm in danger of losing the park."

"Sorry. I'm new to this. I've only been a werewolf for a few months. I'm not even in a pack yet."

"I thought you'd belong to the pack that Changed you."

"I was bitten by a rogue," I said, though "bitten" was putting it mildly. "That means I get to pick a pack at the Gathering next month. That's why I took this vacation — the packs have been courting me relentlessly."

"Naturally," he said.

I looked up at him in surprise. Had that been a compliment? I pushed the idea away. "But back to your problem. You said you have no enemies?"

"Of course I have enemies. I'm over three hundred years old."

"You're how old?" I did some figuring. "Jeez, were you really a pirate?"

"Not by choice," he said softly. "So I sympathize with your curse."

"My curse? You mean being a werewolf?"

He nodded.

"It's not a curse — I love being a were-wolf." I loved roaming the woods with every sense on overload. I loved the strength in my body, the power in my movements. And God knew I loved being able to eat whatever I wanted and then run it off effortlessly. "The pack lifestyle is going to take some getting used to," I admitted, "but being a werewolf rocks." I was about to ask how he felt about being a vampire, but the float had come to the end of the route.

Pirate Dave helped me descend much more gently than he'd helped me ascend.

"I am sorry for suspecting you," he said, "and when this is all over, I would very much like to spend more time with you."

"As long as it doesn't involve a cage."

"Not until we know each other better," he said with the wicked grin that I'd dreamt of.

It was the grin that made me reluctant to leave. "Isn't there anything else I can do to help?"

He cocked his head to one side. "Not that

I don't appreciate your concern, but why? We've barely met."

"True, but in a way I've known you for years. My family used to come to Lake Bartholomew every year, and coming to the park was the best part." I left out the part about praying I'd catch the golden doubloon. "I love this place."

He smiled incredibly sweetly. "Thank you."

Dave leaned forward, and I was sure I was about to have another part of my dream come true, but an employee came running up. "The Octopus is making funny noises!"

With a quick squeeze of my hand, Pirate Dave took off, with the flunky trying in vain to keep up.

I started to follow, then stopped to think about the possibilities. If the sabotage had just happened, then the saboteur might still be around, which meant I might have a shot at sniffing him out, but it wouldn't hurt to improve my chances. I went to a nearby souvenir booth, grabbed what I needed, and threw money at the cashier on my way to the closest ladies' room. It took only a minute to strip and stuff my belongings into the tote bag I'd just bought — a canvas number with *Keep to the Code!* emblazoned across it. After a moment's consideration, I

Changed into a Scottish terrier so as not to look threatening, then zipped out of the bathroom, dragging the bag behind me. The only one who noticed me was a little girl waiting while her parents argued over whether or not to stay for the fireworks.

First I found some bushes to leave the bag under, hoping that nobody would find it. Then I pranced into the park, acting cute and friendly and perky as hell while I sniffed everybody I passed. I got whiffs of grape slushie, chocolate ice cream, numerous brands of sunscreen, and of course, body odor. I smelled smoke — both tobacco and other, beers that were being concealed in water bottles, and one diaper that really needed to be changed. But it was all human.

A small crowd was gathered at the Octopus, but I didn't smell any blood, which was a good thing, and there didn't seem to be any signs of panic, just major annoyance. Dave was speaking earnestly to a barrel-chested man with a sour expression, but the expression gradually turned almost jovial, and I had a hunch Dave was using the glamour that hadn't worked on me.

I'd always heard that criminals can't resist returning to the scene of the crime, so I took my time sniffing all the people clustered about. I got popcorn and soda from the guests, and various metallic, oily, and acrid scents from the employees, presumably from running rides. But again, nothing supernatural.

Eventually Pirate Dave saw me and did a double take. I wagged my tail furiously, hoping he'd realize it was me and not some random pooch. A couple of guests noticed me, too, and I heard a little boy say indignantly, "Dad, you said I couldn't bring Hershey to the park! You said dogs weren't allowed!"

"That be my dog," Pirate Dave said. "Ye must have heard tell of old sea dogs! That's Salty, the Sea Dog!"

Okay, the "old" part didn't thrill me, but I barked appealingly and came to rub my head against Dave's leg until he patted me. The kid seemed satisfied, and though I saw a couple of employees looking confused, apparently a brand-new mascot wasn't enough to worry them in the middle of other concerns.

Dave continued to appease the guests, using a mixture of glamour and comp tickets, while I worked the crowd. It took a good half hour for Dave to make everybody happy, and then he clapped the employees on the back, told them to keep up the good work, and whistled for "Salty" to come along.

When we were out of everybody's earshot, Dave said, "Did you find anything?"

I understand some werewolves can manage speech in canine form, but I haven't mastered the technique. So I whined in response.

"Bugger!"

After a quick stop for me to drag out my tote bag, which Dave then carried for me, he led me back to the admin building. Not the basement, I was happy to see, but his office. Unsurprisingly, it was decorated with nautical knickknacks and a glorious selection of Adventure Cove souvenirs.

"I thought you could use a place to Change," he said.

I nodded, then looked at him expectantly. Eventually he got the idea and turned around. I quickly Changed back to human and pulled my clothes back on. "I'm sorry," I said once I could speak again.

"At least nobody was hurt this time," he said, and sat at his desk. "The devil of it is that one of those people is a reporter. I tried to glamour him, but he's a hard-nosed sort and I don't think it took."

"I'm sorry," I said again.

He rubbed his eyes wearily. "I may as well

close the park down now and get it over with."

I really just intended to pat his shoulder comfortingly when I went to stand behind him. The one-armed hug was a natural extension. Ditto for stroking his back. I think I went over the line when I started playing with his hair, and inhaling that increasingly addictive scent of his was no help. But he's the one who kissed me, and that was enough to set our course. Every man should practice kissing for three hundred years.

We were about to move on to bigger and better things when there was a knock on the door. We hastily rearranged ourselves and our clothing, and Dave said, "Come in."

A man in coveralls with that same acrid smell I'd sniffed in the park came in. "I heard about the trouble earlier. You sure you want to go ahead with tonight's show?"

Dave shrugged. "We may as well. It'll probably be the last, so make it a good one."

"You bet," he said. As he turned, I saw a company logo on the back for "Great Balls of Fire Pyrotechnics."

After that, the mood was broken. "Time for one last Pirate Dave appearance," he said. "Since you missed the fireworks last night, would you care to join me tonight?"

"I'd love to."

We didn't speak on the way to the fireworks pavilion. Of course, the fireworks would be visible from anywhere in the park, but the best place was the pavilion, a semicircle of bleachers in front of a small stage where Pirate Dave would announce the show. Directly behind the stage was the man-made lake that was the center of the park, and the moored barge from which the fireworks were shot.

We were about halfway there when the silence got to me and for lack of anything else to talk about, I said, "I never realized gunpowder had such a distinctive odor."

"Oh?" Dave said politely.

"I assume that's what I was smelling on the pyrotechnics guy."

No response, not even an *Arr, that be the way of it.*

"I'd never smelled anything like that before tonight, but I noticed it on one of the other fireworks guys out in the park."

"Hmm . . ." Dave said absentmindedly. Then he stopped. "What did you say?"

"I said that fireworks smell really strong, and I noticed them on one of the employees earlier."

"None of the park employees have anything to do with the fireworks because of insurance regulations. We have a contract with a pyrotechnics company, and they never come until just before the show."

We looked at each other as we both came to the same awful conclusion. The saboteur had done something to the fireworks! Dave took off, moving so fast I could barely see him, let alone keep up.

Since there was no way I could catch him, I ran into the nearest souvenir shop and buttonholed the salesclerk. "Have you got a walkie-talkie or a phone? Some way of getting in touch with security?"

"Yeah, but —"

"Tell them to stop the fireworks! Tell them there's something wrong with them! Now!"

I was going to have to tell Dave to give that gal a raise, because she didn't even hesitate.

I left her to it and started toward the pavilion. Then I stopped. Even if I could get to the fireworks in time, I wouldn't know what to do when I got there, short of Changing and peeing on the lit fuses. Dave would take care of that part. In the meantime, I was willing to lay odds that the saboteur was waiting impatiently for disaster to strike. And I had his scent!

I ran back into the souvenir shop, to the

door marked *Ship's Crewmembers Only.* The cashier was busy on the phone and didn't notice me ducking into the back room, but she sure noticed when I burst back out after Changing.

Which way to go? I was going to assume that the saboteur was sticking around to see the havoc he'd caused, just as he had after the Octopus broke down. But I was also assuming he wasn't suicidal, so he wouldn't want to be too close to where the fireworks were going to explode or misfire or whatever he'd planned. Presumably he'd be somewhat close to the exit. What was the best place to watch the fireworks that was close to the exit?

Had I still had fingers, I'd have snapped them. The crow's nest! The mocked-up section of a ship where the daytime Pirate Dave stood was high enough to see the fireworks from and right in front of the exit. And, unfortunately, halfway across the park. Still, though I may not have been as fast as a vampire, I wasn't exactly slow, and I was close enough to see a shadowy figure in the crow's nest when the first firework went off. As the purple chrysanthemum lit up the sky, I saw he was dressed in black from head to toe, complete with a black face mask, like a ninja. Did ninja count as supernatural?

I was listening for screams or some sign that something had gone wrong, but there was nothing. A minute later, I realized there'd been no second explosion either. Either Dave or the helpful cashier had stopped them in time!

The saboteur must also have figured out his plan had gone awry because he clambered down the ladder and sprinted for the exit. I put on a burst of speed and tackled him, and both of us rolled over from the impact. Lucky for me, I ended up on top, straddling him and growling. He looked up at me, covered his face with his hands, and whimpered.

Though I hated to admit it, just for an instant I felt a taste of that ravening beast Dave had accused me of being. I wanted to rip the bastard's throat out, and I howled in pure triumph. Chihuahuas and Scotties are all well and good, but when you really want to make an impression, there's nothing like a wolf.

Before the temptation to rip and devour could take over, the guy fainted. And peed himself.

That's how Dave found us a few minutes later. Well, I'd switched back to Salty the Sea Dog, to keep from freaking out anybody else, but the saboteur was still unconscious.

Dave took in enough of the situation to throw the guy over his shoulder without stopping to ask questions. I trotted along beside him until we got to his office.

Dave said, "Do you want to Change to human?"

I cleared my doggie throat and made a show of looking around. Though I was certainly considering the idea of being naked around Dave in the near future, it wasn't the time.

"Oh, sorry." He rummaged in a drawer and found an Adventure Cove T-shirt big enough to cover the basics and turned his back while I Changed and pulled it on.

"You stopped the fireworks in time?" I said, once I could.

"Barely. The pyrotechnician said he would have gotten to the shell that would have burned down the park in another four minutes."

"Wow."

"I take it this is the saboteur."

"He smells like gunpowder, was standing in the crow's nest watching the show, and started to leave after the second burst didn't go off. And he's dressed like a ninja. So I'm thinking yes."

"Shall we see who or what it is?" He grabbed the mask and pulled it down from the guy's face. "Son of a whore!"

"Do you know him?"

"Don't you?"

I looked more closely but shook my head.

Dave reached for a cheap felt tricorner hat and put it on the guy, and then I recognized him.

"Oh my God, it's Pirate Dave!"

My Pirate Dave made a sound that was suspiciously close to one of my growls.

"I mean, he's the fake Pirate Dave." The first time I'd seen this guy, he'd been dressed in full Captain Jack Sparrow regalia, greeting guests as they came into the park.

The ninja started to stir and opened his eyes. "Where am I?" he croaked.

Instead of answering, Dave fixed him with his gaze, and the hair on my arms stood up as the vampire spoke. "Why have you been ruining my park?"

It was like he'd flipped a switch, and the ninja — whose real name was Randy — let it all come out. "It's your fault! If you'd let me take the night shift once in a while, I wouldn't have done anything!" He saw me watching. "Great, another one of your Sea Queens. How many do you need, dude? Couldn't you share? If you'd let me throw the effing doubloon once in a while, I could have gotten a piece of that."

"As if!" I sniffed.

Randy went on. "How long does a guy have to work here to get a shot at the Sea Queens? Ever since high school, I've worked my ass off all summer long. When I hit college, I could have gotten a nice cushy internship, but no, I came back here to play Pirate Dave. Only you wouldn't let me take the night shift, not once. For three summers, I've been sweating buckets in that damned wig while you swoop in as soon as it cools off and make off with the Sea Queens. Next year I graduate and get a real job, so this was my last chance. All I wanted was for you to switch shifts with me for one lousy season! But you wouldn't even discuss it! Why wouldn't you let me have a shot?"

Of course, it was obvious why once you knew Dave was a vampire, but just as obviously, Randy didn't know.

"I thought if there were problems in the park, you'd be too busy to dress up every night, and you'd have to give me a shot." He went on to describe how his years in the park had taught him the best ways to cause trouble and how to dodge the security guards. "But no matter what I did, you had to keep the spotlight to yourself. The park was going to close, and you didn't care. Even when those kids got hurt, you still had to be in the parade!"

I couldn't stop myself from blurting, "You jerk, you're the one who hurt those kids, not —"

Dave held up a hand to stop me and said, "Go on, Randy."

"So if I couldn't be Pirate Dave, then I was going to fix it so you couldn't either. I'm a chemistry major — fucking up the fireworks was easy."

He actually smirked, and it was all I could do to keep from Changing back to a wolf and scaring it off of him. Dave had more control and got the rest of the details, including the fact that the ninja mask was just a black Captain Jack T-shirt turned inside out and tied around his head.

I think Dave really wanted to find something supernatural in the whole sordid mess. No grown-up would want to admit to being confounded by a horny college boy, and it was even worse for a three-hundred-year-old. Then again, it seemed to me that a college boy in need of sexual relief was pretty darned close to supernatural.

At any rate, Dave didn't stop the interrogation until Randy was drained dry.

Not literally. I don't think Dave would have had Randy for dinner if I hadn't been there, but . . . Well, he was a pirate. At any rate, I was there and he restricted himself to glamouring Randy enough to make him forget about the wolf running loose in the park and to convince him that confession was good for the soul. Then he called the police.

In short order, the cops came, investigated, and left with Randy.

Afterward Pirate Dave showed me the captain's quarters, and we had fireworks that night after all.

Unsurprisingly, I slept late the next day, and since I was due to check out of my cabin and head back home, most of the day was spent packing and distributing the accumulation of fruit baskets and cookie trays to the hotel staff. Then I loaded up my car before heading back to Adventure Cove.

The park was closed, temporarily according to the sign on the ticket booth, but I had my suspicions. I found a shady spot to park in, and sat and thought about the situation for the next few hours. As soon as it was dark, Pirate Dave came to me, wearing blue jeans, of all things.

"Ahoy," I said as I got out of the car.

"Hi," he said almost shyly. "I suppose you'll be on your way out of town."

"That was the plan. What's the word?"

"Randy told the police everything."

"And the park?"

He shrugged. "The newspaper printed the whole story, which I hope will reassure people, but there's been a lot of damage to our reputation. People don't want to come to an unsafe amusement park. I thought I'd close for a week, and then decide what to do." He looked over at the concrete pirate ship. "Maybe it's time for me to weigh anchor."

"Bullshit!" I said. "You are not going to let some phony pirate chase you off your own ship. I mean, away from your home. Sure, you've had some bad publicity, but you can turn this around to your favor. Go ahead and stay closed for a week, but spend the time cleaning, freshening up the rides, brainstorming new attractions. I've got some ideas, too." I pulled out the back of the envelope on which I'd been making notes. "I know this season is going to be mostly a bust, but what about staying open later in the year? A lot of parks do Halloween events — pirates are a natural for that. Not to mention vampires."

"Pirate Dave's Haunted Cove?"

"Why not?"

"You've given this a lot of thought."

"I told you I'm in marketing. I've never worked with an amusement park before, but

I could learn."

"Are you asking me for a job?"

"Permission to come aboard?"

"What about the packs? Will they let you work with a vampire?"

"What I do is none of their business. This whole pack thing just doesn't do it for me. I don't even like fruit baskets!"

I could tell Dave was having trouble following my reasoning, but either he caught on or decided he didn't care, because he switched from conversation to kissing.

After a wonderful few minutes, he said, "And tonight?"

"I thought we could go out for a bite. And for dessert, we can come back here for a bite."

"Prepare to be boarded," he said with the patented Pirate Dave gleam in his eye.

A week later, the park reopened, bright and shiny, and thanks to some hard work on my part and a little glamour on Dave's, we had a good-sized crowd waiting to appreciate our efforts. We hadn't had time for much more than cosmetic changes, but the employees were enthusiastic again, which made all the difference in the world.

The one big change we had made was the whole Sea Queen ritual. Pirate Dave still picked a Sea Queen during the parade, but now his selections were little girls, so naturally he'd stopped the suggestive banter. And if any of the Queens got nervous about being near the handsome pirate, they had Salty the Sea Dog right there to distract them. I still couldn't really speak while in canine form, but I could manage to bark appropriately: "Arr-fff!"

COPYRIGHTS

ABOUT THE AUTHORS

Charlaine Harris is the author of the #1 *New York Times* bestselling paranormal fantasy series featuring Sooki Stackhouse (the basis for the HBO series *True Blood*), the *New York Times* bestselling mystery series featuring lightning-struck corpse locator Harper Conelly, and other acclaimed novels.

Toni L. P. Kelner is the author of the "Where Are They Now?" mysteries and the Laura Fleming mystery series. She has won an Agatha Award and a Romantic Times Career Achievement Award, and has been nominated for the Anthony and Macavity awards.

The employees of Thorndike Press hope you have enjoyed this Large Print book. All our Thorndike, Wheeler, and Kennebec Large Print titles are designed for easy reading, and all our books are made to last. Other Thorndike Press Large Print books are available at your library, through selected bookstores, or directly from us.

For information about titles, please call:
   (800) 223-1244

or visit our Web site at:
   http://gale.cengage.com/thorndike

To share your comments, please write:
   Publisher
   Thorndike Press
   295 Kennedy Memorial Drive
   Waterville, ME 04901